Janice Prest ... heartwarming ... novels are standalone reads, she loves to write stories set in the same Regency world, and many of her books include book-hopping characters. When Janice isn't writing she enjoys reading, pottering in the garden when the sun is shining, and travelling when she can. She fuels her imagination with endless cups of coffee, is far too keen on unhealthy food, and is an expert procrastinator.

Regency Secrets

July 2022
Those Scandalous
Stricklands

August 2022
The Governess Swap

September 2022
Penniless Brides of
Convenience

October 2022
The Cornish Dukes

November 2022
Breaking the Marriage Rules

December 2022
The Beauchamp Heirs

January 2023
The Wild Warriners

February 2023
Brides for Bachelors

March 2023
Secret Lives of the Ton

April 2023
The Widows of
Westram

May 2023
Saved from Disgrace

June 2023
The Return of the
Rogues

Regency Secrets:

The Beauchamp Heirs

JANICE PRESTON

MILLS & BOON

First Published in Great Britain 2022
By Mills & Boon, an imprint of HarperCollins*Publishers*
1 London Bridge Street, London, SE1 9GF

www.harpercollins.co.uk

HarperCollins*Publishers*
Macken House, 39/40 Mayor Street Upper,
Dublin 1, D01 C9W8

REGENCY SECRETS: THE BEAUCHAMP HEIRS
© 2022 Harlequin Enterprises ULC.

Lady Olivia and the Infamous Rake © 2018 Janice Preston
Daring to Love the Duke's Heir © 2019 Janice Preston

ISBN: 978-0-263-31807-4

LADY OLIVIA AND THE INFAMOUS RAKE

To Ian. Thank you for understanding when
I disappear into my own little world.

Chapter One

'Where have you *been*? Do you know how long we've been waiting? We were about to give up.'

'It's not my fault,' Lady Olivia Beauchamp retorted to her brother, Alexander. 'Do you even *know* how hard it is to sneak out without bumping into a servant? They're everywhere. And what do you mean...*we*?'

'Never mind that now.' Alex grabbed her arm and bundled her unceremoniously towards the waiting hackney. 'Hurry up. If anyone should catch us, there'll be hell to pay.'

Huffing at his cavalier treatment of her, Olivia clambered inside, then stopped short at the sight of a figure already seated within. Alex put his hand between her shoulder blades and shoved. 'Move. It's only Nev. He's come to help me keep you out of trouble.'

Olivia sprawled inelegantly on the seat opposite Neville Wolfe as her brother leapt in behind her and slammed the door. Immediately, the hackney rocked into motion, causing Olivia, by now half-upright, to tip over once more.

'Alex,' she wailed.

Neville's hand covered his mouth, but he failed to muffle his snort of laughter. Olivia glared across the carriage at him.

'Oh, God,' Alex muttered, as he reached across and hauled her upright. 'Tonight is bound to be a disaster.'

Neville passed a flask to Alex, who drank before handing it back.

'Can I have a drink?' Olivia asked.

'No, you cannot,' Alex retorted. 'That's all I need… you half-cut!' He eyed Olivia sternly. 'Two hours and not a minute longer, d'you hear? We've got better things to do tonight than dance attendance on a troublesome chit like you.'

The carriage passed under one of the new gas street lamps at that moment and Alex's eyes widened as the light caught the ruby and diamond bracelet on Olivia's gloved wrist. He reached across and grabbed her hand, holding it up to examine it.

'That's from Mama's parure. What the devil are you about? What else have you got on?'

He yanked down the hood of her cloak, revealing the pair of exquisite eardrops and the matching necklace she wore. The set had been a wedding gift from their father, the Duke of Cheriton, to their late mother. Olivia fingered the necklace—remembering how beautiful Mama had looked, all dressed up and wearing the parure—before battening down the guilt that stirred her conscience. She stuck her nose in the air.

'They belong to me, not Rosalind.' Rosalind was their new stepmother and Olivia was finding it hard to adjust to calling her Stepmama, although she took care not to call her Rosalind to her face. Or in front of her father. 'Papa said that Mama would have wanted me to have them.'

'He *also* said you're not allowed to wear them. They're totally unsuitable for a chit in her first Season.'

'Exactly! So when people see a masked lady tonight, wearing such fine jewellery, it will help my disguise. No one will guess I am your younger sister. They will think I am your light o' love.'

'*That's enough.* Where *did* you hear such language?'

'From you,' she retorted.

Really! Alex is such *a hypocrite!*

'God's teeth, Olivia, you'd try the patience of a saint. How did you get the jewels, anyway? I thought Father kept them locked up in his safe.'

'He does.' But she also knew where Papa kept the key.

'What do you imagine he'll do when he discovers they're missing, you little idiot? He'll have the Runners out.'

'Idiot yourself! I'll have them back long before he returns from Birmingham. He'll never know.'

'Well, you be sure to keep them covered up at Vauxhall. You'll be a magnet for every fingersmith and gallows bird there tonight. I must have rocks in my head to ever agree to such a madcap stunt as this.'

'Well, you did not agree. I won our wager fair and square and—as you always tell me, Brother dear—gambling debts are debts of honour, so you had no choice. *We* had a bet and *you* lost!'

Alex muttered something that sounded suspiciously like *spoilt brat* before lapsing into a sullen silence.

A minute later, out of the dark, came a mocking, 'Good evening, Lady Olivia.'

Olivia—miffed at having been betrayed into such unladylike behaviour in front of Alex's friend, even though she had known him for years—responded with a hissed, 'And if you tell a *single soul* about tonight, Neville Wolfe, your life will not be worth living.'

They crossed the Thames by boat and her first sight of Vauxhall Gardens utterly enchanted Olivia as they en-

tered via the water entrance. Papa was exceedingly unfair to refuse to allow her to come to here—apart from
one *very* fleeting visit, with him and Rosalind—early one
evening, before it was even dark enough to fully admire
all the lanterns. He had kept her close to his side the *entire* time and then whisked her and Nell—her very best
friend and now her step-aunt because she was Rosalind's
stepsister—home *immediately* after they had watched
the marvel of the mechanical cascade and just as it was
beginning to get crowded and the excitement started to
build. It was so unfair. Alex and Dominic—their eldest
brother, Lord Avon—came here all the time and Olivia
knew for a fact that Papa and Rosalind had visited the
Gardens again since then, leaving Olivia and Nell to endure yet another insipid evening at Almack's in the charge
of Aunt Cecily—an activity Papa considered more suited
to young ladies.

Not for the first time, Olivia wished she had been born
a boy.

They have all the fun and all the freedom. It's not fair.

They climbed the Vauxhall Stairs and entered the Gardens, which were lit by thousands of coloured lanterns,
hanging in festoons between the trees. Her squabble with
Alex was quickly forgotten, as always, and Olivia linked
arms with her brother. With Neville bringing up the rear, she
had no qualms about her safety and neither did she worry
that she would be recognised. Her midnight-blue velvet
domino, with its hood and matching mask—which left only
the tip of her nose and her mouth and chin visible—would
surely pass the closest scrutiny.

They strolled the well-lit paths, avoiding the more secluded walks—walks that rejoiced in names like the Dark
Walk and Lovers' Walk. Olivia peered down these dark
and mysterious ways, catching glimpses of couples stand-

ing close together in the shadows and groups of young bucks—noisy in their cups—patrolling the walks. Alex had warned her she was on no account to enter any of these walks, hinting at dire consequences if she did not obey him.

She huffed quietly to herself. He should know she had more sense than *that* and as for her father's tendency for overprotectiveness…well! It was totally uncalled-for, as far as Olivia was concerned. She was more than capable of looking after herself. She brushed aside the whisper of conscience that reminded her why Papa was so protective. She did not want to remember what had happened to Mama. Not tonight. She was determined to enjoy this evening, not dwell on past pain.

Papa is so old-fashioned. As if anything could happen to me in among all these people.

They stopped to admire the picturesque caves, grottos and waterfalls, Olivia staring in wonder at the sights, then continued until they reached the central square, where jugglers and tightrope walkers entertained the crowds and an orchestra played, the music struggling to be heard above the chatter and laughter of the crowds dancing, strolling and finishing their supper in the many supper boxes.

As they continued to stroll, arm in arm—Neville still ambling along in their wake—a female voice called Alex's name. They turned as one and Olivia sensed her brother's sudden tension. She had no difficulty in recognising the lady who had hailed him—Lady Shelton, the beautiful widow of Baron Shelton of Rutland. She indicated a supper box—in which several ladies and gentlemen were already seated—and beckoned Alex with a smile of enticement that set Olivia's teeth on edge. She'd never been introduced to Lady Shelton nor, she realised as she scanned the occupants of that box, to any of the others, apart from Lords Clevedon and Sudbury. They were of an older set than the young gentleman and ladies she normally socialised with. A shiver chased down her spine. She chose to interpret it as a shiver of excitement rather than apprehension. At last she would experience a little of *real* life…the life outside the confined world of debutantes and chaperons and balls and Almack's.

'You don't mind if we join them, do you, Livvy?' Alex said, his eyes glued to Lady Shelton.

'Beatrice! I'm *Beatrice*, remember?'

'What? Oh, yes, of course. But you don't mind, do you?'

Neville stepped forward and cleared his throat. 'Alex. Have you forgotten what you said?'

'What?' Alex tore his gaze from the buxom blonde and stared at Neville.

Neville's jaw firmed. 'It's no good givin' me the evil eye. You said on no account was I to be tempted to join up with any of our pals while your sister is under our protection. We was to walk around a while, have a bite of supper if it's not too late—'

'Well, it *is* too late, 'cause *she* kept us waiting for ever.'

'And then take her straight home.' Neville spoke over Alex's grumble. '*That's* what you said. And they—' he indicated the occupants of the box with a flick of his head '—ain't even our pals. And they ain't fitting company for your sister, neither.'

'Oh, never mind that now,' said Alex. 'We shan't stay above five minutes—ten, at the most. Do try not to be so faint-hearted. You'll be all right, won't you, Liv—Beatrice? We'll both be with you. There's no need to be afraid.'

'Afraid? Why should I be afraid? Don't be so stuffy, Neville. Really, you are as bad as Papa, fussing over every little thing. How can there be any risk? They'll never recognise me.'

They approached Lady Shelton.

'Lord Alexander, Mr Wolfe,' she purred. 'How lovely to see you both. I hoped I might persuade you to join our little party tonight?' She indicated the box behind her and the neighbouring box. 'Just a few select friends gathered here to celebrate Lord Clevedon's birthday.' Her gaze skimmed Olivia, who detected curiosity, but also a touch of scorn, in her ladyship's blue eyes. 'Will you introduce your companion?' She leaned closer and her strong perfume wafted up Olivia's nose, making it twitch. She held her breath, desperate not to sneeze. Lady Shelton fingered the edge of the hood covering Olivia's head. 'There really is no need to be bashful with us, my dear,' she added, with an amused smile. 'You will be among friends. We do not judge.'

'Oh, this is Beatrice…er…well, just Beatrice,' Alex said, dismissively, as he handed her into the less crowded of the two supper boxes. 'She's…er…well, she's here incognito as a wager. Yes, that's it. A wager.'

Olivia sat down, fuming. Really, Alex couldn't dissemble convincingly if he tried. No one, listening to him, would believe she was his lady-love now. And that might cause them to wonder who else she might be. She might be willing to rebel now and then, and to take a few risks, but she had no wish for her behaviour to become common knowledge. She knew very well what was expected of her and, in public, she was every inch the perfectly behaved young aristocratic lady. She inched along the bench and smiled invitingly at Neville as she patted the space next to hers. He would do as a decoy. He eyed her warily and then, with a shrug, he sat next to her while Alex squeezed in next to Lady Shelton with a triumphant grin.

'You gentlemen will already be acquainted with my companions,' Lady Shelton said, 'but, for Beatrice's sake, allow me to introduce Lady Sale, Lords Clevedon and Sudbury, Lord Hugo Alastair, Mr and Mrs Bartlett and Mr Douglas Randall.'

A whisper of caution warned Olivia that these people were very different from those she was used to. She scanned their faces again, suddenly anxious, but there was nothing she could do...having accepted her ladyship's invitation she could not now ask Alex to leave without drawing attention and speculation. She drew in a steadying breath. Ten minutes, he had said. She could manage ten minutes.

A glass was placed before her and a male hand, a ruby ring on one finger, tipped liquid from a jug, filling the glass. She raised her gaze, which had been fixed to the white tablecloth—soiled with crumbs, bearing witness to the supper recently consumed—and met the dark gaze of Lord Hugo Alastair. She felt the blood rush to her face as she forced herself to hold eye contact...there was something about his challenging scrutiny that attracted her and yet made her nervous at the same time...tingles of awareness chasing along every nerve in her body, urging her to flee. Or to find out more. His perfectly shaped mouth curved in a smile.

'What is this drink, sir?' Olivia raised the glass, eyeing the amber liquid.

'Arrack punch. Not too potent for you, is it?' There was a barely perceptible pause and she caught the twitch of his lips before he added, 'Beatrice.'

She swallowed a sudden swell of nerves. He couldn't possibly know her identity. Could he? She raised the glass to her lips, conscious the whole time of Lord Hugo's scrutiny. She'd never tried arrack punch before. She sipped, and barely prevented her nose from wrinkling. It *was* strong. But she would not allow this…this…mocking *coxcomb* the satisfaction of believing her weak. Or lacking in experience.

'It is delicious, thank you.'

She tilted her chin. He was as bad as her brothers…all her life she'd had to prove herself to them—prove herself capable of matching whatever they could do. She drank again. It tasted better this time and she felt the warmth hit her stomach, reminding her that she'd been so excited about tonight she'd barely eaten a thing at dinner and now—she glanced around the table—they were clearly too late for any supper here. She was conscious of the weight of Lord Hugo's gaze upon her. She knew him by sight, but they'd never been introduced—he was not the sort of man who attended come-out balls or who frequented Almack's. In fact, he was exactly the sort of man her Aunt Cecily would warn her to avoid: a disreputable rake and definitely an unsuitable acquaintance for a young lady in her first Season. She glanced at his lordship and saw his attention had been diverted by Mrs Bartlett, his head cocked towards her as she spoke into his ear. He smiled at her words and from looking rather dangerous—with his dark, sardonic good looks—his features were transformed. He looked much younger as his eyes crinkled—lines fanning out from the corners—and his lips parted to reveal strong white teeth. His right hand rested on the white tablecloth, his fingers moving—drumming lightly, as though he was restless—and that ruby ring on his third finger caught the light.

Olivia found her gaze riveted to those reflected darts of colour as she drank again and she realised, with a sense of shock, that she had drained the whole glass. Lord Hugo's hand moved, picked up the jug and refilled her glass.

Startled, she met his gaze again and a curious shock rippled through her. Again, she recognised nervousness and excitement all tangled up together. And something more. Something…deeper and slightly thrilling.

Anticipation?

His smile turned arrogant. Knowing. She recognised the look from that of her brothers when they were being particularly annoying—convinced they knew her better than she knew herself. Her brows twitched into a frown and she wrenched her eyes from Lord Hugo. Across the table, Lady Shelton was draped all over Alex, so Olivia avoided looking at them, too, embarrassed by their lack of shame in behaving in such a way in public—kissing and…and…*fondling* like that. Even Neville was taking no notice of her; he was too busy flirting with a gaudily made-up woman—clearly no lady—who had paused outside their box. She was starting to wish she had never goaded Alex into that wager. This was not as much fun as she had thought it would be.

'Oh!'

Lady Shelton's gasp brought Olivia's attention back to her.

'Oh, heavens.' Lady Shelton fanned herself vigorously. 'It is so very hot. I wonder, Alexander, would you be an absolute angel and escort me outside for some air?' Her free hand disappeared beneath the table. 'Perhaps we could dance…or something?'

Alex leapt to his feet, his cheeks flushed. 'It would be my pleasure, ma'am.'

He helped her from the box, then appeared to remember Olivia, for he leaned across Neville and whispered, 'I shan't be gone long. You'll be safe enough here with Nev. Just don't be tempted to wander off. With *anyone*.'

And he disappeared into the crowd, Lady Shelton on his

arm. Soon afterwards, Lord Sudbury, Mr and Mrs Bartlett and Lady Sale followed them, leaving Olivia alone with Lord Clevedon, Mr Randall, Lord Hugo and Neville. She edged closer to Neville, even though he was still flirting with that same woman. The prickles of awareness chasing over her skin warned her that Lord Hugo's attention was once more upon her, so she studiously avoided looking in his direction. In doing so, however, she inadvertently caught Mr Randall's eye. He was a bulky man of around five-and-thirty and he immediately moved, coming to sit on her side of the table, sliding along the bench until he sat right next to her, his thigh pressing against hers as he twisted his upper body to face her and fingered the edge of her hood.

Then his hand swooped down to land on her thigh and she squeaked a protest, knocking his hand away.

'Just a bit of fun, darling,' he whispered into her ear. 'Why not?'

'Randall.' There was a note of warning in Lord Hugo's voice.

'Alastair?'

'The lady does not appear to welcome your attentions.'

'What business is it of yours?'

Mr Randall then fell silent as Lord Clevedon rose to his feet. Olivia did not know whether to be relieved or alarmed. She was acquainted with Lord Clevedon, having met him at several functions—so he was clearly a respectable gentleman—but she was anxious he did not recognise her and this was drawing far too much of his attention. Up until now he had been too busy talking with Lord Sudbury to take much notice of anyone else. His gaze wandered casually over Olivia.

'My guest is clearly a lady, Randall. You will oblige me by treating her as such at *my* birthday party.'

'My apologies,' Randall muttered. He was so close Olivia could smell the spirits on his breath and his cheeks were flagged with hectic colour. He shifted away until he no longer crowded her and she smiled at his lordship.

'Thank you, my lord.'

His eyes narrowed slightly. Then he bowed, a smile playing on his full lips.

'The pleasure is all mine, my dear.' He gestured at Lord Hugo. 'I shall leave it to you to ensure our glasses are kept topped up, Alastair. I cannot have it said that I am an ungenerous host.'

Lord Hugo—with a sardonic grin—obliged and, because she was overly warm in her velvet domino, Olivia continued to sip the punch. She dare not remove her domino, for that would uncover her hair—distinctive with its blue-black sheen—and she was now desperate not to be identified. She reached for the bow at her throat and pulled it loose, parting the front of the cloak to allow some air to reach her skin, but still leaving her head covered. As she did so, she glanced across the table at Lord Hugo.

Dark eyes lazily surveyed her chest area, then rose to linger on her lips and she trembled. She'd thought this would be an adventure. Now, it just felt dangerous and she felt very foolish and very inexperienced. She broke out in a light sweat even as her mouth dried and she snatched up her glass again and drank thirstily. She might never have been introduced to Lord Hugo, but she knew his reputation as a devil-may-care rake. A shiver tiptoed down her spine as she recalled some of the tales she had heard…stories she could well believe of the man who lounged opposite, a mocking edge to his hard gaze as he drank liberally and refilled the glasses on the table—including hers—at frequent intervals.

Uneasy at being alone in the box with the four men—

even though one of them was Neville—Olivia distracted herself by drinking as the men chatted idly and made pithy comments about the people passing by. Gradually, though, she relaxed and she regained her normal, bubbly spirits, giving her the confidence to join the conversation.

Chapter Two

Some time later, Lord Clevedon produced a pack of cards from his pocket and he smiled at Olivia. 'May I challenge you to a few hands of piquet, my dear? I cannot offer an alternative game, for I only have the reduced pack here.'

Olivia had often played piquet with her family, and prided herself on her skill, but she hesitated, knowing that playing cards in a public place was not at all the same as playing cards at a private function. Neville dug his elbow into her ribs at that point and muttered, 'Not at all the thing, La—Beatrice' under his breath.

Olivia glared at him. Then stuck her nose in the air. If she wished to play a hand or two of cards with Lord Clevedon, why should she not? Nobody knew it was her, except Neville, and he did not count.

His lordship shuffled the cards before fanning them between long, elegant fingers. 'Do not concern yourself, Wolfe. We shall play the classic game—the first to gain one hundred points wins. Your…er…*friend* has already proved herself admirably bold, venturing here with two escorts, neither of whom, I'll wager, are members of her family.'

His words reassured Olivia that he had not guessed her

identity and, ignoring Neville's desperate grimaces, she said, 'Very well, then. I accept your challenge, sir.'

At that point, Mr Randall exited the box after mumbling an excuse. Olivia was pleased to see the back of him—she just wished Lord Hugo would also leave, with his unsettling gaze that seemed to penetrate deep inside her to winkle out her secrets.

'What stakes shall we say?'

Olivia bit her lip. 'I have no money with me with which to wager.'

'No matter, my dear. Let us hope Lady Luck will smile upon you and, if she should not, I will happily accept your vowel, you know. Of course, if you fear to take the risk, we can play for a penny a point. I am sure one of your two cavaliers will be happy to cover any losses.'

Olivia—discovering in herself a sudden desire not to risk her money on a skill she suddenly doubted—thought a penny a point might be just the answer. Before she could accept Clevedon's offer, however, Lord Hugo, his deep voice an amused drawl, said, 'A penny a point? My dear Clevedon, you insult the lady.'

Olivia glared at him. The sight of that mocking smile fired her anger, egging her on, and she elevated her chin.

'My thoughts exactly, sir. Why, a penny a point is hardly worth bothering with. What do you say to…to…?' Frantically, she tried to decide what would be deemed a reasonable wager without her having to risk *too* much.

'A guinea a point,' Lord Hugo said, with a lift of his brow.

She held his gaze defiantly. 'Perfect.'

'Deal the hand, Clevedon,' Lord Hugo drawled. 'I have an extraordinary desire to see the outcome of this game before I take my leave.'

Light-headed from the effects of the punch and with

the enormity of what she had agreed to, Olivia frowned as she forced her somewhat fuzzy attention on her hand. She won the first deal, but she was soon out of her depth. Clevedon played ruthlessly and Olivia was left reeling at the speed at which his points stacked up. Neville, his face grimmer by the second, shot her an encouraging smile.

'I'll go and find Alex.'

He stood and, none too steady on his feet, left the box. Olivia watched him go until he was absorbed into the crowd, then turned her attention to the remaining two men in the supper box and to the new hand dealt to her.

'I… I think I would rather not play any more,' she said, her stomach churning.

'Such a shame you have suffered an unfortunate run of cards,' Clevedon said, smiling. 'But we cannot stop now— we are *so* close to the finish. One more deal should do it.'

Pride alone stopped her from refusing to finish the game. She lost as, deep down, she had known she would.

'Never mind. Perhaps, if we play on, your luck might change, Beatrice, my dear.'

The breath left Olivia's lungs in a whoosh. *Beatrice.* She had forgotten. She felt the blood drain from her face as she realised the dilemma she faced: she could not give Clevedon her vowel. She was here incognito. She could not risk this escapade becoming common knowledge—it would destroy her reputation and her father…

Sick dread pooled in her stomach. *She* would be in trouble, yes, but that was not the worst of it.

Oh, dear God. What have I done? Papa will blame Alex and then—

She thrust aside that frantic voice inside her head as Clevedon raised the pack of cards, his brows raised, waiting for her reply.

'I…no. I do not care to play again, thank you.' She

sucked in a shaky breath and continued, 'I will pay you your money by the end of next week, my lord, if you would be so good as to give me until then to settle my debt?'

'But of course, my dear. Just give me your vowel and then I shall call upon you—shall we say next Saturday evening—and you can repay me. I shall, of course, need your address.'

Panic threatened to overcome her, squeezing her lungs until she could barely breathe. 'I… I… I cannot give you my vowel, sir. But I give you my word that you will be paid on time.'

Clevedon's smile was sympathetic, but there was a hard edge to it now. And how could she blame him? He had no idea of her identity. Why should he trust her? She scanned the people thronging the square.

Oh, where is Alex? Or Neville? Why have they not returned?

'I am sorry, my dear, but…a debt of honour, you know. And an unknown adversary. I am afraid that I must insist on a signed vowel or—perhaps—payment of a different kind?'

Her throat constricted. Her gaze flew without volition to Lord Hugo, but he was staring out across the square, seemingly taking no notice of their conversation.

'D-different kind? I do not understand.'

Clevedon proffered his hand and, as if in a dream, she took it and rose to her feet.

'Come walk with me, Beatrice. A kiss. Or two. That is all I ask. There are private nooks aplenty in the Dark Walks.'

His eyes lowered to her décolletage. She snatched her hand from his and pulled her domino tightly across her chest, her hand at her throat.

'I…no. I should rather not. Thank you, sir.'

'Your address, then? Or how shall I know where to apply for my winnings?'

Beneath her fingers was the hard outline of Mama's necklace. In a panic, she slid her hands inside her hood and reached behind to unclasp the necklace. She tugged it free and almost flung it on the table.

'There. You may take that as my promise to pay my debt. And, when I do, you must return my necklace.'

A low whistle reached her ears. Lord Hugo's eyes had widened at the sight of the necklace. Belatedly, Olivia recalled she could have offered the bracelet or even the eardrops—either would have covered the amount she owed and both were worth far less than the necklace.

And Papa is far more likely to notice the necklace is missing than he would the others.

But it was too late to change her offer now for Clevedon had already pocketed the necklace, saying, 'A pledge? Hmmm… I should have preferred a kiss, but very well. I accept your pledge. I shall still require your address, however.'

'No! Why?'

His brows rose. 'No? But how, my dear, are you to pay my winnings and how am I to return your necklace? Unless…but of course. You may call upon me at my house in Dover Street. If you wear your domino, then it is unlikely you will be recognised. Shall we say, Saturday evening at seven o'clock? Bring the money—and your delightful self for dinner—and I shall return the necklace.'

'Dinner? No. I could not possibly—our agreement was for me to pay my debt, nothing more.'

'There is the little matter of interest payable, my dear. I shall hold the necklace for you until Saturday, but should you fail me I shall have no choice but to sell it to defray expenses. You do understand, I trust? Don't be late.'

She could stay there no longer. Sick at heart, she fled the box, stumbling a little in her haste, and plunged into the dense mass of people thronging the square, desperately searching for Alex or Neville.

Lord Hugo Alastair watched the mysterious Beatrice vanish among the crush of people, who were growing rowdier by the minute, and he hoped she would quickly find safety with Beauchamp or Wolfe—he'd wager she was younger than she'd tried to appear, but she was without doubt a lady. He bit back a cynical smile—yet another young wife, unrecognisable in her hooded domino and lace-edged mask, out with her lover, proving yet again that matrimony was for fools. Hugo had had his fair share of disenchanted wives on his arm in the past. Although— now he considered it—neither Beauchamp nor Wolfe had paid her much attention. If either of those young greenheads was her lover, they weren't making a very good fist of it.

He scanned the densely packed square and disquiet threaded through him. A female on her own would prove an easy target for the many predators prowling the Gardens— thieves, pickpockets…and worse.

He frowned, recalling the way Beatrice had taken fright at Clevedon's suggestion of a kiss or two. That was not the reaction of a married lady out with her lover. And, now he came to think about it, neither was Clevedon's suggestion one that Hugo would ever have expected of the man who was now examining that ruby and diamond necklace with a look of pure satisfaction on his face.

'Care to enlighten me as to who the mysterious Beatrice is, Clevedon?'

Clevedon smiled smugly. 'My salvation, dear boy. My future wife.'

'Your *wife*?' Hugo's astonishment was perhaps too overt and Clevedon looked up with suddenly narrowed eyes.

'Why ever not?' he said, evenly. 'A man in my position must marry eventually. The Beauchamp chit is as good as any.'

Hugo racked his brain to come up with a mental picture of Cheriton's daughter. Their paths rarely crossed; young ladies in their first Season held no appeal for him and he, as a younger son with no prospects, held even less appeal for them. Or for their parents. Lady Olivia Beauchamp. He remembered her now: a true beauty, with a willowy figure and the same black hair and silver-grey eyes as her sire. And utterly innocent. Anger stirred, deep in his gut.

What the hell is Beauchamp about, bringing his sister here and then abandoning her?

'I never had you down as the marrying kind, Clevedon.'

Hugo had always suspected the other man's proclivities, but that was a delicate—not to say, illegal—matter and not one he could even mention, although he was aware Clevedon was not the first man to prefer the company of other men and neither would he be the last. He could see now that Clevedon's suggestion of a kiss in payment for the debt had been an elaborate ruse… Clevedon had known damned well that the Lady Olivia Beauchamp would never consent to walking down those shady pathways with him. He had well and truly hooked her in.

Clevedon shrugged. 'It is not by choice, dear boy, but I find myself in need of a wife with a wealthy father. And they don't come much wealthier than Cheriton. Besides, our marriage would be one of pure convenience. My life need not change.'

Distaste mushroomed in Hugo's gut. Lady Olivia might be a spoilt little rich girl who wanted for nothing—and a foolish chit for taking the risks she had tonight—and yet he could still find sympathy for a young girl who would marry with high hopes only to find her dreams dashed by the indifference and neglect of her husband.

His face must have revealed his feelings because Clevedon laughed out loud.

'Scruples, my dear Hugo? Surely not.'

Hugo stood up. 'I don't approve of playing games with innocents.'

'Needs must, dear boy. Needs must. It would not be my choice were things different, but her dowry will compensate for the inconvenience. And, of course, there will be the added bonus of marrying into such a powerful family.'

'You think you can force Cheriton into agreeing to a marriage?'

Clevedon shrugged again. 'Why not? When a juicy plum like the Catch of the Season drops into one's lap, it would be remiss not to take advantage. And now, with this,' he held the sparkling necklace aloft, 'I have the means to exert a little additional persuasion, shall we say.'

Hugo tried to mask his revulsion at what Clevedon had in store for the girl. Marrying money was one thing. Ruining a girl's reputation and innocence in order to force a wedding was beyond the pale, particularly when the man had no taste for female flesh.

'Look here, Alastair. It was her decision to come here, presumably against Cheriton's orders.' Clevedon shrugged. 'If she wants to play with the grown-ups, she must accept the consequences, as must her fool of a brother. He, too, will get his comeuppance very soon, if I'm not mistaken.'

His words resurrected a memory from earlier that evening—Sir Peter Tadlow cajoling Marie Shelton, *'Please, Marie'*, until Marie, with an irritated huff, had flounced out of the supper box and intercepted Beauchamp, Wolfe and their female companion. Tadlow had

followed Marie from the box and not returned. Not that
that was any loss—Hugo never had taken to the man.
But he had wondered at the time why Marie—mercenary
to her core—was bothering with Lord Alexander Beauchamp, whose pockets always seemed to be to let, even
with a father like the Duke of Cheriton, who was rich
as Croesus. Why had she draped herself all over Beauchamp and plied him with punch before enticing him
away from the supper box? And where did Tadlow fit in?

'What was Marie up to, with young Beauchamp?'

Clevedon's eyes gleamed. 'What do you think? Use
your imagination, Alastair, do. I declare, you are growing dull of late.'

'Yes. But why?' Watching young Beauchamp had put
Hugo in mind of his younger self—a young man on the
path to self-destruction. 'And where did Tadlow disappear to?'

Clevedon sighed. 'You are like a dog with a bone,
Alastair.' He slipped the necklace into his pocket. 'Tadlow,' he said, with exaggerated patience, 'was keen to avoid
being seen by Beauchamp. He's got some scheme or other
planned.'

'Scheme?'

Clevedon shrugged. 'Something about revenge on
Cheriton—seems he interfered in some plan Tadlow had
to wed Bulbridge to Lady Helena Caldicot. Tadlow's her
uncle on her mother's side.'

Sir Peter Tadlow and Viscount Bulbridge—and Bulbridge's cousin, Douglas Randall—were recent additions
to Hugo's circle and he could not like any of them. All
three were the sort of dissolute fellows that should serve
as a stellar warning to unwary young bucks: *Look closely,
lads, for here lies your future.* An unwary young buck such
as he had been at the age of seventeen when he had set out

to squeeze every last drop of pleasure from life without regard to the consequences.

Dear God. That was nine years ago!

'Anyway,' Clevedon continued, 'Cheriton stuck his nose in, as is his wont, and put a stop to it so they're out to bleed him through his son. Tadlow reckons Cheriton owes him. And young Beauchamp can look after himself—it's no different for him than it is for his silly sister. If they come out to play with the adults, they must be prepared.' He smiled wolfishly. 'Now, much as I enjoy your oh-so-charming company, Alastair, old man, I think I shall join the others next door. Coming?'

Hugo could stomach no more tonight.

'No. I'm off to my club. I'll say goodnight.'

He left the box and plunged into the crowds, sick with disgust as he wondered why the hell he was still hanging around with Clevedon and his ilk, with their louche, care-for-nothing ways. Hugo might have always been wild and reckless, but he would never deliberately ruin an innocent girl for the sake of money and he would never stoop to using a young man to wreak revenge on his father. It was almost as though a veil had lifted from his eyes and he saw for the first time some of their true characters.

He had only attended tonight because it was Clevedon's birthday, but he'd already decided it was time to stop socialising with this crowd altogether. In the past year or so he had gradually clawed his way out of the swamp of vices that had held him captive for so long, but he was aware it would be all too easy to slide back into the mire. A few too many drinks, and judgement and common sense were pissed down the gutter along with the alcohol.

Anger at the way the two youngsters had been targeted by Tadlow and Clevedon continued to gnaw at Hugo as he strolled through the hordes gathering to enjoy the fire-

works display. Of the two, Clevedon was the most dangerous because he was welcomed almost everywhere in the
ton and far more readily than Hugo himself was accepted.
Parents fawned over him, eager for a title for their daughters and, if his plan to compromise her succeeded, he was
the sort of man Cheriton might very well accept as a husband for his daughter.

Even though he told himself he would not put himself
out—it was none of his business, after all—still Hugo
found himself watching out for a figure in a midnight-
blue velvet domino.

She'd said she had no money. Had she found her brother?
Or Wolfe? They'd both been well on the way to being foxed
anyway, as had Lady Olivia. And guilt mixed in with the
disquiet as it continued to spiral through him—guilt over
his own part in topping up her glass, time after time. It
made no difference to tell himself he wouldn't have done
it if he'd realised who she was…how young she was…how
innocent. He still felt responsible.

And it is my *doing that she lost so heavily. I provoked
her into agreeing those high stakes.*

He stopped dead. People jostled around him, loudly
complaining, but he ignored them. Then he cursed, fluently, beneath his breath. It went against the grain, but he
felt compelled to look. To at least try to make sure she was
all right…that she had found her brother. He gazed around.
But how on earth could he locate her in this heaving mass
of humanity? Where would she go? He bit back another
curse as realisation dawned. She would stay near the supper box, in the hope that either her brother or Wolfe would
return for her. He turned and shoved his way back through
the crowd, until Clevedon's box was in sight, and…*there.*

'Bloody hellfire!'

She was close to the box, but not close enough to be

visible to the occupants, and she was surrounded by several young men. One of them had his arm around her shoulders and was trying to pull down her hood, but she was fighting him off—verbally as well as physically, from what Hugo could make out. The lads surrounding Olivia were not gentlemen—probably clerks or some such, out for a good time—which was just as well because by the time Hugo reached them, Olivia's hood was down, her hair was awry and her face unmasked. Her eyes were huge in her pale face, but they nevertheless fired ice shards at her tormentors as she berated them. As he came within hearing distance, Hugo bit back a grin to hear her spitting a variety of insults.

'You vile worms! Churls! Scabs! Sodden-witted knaves! Leave me alone, or I'll kick you so hard you won't remember your own name for a month!'

The surrounding youths were laughing at her…mocking…and Hugo could see the effort it cost her to hold tears at bay.

He stepped into the fray.

Chapter Three

'Enough!' He faced the lad who was taunting Olivia by waving her mask above his head, its ribbons dangling and dancing. He held out one hand. 'I'll take that.'

The lad exchanged looks with his friends. 'And who might you be? The little tart gave it me as a tro— *Argh...*'

Hugo's fingers tightened around the youth's throat, causing his eyes to bulge.

'I said... I. Will. Take. That.'

A ragged but muted cheer sounded from some of the on-lookers as Hugo continued to hold the youth high, by the neck, allowing just the tips of his toes to scrape the ground. It took no time for the lad to capitulate. He thrust the mask into Hugo's face. Hugo took it, releasing him, and, as her tormentor slumped to the ground, Hugo faced Olivia. She was shaking, her eyes suspiciously luminous, but she held herself straight, her nose in the air, as she accepted the mask, tied it back in place and pulled her hood over her head.

'Thank you.' She began to walk away.

For God's sake! Where does *she think she is going?*

With two strides he caught up with her and grabbed her by the arm, spinning her around to face him. She wrenched her arm free.

'Leave me alone.'

'How do you mean to get home?'

'I shall find my brother.'

'And if you don't? And if you get accosted again? The next men might not be inclined to leave it at teasing.'

She elevated her nose. Again. Really, she was beyond hoity. He was almost inclined to leave her to it, if she was this stubborn.

Almost.

'I shall escort you home.'

She was slowly but surely backing away from him. With a growl that originated deep, deep inside him, Hugo followed her and grabbed her arm again.

'Let go of me.'

Those amazing eyes of hers shot icy slivers at him. What would they look like, fired with passion rather than fury? Would they—? He batted those errant thoughts aside. She was eighteen years old...had only just made her debut in society.

'With what will you pay a jarvey to drive you home, Lady Olivia?'

He used her name deliberately, so she would know he recognised her. Her eyes flared.

'You have no money, or you would have paid Clevedon,' he reminded her.

She gasped at that, her worry palpable. 'D-does Lord Clevedon know it was me? What if he tells my father?'

'No. He does not know.' The urge to soothe her took him unawares. Besides, there was no point in her fretting when he knew damned well Clevedon would never tell her father about tonight.

'So, how will you get home if you don't find your brother?' he went on, ruthlessly. 'Will you pay your fare with your bracelet?'

He raised her arm and the jewels caught the light, winking ice and fire.

'Or maybe an eardrop?'

He slid his hand under her hood, skimming the satin-soft skin of her neck, and found her earlobe, tugging at it gently. Her breath quickened, her bosom heaving, and he snatched his hand away before he gave in to his instincts…the ones clamouring at him to haul her into his arms and to kiss some sense into her. He grasped her wrist. Firmly.

'You're coming with me,' he rasped out and began to stride in the direction of the water gate, towing her along behind him.

'Wh-where are you taking me?'

The fear in her voice had him slamming to a halt. He clenched his jaw.

'Home,' he gritted out. 'And, before you ask, yes…*your* home.'

'I… I won't go without my brother.'

'Your brother? Well, and where is he?' Hugo flung his arm wide, almost knocking a passing gentleman's hat from his head. 'If he is supposed to be looking out for you tonight, he's making a poor fist of it, that's all I can say. I am not spending all night searching for your ramshackle brother when he clearly doesn't give a da—hoot that he's left you on your own in among this sort of crowd. I'm taking you home. Then I can return to my own plans for the evening.'

With that, he whirled around and set off again, his hand still clamped around her wrist.

He did not dare to slow his stride—she would only argue again. The sooner he delivered the troublesome minx home, the sooner he could forget all about her and her risk-taking, and her luminous, hypnotic eyes that reminded him of the moon and were fringed by the thickest, darkest, longest lashes he had ever seen.

Temptress eyes.

They soon reached Vauxhall Stairs and the water gate. A boat was already waiting and they embarked, along with several other passengers, some of whom Hugo knew. He nodded a greeting, but then pointedly directed his gaze across the river to discourage conversation. If any of them should recognise Olivia…his stomach clenched. She would be well and truly compromised and there was no way he ever intended to wed, not after the wretched example of his parents' union.

'But what—?'

'Be quiet,' he growled, glaring down into those wide eyes that glittered at him from behind her mask. 'We'll talk later.'

He ignored her loud puff of exasperation, concentrating instead on the dark ripples of the Thames slipping past the boat as the oarsmen strained to reach the opposite bank.

They disembarked, still in silence. Olivia stumbled and Hugo steadied her, wrapping his arm around her waist.

'Oops,' she said, stifling a giggle.

She straightened and pulled away from him, but her progress was erratic as she made for a waiting hackney. Hardly surprising, given the number of times he had refilled her glass—and her readiness to drain it every time. Hugo instructed the jarvey to take them to Grosvenor Square, where Beauchamp House—the Duke of Cheriton's London residence—was located, then he handed Olivia up the step and climbed in behind her.

'Why did you stop me from speaking in the boat?' Her voice quivered with indignation. 'Who are you to tell me what to do?'

Hugo shifted on the seat so he was half-facing her, and folded his arms across his chest.

'I am the man who is saving you from the results of your own folly.'

She pushed back her hood and tore off her mask. 'Hmmph. Some saviour you are. I should not be alone with you like this. It is scandalous.'

Her pert little nose was in the air again—she really was the most infuriating wench he had ever met.

'More scandalous than you getting drunk and wandering around Vauxhall unescorted?'

'I am *not* drunk. And I am masked. No one could recognise me. I know your reputation, Lord Hugo Alastair. You are the sort of man my aunt always warns me about. Well, you need not think you may take advantage of me, for I shall fight you and scream *very loudly* if you try to touch me.'

Her words might be full of bravado, but Hugo did not miss the way she shrank back into the corner of the hackney as she spoke them and the intermittent illumination from the street lamps as they passed revealed her hands gripping one another so tightly they shook.

He sighed. 'I have no intention of touching you, Lady Olivia. I prefer my ladies willing. And experienced.'

Her eyes flashed at that but, thankfully, she remained silent.

'I was impressed by your vocabulary back there,' he said. Talking would, surely, help take her mind from their situation. And his. 'Where did you learn such insults?'

'Shakespeare,' she replied, haughtily. 'I am surprised you did not recognise them. I presume you did study his works at school?'

Impertinent little... He swallowed his irritation. 'I did. Although I believe it is sodden-witted *lords*, not knaves.'

She glared at him. 'Why would I call them *lords*? I was insulting them.'

'They are not the typical words one might expect from a young lady.'

She shrugged. 'I've heard Alex use them.'

Her brother again: Lord Alexander Beauchamp... younger son of the Duke of Cheriton and as wild as they come. Although what *his* excuse might be, with such a decent and supportive father, unlike Hugo's—

He clamped down on that memory there and then. He would not allow himself to remember his childhood or his brutal father. It was shut up tight in a dark corner of his memory—a corner he refused to revisit.

'Your brother should have more sense than to utter such words in your hearing.'

'You sound just like Dominic. That's what he always says. But Alex...you do not understand. Alex is...'

Her smooth forehead furrowed as she chewed her full bottom lip. Hugo waited, loath to say anything that might distract her from the confidence he sensed she was about to share. Her earlier tension had gone, to be replaced by agitation. Her hands now writhed in her lap. Hugo was certain he was not the cause this time. This was connected to her brother.

'Alex has always been troubled,' she said, eventually, her voice subdued. 'He... I do not understand why, but he has always had a difficult relationship with Papa. Ever since...' Her voice dropped to a near whisper and Hugo got the impression she had almost forgotten his presence. Then she drew in a hasty breath, and straightened. 'Well, never mind that. The family look out for him. That is all.'

The family. Did she realise how fortunate she was to have such a tightly knit family to support her? And yet the silly chit risked disgrace and worse by this foolhardy escapade.

'Your father will not be happy when he learns of your antics tonight.'

Her gaze flew to his. '*No.* You cannot tell Papa.' She grabbed his hands. 'Please. You cannot.'

'He needs to know the danger your brother put you in.'

Hugo marvelled at the words coming from his mouth. Him…the wildest and most reckless of them all…ready to test any boundary for the sake of having fun. And now here he was, attempting to imbue some common sense into a troublesome young lady like Lady Olivia Beauchamp.

'Please. Do not tell Papa. Not for my sake, but for Alex's.' Her eyes searched his. 'Please?' Her hands tightened their grip.

He locked in the words '*persuade me*'. Reined back his sudden urge to seize her mouth, taste her lips. He extricated his hands from hers, suddenly uncomfortable…too viscerally aware of her nearness, the way she gazed up at him with parted lips. And those eyes…

He twisted to look out of the window. Piccadilly. They would soon reach Grosvenor Square.

'Why should I care about protecting your brother?'

'Alex…he is difficult, I know. He drinks. He gambles. He fights. But he is unhappy. At least, everyone *else* thinks he is upset by what happened. *I* believe he's angry. But I do not understand why.'

It was the second time she had said that. Curiosity stirred within Hugo…what had happened in the Beauchamps' past? He made a mental note to quiz his mother.

'The only thing that takes him away from all those… those *vices* is horses. He adores horses and they adore him. He has an almost magical connection with them. Give him an untameable horse and he will gentle it until it follows him around like a puppy.'

'That does not explain why I should not tell your father.'

'But you cannot. Not when Alex finally has a chance to settle down…when he has the chance to have something of his own that will make him content.' She chewed at her lip again. 'It is not yet common knowledge, but Papa has purchased Sir William Rockbeare's estate in Buckinghamshire. Do you know Sir William?'

'I know of him.' Everyone knew Rockbeare's cattle were the best riding and carriage horses in the country. 'I heard he'd sold up.'

'Well, Alex got into trouble while Papa was away in Buckinghamshire. And Papa told him if he could stay out of trouble for the rest of the Season, then he could move to Foxbourne and run the stud and training stables. If he proves himself, in a few years Papa will sign the estate and all the horses over to him. Do you not see?'

She sat forward, her silver gaze intent upon his, sending strange impulses quivering through him. Not the impulse to seize and to take this time, but…the desire to protect. He frowned, dragging his attention away from his feelings and back to her words. Too much thought about his feelings always made him fidgety and out of sorts. That's why he was usually careful to avoid such namby-pamby nonsense.

'It is a wonderful chance for Alex and he wants it *sooo* much, and he has been trying so hard to keep out of trouble and if Papa finds out about tonight…' She hung her head. 'It was all my fault.' He caught the sound of a tiny sniff. 'I won a bet and Alex lost which meant he had no choice but to take me to Vauxhall. But it was not a fair bet. I *knew* I could not lose, because Uncle Vernon had already agreed to allow me to drive his blacks in the Park, but Alex didn't know that, and he thought it a safe bet because Vernon never allows *anyone* to drive his blacks.'

Hugo frowned, trying to make sense of her jumbled tale. 'Then why did your uncle allow *you* to drive his blacks?'

He knew the pair she meant and he knew how proud and protective her uncle, Lord Vernon Beauchamp, was of them.

'Because I tricked him. He upset Aunt Cecily—he was teasing her and she was in a snit with him, but he needed her to do him a favour because Lady Slough was pursuing him relentlessly, he said—'

'Lady *Slough*?' An image of the lady in question—short, stout, fifty if she was a day—formed in Hugo's head. 'Lady Slough was pursuing your *uncle*?'

Lord Vernon Beauchamp was one of the most eligible bachelors in the *ton*—much sought after and very popular with the ladies.

'Well, not for *herself*, of course.' She tutted. Hugo could barely contain a chuckle. She really was an entertaining miss—an unexpected mixture of naivety and shrewdness. 'For her *daughter*. Anyway, Uncle Vernon needed my Aunt Cecily to seat him as far away from Lady Slough and Amelia as possible when they came to dinner—'

'But…why would they be invited to dinner?'

'Because Lady Slough is my stepmama's aunt—even though she used to disown Stepmama but now she is toadying up to Stepmama for all she is worth—and she really believes Uncle Vernon will marry her spotty daughter. Which he won't, I can tell you, because Uncle Vernon will *never* get married, he says.'

Hugo had every sympathy with that point of view.

'Anyway, I was telling you all about my bet with Alex… so, Uncle Vernon *begged* me to persuade Aunt Cecily not to sit Lady Slough or Amelia next to him—because she threatened to do exactly that—and *I* said I would persuade her, but that he would owe me a favour. And he said, *Anything*. And then, the next day, when I reminded him he tried to wriggle out of it, but Papa was a witness and told Uncle Vernon he should be more careful about making such vague promises. So Vernon had already agreed, but Alex didn't know…and Dominic is right! I *am* a horrid, manipulative creature.'

'Dominic?' It was the second time she had mentioned this Dominic.

'Avon.'

'Of course.' Dominic, Lord Avon, was Olivia's eldest brother and heir to the Dukedom. 'So you don't get on with Avon?'

She pouted. 'Well, I do. He is nice enough when he's not teasing me. But he does take himself and his position as Papa's heir exceedingly serious. He is opposite to Alex. Poor Alex.' She slumped back into the corner. 'I shall *never* forgive myself if he loses the chance to have Foxbourne because of me.'

'Why do you care so much?'

She stared. 'He's my *brother*. Of course I care. I *love* him.'

Envy stirred. Everyone knew the Beauchamps were a close family. What must it be like, to have complete and utter faith and trust in your own father? Hugo had never known such security, even though his mother had tried her best to protect him and Lucas, his older brother, from their violent father. Neither of them had returned to Rothley Hall, the family estate up in Northumberland, after they left university. Lucas had made his home in London and Hugo had spent more time with Lucas than at Oxford, finding his elder brother's life of excess and debauchery much more exciting than a life of study. They had been wild years—until Lucas had been betrayed by the woman he loved and a man he thought his friend and had left London abruptly, a bitter man. Later, following their father's death, Lucas had become the Marquis of Rothley and led the life of a joyless recluse.

Since then, Hugo had been on his own, continuing with all those same rakish excesses and vices until this past year or so, when that way of life had begun to pall, almost without him realising it. He had even—God help him—invested some of his recent winnings in government bonds. *That* was the influence of Sir Horace Todmorden, his new stepfather, whose seemingly unshakeable faith in Hugo was beginning to change him.

'What are you thinking about? You look…sad.'

The soft query jerked him from his thoughts. 'Nothing.' Then, at her crestfallen expression, he gentled his voice. 'I was thinking about my father and how fortunate you are in yours.'

Her hand covered his. 'You must miss him dreadfully.'

'Hardly.' He huffed a laugh. 'He was a brute.'

'Oh.' Her fine, dark brows drew together as she withdrew her hand. 'But…you still have other family, do you not?'

'My mother and my brother, Rothley.'

He'd said enough. She could have no real interest in his family. Once he had delivered her home, their paths were unlikely to cross very often. But their conversation had stirred hope within him, for not only had Mama married Sir Horace last year, but Lucas, too, had now wed. He and Mary, his new wife, and Mary's two young children, would arrive in London very soon for a prolonged visit. And then…pleasure glowed deep inside at the thought that, maybe, he would finally be part of a close-knit family himself.

He shook all thoughts of his family from his head as the hackney rocked to a halt.

'We're here.' Hugo glanced up at Beauchamp House. Belatedly, he realised he should have instructed the jarvey to stop around the corner. 'Put that mask back on and pull up your hood.'

Olivia stared at him, an unfathomable expression on her face before, with yet another pout, tying her mask in place. Hugo jumped from the hackney. The front door of the house now stood open, a footman silhouetted within the frame. Hugo waved him away.

'Wrong address,' he called.

The man raised his hand in acknowledgement and retreated into the house, closing the door behind him. Hugo leaned back inside the carriage.

'How did you intend to get back inside?'

'Around the back. There's a window... Alex makes sure it's unlocked whenever he goes out at night and doesn't want anyone to know.'

'And he told his younger sister about it?'

'No. Nobody ever tells me *anything*. But I usually find out anyway.'

The hint of pride in her tone made him smile. Again, he thought of her as an odd mixture of naivety and intuition, but that didn't mean she was up to snuff when dealing with the darker aspects of life...or of society, for that matter. He held out his hand and she took it to climb down to the pavement. Without volition, his fingers closed around hers and he had to force himself to release her.

'Wait for me,' he said to the jarvey. 'I won't be long.' Then to Olivia, he said, 'Come. Show me. But if your father appears, I'm off.'

'Papa's away,' she replied. 'He and my stepmother left yesterday, with her grandfather. They're going to Birmingham to collect his belongings, although…' She frowned. 'I *think* they're meeting Uncle Vernon somewhere first. He wrote to Papa, only Papa would only tell me it was nothing to worry about.'

Yet again, Hugo found himself biting back a smile—this time at her disgruntled tone. She clearly prided herself on knowing everything that was going on within her family. They had reached the corner and turned into a side street. There was a low bark, the click of claws on the pavement, and an enormous dog launched itself at Olivia. Hugo's heart thundered as he threw his arms around its neck, dragging it away.

'Hector!' A tall, slender man, supporting himself on a crutch, lurched towards them.

'Hector!' Far from being petrified, Olivia's squeal was one of delight.

The dog squirmed, its tail waving, as Hugo held it fast.

'You know this monster?' he panted.

'Of course I do. It's Hector. My stepmother's dog and… oh! F-F-Freddie.'

The man had reached them and, with a ferocious scowl at Hugo, he reached out and tugged the hood from Olivia's head.

'What do you think you are doing?' He kept his voice low as he scanned the surrounding street. 'And who the de—who on *earth* are you?'

Chapter Four

Olivia clutched at the man's sleeve. 'Oh, Freddie! *Please.* You must not tell *anyone* you have seen me.'

'Livvy, how can I keep this a secret? I enjoy my work for your father—he trusts me to be honest with him.' He pushed her behind him and glared at Hugo. 'I asked who you are, sir. And you can release the dog. He will not run off. Nor attack you—unless I tell him to.'

Hugo released the huge hound. 'I'm Alastair. And you, sir?'

'Frederick Allen. The Duke's secretary.'

'Allen? You are connected to the new Duchess?'

'Her brother.'

'Well, before you imagine the worst, Allen, let me assure you that I am merely escorting Lady Olivia home from Vauxhall Gardens where, unfortunately, she became separated from her brother, who originally took her there.'

'It's true, Freddie. Alex disappeared and I had no money to get home and Lord Hugo very gallantly offered to escort me so I would not come to any harm.'

'No harm? There will be no end of harm if anyone should spot you.' Freddie glanced around again. 'We must get off the street.' He tugged Olivia towards a flight of steps leading down to the basement area, where a door stood ajar casting a patch of light on to the flagstones. Freddie jerked his head, indicating that Hugo should follow.

Once they were hidden from view, he growled, 'How can you have come to no harm when you're out at this time of night, unchaperoned, with a strange man? Does Nell know?'

'No. I did not wish her to be obliged to lie on my behalf, so I did not tell her. But you must not tell Papa, or Rosalind, or…or…*anyone*. You *know* Alex will get the blame and then he will lose Foxbourne, and he will be devastated and then he will disappear again like he did before, and no one will know where he's gone, and—'

'Olivia!'

She clamped her mouth shut.

'You cannot possibly know what might happen in the future, so please stop imagining the worst all the time.'

Olivia stuck her pert little nose in the air again. Freddie caught Hugo's eye and rolled his eyes and Hugo warmed to the man, who looked to be a similar age to himself.

'Olivia, if you do not wish me to tell your father about this, I suggest you go inside and get to bed, *now*. And take Hector with you. If anyone sees you, tell them you came outside with me and Hector but, for goodness' sake, keep your gown covered and hide that mask. You and I will have further words in the morning, after church.'

Olivia clutched Freddie's arm. 'But what about Alex? What if he's in trouble?'

'Leave Alex to me. Goodnight, Livvy.'

Her lips firmed. 'Very well,' she said, with a pout and a sigh. 'Goodnight, Freddie. Goodnight, Lord Hugo. And thank you for bringing me home.'

Hugo bowed. 'It was my pleasure, my lady. Goodnight.'

She stared at him—slightly resentfully, he thought, but he could not fathom why that might be—then she swung around and, with Hector at her heels, she vanished inside the house. Hugo found himself the object of Freddie's scrutiny.

'What happened?'

Hugo told the other man how Lady Shelton had persuaded Alex, Olivia and Neville to join them.

'You have no idea where he went?'

'No. Only that he wandered off with Lady Shelton on his arm. But that's not all.'

He revealed Tadlow's plan to wreak revenge on the Duke through Alex.

Freddie's brow furrowed. 'That wretch,' he said, in disgust. 'He is my stepsister's uncle. A nasty piece of work. I must warn Alex to beware of him and just hope he'll listen to me. Silly young chump,' he added. 'Let us hope he's not courting more trouble than he can handle.' He sighed. 'I must away to Vauxhall, then. See if I can find him and warn him. Although if he's been drinking he may well be in no mood to listen.'

'Does he not have an incentive to mend his ways now?'

Freddie raised his brows.

'Lady Olivia told me about Foxbourne and how much it means to Alex.'

Freddie nodded. 'It means the world to him, but Alex is young and impetuous. A bit like his sister,' he added with a grin. 'And with both his father and uncle out of town, it's too easy for him to fall back into his old habits. If the Duke finds out Alex took Olivia to Vauxhall against his expressed wishes—let alone that he left her alone with such an unsuitable group of people, if you'll pardon my bluntness—then he will have little choice but to follow up his threat to put a manager into Foxbourne.'

He began to climb the area steps. Laboriously. Sympathy stirred in Hugo's heart, and also something of a feeling of shame—whatever reasons he'd ever had for self-pity, at least he was fit and able. He followed Freddie up to the street.

'I shall come with you,' he said. 'I have a hackney waiting in the Square.'

'There is no need. You've done enough.'

'I intended to return anyway. I'll help you find Beauchamp first, then I have business of my own to attend to.'

Lady Olivia might have forgotten her reckless wager, and the price Clevedon intended to extract, but Hugo had not. Not only was there a wayward brother to track down, but he also had a necklace to retrieve.

Olivia clung on to Hector's collar as they climbed the stairs. After the terror and excitement of the evening, tiredness all at once swamped her. Her legs felt cumbersome, as though they belonged to someone else, as she attempted to move quietly. The familiar surroundings appeared to be somehow distant from her—as though she was viewing them through thick, somewhat distorted glass. She realised she was a touch drunk.

All I need to do is get to my bedchamber without anyone seeing me.

A single candle burned in a wall sconce opposite the head of the stairs, as it did every night, and she resumed her climb up to the second floor and her bedchamber. She stumbled over the final stair as she gained the second landing and she swallowed down a giggle.

'Shhh,' she said to Hector. He looked up at her, somewhat reproachfully, she thought. She weaved a little as she headed along the corridor towards her bedchamber.

'We must not wake Aunt Cecily. Or Lady Glen... Lady Glenlo... Lady G.'

She grimaced at the thought of meeting Nell's formidable aunt, who had been living at Beauchamp House for the past few months, ever since Papa and Rosalind's betrothal and their subsequent marriage.

Without warning, her throat thickened and her eyes blurred. She stopped walking and frowned.

'But I *like* Rosalind... I mean, Stepmama,' she said out loud. 'Why do I feel like crying?'

The click of a door latch roused her and she turned, her heart thumping, afraid it would be Aunt Cecily. Her aunt would never swallow some cock-and-bull story about going outside with Hector. She would see right through Olivia. She released her pent-up breath as Nell peered from her bedchamber.

'I thought you were my aunt,' Olivia said.

'But Cecily's bedchamber is nowhere near here, Livvy,' Nell said. She stepped out into the passageway, a frown creasing her forehead. 'Why are you dressed? You retired hours ago, with the headache.' She scanned Olivia from head to toe. 'Have you been *out*? Where did you get that bracelet? What have you been up to?'

Olivia's stomach somersaulted.

The bracelet. Mama's necklace. *Lord Clevedon.*
How could I have forgotten?

'Livvy?' Nell's voice was laced with concern as she grabbed Olivia's arm. 'Are you ill? Shall I fetch someone?'

Olivia wrenched her horrified thoughts from that dreadful game of piquet. 'No. But I'm in such trouble. Oh, what am I to do, Nell?'

'Shhh.'

Nell dragged Olivia into her bedchamber and thrust her towards the bed, where the rumpled sheets were—Olivia discovered as she slumped to the mattress—still warm. Nell lit a candle on her bedside table and then sat next to Olivia, her arm around her, as Hector padded across to flop down on the fireside rug.

'What is it, Livvy? What happened?'

Olivia tugged at the ties of her domino and let it slide from her shoulders as her hands went to her neck, exploring the bare skin in the vain hope that the entire episode had been a dream—or a nightmare—and, somehow, miraculously, her mother's necklace would reappear. Tears stung her eyes again.

'Oh, I am a wicked, wicked girl.'

'Livvy! You are frightening me. What has *happened*?'

Nell shifted away from Olivia and, grabbing her by the shoulders, she shook her.

'Please. Tell me, Livvy. It cannot be so very bad, but I cannot help if you do not tell me.'

Olivia sunk her head into her hands, her thoughts muddled and sluggish as she tried to remember it all. Slowly, disjointedly, she told Nell about her wager with Alex, their trip to Vauxhall and that disastrous card game with Lord Clevedon.

'Lord *Clevedon*? I am shocked. I thought he was a gentleman.'

'He is. But he did not know it was me. He thought I was a *floozy*. He probably thought I only got what I deserved...but...oh, *Nell*! I could have asked Lord Hugo for help... I am certain he would have helped me. But I forgot all about it because I was so certain he would try to kiss me in the hackney and when he did not—' Olivia sniffed and rubbed her eyes. 'He is as bad as Dominic and Alex. He thinks I am a s-s-silly child and not even p-p-pretty enough to steal a kiss. I was at his mercy, and he...he...'

He was kind.

He listened.

And I...oh, no...

'I told him all about Alex and Foxbourne and *everything*. Why did I tell him? I did not mean to, it just all poured out.'

'But… Livvy…who is Lord Hugo? How is he involved?'

'Lord Hugo Alastair.'

Nell gasped. 'Livvy! Do not tell me you were alone with *him* in a hackney.'

'Yes,' said Olivia, miserably. 'And he did not even *try* to kiss me.'

'But where did you meet him? Where was Alex? Surely Alex did not allow you to go off alone with a rake like Lord Hugo?'

'Alex was not there. He went off with that strumpet Lady Shelton,' Olivia said, tartly. 'He left me with Lord Clevedon and Lord Hugo. But then, after I lost Mama's necklace, I went to look for Alex and Lord Hugo rescued me and he brought me home.'

'Well, it is Alex's fault. Let him retrieve the necklace.'

'I cannot. He already scolded me for wearing it. And he's like to go off and challenge Lord Clevedon to a duel or something. You know how hot-headed he is.'

'We shall confide in Freddie, then. *He* will know what to do,' Nell said.

'Freddie already knows, but he does not know about the necklace and I cannot tell him, because then he will feel he *has* to tell Papa and then he will cast Alex out and it will all be my fault. Oh, Nell. What am I to do? Papa will be home in a few days and he is bound to see it is missing.'

'Well…' Nell frowned, clearly thinking. 'Well. I suggest we sleep on it. I am sure we'll think of something in the morning.'

* * *

Progress was slow when Hugo and Freddie arrived back at Vauxhall Gardens. Hugo matched his pace to that of his companion as they turned down yet another path, searching the faces of the numerous young men in the dimly lit thoroughfare, seeking Alex. Hugo curbed his impatience—Freddie could not help being slow, and Hugo was keen to help him find Alex. Everything he had learned tonight about the Duke's son had reminded him of his younger, wilder self.

And then there was this weird, completely out-of-character compulsion to help Olivia—he made it a rule in life not to burden himself with unnecessary responsibilities—but there was something about her spirit that drew him to her. And the odd glimpse of bewildered child beneath the bold front she exhibited to the world roused his normally well-concealed protective instincts. The decision was made. If he could help the two of them, he would do so.

Hugo scanned the couples they passed, but there was still no sign of young Beauchamp. Freddie was noticeably struggling to cope with the crowds and the distance they needed to walk.

'I have an idea.' Hugo halted as they entered the main area near to the rotunda. 'We could walk around for hours and keep missing Alex. Why do you not wait here…' he indicated a nearby bench '…and I will search the pathways. That way, you will see him if he should happen to pass.'

'And it will take much less time,' Freddie said, with a rueful smile.

Sweat beaded his upper lip and he took out a handkerchief to dry it. Out of nowhere, three youths sped past, knocking him back. They snatched the handkerchief from his hand. Hugo grabbed Freddie to prevent him falling and, as soon as he was steady on his feet, he spun around, ready to chase the thieves.

Freddie held him back. 'Leave it. They have gone.'

Sure enough, they had melted into the crowd.

'Are you hurt?'

Freddie shrugged. 'Only my pride, but I am accustomed— Hoi! Alex!' He had straightened, craning his neck to see over the crowd. 'I saw him, Alastair. Over there.'

Hugo dashed in the direction he pointed and, sure enough, there ahead of him was Lord Alexander Beauchamp and Neville Wolfe.

'Beauchamp,' he roared.

Alex swung around, searching the faces near to him. As he neared, Hugo could read the desperation in his eyes, the tightness in the set of his lips.

Alex grabbed Hugo's arm. 'Do you know where she is? You were with her. Neville here saw you both, but he lost you in the crowd. Where did she go, Alastair? What have you done to—?'

'Hold hard there, Beauchamp.' Hugo wrenched his arm from Alex's grip. 'Do not throw any accusations at me that you are not prepared to back up.'

He held the younger man's gaze. Saw the leap of muscle as Alex clenched his jaw. Then Alex's amber eyes widened and his jaw went slack. 'Freddie? You here? Where's Livvy?'

Neville Wolfe nudged Alex. 'Not Livvy! Beatrice!'

Oh, God, they can't even get their stories straight. Was I ever as wild and stupid as this pair of buffoons?

'Lady Olivia is safe at home, no thanks to you pair of numbskulls. What the devil were you thinking, bringing your sister here and then abandoning her like that?'

Hot colour swept Alex's face, but he scowled nevertheless.

'There's no harm done,' he muttered. 'I didn't want to bring her…you don't know what she's like…kept going on about debts of honour and the word of a gentleman. I didn't think there'd be any harm in it. She was *supposed* to stay put. She's safe at home now, you say?'

'Yes, thanks to Lord Hugo here,' Freddie said.

Suspicion clouded Alex's face. 'You were alone with her? In a carriage?'

'You would rather I had left her here? Alone and vulnerable?'

'Clevedon said she went off to look for us. He didn't say anything about her leaving with you.'

Hugo tamped down his irritation at young Beauchamp's accusatory tone. He was well into his cups, by the smell of his breath. And it wouldn't help to keep this escapade quiet if they had a stand-up argument here, with so many eyes and ears around.

'I left later. I happened to come across her being accosted by some youths.'

Alex hung his head at that. 'I know I shouldn't have left,' he mumbled, 'but, well… Marie Shelton! You know how it is…'

Hugo did. That was the problem. He knew exactly how it was for Alex because, not so many years ago, that had been him. Only he didn't have an impetuous and, seemingly, fearless younger sister to watch out for.

'You should take care around Marie,' he said. 'She was put up to it by Sir Peter Tadlow, some scheme to get at your father through you. Did you meet up with him again, by chance?'

Alex's flush deepened. 'What if we did?'

'What happened, Alex?' Freddie asked. 'What did Tadlow want?'

'We had a friendly game of hazard, after…after…when

we were on our way back to Clevedon's box. And we were all to go on to a gaming club together, only then I remembered Olivia and I came back for her. It's not *my* fault she took it into her head to wander off alone, is it?'

'You stupid young pup,' Hugo growled. 'Stay away from that pair and from Marie Shelton. They'll fleece you for all—'

'What is it to you?' Alex's eyes blazed as he thrust his face close to Hugo's. 'It's none of your concern what I do and who I do it with. I can take care of myself. C'mon, Nev.'

He pivoted on his heel and stalked away through the crowd. Neville, with an apologetic shrug, followed. Hugo heaved a sigh.

'That,' he said, 'is an unhappy young man.'

Freddie's brows rose and he gave a rueful smile. 'He is. He is…difficult, far too ready to fly up in the boughs. Even his father struggles to get through to him at times. He heeds his aunt, Lady Cecily, and sometimes his uncle, but seems to harbour some deep-rooted hostility towards the Duke. The trouble is… I was asked to keep an eye on him while the Duke and my sister are away, but I simply cannot go to all the places he can.

'That is why I feel I must tell the Duke about tonight, despite what Olivia wants. *Someone* must keep watch over Alex.'

'What about Avon? Surely he is better placed than you.'

Freddie huffed a laugh. 'They're brothers. They get on well enough, but if Dominic tries to tell Alex what to do, Alex is just as likely to do the opposite. He can be like it with his father, too, only not so overtly—he has no choice but to accept *his* authority most of the time, especially now with the carrot of Foxbourne dangling in front of him.'

'I'll help you to keep an eye out for him,' Hugo said, before he could censor his words.

'You?' Freddie eyed him with suspicion. 'Why would you want to do that?'

Why indeed?

Hugo had made it his business in life never to put himself out for anyone and yet here he was…

'He reminds me of myself at his age.' That much was true, at least. 'And it offends me that a man such as Tadlow would use a young man to punish his father. I should like to at least protect him from that. Only until his father returns, of course.'

'In that case, I shall accept your offer with pleasure. The Duke should be back by midweek so it will be a weight off my mind if you can help me watch over him until then. Thank you. You will alert me if there is anything you feel I should know?'

'Of course.'

Freddie bowed and then limped away, leaving Hugo to return to Clevedon's birthday celebrations, which were still in full swing, but without the guest of honour. Nobody could tell Hugo where Clevedon had gone, or how long ago he had left, leaving Hugo with no choice but to resolve to speak to him the next day.

Tadlow and Marie were both there and Hugo joined their conversation. They already trusted him and he hoped to discover their plans for Alex, but Tadlow was too foxed to make much sense and, when his head sank to the table and his eyes closed, Hugo admitted defeat. He would have to try again when the man was sober. He tried to recapture the party spirit, but within half an hour he was stifling yawns and casting a jaded eye over the rest of the company as he wondered idly what the devil he was doing still there. His wandering gaze paused on Marie as her full lips stretched in a come-hither smile, one brow arching in invitation and her blue eyes aglow with promise. Hugo, however, felt not the smallest urge to respond. Instead, a pair of wide, black-fringed silver eyes materialised in his mind's eye.

This time it was a curse he stifled. He drained his glass and stood up. Marie reached out, slipped her hand beneath his coat, and curved her hand around his buttock, squeezing, but Hugo sidestepped, out of her reach. Unsettled, and with a quiet anger humming through him, he could not wait to get away. He was in no mood for more of these people. They could go to hell as far as he was concerned.

'Goodnight,' he said abruptly and walked away.

Chapter Five

Olivia awoke the next morning with a woozy head and a vile taste in her mouth. She grimaced and cranked open her eyes. The maid had been in to open her curtains— she must have slept right through that—and the bright sunlight stabbed at her eyes. She screwed them tight and groaned. Then, as memories of the previous evening filtered into her consciousness, a feeling of sick dread settled in her stomach.

Mama's necklace.

She rolled on to her side and curled into a ball, her head in her hands, fingers rubbing her temples as she tried to think of a solution.

All she could think was: *Thank goodness Papa is away.*

But would Freddie notice the necklace was missing?

She shot up into a sitting position, ignoring the nauseous roil of her stomach, and forced her eyes open. There, on her dressing table, were the bracelet and eardrops. She hadn't even had the sense to put them in a drawer last night when she took them off. Had the maid noticed them? If she had, hopefully she would not realise their significance.

Olivia swung her legs out of the bed and levered herself to her feet, wincing as pain speared her temple.

How much punch did I drink last night?

And she had Lord Hugo Alastair to thank for that. Lord Hugo Alastair…legendary for his exploits, according to Alex and to the gossip of her friends. There had been much giggling and whispering behind their hands on the few occasions his path had crossed that of the young innocents out in society for the first time. And the most recent on dit—that his older brother, Lucas, was due back in town for the first time in six years—had stirred not only much excitement among some of their older sisters, but also the retelling of the most lurid tales of the infamous Alastair brothers—tales intended to act as a dire warning to beware of Lord Hugo and his ilk, but that instead merely intrigued.

No woman was safe, they had been told.

Hmmph. No woman is safe…except me.

She had been ready to fight him off in the hackney, but he had shown no inclination to even flirt with her, let alone *kiss* her.

I prefer my ladies willing. And experienced.

She *supposed* he had acted the gentleman, but it still rankled. She had become accustomed to young men courting her and paying her compliments, not ignoring the charms that others praised. He had scolded her and treated her like his sister. All her life she had striven to prove she was good enough for her brothers, only to be dismissed, time and time again, as a mere female and, even worse, a child. But Alex was only two years older than her, and Dominic three—that wasn't so big a difference. Not like Papa and Uncle Vernon and Aunt Cecily, who was a full *ten years* younger than Papa.

Olivia went to the dressing table and scooped up the jewellery, a sharp memory of her mother rising from the past as she stared down at the rubies and diamonds.

Mama…seated at her dressing table as her maid clasped

the necklace around her neck. The rubies had looked like drops of blood and the diamonds like chips of ice as they sparkled in the candlelight.

It was Olivia's last clear memory of her mother—being pushed impatiently aside as she tried to touch the jewels... her mother snapping, *'Oh, do get the child away from me. She will crease my dress...'* The maid scurrying to the door and calling for Nurse...being bundled from the room in tears at yet another rejection from her mama.

No matter how hard Olivia had tried to be the perfect daughter, Mama had been...uninterested. That was the word. She had been proud of *her boys*, as she had called them—although Olivia couldn't recall her spending much time with her sons—but the only love and approval Olivia could remember from her childhood had come from her father, her uncle and her aunt.

Her throat thickened and she swallowed past the painful lump that had formed. Not long after that memory, she had been told her mother was dead. She had been just five years old...she barely understood at the time but, as she had grown, she had finally understood that she would never now have the chance to make her mother proud of her.

The sound of her door opening shook her from her memories and she quickly opened the drawer in front of her and flung the jewellery inside. She would put them back in the safe later.

'How are you this morning?' Nell's violet eyes were wide with sympathy.

'I am very well.' Olivia ignored the pounding of her head. She did not deserve sympathy. She crossed to Nell and took her hands. 'I am sorry for disturbing you last night, Nell.'

'I do not mind, although I should have preferred it if you

had told me your plans. *Mayhap* I could have persuaded you not to go…that it was a mistake.'

The mischief in Nell's smile suggested she was well aware that Olivia would not have listened to her and, despite the guilt and worry causing Olivia's stomach to alternately clench and roil, she laughed. They had been firm friends ever since their first meeting at the start of the Season, even before Nell's stepsister and Olivia's father had met and fallen in love.

'Have you thought about how to get the necklace back?'

'No.' Olivia rang the bell for Hetty, her maid. 'But I am sure I shall find a solution.'

'And Freddie definitely does not know about the necklace?'

'No. You have not told him, have you?'

'No, not about the necklace, but I did tell him we spoke last night because he looked so worried I was almost afraid he would speak to Lady Cecily about it and she, of course, would be duty bound to tell your papa when he returns.'

'Did Freddie find Alex?'

'Yes, although he stormed off when Lord Hugo scolded him for putting you at risk. Freddie was quite impressed by his lordship… He has promised to help Freddie watch out for Alex until your papa comes home.'

Impressed?

Olivia pictured those lazy, mocking eyes and that hard edge to his smile as he goaded her into agreeing to a guinea a point. Now her head was no longer fuddled with the effects of punch, she realised Lord Hugo had seemed like two completely different men the night before. She had no trouble reconciling the Lord Hugo Alastair of notoriety with the bored, cynical man in the supper box, but the man who had come to her rescue, and who had escorted her home…safely…and who had, according to Nell, agreed to help Freddie watch over Alex...*he* was less easy to define. Which was the real man? She trusted Freddie's judgement, but...what if it was an act and, somehow, Lord Hugo meant Alex harm? She'd told him things last night she would never normally reveal to anyone outside her family. Was he the sort of man who might use those revelations against Alex? One thing was for sure. Somehow, she must contrive to speak to Lord Hugo and try to make sure Alex was at no risk.

It is a pity I cannot so easily deal with Lord Clevedon—unless I reveal all and throw myself upon his mercy.

At the moment, that was her only hope. She had been scared last night by his insistence that she dine with him when she redeemed her necklace but now, having thought it through, she realised her disguise as a female of lax morals had prompted his treatment of her. Clevedon was a respectable and well-respected nobleman—if he knew Beatrice's real identity, he surely would not still insist on her dining with him. Would he?

But...if I reveal to him that Beatrice was me, will he keep my secret? Or will he tell Papa?

Maybe, if she prayed most devoutly at church later, God might show her another way.

The door opened and Hetty came in with a jug of water. Nell squeezed Olivia's hand.

'I shall see you later.'

Reluctance slowed Hugo's steps as he neared the Bruton Street town house where his mother resided with his new stepfather, Sir Horace Todmorden. His lack of enthusiasm did not stem from any disinclination to see his mother—he loved his mother and, despite his initial doubts about their whirlwind courtship and marriage last year, he had to admit Mama and Sir Horace were happy together. And having Mama living closer to hand—instead of at the far end of the country at Rothley—had proved more agreeable than he had anticipated.

No. His reluctance was entirely due to the fact that Mama was nobody's fool. He inhaled deeply and then released that breath with some force. He must do this. He could not leave things as they stood. It was his fault Olivia had ended up playing to such high stakes and had been forced to pledge that necklace and it behoved him to set her mind at rest. He walked on with renewed purpose and rapped on the front door.

'Good morning, Stape,' he said as the door opened. 'I've come to escort my mother to church.'

The butler's eyes widened slightly, then he stepped back and bowed as Hugo strode past him into the house.

'I shall inform her ladyship of your arrival, my lord, if you would care to wait in the salon?'

Not ten minutes later the door opened and Mama swept in, already dressed for church in a dark blue pelisse and matching hat.

'Hugo?' She crossed the room in her normal brisk fashion and placed both hands to his chest. 'You *are* real.' Her dark eyes twinkled as she looked up at him. 'I felt certain Stape had made a mistake. I almost accused him of helping himself to the brandy while dear Horace is away.'

'Mama. Looking as beautiful as ever, I see.'

Hugo kissed her cheek, then gave her a hug, feeling his heart lift.

'But what is this nonsense? You? Escort me to church? Stape must be mistaken about that.'

'There is no mistake, Mama. With Sir Horace away, I thought to offer my services, that is all.'

His stepfather had been called back to his estate near Brighton and was not expected to return until Tuesday.

Mama tilted her head to one side, making her look more than ever like a bright-eyed, inquisitive bird.

'Well, I am delighted to accept, my dear. In fact, nothing would give me greater pleasure than to walk into St George's upon your arm, but…' her eyes narrowed '…I *know* you. You are up to something. And I shall be watching you.'

She smiled, wagging her forefinger at him, and Hugo—who was already wondering how on earth he might contrive a private word with Lady Olivia Beauchamp without setting the gossips of the *ton* on fire—knew that his own mother, with the sharpest eyes of anyone in his acquaintance, would be the first to notice any particular attention. And, worse, she was the *only* person with enough nerve to interrogate him about it.

'Watch all you like, Mama. If a son cannot do his mother a service without an ulterior motive, then what *is* the world coming to?'

Mama smiled serenely as she pulled on her gloves. 'As you say, my dear. Come then. Shall we walk, as it is such a lovely day?'

Hugo bowed and proffered his arm.

As they crossed Hanover Square on their way to St George's he saw her, alighting from Cheriton's town coach. She was with her aunt, Lady Cecily, as well as her eldest brother, Avon, Freddie Allen—the Duchess's brother—and the Allens' stepsister, Lady Helena Caldicot. She and Olivia made a striking pair, both tall and willowy, but as different in colouring as it was possible to be, with Lady Helena's silver-blonde locks contrasting with Olivia's raven-black hair. No sooner had the pair set foot on the pavement than a pack of eager young pups clustered around them: bowing, proffering their arms, clearly striving to be the favoured one. Hugo bit back a derisive snort at the sight. At least he had never made a complete cake of himself over a woman like that.

No. You have made very certain never to risk your heart.

He dismissed that snide inner voice as he watched Olivia laughingly refuse all offers, instead linking arms with...Nell, she had called the other girl last night. They sashayed up the few steps to the church door—two young ladies with the world at their feet: beautiful, well connected and no doubt with generous dowries. It was what the *ton*... the Season...society...was all about. He stared at the pups dogging their footsteps. At least they were a better match for her than a cynical, world-weary man about town such as Clevedon. Or himself.

Which of them will she favour?

He wrenched his attention from the group, irritated by his random thoughts, the last of which he mentally amended to *Which of them will* they *favour?*

Last to emerge from the town coach was Lady Glenlochrie, handed down by Avon. She leaned heavily on her stick as the remainder of the party made their way slowly into church.

'Hugo?'

Startled, he looked down at his mother. Saw the interest in her small, dark eyes. And cursed his inattentiveness that had slowed their pace to a near crawl as he had become absorbed in watching the Beauchamps' arrival.

'My apologies, Mama,' he said smoothly. 'I found myself wondering why Lady Glenlochrie was with the Beauchamps, but then I remembered her connection with the Caldicot chit.'

Mama's lips thinned. 'Chit? Really, Hugo, I do wish you would not use such words. It is most ungentlemanly.'

At his nonchalant shrug of his shoulders, he saw the

interest in his mother's expression fade into one of disappointment. She had made her ambition very clear. Since his brother, Lucas's, nuptials at the end of last year, her one wish was that Hugo would meet a nice young lady and settle down. He huffed a silent laugh. Never. He wasn't the marrying kind and, besides, no *nice young lady* would ever consider him as suitable husband material. But their exchange had reminded him...

'I came across young Alex Beauchamp last night at Vauxhall. He struck me as being an unhappy man. Any idea why?'

His mother's eyes twinkled. 'It amuses me to hear you describe him as such, my son. He is not so very different from you at that age.'

'I am aware of that. I, however, had good reason with the father I had.'

Guilt and pain fused in Mama's expression. 'You did and I am more sorry than you know for not protecting you and Lucas more.'

'Mama.' He put his arm around her shoulders for a quick hug. 'You did everything you could to protect us and we're both more than grateful for that.' The memory of his mother taking the blows intended for her sons reared up and impotent rage raked his gut. His father had been dead three years and was way beyond any revenge or retribution. Hugo hauled his thoughts back to the Beauchamps. 'Someone hinted at something in the past that affected young Beauchamp. I don't believe I've ever heard the story.'

'It was his mother. She was murdered and Alex discovered her body. He was only seven years of age and it affected him really badly. And for some reason—no one quite knows why—he seems to blame his father.' Mama shot a quick look around, then lowered her voice. 'Far be it from me to speak ill of the dead, but it was a release for both the Duke *and* his children. Their mother had no time for them…they were far better off being raised by Lady Cecily. *She* is like a mother to the three of them and has devoted her entire life to them. They are very fortunate to have her.'

So that was what Olivia had alluded to in her jumbled tale of the night before. To know your mother had been murdered—even if she wasn't the perfect mother—must have affected Olivia as much as Alex.

They continued on into the cool interior of St George's.

Olivia squeezed her eyes tight shut as soon as they settled into the Beauchamp family pew at St George's and prayed for a flash of inspiration. She waited, but none came and, finally, she opened her eyes to find her aunt frowning at her.

'Are you unwell, Livvy?' Aunt Cecily took her hand. 'You are very pale. Are you in pain?'

As Olivia opened her mouth to protest her good health, she was distracted by the sight of a tall, dark-haired gentleman walking up the aisle with a tiny, older woman upon his arm. He turned his head, scanning the congregation already seated in the high-sided box pews and, even though she was seated furthest away from him, his gaze lingered on Olivia, a smile tugging at his mouth. She felt her eyes widen.

What is he doing here? What does that look mean? What is he doing with Lady Tod—?

Her thoughts stumbled and tripped over one another as Lord Hugo Alastair handed Lady Todmorden—his mother, who had been Lady Rothley before, Olivia now recalled—into a pew. Never had she seen Lord Hugo attend the church, although Lady Todmorden attended every week and, as she and Aunt Cecily were on friendly terms, they often exchanged a few pleasantries if they met at a function, or in passing on the street, or—and Olivia's heart gave a racketing thump before it began to race—after church.

'Livvy? What is it? You look as though you have seen a ghost.' Aunt Cecily now chafed Olivia's hand between hers.

'I am perfectly all right.' Olivia forced her gaze back to her aunt, praying she hadn't noticed her interest in Hugo. She elevated her nose. 'I was merely indulging in pious reflection. This *is* a church, is it not?'

The bells ceased ringing just as Aunt Cecily tutted and it sounded extraordinarily loud in the sudden, solemn hush inside the church. Olivia cast a sidelong look of reproach at her pink-cheeked aunt because that is precisely how Aunt Cecily would expect her to react, but inside she was a mass of seething conjecture. Alex rarely attended church—he claimed to prefer the services at St James's Church, on Piccadilly, but Olivia was certain he had never set foot in the place. So Hugo was not here today to see Alex, which meant he had come to speak to her. Hope blossomed. Had he recovered her necklace already? She had prayed for a miracle; perhaps this was it.

And, in among that hope was…another emotion she did not recognise. She could put no name to it, but it prompted the frequent urge to slide her gaze sideways until she could just see, from the corner of her eye, his lordship. And, every time, a little jolt of…something…sped through her, making her feel, somehow, more alive. Excitement. But not just any ordinary, everyday excitement. This was… fizzing, bubbly, high—the feeling she always got at her first sip of freshly poured champagne. It made her heart feel somehow hollow and yet full at the same time. She could hardly bear to sit still as the vicar droned on or as she bent her head in prayer. She snatched another glance at Lord Hugo among the kerfuffle as they all stood to sing, drinking in his tall, broad-shouldered frame and the firm line of his jaw.

Olivia waited in a fever of impatience for the service to end, even though she could not see how she could snatch a private word with Lord Hugo. She might enjoy occasional acts of rebellion, but she was not reckless enough to talk openly to a man of his dubious reputation. She was well aware of the behaviour expected of a young lady and she took care to behave with perfect propriety in public.

As the congregation left their pews and moved slowly towards the church door—the Reverend Hodgson prided himself on greeting every one of his parishioners at the door after Sunday service, and always exchanged a few words with each—Hugo caught Olivia's eye with a meaningful look. Her pew steadily emptied and she moved along, behind Aunt Cecily. As they neared the end, she tapped her aunt's arm.

'I've left my reticule behind,' she said.

'I'll wait while you fetch it.'

'There's no need. I shan't be long. I shall see you outside.'

Olivia waited to make sure Aunt Cecily kept moving towards the church door. A surreptitious glance confirmed Lord Hugo also lingered in his pew even though his mother was already halfway to the church door. Olivia went back to fish under the pew for the reticule she had nudged out of sight with her foot.

As soon as the majority of worshippers had exited the church, Olivia made her way back along the pew, emerging into the aisle at the exact time Lord Hugo passed.

Chapter Six

'Why are you here?'

One brow elevated. 'Good morning, Lady Olivia. I trust you suffer no ill effects from last night?'

'Shhh! What if someone was to hear?'

One corner of his mouth quirked as he held her gaze, that infuriating brow still arched enquiringly. Olivia quashed her huff of impatience as they began to walk, slowly and side by side, towards the door at the back of the church.

'Yes. I am very…that is, my head pains me somewhat, but that is of no significance.'

'I wished to set your mind at rest about the necklace. I shall return it to you as soon as I am able to.'

'Oh.' She felt guilt now at her abruptness. 'Then I am most grateful. Have you already spoken to Lord Clevedon?'

'Not as yet, but I shall. Do not worry. I shall deal with him.'

She clutched at his sleeve, forcing him to halt. 'Papa will be home soon. Possibly by Wednesday, my aunt said. It is important I get it back before then.'

He patted her hand, his expression indulgent, firing her indignation as she recalled his gentlemanly behaviour last night in the hackney.

'I shall do my best, but you must be patient.'
Like an adult placating a child.

He was nothing like the Lord Hugo Alastair of legend. Or did he simply not find her attractive? On impulse, Olivia stepped closer to him and gazed up into his eyes.

'You are very kind. How shall I ever repay you?'

She dropped her gaze, but a peek through her lashes caught him in a purely masculine appraisal of her that was completely at odds with his words, telling her that—however much he tried to disguise it—he was absolutely aware of her and attracted to her.

'Consider it my good deed for the year. You had better leave ahead of me.'

He feathered the back of his fingers along the line of her jaw. Her stomach tightened at his touch and, feeling her cheeks heat, she turned and headed for the church door. Outside, Aunt Cecily was quietly conversing with the Reverend Hodgson.

'I am sorry to keep you waiting, Aunt,' she said airily, as Hugo emerged behind her and then sauntered over to stand with his mother, who was chatting to a group of older ladies.

Olivia was relieved to see their coach already waiting at the kerb. Freddie was occupied with assisting Lady Glenlochrie up the steps and would hopefully have missed the coincidence of her and Hugo both leaving the church last, after the events of last night. All she had to do now was wait until Hugo returned her necklace and then all would be well.

'You must be patient, Livvy,' said Nell.

Olivia paced the salon and, for the umpteenth time since Sunday, she said, 'Where is he? Why has he not returned it?'

The suspicion was growing that, perhaps, she should not

have put so much trust in Hugo's promise to retrieve the necklace. She'd heard nothing from him—not one word— and here it was, Tuesday already, and Papa would be home any day. In fact, she counted her blessings he was not already here. At least Freddie had noticed nothing amiss, even though he had access to Papa's safe, but she could not fool herself that Papa would miss its absence.

'What if he thinks it has been stolen?'

'Who?' Nell's fair brows bunched, crinkling her forehead. 'Lord Hugo? I do not—'

'Not Lord Hugo! Papa!' Olivia flung herself down on the sofa next to Nell. 'He will notice it is gone. He—'

She fell silent as the salon door opened and she looked around, almost expecting to see her father there, the empty jewel case in his hand, with a face of fury. The air whooshed from her lungs in a relieved gasp as Aunt Cecily hurried in, a letter in her hand. And then Olivia forgot her own troubles as she took in her aunt's expression. She jumped to her feet.

'Aunt? What is it? Not…it is not bad news?'

Her heart nearly seized in her chest as she mentally reviewed every member of her family—where they were, what disaster might have befallen them. Papa and Rosalind and Mr Allen on a long journey—carriage accidents did happen, as poor Freddie, maimed as a baby, knew to his cost; Uncle Vernon heaven knew where, having left last week on a sudden visit to Worcestershire to look for some boring long-lost cousin; Dominic—he was here in London, and she was confident *he* would be in no trouble…which left…

'Is it Alex? Is he in trouble?'

'No. It is not Alex.'

Aunt Cecily looked—and sounded—most peculiar. Olivia helped her to a chair and, as her aunt sat, she caught a glimpse of the letter, recognising her uncle's dark, sprawling script. Her pulse steadied. If he was well enough to pen a letter, he was not ill. Or—and it was her greatest fear for any member of her family—dead. She did not know whether it was because of the early loss of her mother, but her family meant everything to her and the thought of losing any one of them could send her spiralling into panic.

'It is your Uncle Vernon. I can hardly credit it but…he is getting married.'

'Married? Uncle Vernon?'

Aunt Cecily nodded. 'On Friday. Near to a place called Stourbridge, in Worcestershire.' She jumped to her feet. 'There is so much to do. I must send word to Dominic and Alex. They shall escort us. If we leave early tomorrow, we should be there in time.'

'But…who is he marrying? Is it someone we know?'

Whoever she was, Olivia was already half-inclined to dislike her. Their stable home life—already irreversibly altered by the addition of Rosalind and her family to their household—would now be changed even more. Even though she liked Rosalind and her family, Olivia had still found the recent changes difficult. As the youngest, and a girl, she had always felt she must struggle for her fair share of attention, but now her place in this new, enlarged family seemed even more insecure.

At least Papa still lived at home, but if Uncle Vernon married he would want to live on his own country estate in Devonshire instead of at Cheriton Abbey with the rest of the family and they would hardly ever see him. Resentment squirmed inside her, even though she knew she was being unreasonable. She knew she could not expect everything to remain the same for ever—and, hopefully, she would herself one day marry which would mean she must leave to have her own family—but for both her father and her uncle to marry in the very year of her own come-out into society was just moving too fast.

She felt a little as though she was in a carriage drawn by runaway horses, speeding towards a cliff edge, but she needed a pause while she caught her breath.

'It is a Miss Dorothea Markham, and...' Cecily frowned as she re-read the letter '...he does not say much about her, other than that she is adorable.'

Her brows rose as she exchanged a look with Olivia.

'It sounds,' she added, in a faint voice, 'as though your uncle has fallen in love.'

The dread inside Olivia grew throughout that interminable day until she felt utterly consumed by it. The appearance of Alex midway through the afternoon prompted an idea: she would not see Hugo if she sat waiting meekly at home, but she might very well see him in the Park.

'Alex, dearest, *dearest* brother of mine.'

He eyed her with suspicion. 'What are you after now, brat?'

She let the insult go. 'Will you escort Nell and I to the Park? Please? Aunt Cecily is too busy with the arrangements for the journey tomorrow and Lady G. is having her nap. And, besides, if we go with her, we shall be obliged to go in the carriage. And it is such a lovely day. I long for a little exercise. *Please?*'

'Ask Avon. Walks in the Park are more his style than mine. I've got more important things to do.'

'Dominic has gone to Westfield to tell them he will be out of town for a week or so,' said Olivia.

Westfield School was an orphan asylum and school in Islington that Dominic supported both financially and in person.

'And I thought we might ride to the Park,' she continued.

They could cover more ground that way. 'After all, we shall be stuck in the carriage for the next two days or more, so—'

'Not me,' interrupted Alex. 'I'm not going.'

'Not going? Why not?'

'It's only a wedding, isn't it? I shall meet the bride soon enough, when they come to London. No need to go all the way up there—sounds a dead bore to me. With Papa, Aunt Cecy, you and Avon all there to represent the family, I shan't be missed. And I have commitments here, y'know.'

Olivia frowned. 'What commitments?'

He grinned and tweaked her cheek. 'Never you mind, Livvy. Nothing for a young miss to trouble herself about, you can be sure of that. It's men's business.'

Olivia tamped down her irritation. Men's business indeed.

'*Please*, Alex. You can spare an hour or two, surely? Nell and I are bored with sitting indoors. Our callers have been and gone...' with two eligible and attractive young ladies in the house there was never any dearth of eager male callers '...and now there is nothing to look forward to but dinner and bed.'

Aunt Cecily had already sent their apologies for the soirée they had been to attend that evening.

'Oh, all right,' said her brother, with bad grace. 'I know you...you will go on and on, so I might as well agree now as later.'

Olivia squealed and clapped her hands before tiptoeing up to press a kiss to Alex's cheek. '*Thank* you. I shall send word to the stables and run and get changed.'

Now she must pray that Hugo would be there and that she might contrive to snatch a word with him.

Lord Hugo Alastair strode away from Grosvenor Square after watching young Beauchamp disappear into Beau-

champ House. Hopefully he would stay out of mischief for
a short while at least. Hugo now had a greater understanding of why indolence was his preferred state of being. What
the devil had possessed him to promise Freddie he would
keep an eye on Beauchamp? At least the Duke should be
home some time tomorrow. He hoped. That was what Olivia said on Sunday.

And that was another thing… Olivia. Her and that
blasted necklace. In between watching over Beauchamp—
and he could not believe that young pup's resilience. Had
he ever been that energetic? On the go morning, noon and
night?—he had been trying to locate Clevedon, but he'd
gone to ground. No one had seen him since Saturday night
and even calling at his house had elicited no further information other than that his lordship was out of town and
they did not know when to expect his return.

At least he would be back by Saturday. Of that Hugo was
grimly certain. But his promise to Olivia weighed upon him.
He knew she must be anxiously waiting for news, but a man
such as he could not call upon an innocent miss without inviting gossip and ill-founded conjecture—he was not the sort
of man who called upon young ladies and neither would such
a social call be tolerated by the parents of said young ladies.
And although he had met up with Freddie, despite there being
nothing, as yet, to report on Alex's activities—if Tadlow really did have a plan, it seemed he was in no hurry to imple-
ment it—he could not pass any message to Olivia through
Freddie because he clearly knew nothing about that necklace.
As far as Freddie was concerned, Olivia's escapade was done
and dusted and there was nothing further to worry about.

And therein lay Hugo's main worry. From what he had
learned about Olivia on Saturday evening, she was not the
sort to sit around and simply wait. She was more likely to
meet trouble head on and that made it more than proba-

ble that she would take matters into her own hands before Saturday came around, which is why that bloody necklace was niggling away at Hugo. He needed to get word to her before she did something stupid. But how?

Now Alex was safely home, Hugo had nothing to do until this evening, when he had accepted an invitation from Tadlow to a card party. He knew from past experience it would be high stakes. He suspected Lord Alexander Beauchamp would be on the guest list. Until ten o'clock, then, he was a free man as far as Beauchamp was concerned. He could relax; shrug off the responsibilities he had so unthinkingly taken upon his shoulders and, to that end, he was heading for White's to see who was about.

His steps slowed as he realised that idea held little appeal. He was unusually restless…the mantle of unfinished business pressed down upon him until he could not bear the thought of sitting around and talking of inconsequential matters. With a muttered curse, he halted. He had just left Berkeley Square via Berkeley Street and now he retraced his steps, past the end of Bruton Street—he was in no mood to face one of his mother's inquisitions: she had a way of winkling out how a man was feeling, even though he had no wish to talk of such namby-pamby nonsense—and rounded the next corner into Bruton Place. Since his marriage to Mama, Sir Horace—an ex-cavalryman and a decent enough cove, now Hugo came to think of it—had generously shouldered the expense of stabling a riding horse for his new stepson. A ride in the Park would surely shake some of these fidgets out of his system.

At the stables he found his stepfather, looking tired and dishevelled, unlike his usual dapper self, and deep in conversation with his head man.

'Good afternoon, sir,' he said. 'You just arrived home?'
Sir Horace straightened into his customary upright

stance, squaring his shoulders and straightening his coat, looking every inch the ex-military man. 'Indeed, m'boy. Bennet and I were just discussing that new mare I bought at Tatt's last week.'

'Is there a problem with her?'

'She kicked out at one of the lads the other day and broke his arm. And she's a biter. Bennet said some of the lads are chary of going in the stall with her now.' Sir Horace frowned, his side whiskers bristling as he pursed his lips. 'I must decide what to do with her. I cannot, in good faith, sell her on, but neither can I reconcile myself to destroying her…not until we have tried everything to calm her down. I suspect she was doped for the sale. She was docile enough before I left for Helmstone.'

Sir Horace had been called back to Helmstone—his country estate, situated just outside Brighton—on urgent business on Saturday.

'Who sold her? Can you not return her?'

'*Caveat emptor*, m'boy,' said Sir Horace. 'The animals were sold "as seen". Besides, she really does have exceptional conformation.'

'And *I* reckon she's been ill-treated, milord,' said Bennet. ''Twouldn't be right to send her back, even if we could.' He glanced at Hugo. 'Was you intending to go out on Falcon, milord?'

'Yes.'

'I'll get him saddled and bring him out for you.' Bennet disappeared into the stables.

'I shall have to put my mind to what to do about that mare,' said Sir Horace, a deep frown furrowing his brow as he watched Bennet go. 'I can't have her injuring my lads.'

'Was your trip satisfactory?' asked Hugo in an effort to distract his stepfather. He didn't like to see the old man so troubled. 'Is everything in order at Helmstone?'

'Indeed it is, m'boy. The harvest looks promising…' His voice tailed into silence and he tugged at his whiskers—a sure sign he was agitated, so Mama said.

'Is something else troubling you, sir?'

Even as the words left his mouth, Hugo silently cursed himself. Didn't he already have enough to worry about without adding more? But the old boy looked pretty grey and Hugo was quite fond of him, really. He'd made Mama very happy and that, in Hugo's book, was everything.

'Nothing for you to worry about, son. Nothing you can do—' The old boy's jaw closed with an audible snap as a calculating light dawned in his shrewd grey eyes. He grasped Hugo's arm and steered him to a quiet corner. 'As it happens…' he said, slowly, 'there might be…' His bushy brows bunched over the bridge of his nose. Then his frown cleared. 'Thank you, my boy!'

It was Hugo's turn to frown. 'Why are you thanking me?'

'Why, you offered to help, did you not?'

Hugo thought back. He was almost certain the word *help* had not crossed his lips. A warning rumbled deep in his gut, like the distant growl of thunder on a summer day. Now what had he let himself in for? His eyes narrowed.

'What do you have in mind?'

'Well, I must think this through…but it could be just the solution for the both of us.'

'The both of us?'

This was sounding more and more ominous and caution screamed through him. He owed his stepfather who, to his credit, had never dismissed Hugo as a worthless rake as the rest of society did. Sir Horace, himself childless, had taken time to get to know Hugo when they had first met in the spring of last year and had sought his advice on running his estate—discussing new agricultural developments, as though Hugo knew anything about *them*—and shown every sign of valuing Hugo's opinions. So much so, that Hugo had found himself reading up on such matters in the newssheets and the periodicals at White's.

And that was another thing. Sir Horace had pulled strings and made certain that Hugo's membership of White's was approved, even though it raised a few eyebrows. So now, for the first time in his life, Hugo was a member of the most respected of gentlemen's clubs and, he realised, he was frequenting it more and more often.

His stepfather slapped him on the back, jolting him from that sudden realisation of how much his life was in a state of flux. Satisfaction now gleamed in that shrewd gaze and a heavy weight settled in Hugo's stomach. Somehow, he had embroiled himself in something else that would interfere with his life of idle pleasure. But…curiosity stirred nevertheless.

'Well, well, my boy. I am suddenly feeling much brighter. Yes, indeed. I haven't time to go into the detail now, but I shall see you later. Are you free to come to dinner this evening?'

'Indeed I am. I have a commitment later in the evening, but will dine with you with pleasure, sir.'

'Good, good. We will speak then. For now, though… I am eager to see your mama and I suspect you were on your way elsewhere so I shall detain you no longer.'

With a cheery wave, Sir Horace disappeared from sight. Hugo blew a puff of air from his cheeks as the clatter of hooves on cobbles announced that Falcon, Hugo's bay gelding, was ready.

What the devil *have I let myself in for now?*

Before long Hugo was turning in through the gates to the Park. He turned on to Rotten Row and immediately nudged Falcon into a trot and then—where the carriages thinned out—into a canter, in no mood for conversation as his thoughts leapt forward to that night's card game and what Tadlow might have in store for young Beauchamp. He'd ridden almost the entire circuit when he heard his name.

Chapter Seven

'Hugo!'

Hugo stifled a curse as he looked over his shoulder, but he soon forgot his irritation when he identified the man who had called his name. He reined Falcon to a halt.

'You are not due in town until tomorrow.'

Lucas grinned, and clasped Hugo's outthrust hand in a hard grip. 'We made good time on the journey. We arrived earlier this afternoon. Then Sir Horace came home and told me you'd just ridden out here, so I thought to join you.'

Hugo eyed his brother's mount. 'That's his favourite horse. You *are* honoured. Did you leave Mary and the children in Bruton Street?'

'I did. She and Mama are catching up on all the news from Rothley and Mary isn't keen to leave the children—they've both been asleep since we got here and she doesn't want them to wake up in a strange place alone.'

Lucas's wife, Mary, had been married before and Lucas was now stepfather to her two children—Toby, aged six, and three-year-old Emily.

'Who would have thought it—the original Infamous Alastair, a doting family man.'

The two men turned their horses and rode on side by side.

Lucas laughed. 'I'd forgotten all about that old nick-name.' He nodded at two fashionable young matrons, whose wide eyes and slack jaws followed the brothers' progress as they passed by. 'No wonder we are attracting such attention.'

'The Infamous Alastairs ride again,' said Hugo, with a grin. 'How long is it since you were last in London?'

'Six years now. It seems a lifetime ago. I was two years younger than you are now, Brother. Speaking of which, is it not time you thought about settling down?'

Hugo grimaced. 'You sound just like Mama. In fact, I'll hazard a guess she has already begged you to help her in her campaign to see me wed.'

Lucas smirked. 'She might have mentioned it a time or three. And, as a good dutiful son, I am simply obey-ing her wishes.'

'She has become impossible since your wedding. I only manage to silence her by pointing out I have nothing what-soever to offer a bride, apart from a jaded reputation and a courtesy title.'

'But from what I have been hearing, that is no longer true. You are a member of White's. You have investments. You are *almost* respectable.'

Hugo frowned, then forced a laugh. 'Almost, but not quite, eh?' He knew it would take more than that to banish the *ton's* memory of his hedonistic past. 'I should prob-ably have accepted the younger son's lot a long time ago and gone into the army instead of going to Oxford. God knows I spent little enough time there.'

Lucas laughed. 'That's true. You spent more time with me in London than you did at university.' Then he slid a sly sideways look at Hugo. 'Or you could have gone into the church. I can just see you—in the pulpit every Sunday, preaching to the worthy.'

Hugo tipped his head back and laughed, but when he straightened and directed his gaze forward again, he felt the laugh slide from his face. Olivia, atop a dainty chestnut, her slim figure elegantly clad in a dark blue riding habit with military-style trim, was riding towards him. Hugo wrenched his gaze from her to take in her two companions—her brother, Lord Alexander, and Lady Helena Caldicot.

This would have been an ideal time for Hugo to snatch a word with Olivia and put her mind at rest except that—as the Beauchamp party drew closer—Hugo could read Alex's scowl as he glared at him and he could *feel* the frostiness of Olivia's silver-grey gaze as it swept over him, her hoity nose in the air and her lips set in a tight line. With Lucas at his side, there was no way he would risk an encounter with those two in their current moods.

He stifled a sigh. Alex clearly hadn't forgiven him for Saturday night and Olivia wouldn't know that Clevedon was out of town—she would only wonder why Hugo had not yet returned her necklace as he had promised. He tamped down his frustration as he tipped his hat to the trio and rode on past without as much as a *good afternoon*.

'Care to share, Little Brother?'

Hugo snapped his gaze to meet Lucas's arched brows. The knowing curve to his mouth suggested his perceptive brother hadn't missed the chill in the atmosphere.

'Are you still breaking the hearts of the ladies of the *ton*? I have to say, that dark-haired one was a beauty, but maybe a touch too feisty for comfort. And—' he swivelled in his saddle to look behind them '—I should have thought a touch on the young side for a dalliance with a man of your age and…er…tarnished reputation.'

Hugo felt the growl build in his throat. 'There *is* no dalliance.'

'Could've fooled me,' drawled Lucas. 'Must be losing

my touch—been out of the game too long, I dare say. But, seriously, if not a dalliance, there is definitely something between you. And if I can tell, so will countless others, mind. Never forget the first rule of a satisfactory *affaire*, my lad. Don't get caught. Who is she?'

'*They* are Lord Alexander Beauchamp, his sister, Lady Olivia, and their new step-aunt, Lady Helena Caldicot. Her stepsister has just married Cheriton.'

Lucas whistled. 'Cheriton's brood? My…you *are* mixing with the elite. And why, pray tell, are the Beauchamps looking daggers at you?'

Anger flared. He answered to no one—particularly not the brother who had abandoned him in London at the tender age of twenty. 'I suggest you ask them if you are so curious.'

Hugo dug his heels into Falcon's flanks, pushing him into a canter. Lucas kept pace with him until, his rage subsiding, Hugo slowed. He was behaving like an idiot. He had long ago forgiven Lucas for his abrupt departure from London and he should know better by now than to let his brother's ribbing provoke him. He smiled ruefully at Lucas. His anger was at the situation in which he had found himself, not at his brother.

'Very well. You are right. There is more to it, but it is not what you think and I am not at liberty to tell you more.'

Lucas winked. 'Soul of discretion, eh? I see you haven't forgotten *all* of your lessons.'

'Did you see that?' Olivia ripped off her York tan gloves and dashed them on to her bed. She had managed to contain her fury all the way home, but as soon as she and Nell were alone she let fly. 'Not even the slightest attempt to speak to me and to set my mind at rest.'

'But... Livvy...you heard Alex. He forbade you to stop and speak to Lord Hugo in any case.'

'Pooh. That is no excuse for his *lordship* to not even *try* to talk to me.'

'Who was the gentleman riding with him, do you think, Livvy? Do you think that is Rothley? There was a distinct resemblance, do you not agree? They made a striking pair.'

Olivia waved her hand dismissively. Who cared who he was, when her whole life was in ruins? Anyway, she had barely noticed the other man. She'd had eyes only for Hugo, trying to convey her fury with just one look. For all the good it had done her. He'd not even acknowledged her other than a tip of his hat.

'He does not even know yet that Papa isn't coming home as planned because of Uncle Vernon's wedding.' Her throat was so tight she could hardly breathe. 'Who does he think he is—promising to help me and then brushing me aside like a...a...bothersome fly?'

Nell snorted with laughter and Olivia glared at her. 'Do not laugh at me, Nell. And as for Alex...of all the high-handed, interfering—Oh! I could throttle him! Ordering me about like a...like a...'

'Like a bothersome fly?' Nell spluttered.

'Hmmph!' Olivia threw herself on her bed, her mind whirling with indignant thoughts. 'I'll show him that I don't need him and his...his...top-lofty opinion of himself. I don't need his help. You see if I don't.' Then, gradually, the whirl slowed and steadied, until... 'Oh, Nell!' Hot tears scalded her eyes. 'What am I to do? W-w-w...' She gulped, then sucked in a deep breath. 'We leave in the morning. We won't be back until next week. And Lord Clevedon threatened to sell Mama's necklace if I don't go to his house to pay my debt.'

Nell sat next to Olivia and patted her shoulder. 'I am

sure he will not do so, Livvy. Why do you not write to him and explain? I am sure he will wait until you are back in town.'

Olivia rolled on to her back. 'But he does not know it is me, Nell. I did think about telling him the truth, but how could I trust him to keep my secret? What if he feels honour bound to tell Papa? Then Alex won't get Foxbourne and he will never forgive me.'

With Papa and Uncle Vernon both with new wives, her brothers would be even more important to Olivia. 'Oh, what am I to do?'

Nell chewed her bottom lip. '*I* am not going to the wedding. I suppose I c-could always go to L-Lord Clevedon's house and retrieve the necklace.'

Olivia stared at Nell, her heart swelling as she recognised the fear in her friend's eyes, but also the determined set of her mouth. She sat up and flung her arms around her.

'No, you will not,' she declared. 'This is my mess and I shall deal with it. I'll prove to Lord Hugo that I can manage my own affairs. All I ask of you, dearest Nell, is that you back up my story to Aunt Cecily.'

'What is the matter, Livvy? You have not eaten a single morsel of your dinner.'

'I feel unwell, Aunt.' Olivia allowed her shoulders to slump. She had powdered her face earlier, to ensure she looked pale, and rubbed a little soot from the fire under her eyes to add to the illusion of sickness. 'I cannot face eating anything. I am sorry.'

'You did complain of the headache when we returned from the Park,' said Nell. 'Has it worsened?'

Olivia nodded, then winced, raising her hand to her temple.

'You do look peaked, now I come to think of it. Oh, dear. I am so sorry, Livvy. I have been in such a fluster preparing for our journey tomorrow, I did not notice. Perhaps you should retire early? A sleep will do you the world of good. Grantham?'

The butler bowed. 'Yes, milady?'

'Alert Hetty that Lady Olivia is unwell and is in need of her assistance in her bedchamber, if you please. Goodnight, Livvy. You will no doubt feel better in the morning.'

Grantham left the dining room and a footman came forward to draw back Olivia's chair and allow her to stand. Olivia averted her gaze from her dinner plate as she did so. It was lobster, her favourite, and her empty stomach groaned a protest. She stiffened her resolve. A hungry night was a small price to pay for being able to remain in town and redeem Mama's necklace.

Some time later, Nell slipped into Olivia's bedchamber. She carried a plate piled with fruit, bread and cheese.

'I went to the kitchen and told Cook that I was still hungry.'

'Oh, thank you, Nell. I am *starving*.'

As Olivia ate, she became aware of Nell's gaze on her. 'What is it? Why do you stare at me so?'

Nell's fair brows drew together into a frown. 'Lord Hugo.'

Olivia put her half-eaten peach on the plate. 'What about him?'

'Oh, Livvy. We are friends, are we not? It is only… Today is the first time I have even seen him close to. He is very handsome.'

'He is completely unsuitable for you, Nell. He is a *rake*.'

Olivia cringed inside as she saw the light of laughter in Nell's violet eyes.

'I was right. You *have* developed a *tendre* for him, Livvy. It is as plain as the nose on your face.' She sobered. 'But…if he is not suitable for me, neither would he be suitable for you, Liv. Your papa—'

'I do not have a *tendre* for him, Nell. That is ridiculous. Of course he is unsuitable.'

Utterly unsuitable.

'But he is very handsome,' Nell murmured, teasingly.

And exciting.

'Those eyes—' Nell's voice was dreamy '—so dark and, somehow, soulful.'

His eyes…

Olivia felt again the weight of his gaze in the hackney. The glitter as they passed beneath the streetlamp…as deep and fathomless as a lake in the moonlight. She shivered. Then, to mask her reaction, she picked up her peach and began to eat again.

'What nonsense,' she declared, around her mouthful of fruit.

Hugo presented himself at Sir Horace's town house in Bruton Street for dinner that evening, as promised. He would dine with his family before heading over to Tadlow's place for his card party, where he would keep an eye on Alexander Beauchamp—hopefully not a waste of time, even though it might prove impossible to dissuade that young hothead from getting in over his head yet again.

'Hugo!' Mama hurried towards him, her hands outstretched and her face creased with delight. 'Horace said he had invited you, but I did not allow myself to hope you would come. You lead such a busy life.'

Only Mama could describe my life of idle pleasure as busy.

Hugo bit back his smile as he took her hands and bent

to kiss her cheek. Mama: ever supportive, ever loving, ever protective. She would never hear a word against either of her sons, even during the years when their wild behaviour had set society on its ears. Her loyalty was what made her the wonderful mother she was. Mary was the same—utterly loyal to Lucas and yet unafraid to stand up to him, discreetly, if she deemed him wrong. It was the trait Hugo would seek in a wife, were he to ever to wed. An image of Olivia arose in his mind's eye. She had that same quality. Loyalty. For Alex. For her entire family.

He thrust aside her image and such ridiculous thoughts.

He had no intention of ever marrying—his parents' example had been enough to put him off marriage for life and, besides, what if he should turn out like his father? A violent, foul-tempered husband and father? He glanced across the room to where Lucas was assisting Mary to her feet. *He* showed no sign of their father's traits. Since Mary and the children had come into his life he had turned into, as Hugo had jokingly said earlier, a doting family man.

Irritated by such thoughts, Hugo shook them away. If ever by some miracle he changed his mind, it wouldn't be to saddle himself with a troublesome minx like Olivia Beauchamp, no matter how those luminous eyes of hers tempted him.

He focused again on his mother.

'Mama, I always have time for you. You know that. Besides, I am all eagerness to renew my acquaintance with my sister-in-law and her delightful children.'

'The children are in bed already, I am afraid.' Mary smiled at him as she came to greet him, her neat figure clad in a gown the exact same shade of blue as her eyes. 'They are quite exhausted with the long journey, poor wee lambs. Say you will come to visit us tomorrow—they will be so excited to see you. Toby has spoken of little else than his Uncle Hugo since we left Rothley.'

'I will do my best,' said Hugo.

He kissed Mary's cheek. She was just as he remembered from her wedding to Lucas—in fact, she appeared to have bloomed in the months since. She—in fact, they both—radiated happiness and contentment and, although Hugo was pleased for them, their love for one another on top of his mother's obvious joy in her own wedded bliss with Sir Horace only served to remind him that he was, essentially, alone.

It is my choice, he reminded himself irritably.

He shook hands with both Lucas and Sir Horace.

'And do not forget we have that matter to discuss, my boy,' said Sir Horace. 'In fact, if you are in agreement, we can talk it over now, before dinner is served? Bad form to discuss business at the dinner table with ladies present and I believe you said you have a prior commitment later tonight, so you will not wish to linger afterwards, I dare say.'

'I do indeed, sir. Very well then.' Better to know the worst now, perhaps, than have it hovering over him throughout the evening. 'Do you wish to discuss it here or in private?'

'Oh, no, m'boy. No need for privacy. Your mother is in full agreement and as it will—in a manner of speaking— affect Lucas and Mary as well as you, I should like them to stay.'

Lucas's brows rose. 'Shall we all sit then?'

'Yes. Yes. Do, please.' Sir Horace took up a stance in front of the unlit fireplace and clasped his hands behind his back. 'Now, as you boys know, I do not have children of my own. Never found a lady I wished to spend my life with, until I met my wonderful Lucy here.' He smiled at Mama, then harrumphed loudly, clearing his throat. 'Well,

I am getting on in years now and not only do I find my energy beginning to wane, but also I find myself wishing to spend more of my time with your mother and less time on business.

'With that in mind, Hugo, m'boy, I have a proposition for you. If you will take on the role of my right-hand man and help me with managing the Helmstone estates, then I shall name you as beneficiary in my will. None of my properties are entailed and I should as soon they went to you as to anyone.'

Hugo stirred in his seat. 'But… I know you have no children, but surely you have *some* family, sir?'

He exchanged a glance with Lucas, wondering how his brother would feel about being left out in this way. As the eldest, he had inherited Rothley Hall along with the title, but years of depredation by their father had left the estate in a perilous state. Lucas had spent the three years since their father's death working hard to repair the damage.

'None that I would recognise if I met them in the street,' said Sir Horace. 'No, you and your mama are my family now and I wish to see you right.'

'But what about Lucas?'

'I have the Rothley estates. You have nothing.'

'And I do not intend to neglect your brother,' said Sir Horace. 'I am impressed with what your mama has told me of your dedication and hard work, Lucas. You are a father now and, we hope, you will expand your little family in time. I am a wealthy man and I want for nothing. I have a tidy sum of money in Government Bonds and I, with your mother's blessing, have decided to gift that sum to you to make reparations to the Hall and to put your land in good heart.'

Lucas leapt to his feet. 'Sir! I don't know what to say… really, there is no need…we can manage…'

Sir Horace raised his hands, palms out. 'I know, I know, my boy. Of course you can manage. But allow an old man the chance to help where he may, I beg of you.'

Mary had also risen and now she put her hand on Lucas's arm and said, 'We both thank you from the bottom of our hearts, Sir Horace. We have been managing and we would have continued to manage, but there is no denying this will help. It is most generous of you, sir.'

Sir Horace's cheeks turned pink. 'Good. Good. That is settled then. Well, Hugo? What say you to my idea? You will need to spend much of your time at Helmstone, but it is not so very far from London, so you need not be entirely cut off from your friends. And there is a tidy little house at Cedar Lodge—only six bedrooms, it is true, but big enough, I'll wager, for a young man looking to set up his nursery.'

'My *nursery*?' Hugo ignored Lucas's smirk as he glared at Sir Horace. 'What the deuce gives you the idea I am looking to enter parson's mousetrap?'

Sir Horace looked a little startled. 'But your mother said—'

'Now, Hugo,' said Mama. 'Do not, I beg of you, be difficult. It may have been a little wishful thinking on my part—I dare say I should not have given voice to such a hope, but…well…seeing Lucas and Mary so happy together made me a little sad that you are still on your own. But now, with such an improvement in your prospects I was hopeful you might think about settling down. And just think how wonderful it will be to have grandchildren almost on our doorstep, Horace, my dear.'

'Is this—?'

Lucas tried and failed to hold in his snort of laughter and Hugo scowled at him. All that achieved was to draw a huge guffaw from his older brother.

'Is this a *condition* of your offer, sir?' Lucas ignored Mary's attempts to shush him. 'That my confirmed bachelor brother must set up his nursery? Is there a time limit?' His dark eyes swam with tears of laughter. 'Do you get to approve his choice of bride?'

Hugo gritted his teeth and folded his arms across his chest. He'd rather have nothing than find his life no longer his own.

'No, no, nothing of the sort.' Sir Horace paced a little, his face anxious. He stopped before Hugo. 'You must not think I intend for this to place any obligation on you, other than to help ease the burden on me and your mother. I only mentioned Cedar Lodge because I did not want you to feel obliged to live at Helmstone with us if you choose not to. I can always find another tenant for it if you prefer?'

Hugo's resentment subsided. 'No. Cedar Lodge sounds perfect.' He stood and thrust out his hand, which Sir Horace took. 'Thank you, sir. I shall be delighted to accept your offer. I won't let you down.'

Chapter Eight

As dinner progressed, Hugo grew steadily more accustomed to this change in his circumstances. By the time Mama and Mary withdrew to leave the three men with their port and cigars, he realised he already relished the idea of having more purpose to his life—quite a turnaround for a man who had spent his entire adult life sidestepping any commitment or permanence. Sir Horace's faith in him brought a lump to his throat and a hitherto rarely felt emotion drifted through him. It took several moments before he identified it as pride, laced with gratitude.

It was not long before Sir Horace left to join the ladies, leaving the two brothers alone.

'So where are you off to later?' Lucas eyed Hugo through a cloud of smoke. 'Is it to be the delights of the flesh or delights of the gaming table?'

'The latter, although I'm not sure I'd describe it as a delight.'

'Why go, then?'

'I made a promise to keep an eye on someone for a few nights. He'll be there and so, therefore, will I.'

'Sounds intriguing. Where is there?'

'Sir Peter Tadlow's place. He's hosting a cards party.'

Lucas tapped his cigar ash into an ashtray. 'That reprobate's still around, then? Never did care for him. Who is it you're watching out for?'

'Alex Beauchamp. Cheriton's spare.'

'Ah, he of the murderous glare. Care to tell me why or are you sworn to secrecy?'

'Sworn to secrecy, I'm afraid.'

Lucas's teeth gleamed in a smile. 'And does this have aught to do with the delectable Lady Olivia?'

Hugo forced a nonchalant smile and rose leisurely to his feet. The conversation was becoming entirely too intimate for his liking. 'It is time I went.'

Lucas's eyes narrowed. 'You always were a deep one, Hugo—hiding your true feelings behind that mask of ennui you cultivate. You are like I used to be—wary of letting anyone close, afraid you'll turn out like our old man but, trust me, you are nothing like him. All that belief gained me was years of loneliness and misery. Give yourself a chance.'

Hugo arched one brow. 'Marriage has turned you into an authority on how I feel, has it?'

'Marriage…love…has opened my eyes.'

Hugo's gut tightened. Lucas was getting as bad as their mother, prying and poking into his private feelings. Well, it was none of their business. He'd managed his life well enough thus far. He could see no reason to change.

'This conversation is irrelevant—your imagination is leading you astray. Now, I must go. Do you care to accompany me? It'll be like old times.'

Lucas tipped his head to one side as he studied Hugo. 'I think not, Brother. I find myself drawn to staying at home with my Mary these days. I did wonder if that might change now we are in town, but—somewhat surprisingly—it seems it has not.' He leant forward and stubbed out his cigar. 'You will have to uphold the Alastair reputation on behalf of us both, I fear.' He winked. 'Enjoy your evening. Goodnight.'

Envy stirred as Hugo left the house after saying his goodbyes to Mama, Sir Horace and Mary. That deep contentment that pervaded both couples...would he ever experience such a thing? A year ago he would not have given a passing thought to that. But now...despite Hugo's denial, Lucas's words had touched a nerve.

He rolled his shoulders as if to shake off that feeling of, somehow, being excluded from a desirable club.

A couple of hours later he stifled a yawn as he and his companions finished yet another hand of whist at the table set up in Tadlow's salon. There were five tables and around thirty guests, of both sexes, including Beauchamp who, so far, had been playing hazard, rolling the dice with moderate success. Hugo kept watch on Alex from a distance. Tadlow noticeably spent much of his time with the young man, clearly keen to gain his trust, but the game appeared honest.

Just before midnight, Lord Clevedon arrived and paused in the doorway, casting a cautious look around the company before venturing further into the room.

Hugo pushed his chair back and stood. 'If you will excuse me, gentlemen, ladies—I shall vacate my seat for another player.'

His chair was filled immediately as he wandered over to Clevedon, delighted the man was finally back in town. Their friendship might be on the wane, but Hugo had a necklace to retrieve and here was his chance. Then, as soon as the Duke returned to London, Hugo could hand over all responsibility for the Beauchamps and concentrate on his own life.

'I haven't seen you since your birthday, Clevedon.'

Clevedon grimaced. 'Had to beat a strategic retreat, dear boy. Got some nasty types on my tail. Thought m'grandmother might stump up enough blunt to help, but she proved remarkably stubborn.'

Hugo frowned. 'Thought you had more sense than to get mixed up with moneylenders?'

'They're not—' Clevedon snapped his jaw shut as a flush coloured his face.

Hugo's heart sank at the whiff of desperation from the other man—it gave him scant hope Clevedon would easily give up his plan to compromise Olivia.

'What d'you say to a hand or two of piquet?'

Clevedon shook his head. 'I'm in no mood to play—I only looked in to see if Sudbury is here but, as he's not, I'll be on my way.'

Damn! There goes any chance of winning *the necklace from him.*

Hugo thought fast. He had an idea…not a brilliant one, but it was all he had. 'That plan of yours,' he said. 'The one involving the Beauchamp girl?'

Clevedon eyed him. 'What of it? You're not turning all moral on me again, are you, Alastair?'

'No…but I got to thinking, after you told me about it. It'll never work, you know.'

And it wouldn't. He could see that now. But what could he suggest to Clevedon as an alternative? He still needed an incentive to return the necklace.

Clevedon cast a glance around the room. 'Come into Tadlow's study. It's more private.'

They left the salon, Hugo's brain working furiously as he examined the ramifications of his idea.

The minute the study door closed behind them, Clevedon demanded, 'Why shouldn't it work?'

'Because the scheme was always flawed and you'd know it if you'd bothered to think it through, you fool. Do you really believe Cheriton would force his daughter to marry against her wishes?'

'She will be ruined if he does not.'

'You've given the girl no reason to trust you. She's likely to dig in her heels and refuse to be forced into marriage and—even if her reputation *is* ruined—there are plenty of other fellows out there who would gladly take her on. Think about it, man. She'll have alternatives and, after the way you treated her at Vauxhall, you are the last man she will choose.'

Clevedon scowled. 'I never thought of that. But what am I to do? I'm up to my neck in it, Alastair.'

'What are you up to your neck in?'

Clevedon tugged at his neckcloth, his mouth thinning. 'Nothing.'

Despite himself, Hugo felt sympathy at the stricken look in the other man's eyes but he hardened his heart, remembering Clevedon's plan to entrap Olivia. The thought of a vibrant young woman like Olivia shackled to a man who could never love her…never satisfy her…enraged him.

'But I must get *some* funds,' Clevedon burst out. 'Or…' He paced across the room and back. 'Maybe the *prospect* of money…yes, that might work. Once my name is linked with hers, maybe they'll give me more time.'

Hugo thought quickly. He must, somehow, persuade Clevedon to return the necklace tonight. His idea wasn't perfect, but it was all he had.

'Then why not court her the traditional way?' It was risky, but surely Olivia would not trust Clevedon after their encounter at Vauxhall? 'You know—dance with her; call upon her; take her flowers; speak to her father? You never know…it might work. You have all the qualities a father would look for on his daughter's behalf.'

It was the truth. Clevedon had a title, a decent reputation and he was charming. He was accepted everywhere. He might not be a man who loved women, but that was not widely known.

'Except that daughter now despises me, as you pointed out.'

'Not if she believes you returned the necklace to her out of the goodness of your heart—a magnanimous gesture to encourage her to think well of you. Except…' Hugo paused.

'Except what?'

'Well…' he spoke slowly, as though thinking out loud '…she would know then that you recognised her all along on Saturday night and that you deliberately targeted her. That will do nothing to endear you to her.'

A frown creased Clevedon's forehead and Hugo waited, hoping he would reach the obvious solution.

'Alastair, my good friend. *You* shall return the necklace on my behalf and collect my winnings.'

'Me? Oh, no.' Hugo shook his head, hiding his satisfaction at having hooked Clevedon. 'How would I explain that?'

'You shall tell the Lady Olivia that my conscience has been troubling me as the necklace is so much more valuable than her debt but, as I did not know Beatrice's true identity, I had no way of changing our arrangement. I confided in you and—as *you* had recognised her on Saturday—you offered to return the necklace and to recoup the winnings on my behalf. And you must make *very certain* to tell her that you did not reveal her identity to me. I do not want her to feel uncomfortable in my company.'

'How will that help you to win her hand?'

'Firstly, she will feel kindly disposed towards me and, secondly, I shall take your advice and pay court to her and encourage her to fall in love with me. You'll see. I'll soon have her eating out of my hand.'

His smug smile, brimming with confidence, made Hugo itch to punch him on the nose.

'And if you fail?'

'I shall *accidentally* compromise her. By then I will have gained her good opinion of me and she will be happy enough to accept me.'

Hugo strove to keep his expression blank. Had he inadvertently made matters worse? He would be able to return the necklace, but at what cost? He had relied on Olivia not fully trusting Clevedon, but hadn't foreseen that the Earl might still try to force a marriage. Hugo vowed to stay close to Clevedon for the few weeks left of the Season to make sure he kept abreast of any further mischief.

'How shall you accidentally compromise her?'

'Details.' Clevedon waved a dismissive hand. 'I shall think of something when the time comes, never fear, dear boy, never fear.'

Guilt wormed its way into Olivia as she lay in bed, the covers up to her chin, facing Aunt Cecily the next morning.

'I have been sick three times in the night.' Her voice sounded suitably weak and wavering. 'I cannot face a carriage journey. *Please* say I may stay at home.'

Aunt Cecily frowned, then raised her nose and gave an audible sniff. Her green eyes narrowed.

'Hetty has been in to clear up,' Olivia added hastily. 'Oh, Aunt Cecily… I cannot face the rocking and the lurching of the carriage. And what if my sickness got worse? I should *hate* to be the cause of you missing Uncle Vernon's wedding.'

She also hated the fact that she would miss Uncle Vernon's wedding, but she knew she could not enjoy it with this business of the necklace hanging above her head. The mattress dipped as Aunt Cecily sat beside Olivia. A cool hand caressed her forehead.

'You do feel rather warm.' Aunt Cecily's green eyes softened. 'Mayhap you are right…we shall have to travel at a fast pace if we are to arrive at Stourwell Court in time for the wedding.' The door behind her opened to admit Olivia's maid. Aunt Cecily leant down to kiss Olivia's cheek. 'I hope you feel better soon and, when you are well enough to go out and about, you are to do as Lady Glenlochrie says, do you hear me, Livvy?'

'Yes, Aunt.'

'It is fortunate she has not yet felt mobile enough to move back to her own house, or I should be compelled to stay behind, too.'

Lady Glenlochrie—Nell's aunt—had broken her ankle at the start of the Season, preventing her from chaperoning Nell for her debut and forcing Rosalind to come to London as her stand in. She had moved to Beauchamp House together with Rosalind, Freddie and Nell after Papa and Rosalind were betrothed.

'I have also instructed Alex that, as he refuses to accompany us, he must hold himself available to escort you, Nell and Lady Glenlochrie to whichever evening entertainments you choose to attend in my absence. He was not—' and her green eyes twinkled '—amused, but he did agree in the end.' Aunt Cecily rose to her feet. 'I shall write to let you know when we are due to return, but I cannot see it being before the end of next week. Now, I must go. The carriage will be outside before long. Goodbye, my dear Livvy. And…*behave.*'

Olivia tried to project an aura of innocence. Aunt Cecily shook her head at her, smiled and left the room.

'Hetty.'

Olivia's maid—round-cheeked and pretty—came to her bedside.

'As soon as the carriage leaves, bring me some chocolate and rolls, will you? I am *starving.*'

'Yes, milady.'

Olivia closed her eyes and tried to come up with a plan to retrieve her necklace without putting either her reputation or her person in danger.

Hugo patted his pocket for the umpteenth time, checking that the necklace was still there as he cast an eye over the colourful, glittering mass of people crowding the Charnwoods' ballroom, seeking the raven tresses of Lady Olivia Beauchamp.

Of course it's still there, you fool.

It had been in his pocket all day as he haunted the places a young lady might possibly frequent, hoping he would see her, but to no avail. The Charnwood ball was his last hope. He raised his glass to his lips and sipped. At least the champagne was acceptable. Charnwood had clearly spared no expense.

Trying hard to control his irritation, Hugo scanned the dancers once more. Balls were not his first choice of entertainment. He didn't care for the noise. He didn't care for the dancing. He didn't care for the reminder that he was *persona non grata* as far as many members of the *haut ton* were concerned. He preferred more down-to-earth pursuits, where a man didn't have to be on his best behaviour at all times. Clevedon was here, he noted, and dancing with Lady Helena Caldicot, so that must mean

Olivia was present although she wasn't currently dancing and he had yet to spot her.

He glanced around at a sudden tug on his sleeve and the delicious scent of violets assailed him. She was walking away from him, her slim hips—sheathed in ivory silk—undulating in a very feminine, sensual movement. His pulse quickened as she glanced over her shoulder and their gazes connected. With a flick of her brow, she communicated her demand that he follow. Hugo tamped down his natural resistance to being commanded to do *anything* by this minx and he prowled in her wake, up the steps leading from the ballroom. He emerged into the reception hall in time to see her disappear upstairs. He clamped his jaw, and followed. On the landing, he looked around, generations of Charnwoods staring down at him with haughty disdain.

Where the devil...?

A flutter of movement caught his eye and her face peered around a door jamb. She beckoned him imperiously and he stalked towards the door and past her, into the room.

A bloody bedchamber. It would be.

'This,' he growled, crossing the room to put as much distance as possible between them, 'is not wise.' He glanced out of the window before turning to face her. It was still light outside—hopefully he could conclude his business with Lady Olivia and then move on. Except, of course, he couldn't. Alex Beauchamp was here tonight and there was still no sign of the Duke having returned from his journey to the Midlands.

'Never mind that. What have you been doing? Why have you not told me what is happening?' She glided across the carpeted floor towards him, elegance personified, her blunt demands completely at odds with her appearance.

'Do you not understand how frantic I've been? Have you got my necklace?'

She halted in front of him, gazing up at him with such innocent trust in her silvery eyes that he felt something shift in his chest.

'Do *you* not understand the risk you run by being in here with me?'

She dismissed his query with a wave of her hand. 'No one will find us here. It is Sophie's room.'

'Sophie?'

'Lady Sophie Wray. The daughter of the house. You must know her. It was her debut this year.'

'No. I do not concern myself with young misses straight out of the schoolroom.' Hurt flashed in her beautiful silver eyes, leaving a blend of satisfaction and shame souring his mouth. 'Besides. That is not what I meant.'

Her eyes flared with sudden awareness. She put her hand on his arm. 'But *you* would not harm me. I know you.'

He fought the urge to knock her hand away as he battled to control other, baser urges. That scent of violets was doing strange things to him…baiting him…drawing him down an avenue he knew could only lead to trouble.

'You do *not* know me.'

He stepped back, needing space between them. He reached into his pocket and extracted the necklace, holding it out to her, expecting her to snatch it from him and to disappear back to the ballroom. The necklace that had caused him nothing but trouble. It would be a relief to be rid of it.

She squealed. And the next thing, his arms were full of warm woman and his senses were full of that violet scent. Her arms were around his neck and she hugged him tight, her smooth silky cheek pressed to his, her curves soft and yielding as her body moulded to his.

Chapter Nine

Instinct had Hugo in its grasp before his mind could catch up. He slipped the necklace back into his pocket and then, with both hands free, he stroked down the delicate curve of her spine to the deliciously rounded swell of her buttocks. His demons urged him on, and his grip tightened, lifting, pulling her closer as his hips flexed instinctively. A sensible, sane corner of his mind warned him to release her, but he thrust it ruthlessly aside. This was his reward. She'd had him running around in circles, trying to help her out of a predicament caused entirely by her own impetuous and scandalous behaviour. She appeared to have an unshakeable belief in her own ability to cope with whatever happened, but the sooner she realised there were some situations she could not control merely by the force of her will, the better.

A kiss was the very least he deserved.

His plan—such as it was—was to shock her. Make her wary. Scare her, even.

He pulled his head back and gazed down at her. She tilted her face to his. Her eyes sparkled; her petal-pink lips were stretched in a smile. The joy and trust in those silver eyes nearly undid him. *Hell and damnation.* Why did his normally well-hidden and tightly controlled protectiveness choose now to surface? He released her bottom, sliding his hands back to her waist. But before he could follow through with his intention to move her back, away from him and away from temptation, her arms tightened around his neck, her lids fluttered down—her sooty lashes a fan against her creamy complexion—and she pressed back into him, rising on tiptoes.

Her lips found his. Soft, lush, beguiling. His fingers flexed on her waist, pulling her close once more, and he lost all conscious thought. The only reality was the slide and glide of her lips over his. The kiss was erotic in its innocent, untutored style. She had never done this before—his experience told him that. Her hands moved, rising to either side of his head, her fingers thrusting though his hair. Battening down his deep sense of foreboding, he traced her mouth with his tongue, gently urging her lips apart. A split second of resistance—of tension beneath his hands—and then, with a very feminine murmur, she relaxed, opening her mouth and allowing him in.

Dear God.

It was a kiss. Only a kiss. But a kiss such as he had never before experienced.

He lost himself in that kiss, his fingertips exploring and caressing everywhere her silky-smooth skin was open to his touch—her face, her neck, her arms.

Her scent surrounded him. Filled him. Lured him.

His heart pounded. He was hard. Painfully hard.

He groaned and gathered her closer still, revelling in that yielding of her supple curves as they pressed to the length of his body. The inexorable feeling rose within him that she was part of him…she *must* be part of him.

That stray thought alone caused his throat to constrict.

It brought emotions—unfamiliar and nerve-racking—to crowd his brain. Self-preservation reared its head and he forced his lips from hers and—too late—he finally succeeded in setting her away from him. He studied her face: her dazed eyes, heavy-lidded, her swollen lips, the flush that washed her skin a delicate pink. And he battled the craving to kiss her again. To go further.

It was a kiss. Only a kiss. But it was a kiss that rocked Hugo to his toes.

She recovered first. She caught her plump bottom lip between her teeth as her eyes—the pupils huge, reducing that ring of silver grey to a sliver—roamed his face. He fought to keep his expression blank, but any concern that she would turn missish on him was banished as she released her lip and her mouth widened into a smile: a satisfied— even slightly smug—smile.

'I enjoyed that,' she said. 'Do you know that is the first time anyone has kissed me?'

It was Hugo's turn to bite his lip. Against the urge to haul her back into his arms and kiss her all over again. Instead, he turned away from her. Resisting temptation.

'I could tell.'

He heard the whisper of a gasp behind him and instantly felt shame at his brutish riposte. He had intended to frighten her a little...to teach her to be cautious around strange men. Instead, it now struck him that he had merely roused her curiosity. There was none of the maidenly bashfulness he had anticipated.

'Did I not do it properly?'

He faced her again. Slowly. She stared up at him, her fine brows arched. He felt his eyes narrow.

'Do you expect me to score your performance?'

'Why are you behaving so oddly? I merely asked a question. I am curious.'

Hugo thrust his hand through his hair. 'The kiss was... acceptable.'

She pouted. 'Well, I do not think that is a very gallant thing to say.'

'You expect me to be gallant?' He stepped closer and curled his hands into fists to stop him grabbing her and shaking her...or hauling her close again. 'I am not one of your brothers, my dear. Do not expect me to behave as such.'

She stuck her nose in the air, spun around and flounced to the door. Hugo gritted his teeth. Lady Olivia Beauchamp was no longer his concern. He had returned the necklace—

'Wait!' He delved into his pocket.

She pivoted to face him.

'Have you not forgotten something?'

He walked towards her, allowing the necklace to swing gently from one finger. This time she snatched it from his grasp and, opening her reticule, she stuffed it inside.

'Thank you.' She turned to go.

Now he had returned the necklace, assuaging his guilt at having provoked her into gambling at such high stakes. His responsibility for her was over, other than to stay close to Clevedon. Which left her brother. Lord Alexander.

'Is your father home?'

Olivia paused, her hand already on the door handle. 'No.' She twisted again to face him. 'Have you not heard?' Her voice sounded brittle. Her temptress eyes glittered with suppressed emotion. 'My uncle is getting married and Papa has stayed in the Midlands to attend the wedding.'

Married? He masked his astonishment. Lord Vernon Beauchamp...married! That little on dit ought to be headline news.

'I had not heard, no.'

'Dominic and Aunt Cecily left this morning to attend

the ceremony. *I*—' her eyes were icy now '—had to pretend I was ill because *you*—' she poked his chest with an accusatory finger '—could not be bothered to let me know you had my necklace.'

'We have not been formally introduced, my dear. I can hardly call upon you and whisper secrets in your ear without causing gossip and speculation.'

'Hmmph. You could have… I don't know…signalled to me or something in the Park yesterday. Instead, you just ignored me as though we had never met.'

'As I said, we have *not* met. Not in the eyes of society. I take it you do not wish to provoke a scandal? Besides, I did not then have the necklace. Clevedon has been out of town. I only retrieved it last night.'

And now—his heart sank at the realisation—not only must he continue to pretend friendship with Clevedon, a man he was growing to despise, but he must also continue to dog the footsteps of her scapegrace brother now the Duke would not be home for several more days. He had given his word.

'You had better return to the ballroom,' he said. 'Before you are missed.'

'Not yet.' She dismissed his concerns with a nonchalant wave of her hand. 'Nell knows to cover for me with Lady G.' She moved towards Hugo and every muscle in his body stiffened. 'I wish to know what you said to Lord Clevedon to persuade him to give up my necklace.'

'I appealed to his better nature. He allowed me to redeem the necklace on your behalf as a gesture of goodwill.'

He had offered to pay Clevedon the one hundred guineas and the man had near bitten his hand off in his eagerness to take the money.

'Does he…did you tell him who Beatrice really is?'

'No. I did not tell him.'

He could see no advantage in her knowing Clevedon had been aware of her identity from the start—it would only worry her to no purpose. She would live in fear of Clevedon revealing her escapade to Vauxhall, not realising her secret was perfectly safe because of Clevedon's plan to court her—a plan that made Hugo's blood run cold. Or made his blood boil. He couldn't quite decide which.

Plus, she was too transparent. If he told Olivia the truth, she would never be able to hide that knowledge from Clevedon, who would lose his trust in Hugo, making it nigh on impossible for Hugo to keep track of any more of his plans.

'But you should stay away from Lord Clevedon in the future,' he added.

Her brows twitched into a frown. 'Why?'

'The reason is not important. Please, just stay away from him.'

Her lips pressed together. Then she sighed.

'Well, I am exceedingly grateful to you for returning my necklace, in any case,' she said.

She reached up to brush back a lock of hair that had fallen over Hugo's forehead and his loins tightened at that intimate, tender gesture.

'We must arrange a time and place to meet,' she continued.

He'd thought he was tense before, but now he was as rigid as a marble statue. 'I *beg* your pardon?'

She sank her teeth into that lush bottom lip of hers again, but her eyes smiled at him.

'Why, Lord Hugo. *What* a fearsome frown.' She tapped his arm in coquettish admonishment. 'I merely meant that I now owe *you* a sum of money.'

He might be frowning, but he felt like smiling. She did that to him…she, somehow, lightened his spirit…her *joie de vivre*…the way she had bounced back after such a stressful ordeal. But he could not afford to relax too much around her. It would be too easy to forget who she was. Who he was.

'I do not—'

She put a gloved finger to his lips. 'No. I shall not renege on my gambling debt. It is a matter of honour. That is what Alex always says. Although…' her dark brows met, furrowing her forehead '… I hope you will agree to my paying in instalments? I promise I shall pay it all, as soon as I can. Nell and I were going to pool what's left of our allowances, but I should prefer not to involve her if you do not object. Will you trust me?'

His heart clenched and then felt as though it expanded until his whole chest was flooded with warmth. 'Of course I trust you.'

Their gazes fused and he saw her eyes darken again as her lips parted, releasing a soft sigh. He wrenched his gaze from hers.

'It is time you went.'

He clasped her upper arms and moved her aside, then reached for the handle. A quick glance ascertained the landing outside was empty. She was at his back. He could hear her breathing. Smell those violets. He could *feel* her presence as every single hair on his body stood to attention. He did not risk looking at her…if he did, he would not answer for the consequences. He reached behind him, grabbed her arm and propelled her from the room. He closed the door behind her and, with a shaky sigh, he bent his head and rested his forehead against the door panel.

What had just happened?

* * *

Olivia stood on the upstairs landing, glaring at the door Lord Hugo Alastair had just shut in her face. *How exceedingly rude.* She huffed a sigh. She'd thought—although, to be sure, she had no experience—but she'd *thought* their kiss was…oh…wonderful…full of shooting stars and bursts of light and firecrackers exploding. But she was wrong. It had meant nothing to him…he had even…well, *almost*…accused her of being useless at kissing. Although he had appeared to enjoy it at the time. It was only afterwards he had pokered up on her.

She rubbed her tingling lips. Her heart was still racing and skipping. She longed to go back inside the room and…

And what? Accost him? Make him *kiss me again? Prove I can do it better? Hmmph.*

She forced her feet in the direction of the staircase. She wouldn't give him the satisfaction. He was as bad as her brothers, dismissing her as a silly little girl and as someone who could be ordered about and who was too insignificant to warrant a rational explanation. She'd had enough of that throughout her childhood: her brothers had left her out, refusing to let her tag along, accused her of spoiling their games, rejected her.

Like Mama…

She felt tears scald her eyes as that all-too-familiar feeling of never quite being good enough invaded her. Well, no more. She was out in society now and she was a success! She would show them she was more than just an insignificant female who could be brushed aside whenever it suited them. She gritted her teeth, brushed the foolish, self-pitying tears away and marched down the stairs, her back straight and head high.

Inside the ballroom an anxious-looking Nell hurried to her side.

'You have been gone such a long time, Livvy.' She frowned, her violet eyes scanning Olivia's face. 'What happened? Are you all right?'

'Of course I am all right, Nell. Why should I not be all right?'

'Did Lord Hugo have the necklace?'

Olivia nodded. 'And now I have it,' she said, patting her reticule.

'We should return to Aunt Glenlochrie, Livvy. She has been asking for you.'

'I shall go and set her mind at rest.' Olivia linked arms with Nell and steered her around the edge of the ballroom, avoiding eye contact with several young gentlemen vying with each other to attract her attention. She had no intention of dancing tonight. She had used her fake illness as an excuse, claiming a lingering lack of energy, but it seemed some young men still harboured hopes. Then Lord Clevedon was before them, bowing, and she had no choice but to stop and to acknowledge him. Her grip tightened involuntarily on her reticule and the incriminating evidence within.

'Good evening, Lady Olivia, Lady Helena.'

They both bobbed curtsies. 'Good evening, Lord Clevedon,' they chorused.

'Might I engage your hand for the next dance, Lady Olivia?'

'I regret I must refuse, my lord. I am not dancing this evening as I have been unwell.'

It had taken all her charm and persuasion to convince Lady Glenlochrie that she was well enough to attend the ball this evening, including a solemn promise that she would not tax her strength by dancing, and thank goodness she had succeeded—the weight that had been lifted from her by the return of her necklace was worth the sacrifice of not dancing for one evening.

'I am sorry to hear that, my lady. I trust you will recover your customary vitality very soon. In the meantime, might I escort you to your chaperon?'

Olivia caught sight of Hugo on the far side of the room. He was talking to his mother, Lady Todmorden, his brother and another lady—presumably his brother's wife—but his attention was on Olivia. She could almost *feel* him commanding her to obey his edict even though he had given her no good reason for such an order. Besides, all Lord Clevedon had done was challenge her to a game of piquet. It was not *his* fault she had lost, or that she had pledged her necklace because she was unable to give him her vowel. And neither was it his fault the wager was so high. No. That was *Hugo's* fault, as was the fact that the arrack punch had flowed so freely. No doubt the strength of that punch had impaired Clevedon's judgement that night as much as it had impaired her own.

How dare he try to dictate how I must behave?

She averted her gaze and bestowed a gracious smile upon Clevedon as she placed her hand on his arm.

'Thank you, my lord.'

See, Lord Hugo Arrogant Alastair! I can make my own decisions and if you do not find me attractive there are other men who do.

Clevedon stayed with them for the remainder of the evening: procuring drinks, escorting them to supper and generally being charming. Olivia kept her reticule—complete with the incriminating necklace—in her tight grasp the entire time, her stomach a tangle of nerves in case it somehow came open and spilled its contents. But now 'Beatrice's' necklace was safely back in her possession—and without any strings attached, which was more than she had dared hope for—Olivia did start to feel more magnanimous towards his lordship.

Hugo disappeared after supper and, somehow, the ball lost any further appeal for Olivia. She felt nothing but relief when Lady Glenlochrie complained she had one of her heads coming on and it was time they went home.

Chapter Ten

Olivia tried her best over the following days to block Hugo and that delicious kiss from her thoughts. He clearly still thought her far beneath his notice, judging by the way he had bundled her out of the door afterwards, and he had made not the slightest attempt to see her since. She had looked for him in vain at church yesterday, but his mother had been escorted by his stepfather, Sir Horace. Lord and Lady Rothley and their two adorable children were there, too, but there was no sign of that despicable, untrustworthy rogue. She was clearly good enough for him to snatch a kiss when the opportunity arose, but not good enough to—

And every time her meandering thoughts reached that point, she hauled sharply on the reins and dragged them to a halt. Good enough to what? What was it she wanted… expected…from Lord Hugo Alastair? She knew enough of their world to know he was not a man any young lady in her position could even contemplate as a suitable paramour, let alone hanker after.

And yet hanker she did.

And would it really hurt him to show her a little attention?

The days had passed in an alternating blur of brooding reflection and splendid daydreams in which a certain dark and sinfully handsome lord cast himself at her feet and declared his undying love. At times she could not resist embellishing the reality of what had happened—adding further imaginary encounters and embraces—and then, with the next breath, she was consumed by indignation at his casual dismissal of her.

Doesn't he know I'm the Catch of the Season?

She'd been told it often enough by the young men who fawned around her, vying for her attention. She did squirm inside as the thought popped into her head, however. It sounded so conceited and she would never dream of saying such a thing aloud—or even thinking it, normally—but she could not deny that it did help bolster her mood whenever her spirits dived.

Which happened all too often. Whenever she thought about Lord Hugo Arrogant Alastair, in fact. Which seemed to be all the time.

'Livvy!'

Olivia's head jerked up. Nell's expression was a picture of exasperation.

'You have just agreed to walk to Brighton with me,' said Nell.

'Brighton? *Walk?* Why on earth would I agree to such a silly suggestion?'

'Why indeed?' Nell sat on the sofa next to Olivia and plucked *La Belle Assemblée* from her lap, casting it aside. 'I *knew* you were not listening to me and you have not turned a page in the past quarter of an hour so you cannot claim you were engrossed in the fashion plates. What is wrong? I thought you would be in alt now the necklace is back in your possession.'

Olivia's neck grew hot and the flush crawled up to heat her cheeks. 'I *am* in alt!'

Nell raised a fair brow. 'I thought we were friends, Livvy. Please tell me what ails you. Is it that you have missed the wedding?'

'No. *Yes.*'

'No? Yes? Make up your mind.'

Olivia rubbed her brow. 'I am sorry I have missed it, but…' She hesitated. She longed to speak of her confusion, but was it fair to burden to Nell with the truth? Nell would keep the secret of that kiss if Olivia was to confide in her, but she would suffer under the weight of keeping it secret from Rosalind. And if Rosalind's suspicions should ever be aroused then she, surely, would see it as her duty to tell Papa. And what if *he* then felt honour bound to challenge Hugo? What then? Olivia's blood ran cold. She could not risk any harm coming to her papa.

'Yes. I am sorry to have missed the wedding, but I have no one to blame but myself and, as I cannot change what I did, I shall try to forget it and pay more attention to you, my dear step-aunt.'

Nell's violet eyes crinkled. 'It never fails to make me smile, to hear you call me that. Now, what I was asking you is this. Sophie Wray has sent round a note asking if we should like to accompany her and her mama on their shopping expedition this morning, as Lady Cecily is away. *I* should like to go—I must confess to feeling unaccountably restless today and I have discovered in myself an urgent desire to fritter some money away on fripperies.' They had been unable to visit the shops since Aunt Cecily's departure as Lady Glenlochrie's ankle was not strong enough to walk very far.

Olivia was delighted by the opportunity to escape her ever-circling and increasingly brooding thoughts. She jumped to her feet. 'I should enjoy that—I shall run and change my gown.'

* * *

Half an hour later, the Earl of Charnwood's barouche drew up outside Beauchamp House. A liveried footman leapt down to open the door and let down carriage steps as Olivia and Nell approached and Sophie—her smiling face framed by dusky curls and a charming rose-pink bonnet—waved.

'Livvy! Nell! I am so pleased you decided to accompany us.'

Lady Charnwood—a slim, stylish woman who bore a startling resemblance to her daughter—said, 'Sophie. Do try for a little more decorum, my dear. Such displays of enthusiasm are entirely unbecoming in a young lady.'

'Oh, Mama. It is only Liv and Nell. You *know* I am the perfect young lady when there are important people within hearing.'

Olivia and Nell exchanged a grin as the footman handed them into the barouche.

'A young lady should curb all tendencies to excess at *all* times,' said her mother. 'That way, the correct behaviour will become second nature and mistakes are less likely to occur. Good morning, Lady Olivia, Lady Helena. I trust you are both well?'

'Yes, thank you, ma'am,' they chimed in unison.

Bond Street was a-bustle with shoppers when the carriage drew up at the kerbside and anticipation stirred inside Olivia. She had yet to become blasé about all the attractions London had to offer after having spent most of her life on Papa's estate in Devonshire. She still could not get enough of the sights, the sounds, the smells—although the latter often left much to be desired—and the entertainments, in which she included the shops and warehouses. The carriage drove away—leaving the footman behind to carry their purchases—the coachman having been given instruc-

tions to collect them in an hour and a half, to take them to
Gunter's Tea Shop, as Lady Charnwood had promised to
treat the girls to ice cream after their shopping excursion.

Nell, Sophie and Lady Charnwood all managed to find
some essentials that they could not resist purchasing, but
Olivia found herself unable to muster any enthusiasm
for shopping now they were actually there. Not one item
tempted her to buy—and telling herself that she must save
her allowance to pay back Hugo simply made her feel more
wretched. She had agreed to the shopping expedition to
forget about that heartless rogue and still she could not
banish him from her thoughts. Still, she smiled and en-
thused about the other three's purchases as they piled them
in the footman's arms and she was certain nobody would
suspect there was aught amiss. Finally, after a very thorough examination of the stock at the premises of Messrs
Harding, Howell & Co., the barouche returned to collect
them and they set off to Gunter's Tea Shop.

Large plane trees grew in the centre of Berkeley Square,
providing welcome shade for those customers of Gunter's
who chose to enjoy their ices from the comfort of their
own carriages. The Charnwood barouche drew up beneath
the canopy of one such tree and a waiter hurried across
the road to take their orders. The three girls settled very
quickly for their favourite strawberry-flavoured ice cream
and it was as Lady Charnwood was deliberating, at some
length, between peach- and pistachio-flavoured ice cream
that Olivia's idly wandering gaze alighted on Hugo, who
was leaning against a run of railings close to the carriage
in front. He was talking with his brother, Lord Rothley.
They were an eye-catching sight—both tall and dark, with
a slight air of danger surrounding them that made her heart
flutter alarmingly. And she was not the only one captivated
by the pair of them together—they attracted plenty of at-

tention from people strolling through Berkeley Square, especially the females, who eyed the two men surreptitiously as they passed them by, she noted with an inner *hmmph*.

As though he sensed her gaze, Hugo turned his head and looked directly at Olivia. He winked as his lips curved into a smile that set her teeth on edge and, to her utter mortification, Rothley glanced over his shoulder, then turned and executed a bow. Somehow, that bow seemed to convey amused irony even though Rothley was entirely straight-faced. Olivia swallowed, thrust her nose in the air and snapped her attention back to Lady Charnwood, who had finally plumped for pistachio.

While they waited for their ice cream to be served, Olivia made every effort to take her part in the conversation and ignore the fact that Hugo and Rothley stood not twenty feet away. Although she had earlier been impatient to see him again after their kiss, now that he was there, in front of her, large as life and twice as handsome as in her memory, she found herself in the throes of an unaccustomed and most unwelcome nervousness. It was not long, however, before movement caught her eye and a sidelong glance revealed Lady Todmorden being handed from the carriage by Rothley. Lady Rothley then descended and the whole party—together with the two small children Olivia had seen in church—then strolled towards the barouche.

Olivia's face flamed and her skin prickled as she sensed Hugo's eyes upon her. The Alastairs halted by the barouche and Lady Charnwood, suddenly aware of their presence, straightened.

'Lucy, my dear,' she said. 'What a happy coincidence. Are these the grandchildren you were telling me about the other night?'

'They are,' said Hugo's mother. 'We brought them here to

sample Mr Gunter's famous ices as a treat. This is Toby—'
the young boy bowed solemnly '—and this is Emily.'

The little girl clutched her dress in two chubby hands
and bent forward from the waist in a bobbing movement.

'Emily, that's not right.' Toby wagged his finger at his
sister. 'You're a girl. You have to curtsy.'

Emily's face crumpled. Before either of the Rothleys
could react, however, Hugo swept her up into his arms,
saying, 'Well, *I* happen to be an expert on ladies' curtsies,
Emily, and *I* thought it was perfect.' He bussed her on the
cheek, making a rude noise with his lips. Emily squirmed,
erupting into giggles, and Olivia's heart flipped at seeing
this different side of him. The cynical, world-weary man
of the town had disappeared to reveal a younger-seeming,
fun-loving uncle. 'And you, young man,' he added, ruf-
fling Toby's hair, 'showed Lady Charnwood a perfectly
splendid bow.'

Toby's mutinous expression dissolved into a cheeky
grin. 'Chase me, Uncle Hugo.' He grabbed Hugo's hand
and tugged. 'Come on.'

'Toby.' Lady Rothley spoke softly with a faint accent
that Olivia could not quite place. 'Remember what we told
you. You are not at home now and you must mind your
manners, or we shall have to leave you at Grandmama's
house.'

Toby released Hugo's hand immediately. 'Yes, Mama.'

Lady Rothley smiled, her blue eyes twinkling on either side of her tip-tilted, freckled nose. 'Good afternoon,
ladies. Please allow me to apologise for my son's enthusiasm.'

This was Olivia's first chance to see her ladyship close
to and she thought she looked friendly and fun.

'That is perfectly understandable, my dear Lady Rothley,' said Lady Charnwood.

Hugo's brother bowed as he bestowed a charming smile upon Lady Charnwood. 'It is good to see you again, Sally. Thank you again for extending the invitation to your ball to include Mary and me.'

'You are most welcome, Rothley. It is good to see you again after all these years. Now, I know you were all introduced to my daughter, Sophie, the other night, but are you acquainted with Lady Olivia Beauchamp and Lady Helena Caldicot? Girls…' Lady Charnwood smiled at Olivia and Nell '…this is Lord and Lady Rothley, who have just arrived in town…'

Lady Rothley smiled a general greeting, but Lord Rothley's gaze—his ebony eyes the image of Hugo's—travelled without haste over the three girls and Olivia fancied that, as they reached her, his lips compressed as though he suppressed a smile. Her temper stirred as she imagined Hugo confiding their secret kiss to his brother. Rothley bowed again, elegant and assured.

'Delighted, ladies.'

'And this is Lord Hugo Alastair, Lady Todmorden's younger son.'

Olivia, her hackles raised after that lazy appraisal from Rothley, nodded in her most imperious manner and was incensed to see Hugo's lips twitch in amusement as one dark brow rose.

'Enchanted to make your acquaintance, ladies.'

Their gazes fused and—although it might seem fanciful to think such a thing—the very air between them appeared to crackle with tension. Her cheeks heated and she forced herself to break eye contact, knowing she must do everything to avoid raising any speculation that they had already met. As she looked away, however, Olivia found the bright, inquisitive gaze of Lady Todmorden upon her. Immediately upon meeting Olivia's eye Hugo's mother diverted her attention to her grandson, leaving Olivia feeling on edge and vowing to be more careful to mask her reactions in future. She knew only too well that in their world it was imperative for a young lady's actions to be above criticism. What she might say or do in private was very different to how she behaved in public and overfamiliar interaction with a man of Hugo's ilk would do her reputation no good at all.

'Your children are enchanting, Lady Rothley,' said Nell. 'Lady Charnwood? Would you object to me leaving the carriage to speak to them?'

'Of course not, my dear. You may all stroll in the square if you wish, while Lady Todmorden and I talk, but be sure to keep an eye open for your ice cream being served—you would not like it to melt.'

'Olivia? Sophie? Do you care to you join me?' Nell sent a mischievous smile in Olivia's direction and then flicked a glance in Hugo's direction.

Nell stood up and Hugo—nearest to the carriage door—handed out first Nell and then Olivia, Sophie having chosen to remain with her mother. As Hugo's strong fingers closed around Olivia's, tingles chased up her arm and through her body. She glanced up at him, through her lashes, and read the glint of amusement in those dark, half-hooded eyes. She snapped her attention away from him.

Wretch! Making fun of me when I cannot retaliate.

She thanked him briskly, avoiding further eye contact, and then quickly moved away, joining the other ladies and the children. She was relieved that Hugo remained by the carriage, talking to Lady Charnwood. She was not sure her nerves could withstand stilted, polite conversation in a group that included him.

'Of course, Rothley is not Toby and Emily's natural father,' Lady Todmorden was saying, as Nell crouched beside Emily, trying to coax her to talk, 'but he loves them every bit as much as if he were.'

Toby was busily vying for Nell's attention. 'I am six. I can say lots of words. *Much* more than Emily.'

'You're a big boy for six,' said Olivia, to distract him. 'I thought you must be seven years old at the very least. I know a little girl, Susie, who is seven, and you are as tall as she is.'

Toby puffed out his chest. 'Does Susie have her own pony? *I* have my own pony and I can ride him, but it was too far for him to come with us.'

'His little legs would have worn into stumps if you rode him all this way, Toby.'

Olivia's pulse stuttered. Hugo had materialised by her side and now he grasped Toby's hands and swung him around and on to his back, where he clung like a small monkey, giggling. Hugo put his arms behind his back to support Toby, causing his coat to swing open. Without volition, Olivia's gaze travelled downwards from his broad chest to linger on powerfully muscled thighs that a pair of well-cut breeches did nothing to disguise.

She swallowed and averted her gaze, her corset all of a sudden restricting her breathing.

'The waiter is on his way with our ice creams,' said Rothley, for he, too, had joined them. He raised his hat. 'It was a pleasure to meet you, ladies.'

Nell rose to her feet. She and Olivia, still battling to regain her composure, dipped curtsies.

'Say goodbye, Toby,' said Hugo.

'Goodbye! I'm lifting your hat, Uncle Hugo, so you can say it was a pleasure, like Papa.' Toby grabbed Hugo's hat and waved it in the air.

Hugo laughed. 'So you are, Toby. Thank you, for my

hands are rather full of small boy at the moment. Good day, ladies. It was indeed a pleasure.'

He nodded, but he did not look at Olivia and she carefully avoided looking directly at him even though every nerve in her body was afire with awareness of him. Instead she focused her attention on Lady Rothley.

'I am pleased to have made your acquaintance, Lady Rothley. I hope we shall meet again very soon.'

She was rewarded with a warm smile. 'I hope so, too. This is my first ever visit to London and it would be pleasant to get to know a few ladies more my own age.'

'Perhaps you might care to bring the children to visit Susie, the child I mentioned to Toby?' Olivia explained about Susie, who was a recent addition to the Beauchamp household—a runaway girl who Papa and Rosalind had rescued way back in February and then decided to bring up as their own child. 'Susie would love to meet some other children, I'm sure.'

'Thank you, Lady Olivia. That is most kind.'

The farewells completed, each party returned to their own carriage and enjoyed their tasty ices.

Later, after Olivia and Nell had returned to Beauchamp House and spent a pleasant half-hour examining Nell's purchases, Nell suddenly fell quiet as she chewed her bottom lip.

'What is wrong, Nell?'

Nell took Olivia's hand. 'I am sorry. I should not have teased you. Please, Livvy…do take care.'

Olivia frowned, genuinely puzzled. 'Tease me? When?'

'Today, in the carriage. I should never have asked if we could go and talk to the children. It was wrong of me. I thought it would be a bit of fun, to tease you after I noticed how you avoided looking at Lord Hugo. But now…

I feel…oh, I don't know. I feel a bit as though I have put you at risk.'

'At risk? I am not at risk.'

Nell gathered Olivia's hand to her chest. 'Take care, Livvy. He is dangerous.'

'*Dangerous?* What nonsense!'

Never had she felt in danger when she was with Hugo. Nell did not know what she was talking about. He had never made her feel anything other than safe in his company.

'I think perhaps I did not express myself very well. What I meant is not that he is dangerous *per se*, but he *is* a danger to you. When you look at one another…oh, Livvy.' She shook her head. '*Please* be careful. A man such as he…with his reputation…he knows how to entice women. You've heard the tales of the Infamous Alastairs…but I've also heard them called the *Irresistible* Alastairs. And now I understand why.'

Chapter Eleven

'Well. I thought he would never leave.'

It was the following day, in the early afternoon when Olivia and Nell were at home to their callers, and Lord Clevedon had called, complete with a bouquet of flowers for Olivia, and sat with her, Nell and Lady Glenlochrie for a full half-hour.

'Do not be so ungracious, young lady,' said Lady Glenlochrie. 'You should be honoured such a fine-looking gentleman is showing an interest in you. He is an earl and has a fine estate in Derbyshire and he is old enough now to be thinking of setting up his nursery. Yes, I think your father and your aunt will both be quite content to learn of his attentions when they return from Worcestershire.'

'Well, I am not content with his attentions,' said Olivia, rising to her feet and shaking out her skirt, 'and I have no wish to encourage them.'

Her conscience stirred as she blocked Lady Glenlochrie's *'Ungrateful gel'* from her ears. She *had* been guilty of encouraging his lordship a little—but only because he was Hugo's friend and she was desperate to prove that an older, more sophisticated gentleman such as Lord Clevedon could find her attractive and interesting. The few times she had seen Hugo since that kiss she had noticed the best way to attract his attention was through Lord Clevedon and she was willing to try anything.

She crossed the drawing room to gaze out of the window, but the garden held no interest for her. Restless energy surged through her. She wanted to be *doing* something, not sitting at home pursuing ladylike occupations such as playing the pianoforte and embroidering and waiting meekly for gentlemen to deign to call upon her. It was hugely frustrating to have to constantly wait. She wanted… Hugo's face, complete with that infuriating, knowing smile of his, materialised in her thoughts. She huffed impatiently and spun round to face the interior of the room again.

Lady Glenlochrie was in the process of levering herself to her feet while Nell hovered by her side with her walking stick at the ready.

'Help me upstairs to my bedchamber, will you, Nell, dear? I hope that if I rest now I shall be recovered sufficiently for the ball tonight. You young things are quite exhausting.'

Guilt swept aside Olivia's restless yearnings. Poor Lady G. She had travelled from her home in Scotland and taken on the task of launching Nell into society even though she found the hustle and bustle of London exhausting. And then she had broken her ankle, which had resulted in Rosalind coming to London to help. And probably that was good, because then Papa and Rosalind had fallen in love and Rosalind, Nell and Freddie had all come to live at Beauchamp House. But Lady G. was still not sufficiently recovered to face the return journey to Scotland and so she, too, had moved into Beauchamp House. And now, with Papa, Rosalind, Uncle Vernon and Aunt Cecily all absent suddenly, the role of chaperon for not only Nell but also Olivia had landed squarely back on Lady G.'s shoulders.

And Olivia knew—because she did not hide her faults from herself—that was no easy task.

She crossed the room to open the door as Nell assisted her aunt into the hall and then they both helped the elderly lady across the hall to the stairs. Lady Glenlochrie bestowed a smile upon Olivia.

'Thank you, my dear. Nell will manage from here—I shall feel safer if I can hold the banister as I climb the stairs. Nell?'

'Yes, Aunt?'

'Will you read to me until I fall asleep?'

'Of course, Aunt.' Nell caught Olivia's eye. 'I shall go to see Susie afterwards, if you care to join us?' She sighed. 'We see so little of her these days, since Rosalind appointed Miss Pyecroft as her governess. It would be pleasant to take her for a walk in the Park later, but if Alex is not home there will be nobody to escort us.'

Olivia watched Nell and Lady Glenlochrie slowly ascend the staircase until her attention was diverted by the murmur of male voices. She followed the sound. If Alex was in, perhaps she could persuade him to accompany them to the Park after all. The voices were coming from the library. The door was open and Olivia put one eye to the sliver of light showing between the door and the jamb to see who was inside. Then she stiffened as she recognised the classic profile of the one person visible—Lord Hugo Alastair.

What is he *doing here?*

'Would you care for a glass of wine?'

That was Freddie's voice. Olivia frowned. Why was Hugo calling on *Freddie*? She noted he had not sent his card in to Lady Glenlochrie—no doubt scared she would deny him—but it was still…discouraging…that he had not made even the slightest attempt to call upon Olivia even though Papa and Aunt Cecily were out of town. She cast a surreptitious glance around the hallway. There were no servants in sight at the moment, but how long would that last? A misspent childhood of listening to adult conversations she was not meant to be a party to had left Olivia with no qualms about eavesdropping on Hugo and Freddie who, after all, was in Papa's employ so surely she had a *duty* to know what they were discussing.

A chink of glass alerted her that Freddie was pouring his visitor a glass of Madeira from the decanter kept on a table in the corner. Olivia thought quickly. Not far from the door was a high-backed chair that faced the opposite end of the room. If she could creep unnoticed into the room and curl up in that, they would never know she was there. And, if they did happen to see her…well, this was *her* house. She had every right to go into the library and educate her mind by reading. But she did not think they would see her—the door stood open and would conceal her from Hugo, and Freddie would be concentrating on not spilling the drink as he carried it to Hugo. She could see that Hugo's attention was on Freddie and so she took her chance, hugging the wall until she was as near the leather-upholstered chair as possible, then stepping across the gap and sitting down. No challenge came from the men and she curled her legs under and ensured her arms were tucked in before directing her attention to what was being said at the other end of the room.

'I am sorry the task of watching out for Alex is taking longer than either of us envisioned,' said Freddie. A creak of leather signified he had taken the chair on the opposite side of the empty grate to Hugo. 'I genuinely expected his Grace to be home before now.'

'I do not blame you, Allen; nobody could have foreseen Beauchamp donning leg shackles so suddenly.'

His deep, soothing voice sent waves of longing through Olivia. She crossed her arms over her chest and cupped her shoulders, remembering the way he had held her. Her throat ached even as she reminded herself of his rakish reputation—the opposite of the sort of man she could rely upon. Except…she frowned. His actions…hadn't they almost proved the opposite? Weren't she and Freddie both putting their trust in him? And had he let them down?

Freddie laughed. 'Leg shackles! That is what Vernon always called it. Or parson's mousetrap. And always with a theatrical shudder. Reckoned he wasn't the marrying kind.'

He was right, Olivia thought. Uncle Vernon always swore he'd never get trapped but now, suddenly, he was leaving the family behind and forging a new path. Her throat ached with suppressed emotion. Why did changes have to happen?

Hugo was speaking again and she switched her focus to his words.

'Well, he's well and truly caught now, so it seems. It was the same story with my brother, Rothley. Once he met Mary, he knew. He told me love hit him like a thunderbolt and I've never seen him so happy. Rather them than me, that's all I can say. I'm not convinced by all this love-at-first-sight nonsense.'

'Six months ago I'd have agreed with you,' said Freddie. 'But I lived through the effects of such a meeting when my sister first met the Duke and let us say I am no longer as sceptical as I was.'

Hugo huffed a mocking laugh and Olivia found each breath she dragged into her lungs more painful than the last. Love at first sight… She had always scoffed at the idea but she, too, had watched Papa and Rosalind. And now, it felt very much as though she was experiencing it herself, which was all very well, but what if only one person fell in love? What then?

'Now, back to Alex,' said Hugo, briskly. 'I've done as we agreed and kept an eye on him. He's played cards with Tadlow a few times, but so far he's always come out even. I've joined in a few of the games and noticed nothing shady—they've been in different places, but at normal card parties or in legitimate gentlemen's clubs. Tadlow's not a fool; he won't risk cheating against Alex in such places.'

Olivia clamped her hand across her mouth to stifle her gasp. Sir Peter Tadlow was Nell's uncle—a nasty beast who had planned to force his niece to marry Lord Bulbridge in order to pay off his own gambling debts. Luckily, Papa had put paid to Tadlow's evil scheme earlier that year.

'But I have no doubts he is working to gain Alex's trust, ready to fleece him, just as Clevedon told me,' Hugo went on. 'I've made enquiries. Tadlow's got links with a gaming club and brothel called Diablo's. It's got a dubious reputation; it's members only—and it's not an easy club to join—and there's some secrecy over who is behind the place. The manager is a ruffian called Wood, but he's just a front man. I've learned Tadlow's introduced more than one green lad to the place and they soon find themselves in trouble. I suspect his plan is to entice Alex into a game there before long.'

'I've tried to warn Alex again about Tadlow, but he's in no mood to listen to me.'

Olivia could hear the dejection and concern in Freddie's voice.

'I am fond of him,' he continued, 'and I should hate for him to get into further hot water with his father, especially when he has been trying so hard to keep out of trouble. He disappeared without trace for days on end the last time he found himself deep in debt and unable to pay his dues.

That inadvertently resulted in my being offered this job with the Duke and I should hate for another such an episode to result in my losing it, selfish as that may sound.'

'All I can do is to watch out for him as much as I can—as long as I can find out where he is going in the first place. That is not always easy, let me tell you.'

'Well, I can help you out there, Alastair. Before she left, Lady Cecily tasked Alex with escorting the girls and Lady G. to their evening entertainments and, to give him his due, he has done so. Tonight they attend the Denbys' ball, tomorrow is, of course, Almack's and on Thursday they go to the Pendletons' soirée, so at least you know where Alex will be at the start of each evening. By Friday, surely, his Grace will be home and you can relinquish the charge you have so manfully shouldered.'

'I shall speak to Lady Denby about tonight. She is an old…acquaintance, shall we say.' Olivia's teeth ground together at the amused warmth in Hugo's voice. 'I am sure she will be happy to extend an invitation to me, even at this late hour. I can watch for Alex leaving Almack's tomorrow and Mama can, I am certain, ensure my attendance at the Pendletons'.'

The sound of movement behind her had Olivia shrinking into the chair in an attempt to make herself as small as possible. She was elated at the news that Hugo would attend the Denbys' ball tonight and her wayward imagination immediately envisioned him requesting her hand for a dance. She could not wait—she would tell Hetty to lay out her favourite pale blue silk evening gown.

After the door had closed behind the two men, however, Olivia's thoughts turned to Alex and Sir Peter Tadlow, and what she had learned and anger simmered deep inside. She would *never* let her beloved brother fall foul of such a wicked plan and vowed that she, too, would watch over him as much as she could until Papa came home. She could not bear his disappointment if he were to be denied Foxbourne after all his efforts to stay out of trouble.

Later, Olivia told Nell about Sir Peter's scheme to cheat money from Alex and, ultimately, Papa. There was no one else in whom she could confide and no one they could ask for help. Freddie already knew what was going on and neither girl could see any benefit in alerting him to the fact that they knew what Sir Peter was up to, and Lady Glenlochrie was an old lady. *She* could do nothing to help or protect Alex. Olivia couldn't wait for Papa and Aunt Cecily, or even Dominic, to come home. *They* would know what to do and she would not feel so alone and so...*responsible.* She had always worried about Alex and tried to protect him from the worst of his self-destructive ways but the rest of the family had always been there, too. Now, there was only her and she had not realised until now how heavy the burden of ultimate responsibility must weigh upon her papa.

The Denbys' ball was the customary squeeze and, after Lady Glenlochrie settled down at one end of the spacious drawing room on the first floor, ready and eager for a gossip with the other chaperons, Olivia and Nell—their dance cards filling nicely—waited with a group of friends for the dancing to begin. Alex had made his way straight to the card room on the ground floor, telling Olivia to send for him if he was needed. She tried to persuade him to stay upstairs and to dance with some of the young ladies, but he had merely cast her a scathing look and stalked off.

'Livvy.' Nell leaned in to speak. 'I have just seen my Uncle Tadlow. He was headed for the stairs and, presumably, the card room, but I have yet to see Lord Hugo. I thought he told Freddie he would be here to watch over Alex.'

The two girls moved apart from their friends, keeping their voices low.

'Tadlow won't cheat here, Nell. He would not take the risk of getting caught in Lord Denby's house. He would be ruined. No, he will do his worst at some shady gambling club like that Diablo's that Hugo told Freddie about.'

'You are probably right.' Nell did not look convinced. 'And I hope, too, you are right to put so much trust in Lord Hugo. I cannot help but worry—'

'Hugo knows here is not really where he is needed,' interrupted Olivia. She had heard enough of Nell's doubts and warnings about Hugo over the past few days. She knew her friend was only concerned about her, but there was a limit. 'It's after Alex has taken us home that Hugo will be needed to keep watch. *I* am perfectly capable of keeping Alex out of trouble while we're here. All *you* need do is make my excuses if I disappear. You may tell anyone I'm promised to dance with that I have developed the headache and suggest they dance with one of the girls without a partner.'

Olivia scanned the room as she spoke. For all her brave words, she hoped Hugo would arrive soon. The music began and her first partner came to claim her hand. For the time being Alex must look after himself. She smiled at Lord Sudbury and set her mind to making polite conversation with him.

Three dances later, Hugo still had not arrived. As Olivia's partner led her from the floor, she manoeuvred him over to where Nell stood with her next dance partner.

'Excuse my interruption,' said Olivia, as soon as her own partner was out of earshot. 'I have the headache, Nell, so can you please make my excuses to…' she consulted her dance card '… Mr Beaton?'

'I am sorry you are unwell,' said Nell. 'Is there anything I can do to assist?'

'Thank you but, no. I am certain a few moments of peace and quiet away from the music will prove beneficial.'

'I shall make sure to tell Mr Beaton, Livvy. I do hope you feel better soon.'

Nell sent her a speaking look before turning again to her partner and Olivia made her escape, running lightly down the stairs to the entrance hall.

The card room was set up with several tables spread around the room and it took no time at all for Olivia to spot Alex, at a table in the corner with three other men, including Tadlow. Her breath caught as she recognised Mr Randall—that disgusting man who had made advances to her that night at Vauxhall Gardens—and Lord Bulbridge. She only knew the latter because of poor Nell's lucky escape from marriage to the brute.

She breathed a little easier as she recognised the other occupants of the card room—respectable members of the *ton*, most of whom she knew. She was confident Tadlow would not dare to cheat here, but it would not hurt him to know that Alex's sister was keeping an eye on him. Resolutely, she crossed the room and stood by Alex's shoulder. The three other men rose to their feet as Alex twisted his neck to peer up at her. He stared blearily for a moment or two, then struggled to his feet, where he swayed. His eyes appeared unnaturally dark and his eyelids kept drooping, almost as though he were on the verge of sleep. Olivia frowned, foreboding knotting her stomach as he propped both hands on the table as though to support himself. He reminded her of Lady Glenlochrie when she had overdone the laudanum in a bid to ease the pain of her broken ankle.

'Wh-wh-what are you doin' here, Sis?'

'Lady Glenlochrie wishes to speak with you, Alex. Will you come with me?'

'Here, Beauchamp, you can't leave the game in the middle of play, man,' said Tadlow, flicking a disdainful glance at Olivia. 'Let her ladyship wait.'

Olivia raised her chin. '*Thank* you for your contribution to our private discussion, sir. I shall, of course, be happy to wait until the hand is complete.'

Olivia glanced at the various piles of money in front of the four players. Alex's was the smallest of the four, but there was no clear winner and it appeared the stakes were within reason.

'I have seen men emasculated by their wives before, but never by their *younger* sisters,' drawled Tadlow. 'Let us finish this hand in order that Beauchamp can obey Lady Olivia's summons without further delay.'

He smirked as Alex subsided on to his chair and reached for the glass before him with a hand that visibly trembled.

'Allow me to fetch you a chair, Lady Olivia,' said Mr Randall.

She shuddered, recalling his slimy behaviour at Vauxhall Gardens, and barely nodded her thanks as he collected a chair and placed it between his chair and Alex's. Then he bowed.

'We have not been introduced, but...will you do the honours, Beauchamp?'

'No, I won't,' said Alex ungraciously. 'M'sister ain't staying and she d-d-don't need an acquaintance with *you* fellows.

Olivia's face flamed at Alex's rudeness. Not that she had no wish to be introduced to any of these scoundrels, but whatever was the matter with Alex? He was abrupt and disrespectful at home at times, but—like her—he knew enough to watch his manners when out in polite society. This was unlike him. Surely he hadn't had the time to get so drunk since their arrival and even he would not drink to excess at a ball such as this. What he did afterwards, when he was out and about with his pals, was a different matter. Her heart crawled up into her throat and she looked anxiously at the rest of the occupants of the room, but everybody was busy concentrating on their own games, taking no notice of anything else going on. The two footmen on duty to supply the players with drinks stood like sentries near the door, their gazes firmly fixed on the opposite wall.

Olivia lowered her voice and put her hand on her brother's arm. '*Please*, Alex. Come with me. You can play cards again later.'

Alex jerked his arm, dislodging her hand as Tadlow sniggered.

'Yes, go on, Alex. Do as your little sister bids you.'

Alex turned to Olivia. 'Go back…d-dance. I 'shcorted you, di'n't I? What m-m-more ish a man to do?' His words were a disjointed mumble and his hand, as he pushed at her, missed her entirely and flopped to swing by his side for a moment before he heaved it back up to the table and fumbled to pick up his cards.

There was nothing she could do without making a huge fuss, which Alex would hate and which would only make him dig in his heels more stubbornly. She rose from the table, glared at the three other men and stalked to the door. Inside, her nerves churned until she felt quite sick. Something was wrong with Alex. He was not just foxed…she had seen him enough times in that state to recognise the signs. By this time of the evening he should be the life and soul of the party…alcohol seemed to sharpen his wits, not dull them as she had just witnessed. She headed back to the ballroom, crushed, desperate and feeling very alone.

Why did this have to happen now, when Papa was away? She had always prided herself on her resourcefulness, but how could she cope with this on her own? How she missed the security of knowing her family were around her, ready to support her.

She hesitated at the door of the ballroom, scanning the men present. Was there anyone she could confide in? Beg for help? But to do that would be to expose Alex's folly to someone outside her family. Perhaps Neville Wolfe? She'd seen him earlier. He was a loyal friend to Alex and would not spread gossip, but he was young himself, and a bit of a fool at times, as young men often are.

No. Neville would be no match for those men with Alex. She would wait a bit longer, until Hugo arrived. *He* would know what to do. He already knew the danger Tadlow posed to Alex and had proved he could be discreet.

He had promised Freddie he would watch over Alex, so where was he?

Chapter Twelve

Hugo strolled into the Denby ball and halted, adjusting his cuffs as he took stock of the dancers and those watching them: the chaperons, seated together, gossiping behind their fans; the hunters, prowling the perimeter of the ballroom as they surveyed their prey—the young ladies with generous dowries and influential family connections; the wallflowers, clustered together, their heads defiantly high.

He had stayed away as long as he could, delaying the moment when he would see Olivia—beautiful, desirable Olivia who kissed like a dream. He knew tonight he would face a battle to avoid her—that damned kiss had opened a door within his soul that, no matter how he tried, he could not quite shut again. He swallowed down a self-deprecating snort—he was well on the way to behaving in the same way as all the other lovelorn fools who constantly surrounded her.

He hadn't suspected he could feel such a longing to simply *dance* with a woman and now, since Lady Charnwood's introduction, there was not a single thing to stop him asking her. And it wasn't only the desire to dance with her that had caught him entirely unawares. *He* wanted to be the man to escort her to supper. He wanted to talk openly with her and make her laugh…see her smile at him…and only him.

Knowing he ought not to do any of those things gnawed at him. She haunted his thoughts every waking moment and danced through his dreams every night. Hence his tardy arrival. The less time he spent resisting all that temptation, the better.

His roving gaze found her soon enough. She was on the opposite side of the ballroom, standing among a cluster of friends—including, he was irritated to see, Clevedon—looking as though she hadn't a care in the world. Which, of course, she hadn't—she was wealthy, well born and beautiful. Her pale blue gown clung to her, outlining her willowy elegance, and her dark hair was piled on her head, with soft waved tendrils left loose to frame her face. Hugo took his time, enjoying the simple pleasure of just watching her from afar. But gradually he realised she was putting on an act. The people around her were talking, but Olivia only joined in when addressed directly—the rest of the time her gaze darted around the ballroom as she bit into her bottom lip.

And then she saw him and her expression lit up, a smile widening those luscious pink lips. Hugo's body responded to her clear joy at seeing him even as he cautioned himself to take care—her unguarded expression would surely cause any observer to suspect an existing intimacy between them and her reputation would suffer. She was young and naïve and had not yet learned to conceal her true emotions, but she must learn to do so if they were to escape detection in future.

He frowned. There could be no future. He was only interested in women for one purpose and she was too innocent and too highly connected for him to even *think* of her in those terms. She deserved a young swain, not a world-weary cynic like him. Or Clevedon. Hugo had seen the Earl arrive at Beauchamp House earlier, clutching a bouquet, and Hugo—on his way to confer with Freddie Allen—had been forced to hang around outside until Clevedon had left again. He did not want Clevedon to know he was looking out for Alex in case he passed that information on to Tadlow. Hugo prayed Olivia was too clever to fall for Clevedon's courtship. He could not bear to see her joy in life battered and squashed by marriage to a man who could never be a proper husband to her.

He tried to keep his attention on the dancers, but he could not resist sneaking another look at Olivia. Her expression was no longer full of joy, but…she looked desperate. And, as their gazes clashed again across the room, he thought back and realised that her earlier joy had been liberally mixed with relief.

Bloody conceited fool!

He had assumed her glow of happiness when she first saw him was purely down to her pleasure at his arrival. But there was clearly something else troubling her and his heart clenched just with the knowing that she was upset. So, despite his misgivings, he stood his ground as Olivia began to make her way to him, keeping his gaze on the couples forming the next set.

Was it Clevedon? Had he done something else to try to compromise Olivia when he had called on her? He noted the bastard tracking Olivia's progress around the room, but then forgot all about him as Olivia paused next to him, her arm brushing against his sleeve. The hair on the back of his neck rose as the smell of violets awakened his senses. Olivia kept her attention on the dancing couples and her voice low. He had to strain to catch her words.

'Alex is playing cards with Tadlow. I tried to persuade him to leave, but he would not listen.' There was a pause. 'He looks strange, almost as though he is drugged.'

'Stay here. I'll go and check on him.'

Hugo headed downstairs to the card room. And just in time, by the look of it as Tadlow and Bulbridge, with a slumping Alex between them, emerged from the card room. A footman pointed towards the rear of the house and, as Hugo drew closer, he heard the man say, 'Through that door, follow the passage and the door to the back yard is the one at the end, sir. There's a gate through to the mews from there.'

'Thank you, my man,' said Tadlow. 'We cannot have our inebriated friend here kicking up a rumpus. It is far better to remove him discreetly through the back than risk offending your master's guests.'

Some instinct made Hugo glance over his shoulder. Olivia, her troubled gaze fixed on Alex, was hurrying towards him. Hugo waved her back. She kept coming until she was by his side.

'Stay out of this,' he growled.

'He is *my* brother,' she hissed through gritted teeth.

'Stay back. You cannot help. Please. Trust me to look after him.'

He didn't have time to see if she obeyed him. If he didn't act quickly, the men would be gone. They were already heading off towards the door the footman had pointed out, Alex's arms slung over the shoulders of the other men as he stumbled in an effort to keep up with them.

'Tadlow!'

The man's head swivelled to peer back at Hugo. He scowled.

'What is it, Alastair? As you can see, we have our hands rather full here.'

'I am come to relieve you of your burden,' said Hugo. 'Beauchamp's carriage is at the front door.'

'This way is more discreet. My carriage is waiting out this way.'

Hugo lengthened his stride and overtook the trio. He faced them. They kept coming and he found himself walking backwards. Olivia, he was relieved to see, had stayed back and was watching, wide-eyed.

'What is a gentleman's carriage doing at the back entrance, Tadlow? Did you plan to leave this way?'

'Keep your nose out of my affairs,' snarled Tadlow. 'Beauchamp owes me. We have unfinished business.'

One bonus of Hugo's misspent past was that men such as Tadlow assumed he was as indifferent now as he ever was. And that assumption made men indiscreet as they revealed things they might otherwise hide, not realising that the man they knew from before was not the same man today. Hugo could at least now hold his head up that he had begun that process of change, even if it had taken him longer than most young men to come to his senses. If only he could imbue some of that sense into young Beauchamp.

'Beauchamp.' Alex did not respond, his head drooping listlessly although he was taking some of his weight on his legs. 'Alexander!' His head snapped up at that. His wavering gaze fixed on Hugo's face, then he grinned. 'Thought you were m'father for a minute.'

The entire time Tadlow and Bulbridge had continued to advance, and now Hugo found himself with his back against the door at the end of the passageway.

He stepped forward, shoving Tadlow aside to grab Alex's arm. 'Come with me, Beauchamp. You don't want to go with these two, do you?'

'Go? Go?' Alex's head swivelled. 'Where we goin'? Diablo's? Don' wanna go there. *Told* you…it's crooked.'

'You heard the man, Tadlow,' said Hugo. 'I don't want

to cause a scandal here in Denby's house, but you'd best leave Beauchamp be. He's going nowhere.'

'Brave talk for one man against two. Now, get out of our way.' It was Bulbridge who spoke this time, a squat, coarse-featured, unmannerly man. 'I don't know what's got into you, Alastair—interfering in things that are none of your business. Although…' and he glanced behind him before fixing Hugo with a leer on his face '…I can see which part of your anatomy is leading you. You've no chance there, you fool. Stand aside.'

Tadlow pushed between Hugo and Alex. About to grapple with him, Hugo paused. Olivia was still watching and, beyond her, people were still moving to and from the card room. He should take this argument outside rather than risk a scandal in here, in front of witnesses—Olivia in particular. He stood aside, opening the door for the three men as, behind them, Olivia started forward. Hugo waved her back again, more urgently this time. What was likely to happen was not for a lady's eyes. To his astonishment, she obeyed, spinning on her heel before hurrying back towards the main staircase.

Hugo followed the three men into a short passageway, dimly lit by a single candle in a wall sconce. There was a door at the far end and a narrow flight of stairs led down to the right, presumably to the kitchen and other service areas in the basement. They soon reached the door at the end and, as they manoeuvred Alex through and into the yard, Hugo saw Alex revive a touch and start to resist the men who were manhandling him. His head lifted, his legs straightened, and he began to struggle. 'No…back… Livvy…'

Hugo overtook the men again, blocking their way to the gate set into the surrounding wall.

'You heard him. He wants to go back. For the last time, leave him with me and we'll say no more about this.'

Tadlow released Alex, shoving him towards Bulbridge, who swung him round and backed him sharply against the wall. Tadlow came towards Hugo, his hands balled into fists.

'And I say it for the last time, too, Alastair—get out of our way.'

Tadlow did not trouble to keep his voice down and every sinew in Hugo's body hardened as the implication of that—coupled with the sound of the gate behind him creaking open—registered. Even as he began to turn, raising his own fists, a blow to the side of his head sent him staggering back. He kept his feet as Douglas Randall— Bulbridge's cousin—stalked towards him. Hugo feinted with his left and then, as Randall blocked him, he jabbed hard straight at the other man's nose. His fist connected with a satisfying crunch and Randall reeled away. This was no time for gentlemanly conduct. With three against one Hugo could not allow the man time to recover and he followed him up, grabbing his shoulder and swinging him around as he let fly with a roundhouse punch to the side of his face and followed that immediately with a solid punch to the gut that floored him. Then he spun to face Tadlow, but hesitated as Olivia burst through the door into the yard and slammed to a halt by Tadlow's side, her mouth a perfect O of horror.

Tadlow wrapped his arms around Olivia, entrapping both her arms and lifting her so her feet flailed helplessly off the ground. With a roar of rage, Hugo charged at Tadlow, but Bulbridge then thrust Alex away and barged Hugo aside. They grappled and, even as they swayed together, each attempting to loosen the other's hold, Hugo saw Randall attempting to get to his feet and his heart sank.

'Liv!' Suddenly, Alex was on Tadlow's back, his arm around the man's neck as he throttled him. 'Let my sister go, you bastard,' he snarled and Hugo saw him sink his teeth into Tadlow's ear.

That gave Hugo renewed strength and he heaved again at Bulbridge, breaking his hold. He stepped back smartly and jabbed once, twice, three times at the man before he could recover his balance. Blood spurted from Bulbridge's nose and mouth, but still he came at Hugo. The swiftest of glances showed Alex with Olivia, pushing her behind him as he—swaying slightly and with a scowl of pure concentration on his face—stood between her and Tadlow and then all his attention was on Bulbridge as they fought. He must disable the man quickly, for Alex was no match for even Tadlow—the weakest of the three men—in his current state and if Randall recovered enough to get involved, all would be lost.

At least, he thought grimly, *Alex will never again trust Tadlow after this.*

Then the door back into the house opened and Clevedon stepped through into the yard. Everyone seemed to freeze, for the briefest of seconds, as the Earl took in the scene. Then he caught Hugo's eye, nodded and strode across to haul Randall to his feet. He dragged him to the gate and shoved him through before returning to Tadlow. Bulbridge backed away from Hugo, but he followed, jabbing relentlessly until the Viscount's back hit the wall. The man looked almost done and Hugo grasped his collar and hauled him to the gate.

'Don't you dare let me see your ugly face near the Beauchamps again,' he growled before throwing Bulbridge to the cobbled ground of the mews beyond. He was then almost knocked aside as Tadlow rushed past him and grabbed Bulbridge, tugging him to his feet. Hugo started after the men, intending to make sure they did actually leave, but Clevedon gripped his shoulder.

'Allow me to escort these gentlemen off the premises.'

He did not wait for a response but strode off, following the three men hobbling in the direction of the road.

The breath whooshed from Olivia's lungs as Hugo returned to the yard. She rushed to him and framed his face with her hands, peering closely in the dimming twilight. His breathing sounded harsh in the sudden quiet. His hand—large, warm, comforting—slid around her waist, pulling her close.

'Are you hurt?' His deep voice curled around her and through her, heating her blood, making her own breath hitch.

No,' she whispered. 'Hugo. I—'

Her heart clenched as she spied a dark line trickling from the corner of his mouth. She stripped off her evening glove and touched his mouth with trembling fingertips. The indrawn hiss of breath told her all she needed to know. She moved closer, sliding her fingers through his hair, relishing the solid strength of his hard body against hers as his scent filled her. He'd been in danger and she needed to know he was safe.

'It is you who is hurt. I am so sorry.' She brushed her lips across his cheek. Saw his lids close. Felt the swell of his chest as he drew in a long, deep breath.

'You have no reason to apologise.' He bent his head, his forehead touching hers as his warm breath feathered her skin. 'This is not your fault.' His fingers stroked featherlight along her jaw. 'I am so sorry you had to witness that.' He heaved in another breath. 'Oh, God!' His voice cracked. 'When he grabbed you... I felt... I wanted to—'

A groan filled the air and Hugo stiffened, releasing Olivia as he stepped back.

'As I said—' he swept a hand through his hair '—it was not your fault. You can blame your reprobate brother for that.'

He jerked his head towards Alex, who groaned again. Hugo's tone was now matter-of-fact, as though that tender moment had never happened. Hurt and confused by his sudden withdrawal, Olivia went to Alex—who was sitting on the ground, back propped against the wall, knees bent, head buried in both hands—and crouched beside him.

'Alex? Alex? Are you all right?'

'He must be very drunk to be in such a state.'

'My head. Wanna sleep.'

He groaned again and Olivia glanced round at Hugo. 'I know my brother. He can hold his liquor better than this and, for all his careless ways, he would never drink himself into this state when he was responsible for escorting me and Nell.'

'Ahem!'

The cough came from close behind her and Olivia sprang to her feet. Lord Clevedon had returned and now stood by her side, staring down at Alex—and how had she forgotten about him? What if he had come back when she was in Hugo's arms?

'My lord, I trust you are not injured, too? Thank you *so* much for coming to our aid.' She glanced at Hugo, who was scowling at his friend. He really did seem to object to her even talking to Clevedon. Was it because they were friends? Or was it because he viewed Clevedon as a more worthy rival than the younger men who courted her? Whatever the reason, she took heart from it. Perhaps Hugo was not as indifferent to her as he pretended to be.

'I sent a message to Lord Clevedon with a footman,

Lord Hugo. He is your friend and he was the only person I could think of who might help us.'

'It was my pleasure, my lady, and I am uninjured, thankfully.'

Hugo joined them. 'You have my thanks, too, Clevedon. Now, we must decide what to do about young Beauchamp here. He can hardly go back inside as he is.'

He bent and grasped Alex's chin, tilting it up. Alex's eyes were screwed tight and he groaned again. 'Earlier, I thought he had the look of a man who had taken opiates.'

'He would never—' Olivia began indignantly, but Clevedon interrupted her.

'It wouldn't surprise me if those three didn't slip him something in his drink,' he said. 'I've heard of such a thing happening and they were pretty determined to get what they thought they were owed.'

'Is Alex in debt to those men?' Olivia clutched Clevedon's sleeve. 'Tell me, please. I must know.'

'This is hardly an appropriate subject for discussion.'

There was a note of warning in Hugo's voice, but Olivia ignored it. She knew exactly what he meant—it was because she was a female and they deemed this men's business. She bridled at yet again being pushed aside as irrelevant.

'How can I protect him if I do not know the worst? Please, Lord Clevedon. Tell me why they were taking Alex to that place. Diablo's, was it Alex said? What is Diablo's? It does not sound very respectable.'

'Alastair is right, Lady Olivia, and you should forget you ever heard of Diablo's.'

And just like that, the men dismissed her. She was unimportant and didn't need to know the facts. She balled her fists in frustration. She wanted to know. Alex was her brother. It was her responsibility to see he came to no harm. Was he already in debt or had they prevented the worst from happening?

'You cannot go back inside looking like you've been in a brawl, Alastair, so why do you not wait here with Beauchamp? I shall escort Lady Olivia back to her friends and then I shall arrange for the Beauchamp carriage to come round and take Beauchamp home.'

Hugo stepped close to Clevedon, his stance challenging. 'Mind you are discreet. We would not want the lady's reputation to suffer, would we?'

Olivia puzzled over the menacing undercurrent in his voice as he spoke to his friend. Clevedon, however, appeared not to notice.

'But of course, my dear Alastair. Soul of discretion, you have my word. And I shall personally accompany Lady Olivia and her companions home, as their escort is indisposed.'

'Very well.'

Hugo sounded most grudging, but Olivia was grateful to Clevedon for his forethought. Lady Glenlochrie was so old-fashioned she would be horrified at the thought of driving home without a gentleman to escort them.

'Thank you for looking after Alex, Lord Hugo.'

She smiled at him, wishing she could say more…wishing she could touch him. She yearned to feel his strong arms around her but she knew that was not possible and so she must be content with the brief smile he gave her in return. She bent over Alex and kissed the top of his head.

'I'll see you in the morning, Alex, dear,' she whispered and then straightened and walked through the back door and into the short passageway that led to the door into the main part of the house.

Clevedon followed her and then led the way to the inner door and opened it to peer into the house beyond. Fear gripped Olivia as she belatedly understood Hugo's warning to his friend—the consequences of her and Clevedon being seen were too horrible to think about.

'The coast is clear,' Clevedon whispered. 'Follow me.'

They reached the vicinity of the door into the card room without being seen and that awful tension that had gripped Olivia melted away.

'Please promise you will not tell anyone about this.' Relief made her garrulous and the words tumbled from her as Clevedon crooked his arm and Olivia tucked her hand into his elbow. They walked towards the staircase for all the world as though the Earl was merely escorting her from the card room back to the ballroom. 'If Papa should hear about what happened, then he won't let Alex have Foxbourne and then—'

Conscious she was gabbling, she fell silent.

'Foxbourne?'

'I shouldn't have mentioned it. I am sorry.'

'You can trust me, my dear.' Clevedon patted her hand. 'You have my word I shall not breathe a word of any of this to anyone. Foxbourne…now…is that not the name of Rockbeare's place?'

Olivia explained, in the briefest of terms, about Foxbourne and Alex.

They had reached the top of the stairs. In a few moments there would be no more time. 'Tell me, sir, please—is Alex in debt to those men?'

'You really do care about your brother, don't you?'

'Of course I do. I would do anything to help him. Anything. Which is why I must know about Diablo's.'

'He is a fortunate man, to have such a fiercely protective sister, but you may rest assured that after this evening your brother will never trust those scoundrels again.'

Clevedon would be drawn no further and Olivia had to be content with that. The remainder of the ball passed without incident. Hugo did not return and Clevedon escorted Olivia, Nell and Lady Glenlochrie back to Beauchamp House as promised.

Chapter Thirteen

The following morning a somewhat battered and bruised Hugo called upon Freddie Allen to acquaint him with the happenings of the previous evening. He had formulated a plan of sorts to try to keep young Beauchamp out of trouble and away from the gaming tables, and Freddie had been enthusiastic about Hugo's suggestion for winning Alex over. Hugo was very aware that it would take much diplomacy on his part to get Alex to agree to his proposal—a young man's pride, as Hugo well remembered, was a prickly subject. Freddie sent a request to Alex to join them in the library and, after a suitable length of time, the door opened to reveal the younger of the Duke's sons. Hugo watched Alex through narrowed eyes as the young man slouched across the library and flung himself into a leather-upholstered wing chair next to the empty grate. Hugo flicked a glance at Freddie—who was already seated in the matching chair—and read the concern in the furrows of his brow.

Freddie pushed himself to his feet. 'Can I get you a glass of Madeira, Alex?'

Freddie and Hugo already had drinks.

Alex shrugged. 'If you like.'

Sullen. Resentful. Disengaged.

Hugo remembered those traits very well.

Without warning, Lucas's words came back to him.

'You always were a deep one...hiding your true feel-ings...wary of letting anyone close...afraid you'll turn out like our old man...'

Hugo rolled his shoulders as though to rid himself of a sudden weight.

Lucas was wrong. He'd shed that protective shield of sullenness at a younger age than Alex—by the age of twenty he had already moved on to the pleasures of life. Just because he didn't wear his heart on his sleeve didn't mean he was *hiding* his feelings. A man needed *some* pri-vacy, for God's sake. Besides, didn't he have some excuse, growing up with that brute for a father?

Hugo thrust down the memory of his father as Freddie crossed to a side table and poured a glass of Madeira. He forced himself to stay seated and not to go and help the other man, instinctively knowing he would resent the im-plication he could not manage. Hugo hadn't liked to ask the cause of Freddie's lameness and Freddie hadn't offered the information.

Freddie hobbled back, leaning on the crutch he used to help himself get around. He passed the glass to Alex, who accepted it with a muttered 'Thanks', and he sat down again.

Alex looked from Hugo to Freddie and back again. 'I suppose this is where you rip up at me for what happened last night? Are you going to tell my father?'

Hugo sipped his drink. 'That all depends.'

'On what?'

'What you intend to do about avoiding men like Tadlow in the future. Do you accept they were out to fleece you?'

Alex's lips set in a mutinous line. 'S'pose so.'

'And?'

'What d'you want me to say?'

'That you'll avoid them in future?'

Alex surged to his feet and paced around the room. 'I'm not a bloody fool, Alastair. Of course I'll avoid them. Although what business it is of yours I fail to understand. What are you doing here anyway? And how come you got involved last night? Nobody asked for your help. I can look after myself.'

'You were out of your mind, you damn fool.'

'I didn't drink that much. I reckon they slipped me somethin' in my drink.'

'You were *supposed* to be escorting your sister and Lady Helena, but you were more concerned with your own selfish pleasures than with their welfare. What if something had happened to either of them?'

'Oh, so that's it, is it, Alastair?' Alex bent over, thrusting his face close to Hugo, who battled to keep his hands on his lap and not retaliate. 'You're sniffing around her again, are—?'

'Alex!'

Alex snapped upright and stared at Freddie in astonishment.

'If you wish to apportion blame, then place it on my shoulders,' he said. '*I* asked Alastair to keep an eye out for you until your father comes home. You would not heed Alastair's warning the night you took Olivia to Vauxhall Gardens and our only concern is to make sure you do not lose Foxbourne. I have no ulterior motive and neither, believe it or not, does Lord Hugo.'

'Still don't see why he's here now.'

He's so ready to believe the worst of everyone, he'll lose Foxbourne through sheer bloody-mindedness if he's not careful.

'Freddie told me of your skill with horses and about the

prospect of running Foxbourne Manor for your father. It sounds like an ideal opportunity. I wish I'd been given such a purpose to life when I was your age.'

Alex's brows met across the bridge of his nose as he glowered into his drink. Hugo waited. When Alex raised his gaze to Hugo it was with a mix of caution and enthusiasm, almost as though he were holding himself back with the fear of being disappointed.

'Father has promised he will sign the place over to me.'

'*If* you prove yourself,' Freddie interjected.

Alex scowled again. 'He knows I'm good with horses. He won't find anyone better to be in charge.'

'And that is in part why I wished to speak with you,' said Hugo. 'I have a favour to ask of you.'

He sipped his own Madeira. Alert for any nuances of expression from the younger man, he recognised the flash of intrigue in his expression.

'My stepfather, Sir Horace Todmorden, has bought this mare…she's a prime piece of horseflesh, but she has turned nasty, biting and kicking until none of the grooms will go in the stall with her, let alone ride her.'

Alex straightened in his chair, leaning forward as Hugo spoke.

'Where did he buy her?'

'At auction. He suspects she was doped—she was docile enough during the sale and while being led home.'

'Doped and docile, eh?' A sudden grin flashed across Alex's face. 'Bit like me last night—I couldn't summon even a spark of energy to resist Tadlow, even though I didn't want to go anywhere near bloody Diablo's.'

'Well, believe it or not, she is even wilder than you now the drugs have worn off,' said Hugo, with an answering grin. 'Would you be willing to take a look at her? The alternative is to have her shot, but her conformation is superb and Sir Horace is keen to breed from her. Not at the price of injured men, though.'

'Of course. Although town isn't the best place to sort out a horse's problems. 'Tain't a natural way to live, see? I like to work with them in a small paddock. They're less likely to feel threatened if they have the delusion of freedom.'

Hugo found himself nodding in agreement. He'd never really thought about it, but what Alex said made sense.

'Sir Horace is an ex-cavalryman and he has plenty of contacts still at the Horse Guards. I'm sure they can find you a safe area to work with her. Although we'd have to get her there safely first.'

'We'll find a way,' Alex said with confidence. He drained his glass. 'When can I go and look her over?'

'Now, if you'd like to.'

'I'll go and change my clothes, then. Give me ten minutes.' Alex leapt to his feet and strode from the room, a completely different man from the one who had entered.

Freddie also rose. 'If you'll excuse me, I must get on. I don't want to give the Duke any reason to complain about my slacking off work when he comes home.'

'When do you expect him?'

'Either tomorrow or Friday.' Freddie rammed his crutch into his armpit and hobbled towards the door. He turned before he left and smiled. 'I've no doubt you will be the most relieved of us all when he returns.'

Hugo smiled, but after Freddie left he stared into the empty grate, lost in thought, his treacherous mind bringing back the slide of his hand around Olivia's waist, the delicious scent of violets, her gentle hands cradling his face and reliving that near-irresistible urge to seize her, to kiss her, to *take*, despite—or maybe because of—everything that had happened. His rakish instincts had clamoured at him—what did it matter that she was too young, too beautiful, too *innocent*? They had roared their demands, their need for satisfaction. Only Alex's groan had jerked him back to reality and he had, thank God, come to his senses before Clevedon returned. And he must continue to keep those urges on a tight leash and, more importantly, he must learn to keep those unwanted emotions—the yearning, the tenderness, the need to *protect*—safely locked away. Olivia was only on his mind now because he happened to be in her home. Once he had fulfilled his obligation towards her brother, he would soon forget her. There were plenty of warm, willing women out there who knew how to play the game.

'Oh!'

The feminine gasp jerked him from his musings. He looked around into her wide silver eyes and his heart twitched with longing. He set his jaw, battening down that unnerving need to be wanted, to find somewhere to belong.

'You should not be in here, alone with me.' His voice emerged as a growl.

'I did not know you were here.' Her pert nose was in the air as she rounded the sofa and sat by his side. Her scent—not only that hint of violets, but the scent of *her*... of a delicious, delectable, desirable female—filled him.

With longing. With desire. With...

It took time to identify that feeling, but she filled him with hope.

'You should go.'

The words came almost without thought. That same feeling of protectiveness arose within him, quashing any lustful urges. It was up to him to protect her from her own innocence...she surely had no idea... He surveyed her expression and caught the glint of determination in those striking silvery eyes of hers, the irises ringed with dark grey—and he wondered. Was it innocence? Or was she a risk-taker? A tease? Out to entice and then to refuse. He had watched her with her coterie of admirers. She was not innocent of the effect she had on *them*. What she might not realise was the difference between toying with those green lads and playing with a man of his experience—an older man less easily manipulated. There were too many wolves out there, prowling around the young innocents, eager to taste young flesh. *He* might feel compelled to protect her from herself, but others would not be so gentlemanlike.

'That is not what you said last night. You were happy to see me then, happy to accept my help.'

'That was different. An emergency. Olivia…you know you should not be in here with me. Your brother—'

'Liv!'

The roar made them both start. Hugo stood and faced Alex, who strode across the room, a dark scowl on his face…directed firmly at his sister and not at Hugo for a change. Alex grabbed Olivia by the arm and dragged her to her feet, shaking her. Hugo clamped his jaw against a protest and stepped back so he would not act upon his sudden urge to punch Alex on his nose.

'I *told* you Alastair was waiting in here and that you weren't to come in. Why must you persist in being such a bloo—blasted nuisance?' He pushed her in the direction of the door. 'Go on. Out! And *please* have a bit more care for your reputation in future.'

Hugo bit back a smile at the absurdity of Alex lecturing Olivia on correct behaviour. Olivia stuck her nose in the air.

'Without me,' she announced, 'you, Alexander Beauchamp, would be much poorer and, probably, still drunk or drugged, lying insensible in some squalid room somewhere with a dirty, diseased—'

'Silence!' Alex strode towards Olivia and she skipped towards the door, keeping beyond his reach.

'I deserve *some* credit for helping you last night. It was *me* who had the nous to send for Lord Clevedon to help you. Otherwise Lord Hugo would have been overpowered because you, brother dear, could barely stand.'

Alex wagged his head at her, waving his hand as if shooing a dog away. 'Have you got irritating little sisters, Alastair?'

Hugo shook his head. 'I have no sisters, irritating or otherwise. But—although I agree your sister should not have come in here *knowing...*' and he captured Olivia's gaze, raising a brow at her, prompting pink to flush her cheekbones '...that I was in here alone—I am happy to have this opportunity of thanking her for her cool head and her prompt action last night. Without her, as she rightly says, the outcome could have been very different.'

Her beaming smile made him feel a hero.

Alex scowled. 'I suppose you have a point,' he grumbled. 'But, now that's done, let's go. We have important business, Sis. Run along and attend to your sewing or your flowers or whatever other crucial activities await you.'

Sympathy swelled inside Hugo, but he realised that to voice such would not only reignite the squabble between brother and sister, but also encourage Olivia. The *tendre* she had developed for him could lead nowhere. *She* would not see the risk in pursuing it. *He* knew only too well what the result might be if she did not take care.

He bowed. 'Good day to you, Lady Olivia.'

She held his gaze boldly and, a split second before he broke the contact, she bobbed a curtsy.

'And good day to *you*, Lord Hugo.'

'You are in a lively mood, Livvy,' said Nell, as they left Lord and Lady Postbridge's garden party the following afternoon. 'You have left at least three young men nurturing high hopes that they might win your hand before the end of the Season.'

They had attended the garden party with their friend, Lizzie Tubthorpe, and her mother, who had taken Lady Glenlochrie's place as chaperon. Lady Tubthorpe and Lizzie had walked on ahead, giving Nell and Olivia an opportunity to exchange views not only on the party and the other attendees' gowns, but also on the beaux who had clustered around them like bees around nectar.

Olivia was satisfied that she had hidden her low mood successfully. She thought entirely too often about Lord Hugo Alastair even though her common sense *knew* he was totally unsuitable for her. There were plenty of other men just as handsome as and far more acceptable than that rogue, but they simply failed to interest her in the way Hugo did.

'Who is your preferred beau?' Nell continued teasingly.

Olivia waved her hand in the air. 'Those boys? Not one of them. Besides, I am not like you, Nell. I did not come to London with the purpose of finding myself a husband. I mean to spend a year or two enjoying myself before settling down.'

'I might have come here with the original intention of marrying well,' said Nell in an unusually acerbic tone, 'but our circumstances have changed since then, as you well know. Now your papa is my guardian I am no longer in danger from my Uncle Tadlow's scheming and so I am no longer in any rush to wed.'

Olivia slipped her arm through Nell's and hugged it close to her body. 'I am pleased to hear it, my dear step-aunt, for it means we shall continue to have fun together as we coax as many young men as possible to fall hopelessly in love with us and then watch at a distance as they enjoy the agony of their broken hearts.'

Even as she spoke such words, an image of Hugo arose in her mind's eye and her heart ached for him. Was this love? Well, if it was, it was not much fun.

'I did wonder…' Nell fell silent.

They were nearing the carriage now and, as one, their steps slowed.

'What did you wonder?'

'Well. I…now, do not fly up into the boughs, Livvy, but… Lord Hugo…there is something there. Between you.'

Olivia bit back a gasp. Could Nell read her mind?

'I do not know if it is because of what happened at Vauxhall Gardens, but I saw the looks you exchanged last night.' Nell's violet eyes were huge with concern. 'You are both constantly aware of where the other is, even if you are on opposite sides of the room. And I know that you think about him…no, do not deny it, for I know it. You bring his name up in conversation. Your eyes light up when he is present. And when, such as today, he is not there…your gaiety seems almost *too* gay, if that makes sense?'

She would die rather than admit to Nell how her heart yearned for Hugo.

'It does not matter what I think of him. He is a penniless rake and I am…well, I am my father's daughter. I am expected to marry well.'

'He is the son of a marquis. He is almost as high born as you are.'

'My father would not countenance him.'

Olivia's throat ached with suppressed pain. It didn't seem to matter how strong her feelings were, neither Hugo nor Papa would take note of her wishes. It had been the same her entire life—Mama had only noticed her when she misbehaved and her brothers only when she did something outrageous or nagged them. Otherwise they mostly ignored her. She was nothing but an unwanted irritant in their lives. And now Hugo... It seemed the only times he took notice of her was when she annoyed him. Well, if that was what it took to get his attention, that was what she must do.

'Anyway, this conversation is stupid,' she said airily. 'I have no wish to marry. Now, let us hurry. Lady Tubthorpe is beckoning us.'

The carriage deposited them at Beauchamp House and they went inside to an ecstatic welcome from Hector and a skipping Susie, who sang at the top of her voice, 'Dom-in-*ic*. Dom-in-*ic*. Dom-in-*ic*.'

Olivia and Nell exchanged a look.

'Susie!' Olivia caught hold of the little girl. 'Are Dominic and Aunt Cecily home?'

She had missed the calm good sense of her aunt more than she liked to admit. Even though Olivia could not confide what had happened to her aunt, she knew that, somehow, she would feel better with her back home.

'Dom-in-*ic*!' shouted Susie.

The governess, Miss Pyecroft, came hurrying from the back of the house.

'Oh, my goodness, ladies, I am so sorry. We were downstairs and when the news came that Lord Avon had returned, Susie rushed up here before I could stop her. We were making jam tarts together and my hands... I had to wash them. Although I see—' and she grabbed hold of Susie by the wrists '—little Miss Susie had no such compunction. Susie, really...come with me now. You must have left sticky hand marks everywhere.'

As she disappeared into the nether regions of the house, she called over her shoulder, 'Lord Avon is in the drawing room, if you wish to see him.'

Olivia exchanged a look with Nell. 'I wonder if Aunt Cecily is travelling home with Papa and Rosalind.'

They went to the drawing room, where Dominic was chatting to Alex and Freddie. He looked up and smiled as they entered.

'Just in time to save me from telling the tale twice,' he said.

'Did Aunt Cecily not travel back with you?'

Dominic's lips firmed. 'No. She formed a desire to visit Great-Aunt Drusilla, so I dropped her off at Leyton Grange on my way back to London.'

'Great-Aunt *Drusilla*?' Alex grimaced. 'But none of 'em can stand the old battle-axe. What's she gone there for? And how long before she comes home?'

Dominic shrugged. 'I do not know. She and Father— I do not know. But she won't be back for a few weeks at least. Father and Rosalind should arrive home tomorrow, though, and Uncle Vernon and Aunt Thea—for that is what she likes to be called, not Dorothea—will come here in a few weeks' time after their honeymoon trip to the Lakes.'

Dominic soon left the drawing room to go upstairs and change out of his travel-stained clothes. Olivia followed him.

'What were you going to say about Papa and Aunt Cecily, Dom?'

'Nothing,' he said as he took the stairs two at a time.

Olivia hurried after him, lifting her skirts clear of her feet. She caught up with him just before he disappeared into his bedchamber.

'Tell me. Please. Did they argue?'

For that is what it sounded like he had been about to say—even though Papa and Aunt Cecily never argued. Not like Uncle Vernon and Aunt Cecily. Dominic paused, his expression softening as he looked down at Olivia. Her heart quailed, her stomach churning at that look. Dominic was only ever kind to her when he felt she was in need of his big brotherly protection; otherwise he was as bad as Uncle Vernon with his teasing.

'They *did* argue, Dominic. I can tell, so please do not lie to me. When will Aunt Cecily be coming home?'

'Livvy.' He put his hand on her shoulder and squeezed gently. 'It is nothing to worry about. It was only the slightest of disagreements.'

'But why? Why would they quarrel?' To her horror, Olivia felt tears burn behind her eyes. 'They *never* argue. She *will* come home, won't she?'

'Of course she will.'

But something in his eyes as they flicked away from hers…in the uncertain way in which he said those four words…warned Olivia that it was by no means certain.

'Did she send me a message?'

Dominic gave a rueful smile, then pulled her into a hug. 'Sorry, brat, but, no. She was a little…preoccupied.' He pulled back then and smiled down at her. 'But don't fret. You still have Father and me and Alex. We are still a family.'

Except Papa now has Rosalind. He won't have time for me. And if…

Olivia swallowed, her throat aching. If they had children, where would that leave her? Her world seemed to be turning upside down. She could see herself in the future, becoming less and less important to her family as they busied themselves with their new lives.

'Besides, you will probably get married yourself very soon.'

She stared at her brother, shock making her stomach clench as the implication of his words hit her. 'Is Aunt Cecily getting married?'

Surely not…her father, uncle and aunt, all in one year? How could life change so very drastically in such a short time?

'This is strictly between us, brat,' said Dominic, 'but she

may do. Lord Kilburn's estates border Leyton Grange—she refused an offer from him earlier this year but it appears she is having second thoughts.' He patted her cheek. 'Don't worry, Livvy. It may never happen.'

Dominic disappeared into his room and closed the door, leaving Olivia standing alone in the upstairs corridor, fighting tears as she wondered what was happening to her precious family. How *could* Aunt Cecily abandon her like this? She was the only mother she'd known since she was five years old. Her own mother had rejected her, but Aunt Cecily had always been there. Now, though…she had turned her back on Olivia without a thought. Was she really so unimportant? So…*unlovable*?

Angrily, Olivia swiped at the tears that now wet her cheeks.

I do not care. I'll show *them I don't care.*

Chapter Fourteen

Olivia stared at her brothers suspiciously. Since Dominic's return they had been uncommonly protective towards her and that only served to worry her more. That Alex was privy to more information about what went on at Uncle Vernon's wedding was clear. And she hadn't heard her brothers argue once—and that was unheard of. She'd bet they'd argue if she told Dominic what Alex had been up to while he'd been away—but then she remembered that much of that was her fault in the first place, so she did not risk opening that particular topic of conversation.

'You *both* intend to escort us?' she said. 'Why?'

It was the evening of Dominic's return to London, and she had come downstairs, dressed and ready for the Pendletons' soirée. The Pendletons' twin daughters—Lynette and Louisa—had made their debut this year and were friends of both Olivia and Nell. Now here were Dominic and Alex, dressed in their evening finery, waiting in the drawing room for her, Nell and Lady Glenlochrie to be ready to leave.

'You should be grateful to have two such handsome, elegant gentlemen as your escorts,' said Alex, with a swagger and a smirk. 'I promised Aunt Cecily I would escort you while she's out of town and that's what I'm doin'.'

'And I am at a loose end,' said Dominic, 'so I may as well go there as anywhere.'

Olivia eyed him gloomily. 'You do know that whenever you show your face at any of these society events I suddenly become *much* more popular with all the simpering young misses, Dominic?'

He smiled. 'Can I help it if I am irresistible?'

'Hmmph. The question is, Brother dear—is it you who is irresistible, or the prospect of being a future duchess?'

She had been hoping Hugo would be at the soirée to watch over Alex as Papa was still not home; she had hoped she might snatch a quiet word with him—she intended to pay him some of what she owed him—and she had also fantasised that he might, finally, dance with her. There were bound to be a few informal dances for the younger set tonight, while the seniors played cards and gossiped. Those hopes were much less likely to come to fruition with Dominic there. He could be so stuffy at times and she just knew he would object to her even speaking to Hugo.

When Hugo appeared in the doorway, flanked by Lords Clevedon and Sudbury, Olivia's heart seemed to perform a somersault in her chest, leaving her temporarily gasping for breath. He was so handsome. So sophisticated. His dark gaze swept the room—where much of the furniture had been removed to provide space for dancing—and came to rest upon Olivia. His expression seemed to harden and he looked away. Exactly as he had reacted to her when he first caught sight of her at the Denby ball, she realised with a sinking heart.

It was so difficult to understand what he truly thought

or felt. He seemed determined to hide any genuine feelings behind a barrier of alternating disapproval and boredom and yet…she couldn't be so wrong about that kiss. Could she? And then, in those few, unguarded moments after the fight…his anguish…that tender moment…*that* was not her imagination. But now, yet again, he seemed as remote as ever and she felt as confused as ever.

Why do you fool yourself that a worldly sophisticated man like Hugo would be interested in a silly little girl like you? Even your own family don't think you important enough to be told the truth of why your aunt hasn't come home.

Then Lord Clevedon caught Olivia's eye, smiled and said something to Hugo and Lord Sudbury before leaving them in the doorway, clearly making his way towards Olivia. On the brink of returning to the safety of Lady Glenlochrie's side, she hesitated. She could not risk annoying his lordship after his help at the Denby ball. So she waited, trying to fathom Hugo's expression as he tracked Clevedon's progress around the room. His features seemed to have hardened, his lips set, his dark brows lowered. Then he glanced at Olivia and immediately his expression blanked and he directed his attention to Lord Sudbury.

That he was annoyed with his friend was clear, but why? Was it…could it be that he did not want Clevedon to dance with her? Was he jealous, if only a tiny bit? That thought buoyed her hopes, but also stirred her indignation. If he did not want to speak with her or dance with her, that was up to him. But he had no right to object if another man chose to do so.

Then Lord Clevedon was before her, bowing.

'Might I have the pleasure of this dance, Lady Olivia?'

She smiled at him, bobbing a curtsy, then placed her gloved hand in his. She'd show Lord Arrogant Alastair she wasn't about to stand around like a wallflower waiting for him to ask her to dance.

Who does he think he is, anyway? Nothing but a rake, with no title of his own and no land or anything. I can look far higher than Hugo Alastair...

She ignored the inner voice that whispered that she did not want to look higher than him. It was him, and only him, that she wanted, but his casual dismissal of her both hurt and infuriated her.

'Avon has returned, I see,' Clevedon remarked as they circled and met and parted again through the steps of the country dance. 'Does that mean the Duke will soon be home as well?'

Olivia was shaken from her brooding by his question. 'Yes. I believe so. My stepmother's grandfather is travelling with Papa and the Duchess, so they travel at a slower pace than Avon.'

She flicked a glance at the doorway. Hugo was still there, his dark gaze on her, so she smiled up at Clevedon. If flirting and dancing with his friend was the only way to command Hugo's attention, then that was what she would do.

'You present a most charming picture this evening, my lady,' said Clevedon, bowing at the end of the dance. 'It is warm tonight, but you manage to maintain your cool poise when all about you are wilting in the heat.'

Olivia laughed. 'Appearances, my lord, are deceptive in that case. Inside, I am melting.'

He appeared somewhat taken aback and she regretted her choice of words, for that phrase conjured up how she had felt inside when Hugo kissed her. Just the memory of his lips on hers...his tongue in her mouth...heat flushed her chest and neck and crept inexorably to her cheeks.

'Might I procure you a glass of lemonade?'

Clevedon beckoned a footman stationed near the door. Hugo was still watching them, his eyes narrowed, and she tilted her chin. Good. He would see it was not only *young* men who found her of interest. She could attract a sophisticated gentleman like Clevedon, who must be thirty if he was a day, and it was a bonus that he happened to be Hugo's friend.

'Thank you, sir. I am rather thirsty.'

Besides, she was conscious that Clevedon knew enough to cause a scandal for her and for Alex if he chose to talk of what happened at the Denby ball. They were in full view at a ball—how could there be any danger? It would not hurt her to be pleasant to him.

'Would you care to stand over there by the window and catch the breeze, if there is any to be had?'

'Thank you; that would be a relief.'

Clevedon instructed the footman to bring two glasses of lemonade to them in the window embrasure and then steered Olivia towards the window, which was partly shielded from the room by a large urn of flowers. The fresher air admitted by the raised sash was most welcome and Olivia was confident in her ability to manage any unwelcome behaviour by the Earl.

She sipped gratefully at the cool lemonade, savouring the sharp tang of the lemons.

'That is better.' Clevedon leant against the wall of the alcove and eyed her as he drank. 'And we have the advantage that those flowers deflect some of the noise from the room. Tell me, how are you enjoying your first Season?'

'It is everything I hoped it would be,' said Olivia promptly.

He chuckled. 'I hear a "but" in there somewhere.' When she did not respond, he went on, 'You have surely achieved everything every young girl dreams of when coming to town for the first time: you have taken society by storm and, despite what happened at the Denby ball, I have not heard a breath of criticism attached to your name.'

Her gaze flew to his. He smiled reassuringly.

'Your secret is safe, my lady. Never fear.'

He moved closer and Olivia tensed, gripping her glass in two hands and raising it to chest level to prevent him getting too close. His gaze flicked down to that protective manoeuvre and his eyes crinkled as they lifted again to hers. He leaned even closer, his lips close to her ear.

'It is a challenge for a man to snatch a private word with such a popular young lady, not to mention one with two very protective brothers. But I have always relished a challenge. Tell me…can you name one single man who hasn't fallen immediately under your spell? I'll wager you cannot and, if you can, then I denounce that man as a fool.'

An image of Hugo arose in her mind's eye. Did one kiss count as him falling under her spell? Her heart sank. No. For it was she who had kissed him. He had merely responded, as any red-blooded male might, to what she had offered. She eyed Clevedon again and swallowed, suddenly uncertain of allowing him to manoeuvre her into this semi-private spot.

There was no advantage to encouraging Clevedon if Hugo could not see them—she'd only thought to make him a little jealous. Her rambling thoughts froze. Dominic always called her a *manipulative little madam* when she tried to get her own way. And that's exactly what she was doing now…using Clevedon in an attempt to—what was it he had said?—in an attempt to have Hugo *fall under her spell*.

She got that squirming, shameful feeling in her stomach that she often experienced when she knew she was in the wrong.

Clevedon brushed the back of his fingers across her collarbone and she straightened, looking him firmly in the eye.

'Thank you for the lemonade, sir. I am quite refreshed and it is time I returned to my chaperon.'

'As you wish, Lady Olivia. You are right to be cautious. Reputation is everything for a young lady, is it not? You may rely on me not to set tongues wagging.'

His words sent a shiver dancing down her spine. Was that a veiled warning? No. Surely not. Her imagination really did run away with her at times.

Clevedon bowed and stood aside. As she passed him, she felt the brush of his hand on the nape of her neck and down her back. She could do nothing but ignore it. She could not challenge him over his inappropriate caress when she had willingly put herself in a situation where he could take advantage. Aunt Cecily had warned her often enough about *never* going off alone with any man—even into a semi-public situation like that window embrasure.

If you do, your actions are bound to be misconstrued. Never give any man a chance to get you alone.

Those words echoed through her head and her spirits— already low—plummeted further. When would she come home? Olivia *needed* her. Papa and Rosalind were all very well, but it was Aunt Cecily to whom she had always turned. Her calm good sense always helped Olivia make the right decision.

'Might I beg a second dance, my lady?'

She wanted to refuse, but she found herself agreeing to Clevedon's request, wary of provoking him when he knew so much about Alex. His smile told her she'd made the right decision, but she consoled herself that he could pay court to her all he liked, she would never marry him. On that thought, she scanned the room. Hugo was nowhere to be seen and neither was Alex, although Dominic was dancing with Louisa Pendleton and Nell was dancing with Lord Silverdale, one of Uncle Vernon's friends. How she hoped Alex had not been lured into another disastrous card game.

They reached Lady Glenlochrie, and Clevedon scribbled his name against a dance later that evening, bowed, and walked away. Olivia sank into a vacant chair and Lady Glenlochrie leaned towards her, raising her open fan in front of her face to keep her words private.

'That is most encouraging, my dear. You did quite right, not lingering for too long by the window. I kept my eye on his lordship, you may be sure of that, and there was nothing untoward that I could see. Your papa *will* be pleased when he returns tomorrow.'

Olivia battened down her irritation. 'Lady Glenlochrie, I know you mean well, but I have no wish to encourage Lord Clevedon or anyone else for that matter. I do not wish to marry yet.'

'Nonsense! If a man such as Clevedon should offer for you, your papa will bite his hand off, gel, make no mistake. He is a splendid catch. And, as behoves an obedient daughter, I make no doubt you will conform to your father's wishes on the subject of your marriage.'

Olivia only just managed to prevent her eyes rolling at that.

Lady G. is so old-fashioned—she belongs in the last century. Papa would never force me to marry someone I do not care for.

That thought sparked another, however. A less welcome thought. Papa might never force her to marry someone she objected to, but would he be amenable to her marrying the man of her choice if he disapproved of him? She suspected she knew the answer to that and it was not the answer she wanted.

She thrust aside all thought of Hugo and marriage—*not that he is interested in me. He is merely a convenient example, that is all*—and turned to Lady Glenlochrie. There was little point in arguing with her so Olivia simply smiled, collected her reticule from where she had left it while she danced and stood up.

'I need to visit the retiring room, ma'am.'

Lady Glenlochrie inclined her head, then returned her attention to her neighbour and their gossip and Olivia made her escape. She exited the room and stood irresolute on the landing before heading for the card room, situated towards the rear of the house. In the doorway, she almost bumped into Hugo, on his way out of the room. Every nerve ending tingled and her breath grew aggravatingly short. She really wished she could prevent these unwanted reactions to the man. She tightened her grip on her reticule.

'Have you seen Alex?' she asked.

'He's in there.' Hugo flicked his thumb at the card room. 'He's playing with Charnwood and a couple of other decent men. There's no need for you to concern yourself; I'm keeping an eye on him.'

'May I see?'

Olivia stood on tiptoes to try to peer over his shoulder and Hugo's dark eyes crinkled at the corners as he stepped aside to allow her an uninterrupted view of Alex, who looked relaxed and happy.

'Do you not trust my word, my lady?'

Olivia elevated her nose. 'I do not believe you always tell the whole truth, no. And I need to be certain Alex is not gambling with unsavoury characters.'

'I can assure you that Alex has seen the error of his ways and is not likely to get embroiled with men like Tadlow again.'

Then his lips firmed. Olivia found it hard to tear her

gaze from his mouth; found herself longing to kiss him again. Was that very shocking? Of course it was, but she could not help how she felt. And as long as *he* did not realise it, her pride would remain intact and she could hold her high.

'I wish I could say the same about you,' Hugo then muttered.

Startled, Olivia looked up. *'Me?'*

'Yes, you. Look. We cannot talk here, it will be remarked upon. Follow me, but at a distance. And for God's sake, be discreet.'

He stalked away without waiting for an answer and took the stairs to the second floor. Olivia followed—reluctance slowing her pace. She knew that tone of voice—although she did not know what gave Lord Hugo Alastair the right to think he could dictate to her about *anything* she might choose to do. On the landing, she looked around in time to see Hugo disappear behind a pair of floor-length curtains. She followed.

They were in a deep embrasure where the window overlooked the street. A gas lamp outside cast a pale illumination over Hugo's grim expression. She cast her mind wide for words that might lighten his mood...anything to avert the lecture she felt sure he was bursting to deliver.

'I prefer my choice of venue for an illicit *rendezvous*.'

No sooner were the words out than the memory of their encounter in Sophie Wray's bedchamber exploded into her brain, complete with every detail of that kiss. Heat erupted and, without volition, she moved closer, placing one hand on his chest as she tilted her face to his. His chest expanded as he drew in a fractured breath, his eyes dark fathomless pools in his pale face. Then he covered her hand with his and slid it up to rest on his shoulder. His fingers feathered over her collarbone and neck and up to her cheek.

She leaned into his touch and stepped even closer, sliding her other arm inside his coat and around him, stroking his back, breathing in his spicy, masculine scent. Their breath mingled as their gazes fused, and then her eyes drifted shut as that delicious, melting sensation gathered deep inside her, pooling between her thighs.

Lips brushed her skin with the most delicate of touches—dancing along her jaw and the sensitive skin at the side of her neck. She swallowed her moan and tilted her head back as he traced her collarbone and teased along her neckline with lips and tongue, leaving her tingling and craving more. Then his arm snaked around her waist and hauled her close as he seized her lips. She pressed into him, soothing her tight, aching breasts against the solid wall of his chest. She opened her mouth, meeting the thrust of his tongue with her own, matching his every move.

His jaw rasped her fingertips as she stroked and explored his face and her other hand dipped lower, skimming the silk of his waistcoat, tracing his spine as it curved into his waist and then the hard swell of his buttocks—rounded and firm. She felt the shift of his muscles as she squeezed and a low groan rumbled in his throat. He stilled. She didn't want him to pause. Didn't want to give him time to think…to have second thoughts. She thrust her fingers through his hair and cupped the back of his head, holding him still as she angled her head and deepened their kiss. She was rewarded by him gathering her closer still, half-lifting her until her entire body fitted to his and she could feel a hard ridge pressing against the softness of her belly.

And then he stopped.

He straightened, his hands at her waist as he pushed her away. He put his fingers to her lips and his lips to her ear. 'Shhh.'

Jolted back to reality and the outside world, Olivia became aware of voices on the landing, just the other side of the curtain. Nerves jangled as she feared discovery, but then she relaxed as she realised, from their conversation, that the voices belonged to two maids and that they were moving away.

She gathered her wits, leaning her forehead against Hugo's chest as he held her. She felt...content and yet, at the same time, on edge. She had dreamed and fantasised about that second kiss, but her imagination had been nowhere near equal to the reality. She'd lost herself—she'd had no concept of where she ended and he began. They were one. And there was more wonder, more pleasure to discover. She knew it as readily as she knew her own name.

As the maids' voices faded, Hugo moved away from her, his hands dropping to his sides. She immediately felt his loss and wrapped her arms around her own waist in comfort.

'I came here with the intention of talking to you, not to carry on from where we left off the other day.'

He didn't sound angry. Or regretful. But he did sound like one of her brothers might, when they were about to take her to task and not one bit like a man who was captivated by her kisses. She recalled his words, the first evening they met. *I prefer my ladies willing. And experienced.* Her spirits plummeted. Of course he did—he was an experienced rake and although she had proved the first to him he clearly was not impressed by her skill, even though she couldn't help that she wasn't as experienced as other women he might have kissed. Ruthlessly, though, she quashed any hint of sadness. She was with him now—she would not spoil their time together with misery or, even worse, tears. Growing up with her brothers had instilled in her the knowledge that men *hated* females who cried.

She gathered her courage.

'Talk *to* me? Not *with* me?' It took effort to tease him, but anything was better than turning into a watering pot, as Alex would scornfully call it. 'That sounds suspiciously like a lecture to me, Lord Hugo.'

Chapter Fifteen

Hugo chuckled. She surprised him at every turn. For a fleeting second misery had swum in those expressive eyes of hers and her pain had tugged at his conscience and stirred—deep within him—the urge to soothe it away and to put a smile on her face and a laugh in her voice. Then there was no misery, just a teasing light, and the transition had been so swift, so smooth, that he could not be sure he had not imagined the entire change of mood.

'Not quite a lecture, more a warning. About Clevedon.'

A frown tugged at her brows. 'What of him?'

'I saw you—dancing with him. And afterwards, in that alcove.' And he had wanted to tear the bastard apart with his bare hands. He nudged her chin up, trying to instil in her how serious he was. 'Do not think to use him, my sweet. You are playing a dangerous game.'

'I do not know what you mean. I am playing no games.'

But she was. He knew it. He had seen the glances she sent his way. He knew women. He knew when someone was trying to get his attention. If only she realised the effort it cost him to ignore her—but he must be strong, for her sake.

'If you say so.'

'You don't believe me?'

'You play with fire if you are encouraging him to no purpose. Unless, of course, you have a burning desire to be Countess of Clevedon?'

She thumped his chest. 'I do not want a husband. Not yet, anyway.'

Through her indignation, however, he heard embarrassment quiver and he sought to soothe her. Her pride and her self-belief were just two of the things he admired in her.

'All I mean is that you should take care. Leading on a man like him—an older man who is on the lookout for a wealthy wife—is very different to games of flirtation with the young bucks who surround you and who profess to be dying of love for you.' He was envious of those young men, who could court her with impunity. 'But you ought not to encourage Clevedon, or any man of his ilk. Goad a man like that too far and who knows what trouble you might let loose.'

He had trusted that her experience at Vauxhall Gardens would keep her wary of Clevedon, but had his actions at the Denby ball changed her opinion of him? Hugo could not possibly admit the real truth about why Clevedon was so unsuitable. All he could do was try to set her straight, and encourage her to think of the consequences of her actions.

She pouted at his words, then peeked up at him through her lashes.

'Do I goad *you*, my lord?'

That look rocketed through him, heating his blood. She chased every sensible thought from his head. Did she realise the effect she had on men? On him? No, of course she did not. She was an innocent. And yet...

He did not doubt she was an innocent in fact, but she was one of those females instinctively aware of her own sexuality...her own allure. And she knew exactly how to

use it. And if he ever saw her use that look on Clevedon…
his hands clenched again into fists.

No.

He calmed himself. For all her attempts to attract Hugo's attention, he had not once seen her use that kind of lure with Clevedon.

Or with any other man.

Only him.

A knowing smile flirted around those full lips, swollen from his kiss, as her gaze dropped to his hands. He quickly unclenched them as she reached for one and caressed it between both of hers. It was all he could do not to haul her into his arms, kiss her senseless and introduce her there and then to the delights of seduction…show her the pleasures that awaited her…the sensations a skilled lover might coax from a woman's body.

Let Clevedon try to entice her away from *that*.

But that would be unfair. Not to mention immoral. And when had he turned into such a stuffy, strait-laced prig? He resorted to the only response he could to try to get her to see sense.

He laughed.

He gazed down at her, half-hooding his eyes and allowed his top lip to lift in a slight sneer.

'Sweetheart,' he drawled. 'I am merely claiming my reward for acting as nursemaid to you and that brother of yours. This—' he curved one hand around her skull and tilted her head up, taking her lips again in a ruthless assault '—is merely a taster to put me in the mood for later tonight, when you are tucked up in your bed with your innocent dreams.'

She pushed him away and wiped the back of her hand across her mouth, shooting icy shards at him from those extraordinary eyes of hers.

'How *dare* you kiss me like that, without my permission!' Her brows were elevated in haughty disdain, as though she were a queen addressing a subject. Far from angering him, he admired her spirit. 'Until now, Lord Hugo, you have proved useful in enabling me to gain a little experience in the art, but I suggest you do not try again unless *expressly* invited.'

She opened her reticule and withdrew a small but bulging pouch which she then thrust at him. 'This is part of what I owe you, sir. Once I pay the remainder, there will be no need for further contact between us. Good evening.'

She flung aside the curtain—apparently heedless of anyone who might see her—and stalked away. As luck would have it, there was no one else on the landing.

Hugo permitted himself no regrets. This was for her own good. Better that she hate him than continue to harbour that hope that shone so clearly every time she looked at him. Better, too, that he slam the door on his own feelings and that pointless, raw eagerness to see her, even from afar, to talk to her, to ask her dance.

He simply could not see how this…this…whatever it was blossoming between them—he could not see how it could end well for either of them. When her father returned to London he would for certain show an interest—and not in a good way—were he to become aware that a man of Hugo's ilk was paying *any* kind of attention to his daughter.

Hugo would still protect her from Clevedon, but only by dint of staying close to his erstwhile friend rather than to Olivia. *Someone* needed to protect her—from her own impetuosity as well as from the prowling wolves of the *ton*.

Wolves like Clevedon. And himself.

He made two vows.

He would try to warn her father about Clevedon, even

though the Duke would be highly unlikely to listen to anything Hugo had to say.

And he would avoid any future contact with her.

It took him all of one day to break that second vow. It seemed he couldn't help himself. He was walking around Grosvenor Square, on his way to his mother's house, when a squeal of laughter and a series of frenzied barks from the garden in the centre of the square caught his attention. And the mere sight of her—her jet-black hair gleaming in the sunshine as she chased a giggling child, who trailed a chip straw bonnet from one hand—thumped him in the heart and he found himself gasping for breath.

And instead of obeying his inner common sense that commanded him to walk on by—to leave her angry—he found he could not bear for her to think so very badly of him and so he changed direction and strolled into the garden, the gate nearest to Beauchamp House having been left unlocked. A footman standing just inside the gate stared at him, but the recognition was mutual—it was the same man who had admitted him to Beauchamp House when he called on Freddie—and although he kept his eye on Hugo, the man made no attempt to stop him.

That gigantic hound that belonged to the Duchess was gambolling at Olivia's heels and he was the first to notice Hugo. He charged up to him and Hugo—even though he knew the dog to be friendly—still had to steel himself not to flinch in the face of the sheer size of him. Hector's disappearance from their game captured Olivia's attention and she slowed, glancing after the dog. Then she slammed to a halt, her mouth a perfect O of surprise. Her cheeks glowed pink and, without her hat, her hair had worked loose from the controlling hair pins.

This is how she would look after a night of bed sport.

Hugo felt his body respond to that wayward thought as he walked up to her and he cursed his newly discovered streak of morality—the voice of conscience that urged him to protect her rather than to seduce. Seduction was his speciality—he knew exactly how to please and satisfy a woman with his body and there were many, many women in the *ton* who could testify to his skill. How much easier it would be, and more agreeable, to follow his male instincts to take and be damned to the consequences. But knowing the consequences for Olivia would far outweigh the consequences for him meant he could not—for the first time in his adult life—pursue his own desires.

Which had left him floundering in, for him, unfamiliar territory.

'Good afternoon, Lady Olivia.' He tipped his hat.

Olivia dipped a curtsy, but the tip of her chin and the martial light in those temptress eyes of hers suggested she had not forgiven him for his behaviour the night before. And he could not blame her. He had behaved exactly like the rake she believed him to be. Except she had no idea of the restraint he had exercised and he could not tell her.

'Good afternoon, my lord.'

Her voice was decidedly frosty, but the effect was wasted when the fact she was panting ever so slightly put him even more in mind of pleasurable romps and beds and—

He swiped those thoughts away. He was not here to rekindle her feelings for him—was he?—but to…his thoughts lurched to a halt. He did not know quite why he was here. Or, indeed, why he had chosen to walk to Mama's house via Grosvenor Square when there were several other routes he might have taken. But he was here now…

He smiled. 'Would you care to introduce me to your friend?'

Olivia elevated her chin, but she beckoned to the child, who eyed Hugo shyly as she came forward. Olivia held out her hand for her bonnet and put it on—tucking the loose tresses away—before introducing the child as Susie, her father and stepmother's adopted daughter. Susie stuck her thumb in her mouth and mumbled around it.

'She is still a little worried by men in tall hats.' Olivia, arms folded, watched Susie rather than looking at Hugo. 'She was raised by her foster parents on an isolated farm and I don't believe she had ever seen a fashionable gentleman until she met Papa.'

'She does not appear to be intimidated by that great brute, however,' said Hugo, as Susie, losing interest in the adults, ran after Hector to fling her arms around his neck. 'He is almost as tall as her, but she shows no fear.'

'That is because she trusts Hector. She knows *he* would never hurt her.'

He supposed he deserved that subtle dig.

'How did she end up with your family?'

'Her foster parents were cruel and she ran away from them.'

'She is fortunate to be taken in by your father. Speaking of whom, can you tell me when you expect him back in town?'

'Some time—' Olivia's jaw snapped shut and her eyes widened as her attention latched on to something beyond Hugo's left shoulder '—today,' she finished.

Hugo spun on his heel. Sure enough, a travel-soiled carriage with the Duke's crest emblazoned on the door had pulled up in front of Beauchamp House.

'We must go.' She did deign to flick a glance at him then. 'Please wait until we are indoors before you leave the garden.'

It was a demand rather than a plea. She certainly had

spirit; not by a flicker did she betray any embarrassment over what had happened between them in that window embrasure.

'You are asking me to skulk in the bushes?' He hardly knew whether to be amused or offended.

'I have no wish for Papa to know we are acquainted. I will not risk him finding out about Vauxhall because he will blame Alex and then—'

'Yes. Very well. I get the gist—you will do anything to protect that scapegrace brother of yours, will you not?'

She gave a slight shrug of her shoulders. 'Of course. Do not think I am ungrateful for your assistance but...yes. I will. At least you no longer need concern yourself with my family. You have proved useful, but you may return to your carefree life without guilt.

'Now, come, Susie. Let us go and welcome Papa home.'

Olivia left the garden without a backward glance and Hugo followed her progress across the road to the carriage. Had he got her completely wrong? Had she just been playing with him, the same as he had accused her of doing with Clevedon? If she had, the reason why was clear enough— she had needed his help to watch out for Alex.

Although that still did not explain why she had kissed him so enthusiastically.

The Lady Olivia who had—almost carelessly—dismissed him just now was not the Lady Olivia who had clung to him and sighed in his arms last night, before he had intentionally infuriated her. But...*could* he have been wrong? An old saying came to mind—while the cat's away, the mice will play. Quite apart from the need to protect her brother, had Olivia merely made the most of the Duke's absence to experience a bit more of life? Had he allowed himself to be reeled in with the rest of her admirers—believing she had feelings for him when in reality she was simply enjoying herself and gaining experience? Was he just another damned gullible fool?

He had never felt so wrong-footed by a woman. Who was she really? The naïve girl or the scheming woman?

Anger tore at his gut, but he forced himself to remain out of sight until the Beauchamps disappeared inside the house. He would do that much for her. Then he strode from the garden, nodding to the footman to relock the gate as he passed. As he neared his mother's house, though, his steps slowed. No matter what Olivia's purpose had been in kissing him—in enticing him to feel more for her than he had ever felt for another woman—the fact remained that he did care for her. And—amazingly for a man who had mostly only ever considered his own pleasures—the compulsion to protect her still hummed in his blood.

She was so busy watching over Alex—but who was watching over her? Hugo would do one last thing for her—he would warn the Duke to keep a closer eye on her. Hell, if she was in Hugo's care, he would have her under permanent lock and key because that was the only way he could ever be certain she was not up to mischief.

The problem now was—how, precisely, did he warn the Duke without landing both Olivia and Alex in trouble?

And *that* particular dilemma was resolved as early as the next day, when he walked into the morning room at White's and there, by the fire, sat the Duke of Cheriton. Hugo gave himself no time for second thoughts. He crossed the room and cleared his throat. The Duke glanced up and his expression changed from one of polite enquiry to recognition and then to curiosity. He folded his newspaper with a rustle and placed it on the table by his side.

'Alastair.' He nodded as his silvery-grey eyes—so like his daughter's—narrowed. 'To what do I owe this privilege?'

'Mind if I join you?'

'Please do.' Politeness rather than warmth coloured the Duke's tone.

Hugo sat in a nearby chair and signalled to a footman to bring him a drink. Now that the moment had arrived, he felt somewhat awkward. It was one thing, vowing to do the right thing, quite another to do it when faced with Olivia's powerful father.

After several silent minutes, Cheriton enquired: 'And what might I do for you?'

Hugo's gaze jumped from the glass of brandy he had been contemplating to the Duke's face. This was more difficult than he had anticipated. He could not see how Cheriton would fail to wonder at Hugo's sudden interest in his family.

'It is more a case of what I might do for you,' he said at last. 'Something I overheard and thought you should know, that's all.'

'Well?'

'It concerns your daughter—Lady Olivia.'

Cheriton's eyes turned icy. 'What about her?'

'Best keep an eye on her, that's all. There are some unsavoury types sniffing around her.'

Hugo started to rise, but Cheriton reached out and caught his wrist in a steely grip.

'Explain yourself,' he growled.

Hugo stilled. He looked down at the hand gripping his arm, then raised his eyes to the Duke's and raised his brows.

Cheriton held his gaze for a fraught number of seconds, then released his grip and leaned back in his chair.

'What do you know?' he asked in a more conciliatory tone.

Hugo hesitated. It went against his code of honour to

name Clevedon but…his need to protect Olivia was stronger. He had no choice.

'Clevedon.'

Cheriton's brows shot up. 'Clevedon? Unsavoury?'

He looked Hugo up and down, and he didn't need to add—*who are you to call the Earl of Clevedon unsavoury?* His opinion of Hugo was clear in that disdainful look.

Hugo gritted his teeth. 'He's in love with someone else—' He could not bring himself to admit it was Lord Sudbury. Who knew if Cheriton could be trusted with such sensitive information? 'He needs a wealthy wife and he's set his sights on your daughter. He'll break her heart.'

The Duke's eyes narrowed and he studied Hugo, who battled to keep his expression blank. When he spoke again, his voice was very quiet, sending a shiver down Hugo's spine.

'And why, I ask myself, are you concerning yourself with my *eighteen-year-old* daughter's welfare, Alastair?'

Hugo stood. 'I don't approve of naïve little chits being used as pawns, that's all. Just watch out for her.'

As he strode away he heard the Duke say, 'Oh, I shall do, Alastair. You may be sure of that.'

Chapter Sixteen

'You wished to speak to me, Papa?'

Her father stood up as Olivia entered his study. 'I do. Thank you, Freddie. That will be all for now.'

Olivia waited until Freddie had gathered up his papers and limped from the room, trepidation coiling inside her. What had Papa found out? Did he know about Alex? But, no. Or he would be speaking to her brother, not to her. So why had he sent for her?

Hugo.

Her insides somersaulted as his name popped into her head. As they always did. Even though she tried very, very hard to never think of him, somehow he was always there. At the edge of her consciousness, just waiting to catch her unawares…waiting until she forgot to brace herself and forcibly keep his memory at bay. And then the memories would erupt, right into the centre of her thoughts, and the black cloud would descend, reminding her of her splintered heart and her shattered dreams.

He had returned her kiss at the Pendletons' soirée. He had *groaned*. She had been sure he had felt something. But then, afterwards, he had reverted to that same cool, detached, arrogant way of his and taken no notice of her *whatsoever.* It was no longer a matter of him not asking her to dance, or taking her to supper. He did not even *look* at her. Not once. He had kissed her and then dismissed her. And she had vowed to do the same with him. And she had been proud of her effort in the Square yesterday. She had been as cool as cool could be. And *she* had dismissed *him* this time. Take *that*, Lord Arrogant Alastair.

But that did not stop him invading her thoughts whenever she was unwise enough to allow her guard to drop. Well, she would keep—

'Livvy?'

The gentle enquiry jerked her from her thoughts. Papa was holding a chair for her, waiting for her to sit down. She plastered an airy smile on to her face.

'I am sorry, Papa. I was debating which gown to wear to the opera this evening.'

Papa raised a single brow. Olivia wished she could master the art—she had spent hours in front of a mirror trying to mimic that look, but to no avail. Pity—it was a very effective expression, suggesting just the right degree of cynicism. She'd love to be able to quell Lord Arrogant Alastair with just one such look—she thrust him from her thoughts and sat down. Papa pulled another chair close and took her hand.

Olivia's heart plummeted as fear rocketed through her.

'Is it Aunt Cecily? Has something happened?'

A frown darkened Papa's expression. 'No, nothing has happened and it does not concern your aunt. Why should you think that?'

She could not confess that deep panicky feeling she always experienced whenever the thought of losing one of her family came into her head. That was *her* secret and Papa had enough to worry about.

'No one will tell me why you have squabbled.'

Papa sighed. 'Livvy. We have not squabbled. We are rational adults—we do not have squabbles.'

Olivia put her nose in the air. No one *ever* told her anything, just because she was the youngest. And female. And then they wondered why she had become adept at winkling out secrets!

'Now, I wish to ask you about somebody, but I need to trust you not to reveal this to anyone else. Can you be discreet?'

Her curiosity aroused, Olivia nodded eagerly. From thinking that no one ever told her anything, it seemed Papa was about to confide in her. She preened at the thought he was treating her as an adult—someone to be consulted, rather than a child to be tolerated or ordered about.

'Who is it, Papa?'

'Lord Clevedon.'

'Clevedon?'

Sick dread crowded her throat. *Had* Papa found out? Had he already sent Alex away?

'Yes,' Papa went on. 'I have already spoken to Lady Glenlochrie and she told me that his lordship has called upon you and that you often dance with him.'

The air left her lungs in a relieved whoosh. 'Yes, that is true…' A horrible thought occurred to her. 'Papa? Lord Clevedon has not offered for me, has he? Because if he has, despite what Lady G. says, I do *not* wish to marry him. You will not make me, will you?'

Relief flashed across Papa's face as he gathered her other hand in his. 'No, no, I have not even seen Clevedon. And you must know I would never force you to wed against your wishes, Livvy.'

'Thank you, Papa.'

'That is all I wished to ask you.'

Olivia stood to go. 'Papa?'

'Yes?' He was already halfway around his desk, his attention on a stack of correspondence.

'What made you ask Lady G. about Lord Clevedon?'

'Oh…' Papa stared at her, a distracted frown on his face. 'It was…someone warned me to watch out for his lordship, that is all. You have good birth and a large dowry. There will be fortune hunters among your suitors—you know the ways of our world and I know your aunt has warned you of such men. They can be charming and declare their undying love, until they have their hands on your dowry. Such marriages, where one spouse cares more than the other, can be…lonely.' The fleeting sorrow that crossed Papa's face told Olivia that he was remembering her mother and his first marriage. 'I have been warned Clevedon is one such man.' He shrugged. 'Who knows if it is true, but as you do not care for him it is, I am pleased to say, immaterial.'

'Yes, but who would tell you such a thing, Papa? Do I have a guardian angel?'

He barked a laugh. '*Angel?* He is no angel, sweetheart, believe me. And it's best you do not know his identity. I don't know why he chose to warn me, but I shall be keeping my eye on him as well as on Clevedon, you may be sure of that.' He stared at Olivia and the harsh planes of his face softened. He rounded the desk in long strides and pulled her into a fierce hug. 'No one will harm you, sweetheart. Not while there is breath in my body.'

Olivia left the study, her thoughts in a whirl. It had to be Hugo. Who did he think he was, kissing her one minute and then lecturing her about Lord Clevedon the next and even warning Papa against him? It seemed *he* did not want her—unless it was to kiss her in dark corners—but he did not want anyone else to show an interest in her either.

That was called being a dog in a manger.

Unless, of course…hope sprang to life again, deep in her heart.

Unless he did want her for himself.

The following few weeks soon disabused her of *that* notion.

Following Papa's return, it proved nigh on impossible for Olivia to contrive a private encounter with Hugo—Papa and Rosalind were more mobile than Lady Glenlochrie and it was hard to give them the slip. And then Aunt Cecily came home as well—well, Papa had stormed off to Oxfordshire to fetch her and there was definitely something wrong, but no one would tell Olivia what had happened. Aunt Cecily was tight-lipped and unhappy as she tried to pretend everything was normal and whenever Olivia tried to talk to Papa about it, he just chucked her under the chin and told her it was nothing to worry about. Why could they not understand that telling her that made everything worse? Caused her to worry all the more?

And so now there were three of them to watch her. It was so frustrating. Dominic and Alex never had this trouble. Anxiety was her constant companion, her insides winding tighter and tighter with every day that passed, until she felt ready to explode. Why did everyone treat her as though she was a child not to be trusted with the truth?

And trying to accept that Hugo simply didn't care a jot for her made her feel infinitely worse, particularly when she couldn't fully bring herself to believe that either. With his brother and sister-in-law in town, Hugo now attended many of the same events as Olivia, but he avoided her; he never asked her to dance or engaged her in conversation or asked to escort her to supper. And none of that really surprised her, but it still hurt. If they did happen to meet face to face, he bowed and greeted her politely, but he sent her no secret signals to encourage her to still hope.

And yet…and yet…there were times—many times—when she caught him watching her as she talked and laughed and danced with other gentlemen. He would quickly avert his eyes when she saw him, but those times kept alive a tiny flicker hope in her heart.

'Dominic?' Olivia ignored her brother's blatant exasperation as he looked up from the book he was reading. 'I desperately want to go for a ride in the Park, but there is no one to accompany me. *Please*, Dominic. Say you will go with me.'

'Ask Alex. I'm in no mood and, besides, it is starting to rain.'

Olivia peered out of the library window. The sky was grey and it was true that one or two drops had spattered on to the glass.

'Alex is out.'

'Are you certain? I heard him not ten minutes ago.'

'Yes, I'm sure.'

She'd watched him leave, after overhearing him tell Freddie he was riding in the Park with Hugo—something about one of Hugo's stepfather's horses that Alex had been helping him with. She needed to go the Park and see Hugo and, hopefully, talk to him. She missed him.

'Please, Dom. I am bored and I want to *do* something. Please take me. Stepmama and Aunt Cecily are too busy with the preparations for tonight.'

Papa had managed to persuade the renowned opera singer, Angelica Catalani, to sing at Beauchamp House that evening, but that had meant a mountain of last-minute preparations, even though the guest list had been kept short and very select—*intimate* and *exclusive*, according to Aunt

Cecily. It seemed everywhere Olivia went, she was beneath somebody's feet.

Dominic's attention was fixed once again on the book in his hands.

'Ask Lady G. to take you in the carriage,' he said without looking up. 'You'll keep dry that way.'

'But you aren't busy and I want to ride. You have no idea how frustrating it is, not to be able to go anywhere or do anything on my own. You are so lucky. Ple-e-ease, Dominic, my darling, my most favourite brother.'

He looked up again at that, but only to purse his lips and shake his head at her. She felt like stamping her foot, but she refrained. If she fell out with him, he'd never agree to escort her.

'Papa says I have too much energy and I shall be expected to sit still tonight when Signora Catalani performs, and no one will allow me to help them. *Please*, Dominic.' Olivia eyed her handsome brother as he turned a page and reached for the glass of wine by his side. 'Surely you are not afraid of a few spots of rain? What would your harem of admirers make of that, I wonder? The bold Marquess of Avon afraid of getting his hair wet.'

That caught his attention.

'Firstly, I am not afraid of getting wet and, secondly, my hair would be protected by my hat, as you well know.' He put a mark in his page and laid the book aside with a sigh. 'You are not going to give up until I agree, are you?'

Olivia hid her triumphant smile as he unfolded his tall frame from the chair.

'Come along then.' He looked her up and down. 'You are already changed, I see. I'll tell Grantham to send word for the horses to be brought round.'

Olivia let her grin spread at that. 'No need,' she flung over her shoulder as she exited the library ahead of him.

'I already did that. The horses should be ready and waiting for us outside.'

'You little—!'

Olivia laughed and skipped quickly out of her brother's reach as he swatted at her backside.

Olivia soon spotted Hugo and Alex, together with four other riders, who were grouped together in a quiet corner of the Park. Alex was riding a beautiful black horse in a large circle while the others watched.

'Why is Alex doing that?' she asked Dominic, turning her own horse's head in their direction. 'Is that the horse that belongs to Hugo's stepfather? What is wrong with it—it looks like Alex is schooling it.'

'He is.' Dominic reached across and grasped Olivia's rein, halting her mare. 'Hugo?'

Blast.

Dominic frowned at her. 'Hugo?' he repeated.

Olivia shrugged. 'Slip of the tongue. I heard Alex call him that. I meant Lord Hugo, of course.'

'You are not to go over there and disturb them,' said Dominic, releasing her rein. 'The horse is a bit wild from what Alex told me. It's taken him several days to persuade her to trust him. This is the first time he's ridden her out.'

'Well, I had no intention of riding up to *Alex*. I just wanted to go a little closer to watch. You *know* how I love to watch him working the horses.'

Olivia nudged Sprite with her heels and simultaneously tickled the flank of Dominic's horse with her whip. The horses ambled forward. Dominic, his attention on Olivia, did not halt them again.

'Since when?'

'Since…well, since Papa has promised him Foxbourne,

that's since when, clever-boots. It's important to me to see Alex settled and happy. Isn't it important to you?'

'Of course it is. But we do not need to mix with Alastair's sort to do that.'

'*Alastair's* sort? Why, whatever do you mean?' They were now close enough to the group watching Alex for Olivia to recognise the men who were with Hugo. 'Do you refer to Lord Clevedon? Or perhaps it's Sir Horace himself that you object to. Or the Marquis of Rothley?' The fourth man was a stranger, but from his clothing she guessed him to be a groom. 'Really, Dominic. You can be obnoxiously top-lofty at times.'

'And you are a manipulative minx,' grumbled Dominic. 'Do not think I haven't noticed what you are up to—and don't think I don't realise that Clevedon has been paying you court of late. Although why such a sensible chap should be interested in a little menace like you, I quite fail to understand.'

Olivia elevated her nose. 'I always did think you somewhat slow on the uptake, Brother,' she said, safe in the knowledge that they were now too close to the others for Dominic to clip her around the ear as he used to when they were younger. 'I, in case you have failed to notice it, have been declared Catch of the Season. *That* is why Lord Clevedon is interested in me.'

'I'd be doing him a favour if I set him straight,' Dominic muttered as they drew even closer to the group of men. 'No one deserves a lifetime with you, you little madam.'

Olivia huffed, but could not reply as they were now within hearing distance.

Maybe she *was* manipulative, but it had been seven days since that kiss and she had not once had an opportunity to even speak to Hugo. It was up to her to make sure they met and had the opportunity to speak, or how would he ever realise...?

Her thoughts stuttered to a halt. Realise what?

That we are made for each other.

She swallowed. She was a scandal waiting to happen. She knew it. And yet...she simply could not help herself. Her restlessness grew by the day as the end of the Season approached. Her family was changing and she felt as though she did not quite belong anywhere any more. Quiet dread churned constantly, low in her stomach, and she simply could not meekly sit and wait for things to happen—she was compelled to get out there and move them along. She brushed aside her doubts, buried her fears. There would be time to nurse her wounded pride later, if Hugo continued to ignore her. For now, she owed it to herself to do all that she could to get him to notice her. Besides, she still owed him the final instalment of the money she owed him. That thought buoyed her. It was the perfect excuse.

The men acknowledged their arrival with nods and smiles.

'Good afternoon, sirs,' said Olivia, smiling straight at Hugo.

He simply looked bored and her hopes—so high a few minutes ago—were dashed.

Clevedon reined his horse around to line it up on the opposite side of Olivia to Dominic. 'Well met, Lady Olivia. Have you come to watch your brother work his magic?'

She had little interest in talking to the Earl, but Hugo was now speaking in a quiet voice to his brother and taking no notice whatsoever of Olivia. *Hmmph.* What did she have to do to get his attention? It was ironic that she was surrounded much of the time by admirers, but the one man whose attention she craved seemed totally uninterested.

'Indeed,' she said in a bright voice. 'Alex is *such* a marvel with horses. I simply adore watching him at work.'

Attuned to Hugo and his every move, she noticed the swift sideways glance in her direction. Good. He wasn't completely unaware of her then.

'What made you come along today, my lord?'

'Oh, I was merely passing and stopped to watch. Quite fascinating. I never suspected your brother possessed such skill. Sir Horace has been telling me about the trouble they've had with that mare since he bought her and how Alex has changed her. I understand from Sir Horace that your father has purchased Rockbeare's place in Buckinghamshire with the intention that Alex will run it on his behalf?'

'But I—' Just in time, she stopped herself from reminding him that she had told him about Foxbourne after that fight at the Denby ball. Conscious of Dominic listening on her other side, she continued, 'that is... I thought no one was to know about that yet?' She glanced at Dominic for confirmation.

He shrugged. 'If Alex wishes to risk people knowing all about it when the entire deal might still fall apart, that's up to him. He always treads his own path, you know that, Sis.'

He then rode his horse over to join Sir Horace, leaving Olivia with Clevedon and thus affording them the opportunity to talk without being overheard. Not that she wished for such a thing. She bit back her *humph* of disgust. Trust Dominic! She'd wager a whole month's allowance he wouldn't have left her alone like this with Hugo.

'Alex is a fortunate man,' said Clevedon. 'Many fathers would have withdrawn his allowance after some of the trouble he's caused, let alone rewarded him with an estate and a thriving business. Let us hope he manages to keep his nose clean long enough for the deal to be finalised.'

'Oh, he will.' Olivia put her nose in the air. 'I shall do everything in my power to keep him out of trouble for the next few weeks. In fact—' she indicated Dominic with a flick of her head '—we both will. We stick together in our family.'

'That is what family is for, is it not?' he said. 'Now, if you will excuse me, my lady, I spy Sudbury over yonder and I have a message for him. Until we meet again.' He raised his hat and nodded before setting off at a trot.

Olivia could not believe her good fortune. Here was the perfect opportunity and she rode over to Hugo and Rothley, her brain working furiously to think of an excuse for joining them. Hugo's expression blanked as she halted Sprite facing them, but Rothley smiled and raised his hat again. Undaunted—well, a touch daunted, maybe, but she did not have the time to nurse bruised sensibilities when with each day that passed the end of the Season drew closer—she pressed ahead, a last-minute idea occurring to her just in time.

'Excuse my interruption, gentlemen, but I wonder if you have heard about our musical soirée this evening? It is all rather last minute, but my father managed to prevail upon Signora Catalani to sing at Beauchamp House tonight.'

'Catalani?'

Good. At least Rothley sounds suitably impressed.

Hugo, however, merely regarded her, one supercilious brow raised as if to say *I see right through you.*

'It is years since I heard her perform,' Rothley continued. 'Is her voice as good as it was?'

'Better, I should say,' said Hugo.

'I am persuaded Lady Rothley would love to hear her sing and I therefore invite you all to join us this evening.' Surely it would not matter if the event was a little bigger than the gathering Rosalind and Aunt Cecily had planned? Surely they wouldn't begrudge one or two additional guests?

Hugo's lips compressed and she saw his chest expand as he drew in a long breath. 'You should accept, Luke. Mary will love it.'

Rothley's dark gaze flitted between Olivia and Hugo, and she swore she saw him bite back a smile before he said, 'The invitation is for you, too, Brother. It would not be the same experience without you there, is that not correct, Lady Olivia?'

'Indeed, sir.'

'And Mama will be thrilled to have us both there together. You know how she always puffed us off in society, even when we were the biggest rogues out there.'

Hugo laughed at that. 'Dearest Mama. Always ready to defend her sons, no matter what.'

'What's that about your mother, boys?'

Sir Horace and Dominic had joined them. Olivia's heart sank. Would Dominic see through her ploy? She'd committed herself too far now to retreat and so she told Sir Horace all about Signora Catalani and repeated her invitation to Beauchamp House that evening.

'Oh, that is most kind. Lady Todmorden is exceedingly partial to a spot of opera. I do wonder, though…such an invitation, proffered without your parents' knowledge…?' Sir Horace raised his grey, bristly brows at Dominic.

Dominic, to give him credit, did not hesitate. 'In my father's stead, please allow me to confirm my sister's invitation to you and your family, Sir Horace.'

'Much appreciated, Avon. I accept on behalf of us all.'

Pure delight spread through Olivia at the thought of the entire evening with Hugo in her own home. Now she must work out how she might speak privately with him without her family noticing. She had the perfect excuse—she had borrowed and scraped together enough money to pay the remainder of what she owed him.

She knew she must take extra-special care to hide any interest in Hugo from her family this evening. The constant effort required to hide her aching heart behind a smiling face had proved exhausting and she suspected she was no more skilled than Aunt Cecily at disguising her unhappiness. She would be utterly mortified if any of her family were to guess it was Hugo who was the cause of her low moods.

But Hugo would be there…tonight…in the same room as her. She hugged that little nugget close to her heart as anticipation swirled deep inside her. Her behaviour *was* outrageous, she knew, but the Season would soon end and then she would not see him again until next year. That thought wrenched at her heart. She could not bear the thought of not even seeing him, even though it was increasingly clear that he did not feel the same compulsion to see her.

Chapter Seventeen

You're a damned fool.

He knew it and yet still he would go tonight. And he would go because—ridiculous, lovelorn idiot that he was—he had missed her. Hugo stared unseeingly at his reflection in the mirror as his valet brushed off his black tailcoat in readiness for the musicale that evening. The past week had dragged unbearably, but he had consoled himself that it was for the best if he gave her a wide berth. Now at least he had the satisfaction of knowing that *that* decision had been wise—look at what had happened this afternoon when they had met quite unexpectedly in the Park. Her face was an open book and Lucas's earlier suspicions of a mutual attraction had been confirmed as fact, but Mama, it seemed, had *already* noticed...

They had arrived back in Bruton Street and Sir Horace had been full of that unexpected invitation to Beauchamp House.

'A small and most exclusive gathering, my dear Lucy, and we are *all* invited.'

'Catalani!' Mama clasped her hands at her breast. 'Oh, how wonderful. But...what on earth prompted Lord Avon to invite us?'

'Oh, it wasn't Avon, my love. At least—it was not he who originally invited us. It was Lady Olivia. Very sweet of her—she thought of Mary, you see, and how much she would enjoy hearing Catalani sing.

'But I have never attended an opera in my life,' said Mary. 'I do not know why Lady Olivia should think of me.'

'I suspect,' Mama had then said, her eyes sparkling as she smiled at Hugo, 'that Lady Olivia had *quite* another purpose in inviting our family.'

And now, thanks to his incorrigible mother, the entire family were aware that there was…*something*. A growl vibrated in his throat but, out of respect for his valet as he helped Hugo into his form-fitting tailcoat, he swallowed it back. He only hoped Mama would be discreet around the Duke.

Safety in numbers. He repeated the mantra as he trod down the staircase of the house in which his chambers were situated and again as he waited for the rest of his family to collect him in the carriage. And he repeated it again as he followed Lucas and Mary and Mama and Sir Horace up the magnificent marble staircase of Beauchamp House. As long as they were within sight of others, he knew Olivia would not directly approach him.

It was a *most* select gathering, he saw, when they were shown into the salon. A space at one end had been cleared for the musicians and the singer, and chairs—Hugo counted twenty-one in all—had been spaced throughout the remainder of the room to accommodate the guests. It was quite some coup for Cheriton to persuade the oft-times capricious Catalani to perform at a private musical soirée. The London theatres—Catalani was the resident soprano at the King's Theatre in Haymarket—would now close until the winter and it was her habit to tour a few of the provincial towns during the summer.

She had not yet arrived, it seemed. The musicians were in place, playing quietly as the guests mingled and chatted. A footman offered a glass of wine from a tray, which Hugo accepted and then cast his gaze around the company. He stilled when he saw her. She was stunning, sheathed in a gown that clung to her slender form and set off her pale skin and black hair to perfection. She stole his breath… he wished—

A nudge dragged him back to a sense of his surroundings.

'Close your mouth, Brother. You look like you're catching flies.'

He snapped his jaw shut and glared at Lucas, who shrugged. 'She is gorgeous, I grant you. But you need to decide if she's worth the hassle you'll get from her father if he gets wind you're interested.'

'I am *not* interested.'

Lucas raised a brow.

'Not in the way *you* mean,' Hugo growled.

'With a lady like her, Little Brother, there *is* no other way to be interested, if you get my meaning.'

Freddie limped towards them then, a welcoming smile on his face. Hugo introduced him to Lucas.

'I hear Alex is doing a grand job with Sir Horace's mare,' said Freddie and Hugo gratefully followed his lead into a general conversation about horseflesh.

He was relieved when Angelica Catalani finally swept into the room and he selected a chair towards the rear of the salon, after watching Olivia sit near to the front. The trills and swells of Angelica's remarkable voice washed through him almost unnoticed as he spent the entire time watching Olivia. At a break in the entertainment drinks were again served and Hugo snatched a glass of wine and headed for the terrace outside before anyone could engage him in conversation. He could not trust himself to discuss the singing that he had barely heard. He would be hard pressed to name one piece Catalani had sung. He crossed the narrow terrace and stared out across the darkening garden, as rigid as one of the dimly seen statues dotted below. Eventually, he released his pent-up breath with a whoosh, raised his glass, tipped back his head and drained it with one gulp.

'*Here* you are.'

He stiffened, and carefully set his wineglass on to the stone balustrade before he turned. They were a mere ten feet from the open window and the room beyond.

'What are you doing? Your entire family is in there.' He jerked his chin towards the salon.

'We are quite safe. Papa is discussing politics with Lord Castlereagh. Once they get started, they will not stop until Signora Catalani is ready to sing again. And my aunt and stepmother are talking to your brother and his wife.'

'That is not what I call safe,' he growled.

Frustration sent his blood surging around his body. He wished he might claim his frustration was due to anger at her risk-taking, but the tightening of his trousers suggested it was a different sort of frustration altogether. She looked so…*edible*…standing there, her silvery eyes glowing as she looked into his.

'Nell is keeping watch. If anyone looks like they might venture outside, she will come out quickly and join us.'

He scanned the windows. Sure enough, he could see Lady Helena, her back to the window as she faced the room.

'It is still an unnecessary risk. Why did you follow me out here?'

'Why?' Her voice rose. 'Because I—' She stopped and he saw her bring herself back under control. His heart ached for her, but he would do nothing to foster false hope in her. When she spoke again her words were measured, the only sign of agitation a crease between her dark brows. 'I wanted to see you. I *needed* to see you.'

Hugo rubbed his hand across his jaw. She appeared to believe herself equal to anything. How on earth could he get through to her that she must take better care of her reputation?

'That is no reason. You know the ways of our world—it is scandalous for us to meet unchaperoned and you would be ruined if we were discovered. You cannot always have what you want, Olivia. You are old enough to understand that.'

'But why not? You are the son of a marquis. I am the daughter of a duke. We are very nearly equal and I assure you I do not aspire to be a duchess.'

'*Even* if I wanted you, it is not a case of our respective births, as you well know.' He swept a hand through his hair in utter frustration. 'My past is sufficient to send any respectable father rushing to barricade his daughter behind locked doors. You must have heard the renewed stories about Rothley and me.'

Lucas's reappearance in society had resurrected all the old tales of wild and scandalous behaviour.

'Those are ancient history.'

'Hey!' He laughed, swatting gently at her. 'Less of the ancient, if you please.'

She laughed back and he battled the urge to sweep her into his arms and to kiss her.

She needs to be protected. From me and from herself.

'I did not mean *you* are ancient, simply that those stories are the past. You are only eight years older than me. It is not so much. Papa is *ten* years older than my new stepmother.'

'And, as your papa would no doubt point out very quickly, I have no prospects.' He would not tell her about

Sir Horace's offer of Helmstone—that was way off in the future and would only feed her hope when he must starve it. 'And I am in constant debt—my allowance is paltry. It would be barely enough to keep you in hats, my sweet.'

'I do not care about hats. Or about m-money.'

Only because you have never had to go without either of those things.

He hardened his heart and turned to pace along the terrace and then back to her. 'Besides, you need to understand this—I have no desire for matrimony, not to you or to anyone. I have an enviable life—I answer to no one.'

There was a pause. 'That does not sound enviable to me.' She sounded thoughtful. 'And neither is it true.'

She's right. And it's not true.

But they were words he could not say. He cocked a haughty brow in reply, but she merely shook her head at him.

'If you answer to no one, it implies you have no one to care about you and no one that you care for. And yet you have your mother and your stepfather. And your brother and his wife. And me.'

And if only that *were true.*

He waved his arm. 'Unnecessary emotional baggage. And unwanted.'

'I do not believe you.' She placed her hand on his chest and his heart twitched at the gentle pressure. 'You have changed. The man in those stories…that is not who you are now.'

Why would she not listen? What she wanted…what she asked…it was impossible.

'What is it you want from me?' The words burst from him. He swung around and braced his hands on the balustrade, leaning his weight on them as his chest heaved with each tortured breath. He swung round to face her. 'Should

I take you to my bed? Is *that* what you want? Because that is where we are heading if you do not stop this. There is only so much I can take, only so many times I can resist you and what you offer.'

His fury subsided as he took in her stricken expression… the pale hand that rose to splay across her chest…the movement of her slender throat as she visibly swallowed. He steeled himself against the longing to haul her close—to hold her and soothe away her pain—as he glared down into her silver-grey eyes.

'You *must* stop this for both our sakes.' She visibly flinched at his harsh words. 'The only future acceptable for a lady of your breeding is marriage and I am *not* the marrying kind.' He could resist touching her no longer and reached for her hands as he gentled his voice. 'If you continue to contrive such clandestine meetings it can only be a matter of time before we are caught. You will bring shame on your family and ruin upon yourself and all for nothing. You *know* your father would never, ever countenance a match between us and *I* know you would accept nothing less than marriage, despite appearances to the contrary.'

She bent her head at that, staring down at their joined hands. Then a single teardrop splashed on his skin.

'But I cannot help myself,' she whispered. 'I long to spend time with you and you will barely even acknowledge me when anyone else is around. What am I supposed to do?'

'You are *supposed* to remember your upbringing and what is expected of you as the daughter of a duke. You are *supposed* to conform to society's edicts. You are *supposed* to be the perfect young lady and to marry appropriately when the time comes.'

'So I am expected to wait patiently and never even *try*

to follow my heart simply because I was born a woman? It's not fair.'

'Life *isn't* fair.'

The truth of that ripped at him, leaving him raw and vulnerable as the memory of his father and his violent childhood loomed large.

A sob tore from her. 'But I love you. And do not tell me that I am too young to know what love is.' She tilted her face to his, tears spilling. 'I am *not* too young to know how I feel and I am woman enough to recognise how you feel about me. I might lack certain experience, but I am wise enough to know that if you did not care for me, you would have tried to bed me long ago. But you did not. Instead, you have done your utmost to protect me—not only from the folly of my own actions, but also from *yourself.*'

He stiffened, then stepped back, flinging her hands from his as he hardened his heart, knowing he must, once and for all, make her *believe* he did not care.

'You have no experience in what goes on between a man and a woman,' he said through clenched teeth. 'You are a beautiful and desirable young lady and I respond to you as a man would to *any* such woman. You are too young and too inexperienced to distinguish between lust and love and your naivety will lead you into trouble if you do not grow up very quickly. *Stay away from me.*'

He fought to maintain his forbidding frown as she touched his mouth, the pad of her thumb drifting across his lips. She lowered her hand and stepped back and he suffered the bleak reality of loss.

She stood tall.

Proud.

Every inch the daughter of a duke.

'Very well. You have made your position clear. It is time to accept I cannot always have what I want and I must stop making this impossible for us both.' The sadness in her eyes tore at his heart. She removed a small drawstring bag that had dangled from her left wrist and thrust it at him. 'This is the last of the money I owe you.'

She turned away and walked to the salon window where she paused for a minute and raised her gloved hands to her face, patting at her cheeks. Then, back straight, she disappeared into the salon, as the opening strains of an aria from *The Magic Flute* drifted out of the open windows into the night.

It was the outcome he had planned, so why then did he feel so wretched? It wasn't just her tears—although they had tugged at his heartstrings. How he felt now was not even about Olivia, as such. It was about him. His feelings weren't the result of guilt or shame that he had upset her. This tearing, heart-wrenching desolation was for himself. It was pure misery. It was the knowledge that he had just sent away the woman he loved with his whole heart and being, and it was the deep gut-wrenching knowledge that he could do not one damn thing about it. He would have to continue his life without her.

He waited ten minutes before following her inside and resuming his seat at the back of the room. The only person who noticed him slip back into his chair was his mother and his heart sank as her beady gaze wandered from him to Olivia, who had regained her seat at the front of the audience. His mother might believe she was being discreet, but he knew her only too well and she had clearly taken note of both Olivia's and his absence and would be, without a doubt, drawing her own conclusions.

After the final song Catalani finished to huge applause, with the audience on their feet. She lapped up the adulation as her due, bowing and smiling graciously.

Hugo kept an eye on Olivia as the guests again mingled while waiting for supper to be served. Although she conversed with others easily enough she was clearly unhappy, earning her worried looks from both her father and her aunt. He set his jaw. There was no more he could do. Olivia would get over her infatuation with him eventually.

As for what he felt for her...his feelings were so muddled he could no longer think straight. If he had ever thought in the past about permanence...marriage...it had been a thought speedily dismissed. The memories of his father had ensured that. He wanted none of that misery. And he—like Lucas, until he had fallen in love with his Mary—had vowed never to wed.

And now? If he could stand aside and counsel himself, his advice would be to stay well away from Olivia, despite—if he were brutally honest—suspecting that what he was suffering from was not unrequited lust but something much, much more profound.

Love.

The word crept into his thoughts. Swelled his heart. Made his pulse pound and sweat prickle his back. Could it be? For either of them? For despite what Olivia had said, he could not believe she knew what love was. Hell, *he* did not know what love was and he was eight years older than her.

He sat with his family to eat supper and Olivia sat with hers. After ascertaining her whereabouts he did not look in that direction again, but mindlessly ate his food as the conversation washed over him. Then a shadow fell across him and the talk at the table ceased. He looked up, straight into the silvery gaze of the Duke.

'Might I have a word, Alastair?'

'Of course.'

Hugo pushed back his chair and stood, wondering what

on earth Cheriton wanted with him. He followed him out
on to the terrace.

'I wanted to thank you for what you have done for Alexander.'

The breath left his lungs in a silent gust of relief. He'd
steeled himself against an accusation about Olivia, certain someone had seen them earlier and told her father.
He silently reiterated his vow to keep his distance. This
man standing before him—a hugely powerful man used
to commanding his world—would want more for his beloved daughter than a cynical, world-weary rake of a second son with only his stepfather's goodwill, which could
be withdrawn at any time, to secure his future.

*Hell, of course she deserves better than me. All that
youth, beauty and innocence...she deserves the very best
in the land.*

'How did you know?'

'Sir Horace has been regaling me with tales of the won-
ders Alex has wrought with that mare. He told me it was
your idea and, again, I thank you for thinking of it.'

He thrust out his hand and Hugo shook it. Then he took
a huge breath. He owed Olivia this much. He would avoid
her, for both their sakes, but someone needed to continue
to watch over her.

'That matter we spoke of once before,' he said.

The Duke frowned. 'Clevedon? I have spoken to my
daughter. She has shown no interest in the man so you do
not need to concern yourself further, Alastair.'

'But Clevedon still has an interest. You sh—'

He fell silent as Cheriton lifted his hand, palm facing
Hugo.

'It is a family matter, Alastair. My sister is home now
and, between us, you may rest assured my daughter has
all the protection she needs.'

The Duke nodded, swung around and strode back to the house, leaving Hugo frustrated that he had not put his case more clearly.

Olivia waited until she was alone in her bed that night. Until then, she went through the motions and behaved as though there was nothing amiss, shrugging aside Nell's anxious enquiry about what she had said to Hugo. And what he had said to her. Nell, at least, would be relieved. She would no longer be asked to cover for Olivia while she pursued her silly childish daydream of an all-time love with Lord Hugo Alastair.

Once alone in her bed, however, she relived that final interview and, though her heart felt as though it was being shredded with the sharpest of claws, she knew she must grow up and accept that Hugo simply did not want her— not in the way she had dreamt of, anyway. That had been a fantasy of her own making. And she would not be his lover—she could never follow that path, not even for him.

So she lay in her bed and she did not allow herself to shrink from facing up to her stupid juvenile behaviour. It was the least she could do. She must accept that she could not have what she wanted simply by force of will. Real life wasn't like that. Other people, such as Hugo, had opinions and desires and needs and expectations, just as she did. And she must respect all those things, even though they differed from hers.

She had asked him once, teasingly, if she goaded him. Now she knew the answer.

She heard again the helpless fury in his outburst. *What is it you want from me?* She pictured again his haunted eyes in haggard features. She had pushed him too far. Did she never learn? She had always done the same with her brothers…badgered them until, finally, they lost their tempers. Or gave in.

And then, as she had struggled to control the emotions that threatened to choke her, his anger had receded, revealing a glimpse of tenderness as he had taken her hands. But it had been an implacable tenderness. He had been resolute and—she now realised—she respected him more for that inner strength. The same solid aching lump filled her throat now as then.

She must move on from believing that, if only she persisted, Hugo would come to realise the depth of his feelings for her and find some way for them to be together. She could not force him to feel more for her than he did and, besides, a miracle would be needed for her father to consider a man like Hugo as a suitable son-in-law. Dominic was right—she must stop trying to manipulate everyone in the hope they would eventually give in and see things her way. She must stand back and allow others to do as they wish.

She could not blame Hugo for her ridiculous fantasies— it was not his fault she had somehow elevated him to the status of a hero, merely because he had saved her from a horrible situation entirely of her own making.

It was time to face reality and time for her to behave as a woman, not as a girl with foolish daydreams.

Chapter Eighteen

Two days later, Olivia sat on the sofa in the morning room, picking disconsolately at the stitches she had only just set. They were all wrong, just like her life. She sighed.

'Livvy?'

'Yes?' She glanced at Nell, who was sitting on a chair nearby, also sewing. She saw the concern in her friend's violet eyes and her throat thickened. Which made her cross, because it was stupid, blatant self-pity. She bent her head again to concentrate on the handkerchief she was hemming.

'Will you not tell me what is wrong?'

'I am tired.'

Silence reigned. Olivia sighed again. 'I am sorry. I did not mean to snap at you.'

'I do not believe you are simply tired, Liv,' said Nell. 'And I hate to see you so unhappy. Please talk to me. Is it Lord Hugo? What happened the other night? You did not…he did not…?'

Olivia shifted impatiently. 'No. Of course we did not. I am not that foolish.' She bent her head to the handkerchief again and stabbed her needle through the fine lawn. 'Oh, blast it!' She sucked at her finger and cast the handkerchief aside. 'Now I shall have to stop sewing or I shall get blood all over everything.'

Nell reached across for her hand and examined her fingertip. 'It is a mere pinprick. It will soon stop bleeding.'

Unlike my heart.

Her vision blurred.

'Livvy…' Nell rose from her chair and sat next to Olivia, putting her arm around her. 'Is Lord Hugo really worth all this risk?'

The pain in her chest spiked, radiating out. 'I thought he was.'

She hadn't confessed the truth of their conversation at the musical soirée. She had allowed Nell to assume it had been as before—with snatched kisses and murmured endearments. Not that Hugo had ever murmured endearments to her except in her dreams, but she had felt compelled to embellish their meetings somewhat. To make them sound more romantic and less… She scowled down at her lap. If she honestly, truthfully sorted fact from fiction in her head, he had only ever taken what she had offered. Yes, he had resisted taking more than kisses, but not once had he ever uttered words to encourage her instinct that he cared for her on some deep, elemental level. Was she really guilty of allowing her own desires and daydreams to colour reality? The answer, she knew, was yes. Her heart, already bruised and tender, squeezed tight and she bit back a gasp at the pain as tears blurred her vision.

'Olivia?'

The burden of keeping her anguish to herself grew too heavy and she told her friend, in halting terms, the truth of what had happened that night.

'He told me I must stay away from him.' Her tears spilled over. 'Oh, Nell! How can I have been so stupid? I thought I could win him over. I th-th-thought he cared for me, but he does not. Or at least, not enough…not in the same way I care for him. And now…and now…oh, Nell, I cannot face him again.'

'You have no choice, Livvy. You are bound to see him, but you shall ignore him. You are a Beauchamp. You are the Catch of the Season. You shall not even glance in his direction…your orbit flies high above the likes of a disreputable second son.'

Olivia blurted out a sound halfway between a laugh and a sob. 'Oh, Nell. You sound so fierce.'

Nell put her arm around Olivia. 'Whatever you do, do not let him suspect for one moment that you still care. You have more spirit than to let one thoughtless, heartless rake defeat you. Yes, you will see him. But there will be other gentlemen there, too, and you will put on a brave face and you will show Lord Hugo Alastair exactly how popular you are.'

'He already knows. And he does not care.'

This time, Hugo stuck to his promise to himself. He continued to avoid Olivia, declining invitations to events where she was likely to be present. It proved harder than he expected to stay away from her. He could not stop thinking about her, and his mother—as discreet as an elephant in a herd of cows—was not helping.

'Why do you not think of settling down, Hugo?'

'Look how happy and content Lucas is with Mary and the children.'

'I thought maybe there was a hint of something between you and Lady Olivia, son?'

'Now you have Cedar Lodge there is nothing to stop you. It is a perfect place to raise a family.'

'Sir Horace and I would adore having our grandchildren living closer to us. I know it's impossible for Lucas's family, but…'

And she would eye Hugo with her head on one side and those bright eyes of hers until he was almost ready to pack in the whole idea of Cedar Lodge and helping Sir Horace run the Helmstone estates. He did not know how he would stand the entire summer at Helmstone if this was how she kept on. Mama was adamant that Hugo should stay at Helmstone itself and not live on his own out at the Lodge while Lucas and his family were there.

One place he was certain to run into neither his mother nor Olivia was White's. And it was while he was there that Alex slouched across to join him one day.

'Don't often see you in here, Beauchamp,' said Hugo, signalling to a waiter for another glass and a bottle of claret.

'Need a bit of peace to think. Too noisy at home…some crisis or other.'

Hugo stilled. 'Is your sister all right?'

Alex stared. 'Liv? 'Course she's all right. Some ruckus concerning my aunt and—well! That's family business. Not for outsiders.'

Hugo lost interest.

'Why would you think it's about Liv? Have you two fallen out? Not so long ago, you were always skulking around corners together.'

'That,' said Hugo, with as much hauteur as he could muster, 'was when we were desperate to keep you away from Diablo's.'

Alex barked a laugh. 'I don't need telling twice. No fear I'll fall for that again.'

They drank in companionable silence for a while.

'We went over to Foxbourne yesterday,' said Alex. 'My father said that if I stay out of trouble and debt, I can take it on. The house needs a bit of modernisation and I'll move there in September.'

'You've just got to stay away from trouble until then?'

Alex nodded. 'I should thank you for not letting on about that Vauxhall business.'

Hugo shrugged. 'It was nothing. I've been dodging trouble most of my life, so I know what it's like. Although…' He hesitated, but then realised that maybe his experiences might help Alex to realise he wasn't the only one with baggage from the past. 'I've been given a chance at a future now, as well.' He told Alex about Cedar Lodge and Helmstone. 'I sometimes find myself wondering how different I would have been had Sir Horace been my father instead of that…bastard.'

'What was he like, your old man?'

'Evil. A drunkard. Violent. Unpredictable.'

'Is that why you and your brother were so wild?'

Hugo shrugged. 'Yes, I suppose so. But it doesn't work, you know.'

'What doesn't?'

'Wild living. Drink, drugs, gambling, women—they will never fully chase the shadows from your soul. I should know. I tried it long enough.'

And now, the one thing that would finally banish his demons—Olivia—was the one thing he could not have. Hell, if he were her father, he would never let her within half a mile of a creature like him! But only now could he fully admit he loved her; only now, when it was safe to do so because he rarely saw her and never spoke to her.

'Take my advice, Beauchamp. Don't leave it as long as I have to get wise. You love to work with horses, so concentrate all your efforts on making a success of running Foxbourne.'

Alex huffed an uneasy laugh. 'Well, at least I'm trying now to stay away from those vices, though it's deadly dull at times.' Then he brightened. 'That's what I came across to tell you. Sir Horace has invited me to Helmstone for a few weeks, until the Brighton races. Wants me to look at some of his racehorses.'

About to take another mouthful of claret, Hugo slowly lowered his glass and stared at Alex.

'How would you feel about staying with me at Cedar Lodge instead of at Helmstone?'

Mama couldn't possibly quibble with that.

Alex grinned. 'Perfect.'

Olivia watched the grey streets of London slip away as the carriage bowled along the road to Brighton. With each mile her heart grew more leaden. Hugo was back there, in London, and she would not see him again until the spring. No matter how she tried to convince herself that what she felt was an infatuation that would fade, she could not truly believe that.

All she had seen of him since the musical soirée had been fleeting, distant glimpses. It had been painfully obvious he was avoiding her—probably afraid she would force him to kiss her again or some such—and she knew it was for the best, but… She sighed and diverted her thoughts to other matters. She had become quite adept at distracting herself and there had been more than enough happening just within her own family to keep her thoughts from drifting to Hugo more than a dozen or so times a day. So she hardly thought of him at all, really.

The cause of Aunt Cecily's unhappiness had shown up in London in the shape of Zachary Graystoke, the half-Romany son of an earl with whom Cecily had fallen deeply in love. *Their* story had ended happily, with their wedding two days ago. Their marriage, however, meant that Aunt Cecily would no longer be a permanent fixture in Olivia's life and neither would Uncle Vernon. He had returned from his honeymoon with his new wife, Aunt Thea—who was actually lovely, and great fun, even though Olivia had been prepared to thoroughly dislike her for stealing her uncle's heart—but they already had plans to make their home together at Woodbeare, Uncle Vernon's estate in Devonshire—a full fifteen miles from Cheriton Abbey. At least *they* would join the rest of the family in Brighton next week, but now Aunt Cecily and Uncle Zach were away on *their* honeymoon.

Despite Olivia's determination not to be selfish—she truly *was* pleased that both her uncle and her aunt had found such happiness—she still could not help but feel that everyone she loved abandoned her.

Misery squeezed her heart. Mama had found her only daughter boring and now Aunt Cecily was gone. Dominic and Alex—neither of whom were coming to Brighton, preferring instead to visit friends' estates rather than be with their family—found her irritating and of no consequence whatsoever in their lives and her father and her uncle now both had new wives to occupy their time.

She felt like her whole world was crumbling from beneath her feet. Had it all been an illusion? Ever since Mama died, her father, aunt and uncle had been there…her rocks, always on her side, constantly supporting her. But now that solid foundation had shifted and she felt…shaky…vulnerable. She had never before questioned their love for her, but these rapid changes had stirred up doubt. Mama made no secret of her indifference to her only daughter. Were the rest of them simply more adept at hiding their true feelings? Was she as unimportant to them as to her mother?

They would all probably be delighted once she was wed and off their hands, then they could pass all responsibility for her on to her husband and forget all about her.

But that wouldn't be Hugo. Not the man she really, truly

wanted with all her heart. Because even *he* dismissed the way she felt as of no importance, setting her aside without a thought…he did not even care enough for her to *try* to persuade Papa…

She swallowed past a hard ball of despair. She had promised herself she would stop hankering after the unattainable, but it was hard. It was heartbreaking. And it was lonely. She battened down that sense that everyone ended up rejecting her, chiding herself for her self-pity. She had so much; she was very fortunate; she should not be so ungrateful.

None of that helped.

She sighed again.

'What is it, Livvy?' Rosalind was watching her with a worried expression from the opposite seat. 'Is the motion of the carriage making you unwell?'

Olivia forced a smile. 'I am quite well, thank you, Stepmama. I am just tired.'

'It has been a long, eventful Season for us all,' said Rosalind. She sighed, a faraway look in her eyes, as though she were reminiscing. '*Most* eventful.' Her attention snapped back to Olivia and Nell. 'I confess I am looking forward to going to Brighton. A daily walk breathing in that bracing sea air will be just the thing—London is growing far too warm and stuffy for my liking.'

'I doubt London will ever fully meet your approval, Ros,' Nell teased. 'Other than that it is the place where you met the love of your life.'

A light blush settled over Rosalind's cheeks and she flashed a warning look at Nell.

'I am sorry if that was inappropriate,' said Nell, 'but you are still my sister, even if you are also Livvy's stepmama. I cannot censor every word that I say.'

'No. I understand that. It is just…it is a difficult adjustment for me, having three stepchildren who are similar ages to my brothers and sister,' said Rosalind with another sigh. 'I feel more like an older sister than a stepmother. Livvy, my dear… I know I cannot take Cecily's place—she has been a mother to you all these years—but I hope you know that I am always here for you, just as I am for Nell.'

'Thank you, Stepmama.' Olivia forced a smile, swallowing down an upwelling of self-pity. Rosalind was kind, but she could never take Aunt Cecily's place. 'The change of scenery in Brighton will probably do us all good. Papa said there are some splendid rides over the South Downs—it will be a pleasant change to be able to gallop Sprite again.'

'Indeed.' Rosalind's face lit with her smile. 'It will be lovely to give Kamal his head again after our sedate outings in the Park.'

Papa had sent their riding horses—including Rosalind's beautiful Arabian gelding, Kamal, and Olivia's Sprite—down to Brighton with the grooms a few days ago. Olivia felt her spirits lift a little. There would be plenty to occupy her in Brighton—far too many new experiences to give her time to grieve over Hugo.

Maybe out of sight will mean out of mind. I must forget him.

Papa had leased a house on Marine Parade and, had it not been for her despair at the prospect of not seeing Hugo again for several months, Olivia would be completely enchanted by the position of their short-term home overlooking the beach and the ocean. The Brighton Season was in full swing, enlivened by the presence of the Prince of Wales and his set—not that Olivia had any great desire to mingle with *them*, because they were, for the most part, even older than Papa and therefore of little interest to her even if he *was* the Prince Regent and just about the most important man in the land. But still they had balls and routs, soirées and theatre outings to attend, the library and shops to visit, sea bathing to experience for the first time—to shrieks of delight—and the enjoyment of riding across the Downs that stretched for miles behind the town.

More than enough to keep any young lady happy and occupied.

Many of the young gentlemen who had paid both Olivia and Nell such marked attentions in London had also repaired to Brighton and so their social commitments were as hectic as ever. Olivia buried her despair beneath a desperate outward gaiety as she tried to pretend—especially to herself—that everything was all right. But, hidden from sight, her insides continued to wind tighter with each day that passed until she felt ready to explode.

She found herself counting the days until they could return home to Cheriton Abbey—at least there she could find some solitude and not feel obliged to paint on a constant happy smile, even though life at home would be very different with no Aunt Cecily and no Uncle Vernon. But it was Hugo she missed most of all. It was not even as though they'd spent that much time together, but in Brighton there was no thrill when she woke up in the morning, wondering if she would see him later. She knew she would not see him. There was nothing to look forward to.

The week after their arrival in Brighton, however, Olivia's bruised heart suddenly somersaulted in her chest at the sight of Hugo, strolling nonchalantly into the ballroom of the assembly rooms at the Castle Tavern. Her blood sang through her veins and her breath stalled. She raised her fan to her face, plying it gently to help hide her reaction and the sudden flush that heated her skin.

He's followed me! He missed me! He's changed his mind!

There were people all around and too many watchful eyes, so she strove to remain casual. She had her pride after all. Not even Nell must know how her hopes flared from nothing to a roaring blaze within a few seconds of that first sighting. He had entered alone and now he prowled the room, bowing and exchanging a word here and there, but never lingering. He was searching.

For her?

Her heart beat a hectic tattoo as she touched Nell on the elbow to gain her attention. She put her lips to Nell's ear.

'Cover for me, Nell. Please.'

Before she had moved two paces, Nell caught her hand. 'Livvy? Where are you going? Please, let me come with you. Do not take any more risks.'

Olivia clutched Nell's hand between both of hers. 'No. Stay here, please. You have my word I will not leave the building. There is someone I need to speak to, but I will not take any risks, I promise.'

She gave that reassurance without a qualm—she knew beyond any doubt that Hugo would not harm her and there was therefore no risk at all.

'Very well. But for fifteen minutes only. After that, I shall find your papa and tell him you have disappeared. And I am certain you do not wish me to do that.'

'Thank you, Nell. You are the best friend ever.'

Chapter Nineteen

Olivia squeezed Nell's hand before releasing it, then she strolled around the room until she could see Hugo again and could be sure he had seen her. But she would remember her vow and let him take the lead. No longer would she pursue her dream unless she was certain it was his dream as well. And so she waited as he crossed to her side, her pulse racing with pure delight at the sight of him—tall, dark and slightly dangerous-looking in his black evening clothes. She carefully concealed that delight as she bobbed her head in greeting.

'Good evening, Lord Hugo. I am surprised to see you here. I was not aware you had plans to visit Brighton this summer.'

He bowed, then passed a hand around the back of his neck as though he were uneasy. He did not even smile at her, but merely looked bored. Her joyous optimism dimmed somewhat.

'I had no intention of coming into town, but Alex told me that Clevedon is here.'

It was true that Lord Clevedon was in town, but…

'Alex?' Olivia frowned. 'But he is not in Brighton.'

'He comes in from time to time. He is staying with me,

at my house on Sir Horace's estate. It is on the western outskirts of town.'

So the friend Alex was staying with was *Hugo*? Her thoughts whirled as she processed these new facts. These *secrets*. She had known Sir Horace had an estate in Sussex, but she'd had no idea it was so close to Brighton. And she'd no idea Hugo had his own house. Or that he would be in the area during the summer.

Her happiness dipped even lower.

'Alex has been advising my stepfather about his racehorses,' he continued. 'They have become quite close.'

'But…he has not visited us. I thought…well, I did not think he was so close to Brighton. He did not tell me.'

And neither did you. The suspicion she was an utter fool began to take hold of her. *You knew I was coming to Brighton and yet you never mentioned you would be nearby.*

'He is keeping a low profile as far as your father is concerned and he's trying hard to stay away from temptation. After they went to Foxbourne a couple of weeks ago, Alex was left in no doubt that if he gets into any more trouble or debt your father will put a manager in there.' Hugo scratched his jaw, frowning. 'I did not come here to talk about your brother. Come, let us walk as we talk. It will be less likely to be remarked upon.'

Without waiting for her reply, he began to stroll. He did not even proffer his arm. Resentment began to simmer, deep down inside, as she sensed his purpose in seeking her out was not for the pleasure of her company but to— yet again—lecture her.

'Alex has been into town a time or two to meet up with Neville Wolfe, which is when he saw Clevedon.'

Olivia put her nose in the air. 'I fail to see why Lord Clevedon should concern you, sir.'

As it happened, her time had been so fully occupied she

had barely noticed Clevedon's presence in Brighton, but the sea would freeze over before she admitted as much to Hugo. She might not have spoken for all the notice he took.

'You should beware of him. He is not what he seems.'

'That he is a friend of *yours* is warning enough, I assure you.'

Again, she may as well not have spoken.

'You must not encourage him. He has only followed you here because he is desperate.'

'Desperate enough to want me? I see.' Olivia dipped a small curtsy. 'Thank you for revealing your true opinion of me, sir.'

His voice deepened. 'Olivia. You know that is not what I meant.'

Her entire being responded to that deepened tone with a quiver, enraging her all the more. She raised her chin.

'It is *Lady* Olivia to you, sir. And I shall speak to whomever I choose, whether or not that might be construed as encouragement by a random casual observer such as yourself. In fact, if I choose to flirt outrageously with his lordship, I shall do so with no compunction whatsoever and certainly without consideration as to *your* opinion in the matter.'

Hugo thrust a hand through his hair. 'Please. Take care. Talk to him by all means—you will come to no harm as long as you conduct yourself as the proper young lady you were raised to be. But be on your guard. I have told you before, you must take care around men of his ilk. You are too innocent to know what could happen when such men are driven to desperation.'

'How dare you!' Olivia kept her voice low, but she was utterly furious. By what right did he lecture her? Far from encouraging her to be careful, his lecture goaded her into throwing caution to the wind and be damned. 'Your opinion, sir, is nothing to me. You are not a member of my family and you have no right to even *comment* upon how I conduct myself.'

She felt tears of rage scald behind her eyes, but she gritted her teeth. She would never reveal the utter agony erupting inside her, nor the fury—this time with herself—for having allowed hope to blossom yet again.

He doesn't want me, but he doesn't want anyone else to have me either.

Either that, whispered a snide voice in her head, or he thinks you aren't good enough for his friend.

'You, sir, are despicable. You denounce a friend behind his back. You steal kisses when it suits you and then you have the gall to lecture *me* about proper conduct? I never, ever wish to speak to you again.'

Olivia whirled on her heel and stalked away, heading for the ladies' retiring room where she might regain her composure. As she walked, she became aware—from the curious looks she attracted—that she was scowling and that her teeth and her hands were all clenched tight. She hauled in a deep breath and forced herself to relax. She slowed her pace and again made use of her fan to mask her expression and to waft cooling air across her hot face.

'It is a wonder you did not snap your fan, my lady, your grip was so intense.' The amused drawl in her ear brought her to a halt. Lord Clevedon bowed, his smile sympathetic. 'And that would have been a shame…it is a very pretty fan.'

Olivia halted, mortified that anyone, let alone Clevedon, should have witnessed her fury. Behind him, she glimpsed Lord Sudbury strolling away.

'What has put you in such a rage? I am always willing to provide a sympathetic ear…perhaps you would care to join me in the tea room for refreshment?'

I'll show Hugo how little his warnings signify!

'Thank you, sir. That would be most pleasant.'

She hoped devoutly that Hugo was watching as Clevedon settled her at a table and signalled to a waiter to bring tea.

'Would you care to share your concerns? Is your brother in trouble again? Really…' He hesitated, and Olivia raised her brows. 'This,' he went on, 'is not a subject I would normally mention to a lady but I know how you have tried so hard to keep Alex out of debt and I know you must be desperately worried to think he will now lose Foxbourne Manor. He is so very much looking forward to it, is he not? I am sure it will break his heart when your father carries out his threat to put in a manager instead.'

The shock knocked all thoughts of Hugo and his duplicity from Olivia's mind.

'What…? I fail to understand, sir. Are you telling me that Alex has run up more gambling debts?'

Dear God, Papa will be furious, especially after Alex promised him so faithfully.

The very thought of the consequences brought sour, scorching bile into her throat.

This will tear our family apart even more.

'I am so sorry, my lady.' Clevedon looked contrite. 'I saw you with Alastair just now and I assumed he had apprised you of Alex's latest troubles and that was the cause of your anger. I see now I was mistaken. Please forgive me.'

So Hugo knows Alex is in debt again and he did not see fit to warn me?

Anger and resentment swelled. He was as bad as the rest of her family—assuming that she was too young and too delicate to handle the stark truth.

Clevedon sipped his tea, casting his gaze around the room. 'I am pleased to have this opportunity for a quiet chat, my dear. You are so very popular, it is difficult to snatch a few moments of your time. Tell me, how you are enjoying your first visit to Brighton?'

'Very much so, sir.' She recalled Hugo's claim that Clevedon had only come to Brighton in pursuit of her. 'And you, sir? Are you a regular visitor?'

'Oh, indeed. I come every year, for the sea air and for the races.'

So you are wrong, Lord Know-It-All Alastair. But proving him wrong did nothing to quell the deep rage that rumbled inside her and neither did it relieve the ache in her heart. She wrenched her traitorous thoughts away from that untrustworthy rogue.

'Lord Clevedon?'

'Yes, my lady?'

'Will you tell me how much money Alex owes and to whom?'

Clevedon straightened. 'I cannot—'

Olivia held up her hand to silence him. She leaned forward slightly and lowered her voice. '*Please?* I know all about gentlemen not discussing such matters with ladies, but Alex has always confided in me. I want to help him—' *I must help him. I have to keep what's left of my family together* '—but to do that I need to know the worst.'

'And what could you do to help even if I did tell you?'

'I have some of my allowance left.' Not much, after repaying Hugo what she owed, but she did have some. 'Or I could appeal to the gentleman concerned to give Alex more time to pay.'

'I did offer him additional time, but—'

'*You* offered him? You mean to tell me that Alex is in debt to you?'

Clevedon gave her a rueful smile. 'I am more sorry than I can say, my lady. I promise you I tried to dissuade him from continuing to play once he began to lose, but he would not listen to me. The others at the table had no idea of what was at stake, which is why I bought up all his vowels at the end of the night.'

She felt sick. 'How…how much?'

'Close to five thousand guineas, I'm afraid.'

Her head swam and she pressed her fingers to her temple. 'Dear God.' She looked up at Clevedon. 'But…you will give him more time to settle his debt, my lord? I am persuaded you will.'

'Unfortunately, it is a matter of honour for a gentleman to pay his gambling debts immediately and Alex is a proud young man and *most* stubborn. He would accept no longer than two days—until tomorrow at six o'clock. If he is unable to raise the funds, I believe it is his intention to admit the truth to your father.'

'Alex will never find that amount of money in so short a time.'

'Gambling.' Clevedon sighed. 'It is the ruin of so many in our society. It truly is a curse. I feel a sense of shame that I have somehow contributed to your brother's downfall although, as I said, I really did try to discourage him from continuing once he had plunged deep. I wish there was a way I could help that might prove acceptable to Alex. Waiving the debt is not an option, I fear.'

'There must be a way.' Olivia sank into thought.

'I wonder…?'

She looked up.

'You might feel this is a risk after our little…er…encounter at Vauxhall Gardens.'

She gasped, feeling the blood drain from her face. 'But…you did not know that was me.'

'Not at the time or, of course, I should have behaved very differently,' he said. 'But I hope my subsequent action in persuading Alastair to return the necklace to you—and the fact that your little adventure has remained a secret—will persuade you that I am to be trusted?'

Her stomach churned at the knowledge that all the time Clevedon had courted her in London, he was fully aware of what she had done. But he was right. He *had* returned her necklace and he had also kept her secret. She should give him credit for that.

'Go on.'

'I propose a small wager, just between us.'

Olivia's heart quailed. 'I do not wish to play piquet again.'

'No, of course not. Now, let me think. Ah… I believe I have it. Do you have your riding horse here in Brighton?'

'Sprite? Yes. Papa had the horses sent down from London.'

'Perfect. As we are here for the horse races next week, it seems appropriate that we might settle this wager with a race between the two of us. Our horses should be well matched. You have seen my fellow in Hyde Park. He has the longer stride, but I'll warrant your little mare can fly when given her head.'

'She goes like the wind,' said Olivia proudly. She studied Clevedon. 'What wager do you propose?'

He shrugged. 'I am feeling magnanimous. If you win, I shall hand over Alex's vowels.'

'And if I lose?'

He smiled. 'One kiss. That is all.'

It sounded too good to be true. Olivia was completely confident in her riding prowess and in Sprite's ability to outrun Clevedon's lumbering nag. Plus, she would be on horseback—completely safe from any attempt by Clevedon to corner her. It would be lily-livered, surely, to refuse the challenge? Except…

'But I thought *you* were in debt? Such a sum of money…' Her voice trailed into silence as she took in his thundering frown.

'Where did you hear such a slander?'

'I… I… I do not recall. Is it untrue, then?'

'Of course it is. I have no debts other than to a few tradesmen. Certainly nothing to worry over and nothing like that sum.'

Olivia hung her head. 'I am sorry.'

'You are forgiven. What others say is hardly your fault, but you should not believe all you hear. There are any number of people out there who delight in making mischief by embellishing the facts.'

She did not believe Hugo was that sort of man. Although what, truly, did she know about him?

He has always treated you with respect and kindness. Always.

Except he kissed me and then rejected me.

Qualms churned her stomach over what she was about to agree to, but her anger over Hugo's treatment of her and her fear for the future of her family spurred her on.

'Where do we race and when?'

'It will have to be tomorrow, before Alex is driven to admitting his latest folly to your father. Will you be able to get away?'

'I…yes, I believe so.'

They were due to go on a picnic ride tomorrow with Uncle Vernon and Aunt Thea, newly arrived in Brighton. She could feign illness and then, after the others had ridden off, tell the grooms she felt better and would catch up with the party.

'I can be ready just after three o'clock.'

She explained about the picnic ride to Whitehawk Down, where they had planned to ride around the racecourse before the races next week and then go further up on to the Downs to have a gallop and enjoy the spectacular views over the coastline and the sea. Olivia had been looking forward to the outing, but she was willing to sacrifice her pleasure if it saved Alex.

'We should go the other way then. Allow me to think.' Clevedon stared down at his teacup for a few minutes. 'I have it. Have you seen the chalk pit near to St Nicholas's Church?'

'Yes.'

'We shall meet there, at the end of the pit furthest from the town. Our course will head across country, up the hill to the north of the church. There is a windmill up there... do you know it?'

'I do.'

Olivia had noticed that windmill last week when she had ridden past it with her family, on an outing to see the Devil's Dyke—a scenic V-shaped valley popular as an excursion with visitors to Brighton.

'Good. So we race up the hill to the windmill, we ride around it and then head west, towards a stone barn you will see in the distance. We ride straight across the road that leads out to Devil's Dyke and then, when we reach the barn, we ride around it before heading back down to the town along the carriage way that runs past the barn. The first back to the church is the winner.'

Olivia frowned as she committed the course to memory.

Clevedon smirked. 'You need not fear you will get lost—you merely need to follow me.'

'Then it is fortunate that I fear no such thing,' she retorted, 'for *I* shall be in the lead. Sprite and I will be showing you a clean pair of heels, you mark my words.'

'Livvy?'

Olivia twisted around at the sound of her name. She had

been so engrossed she'd forgotten the time and Nell, worry furrowing her brow, had clearly been searching for her. She put her lips to Olivia's ear. 'Fifteen minutes! We agreed.'

Olivia stood up. Clevedon was already on his feet. 'Thank you for the tea, sir. I feel greatly refreshed now. I shall remember what you said.'

As she and Nell made their way back to the ballroom, she scanned the surrounding faces for Hugo, but there was no sign of him.

The following day was bright and sunny, with a blustery wind blowing inshore. As the time for the race approached Olivia grew more and more nervous, but her pride—coupled with her concern over Alex and the impact on the family if he were to be denied Foxbourne—would not allow her to back out, or simply fail to turn up. She wondered what Alex was thinking. Was he worried sick about admitting what he had done to Papa? She could only imagine the pressure he must feel watching the clock slowly tick nearer and nearer to six o'clock. Eventually, just before two o'clock, she came to a decision. She dashed off a note to Alex, telling him not to worry because his debts would soon be clear. *That* would set his mind at rest. She even jokingly suggested that he might come to the church to cheer her to the finishing line.

After writing to Alex, Olivia dressed in her riding habit and tucked the letter into her pocket. She would wait until everyone had gone before sending one of the grooms to deliver it. Uncle Vernon and Aunt Thea had arrived by the time she came downstairs, but then Papa announced he was unable to accompany them—kept at home by urgent business requiring his immediate attention—a complication Olivia could have done without. He disappeared into a parlour he had commandeered as an office—along with Freddie and Medland, his man of business, who had posted down from London with important papers—before the grooms brought their horses to the door.

'Ooh!' Olivia bent slightly, holding her stomach as she groaned. 'Argh!'

'Livvy?' Rosalind was by her side in a trice. 'What is wrong? Have you a pain?'

Olivia nodded, then gasped again for good measure.

'Perhaps we should postpone our outing,' said Uncle Vernon. 'With Leo not able to go and now Livvy not well… someone should surely stay with her?'

'No! I shall be all right,' said Livvy hurriedly.

She caught Rosalind's eye and endeavoured to inject special meaning into her look.

'Oh. Yes, of course,' said Rosalind. 'I had not realised… that is…yes, you go and lie down, Livvy. I am sure it will pass soon enough.'

From the corner of her eye, Livvy saw Aunt Thea tug at Uncle Vernon to get his attention. He bent to her as she whispered into his ear. His cheeks reddened a little and he straightened quickly—women's problems weren't normally even mentioned within a gentleman's hearing, but dear Aunt Thea—not a member of the aristocracy, but a humble glassmaker's daughter—probably didn't realise her faux pas.

Nell was the only one present not to regard her with sympathy. She, instead, sent Olivia a searching look; she knew full well that Olivia's courses were not yet due. But, fortunately, she said nothing and everyone soon left the hall, leaving Olivia behind. She listened for the clatter of hooves as the party rode away—they were accompanied by grooms to care for the horses when they stopped for their afternoon picnic—and some of the indoor servants would follow in a carriage with the food and drink. As soon as she judged it safe, Olivia sped from the house and caught up with Tommy, one of the younger lads, who was leading Sprite back to the stables.

'Wait!'

'Yes, milady?'

'I have changed my mind and I shall go with the others after all. Help me up, will you, Tommy?'

'Do you want me to ride with you, milady? You shouldn't ride alone.'

Olivia waved an airy hand. 'That will not be necessary. It will take me a matter of minutes to catch them up. In the meantime, though, I have an errand for you.' She delved into her pocket and handed him the letter. 'Please deliver this to Lord Alex. He is staying at—' She hesitated as she realised she knew neither the name of Hugo's house nor that of Sir Horace's estate.

'I know where he's staying, milady—Cedar Lodge on the Helmstone estate. It's but a short way out of town. I can be there and back fast enough.'

'Very good, Tommy, and thank you. But make sure you only hand it to my brother. Do you understand?'

She certainly didn't want Hugo getting his hands on it. She wouldn't put it past him to turn up and spoil the race out of some misguided sense of propriety. In fact, she now deeply regretted telling Alex the route of their race. At the time she'd thought only to amuse him with the idea of her beating Clevedon in a contest across country.

Tommy touched the peak of his cap and then linked his hands to boost Olivia on to Sprite's back.

'Are you sure you'll be all right on your own, milady?'

'Of course I shall. This isn't London, after all.'

Chapter Twenty

Olivia rode up a side street, away from Marine Parade—where she might see someone she knew—and then turned along St James's Street. She trotted Sprite briskly across the Steyne and into North Street, which would take her to the chalk pit and St Nicholas's Church. Apart from one or two curious stares—all from strangers and, by their appearance, townsfolk—no one took any notice of her, much to her relief.

Clevedon was waiting for her, as arranged, a smile on his face. Olivia quashed any lingering doubts as she eyed his grey gelding. There was no way that animal could out-run Sprite. He barely looked fit enough to gallop a furlong, let alone a mile or more. They rode side by side until they turned off the road.

'When you are ready, say the word and the race will be on.'

Olivia slid a sideways look at Clevedon and quashed the uneasy feeling coiling deep inside. There was nothing he could do to her. She could see the windmill up the hill ahead of her and, in the distance, away off to the left, she could see a stone building, flanked by a huge tree.

'Is that the barn you spoke of?'

'It is.'

'Very well then. Are you ready…? Go!'

By the time they reached the windmill, Sprite was pulling ahead of Clevedon's grey, who was puffing hard. Now was the time to build a lead, before the grey could recover his wind. The final, downhill stretch would favour his longer stride—although Sprite was the more nimble animal which would prove an advantage. As she steered Sprite around the windmill, Olivia glanced back over her shoulder. The grey was not as far behind as she would have liked and she urged Sprite on, setting her in a straight line for the barn in the distance. Fortunately the Devil's Dyke road, as they crossed it, was clear of traffic and a quick scan of the surrounding countryside showed it to be devoid of human life.

With any luck, she would get away with this and no one would be any the wiser.

She leaned forward to urge Sprite to greater effort. At this angle, if she lifted her gaze, she could see the sea, the sun creating a lattice of sparkles on the waves whipped up by the wind. There was no time to sightsee, however. She had a race to win.

Another glance behind. Good. She was now four or five lengths clear of the grey, whose neck and chest were dark with sweat.

The barn ahead was an imposing stone building with a clay-tiled roof, built by the side of a curving carriageway and overhung by that massive tree, an oak. As Sprite drew level with the barn, Olivia steadied her, ready to steer her around the far end and begin the last leg of the race back down to the church.

'Aaaargghhhh!'

Her heart, already racing with exhilaration, leapt into her throat and she flicked another glance behind.

'Oh, no!'

She reined Sprite to a halt and jumped to the ground before running back to the prone figure of the Earl of Clevedon. She slid to a halt and dropped to her knees.

'My lord! Clevedon!' She grabbed his shoulders and shook him. 'Are you all right?'

His eyes flew open and, before Olivia could reassemble her wits, he had grabbed her wrists.

'What?' She tugged and twisted to no avail as she attempted to scramble back, away from him. 'Let go of me!'

He sat up, his hard grip not slackening for a moment. Then he leapt to his feet, still holding on to her.

'Calm yourself. You might as well accept this—there is no one here to save you and—' he dragged her close and wrapped one arm around her waist '—as you can see, your strength is no match for mine.'

Olivia stopped struggling at his words, knowing he was right. She fought to control her breathing and stiffened her spine. She would not show her fear. 'What is the purpose of this, my lord?' Her voice dripped scorn. 'You realised you could not win and thought to take a kiss anyway?'

He threw his head back and laughed. 'A kiss, my precious, is the least of my intentions. By tomorrow, both you and your arrogant father will be *begging* me to make an honest woman of you. At least you have *some* spirit and you are—' he released her hand to spear his hand through her hair, knocking her hat to the ground '—enticing enough. Let us hope our children will inherit those traits.'

His grip around the back of her skull was like iron, holding her head immobile as he kissed her. His thick tongue invaded her mouth and it was all she could do not to gag. Then his other hand slid low, to cup her bottom, and she felt him pull at her skirt, gathering it, until his hand was on her skin and one finger traced the crease between her cheeks.

He slid his mouth around to her ear. 'Yes,' he whispered. 'Enticing enough. We shall do very well and your dowry will pay off Bulbridge and his blood-sucking leeches.'

Sick dread coiled in her stomach. What he planned… the thought of being…*intimate*…with *him*…

His mouth again covered hers and, as he continued to fondle her bottom, she battled to control her nausea, swallowing repeatedly to keep the contents of her stomach down, fearing the consequence were she to succumb to the urge to vomit.

She listened, hoping against hope to hear a horse or a carriage passing by. Something. Anything. But the only sound was the wind as it whipped through the branches and leaves of that oak tree. Her mind went shooting off at tangents as she silently berated herself for landing in such a stupidly risky position. This was what everyone had warned her of—Papa, Aunt Cecily, Nell. Even Hugo… Her heart shredded at the thought of him and her throat thickened with unshed tears. They had warned her of the consequences of her impetuous behaviour, but she had thought she was up to every trick in the book. She'd thought she could handle everything.

Realising that the fear spiralling through her would effectively paralyse her, she desperately tried to divert her thoughts away from what *might* happen and to concentrate on what was actually happening at this moment. Her thoughts whirled, seeking a way out. If she could keep him talking, maybe she could escape him, but that would only be by cunning for he was right—she was no match for him physically, a fact brought home to her as he began to drag her towards the barn, his arm yet again wrapped tightly around her waist.

Olivia resisted at first but, realising that would get her

nowhere, she relaxed, going with him. Surprised, Clevedon paused. He frowned down at her.

'There is something I wish to say.'

Olivia injected as much ice as possible into her words and put her nose in the air, playing the outraged lady for all she was worth. She moved slightly so she was facing more towards him and, as she had hoped, his arm loosened a little, allowing her the freedom to turn more. She couldn't delay until she was in a better position lest he realise her plan, so she angled her right leg back, then swung it forward hard, bending her knee, aiming at his 'wedding tackle', as Alex called a man's private parts.

She was sure she'd succeed but, at the last minute, Clevedon twisted and her knee connected harmlessly with his hip. She could have cried with frustration as he grabbed her by the upper arms, shaking her. But he wasn't angry, he was grinning.

'As I said, I like spirit, my dear.' Almost casually, it seemed, he raised one hand. 'But I cannot allow such defiance to risk spoiling my plans.'

His palm connected with Olivia's cheek and pain exploded through her head as it whipped sideways with the force of the blow. Tears sprang to her eyes and her tongue exploded in agony where she had bitten it. Her ears rang and a sob tore to the surface, rasping up through her throat, as she felt her knees buckle.

'Clevedon!'

The roar shattered the surrounding silence and Olivia's insides tangled and jumbled together until the only cogent thought in her head was *Hugo*.

Rage the like of which he had never known seized Hugo. As he had galloped along the carriageway that led from Helmstone down to the Dyke road he had seen

Olivia fail in her attempt to knee Clevedon in the balls. Then, as he wheeled Falcon around the corner of the barn, the bastard raised his hand and the sound—like a whip crack—ricocheted through Hugo as Clevedon hit Olivia. Her head jerked sideways with the force of that blow and she slumped. Some deep, primal instinct surged to the surface as, yelling his challenge, he hauled on the reins and leapt from the saddle even before his horse stopped.

He was in no mood for talk or explanations. He grabbed Clevedon by the shoulder, hauled him around as his right arm, fist clenched, drew back. And paused. Clevedon, in that split second, hefted Olivia to her feet and held her in front of him, his forearm crooked around her slender neck. Her beautiful silver eyes—always so full of sparkling life—were dazed and her smooth, delicate skin was imprinted with an angry red mark the shape of a hand. She looked horribly vulnerable and his heart clenched.

'Let go of her.'

His breathing came in hard, shallow pants. Fear clutched at his gut, but he ignored it. She was hurt, but she was alive. Nothing worse would happen to her now he was here. He vowed that his life from this point on would be spent protecting her. Loving her.

'You've failed, Clevedon. Let her go.'

Clevedon's lip curled. 'What is she to you, Alastair? You barely know the chit. And you were the one who suggested I court her in the first place.' He moved back a pace, dragging her with him. 'I need her. I need the money. She has to marry some time—popping out brats is all women are good for and she may as well pop out mine as anyone's.'

All the rage that had fired him up—that flaming, explosive rage—swirled tighter and faster, spinning around a point deep in his core where fury was coalescing into a cold, hard, solid mass. That fury was controlled, but it was a thousand…a million…times more deadly than all that hot, spouting rage. He took a step towards Clevedon and something shifted behind the Earl's eyes—an uncertainty…a shaft of fear…as he held Hugo's gaze.

Hugo closed the gap. Slowly. Relentlessly. Clevedon continued to shuffle backwards, hampered by Olivia as she sagged in his arms.

'Let. Her. Go.'

'What's it to you? What does it matter, if I have her?' Clevedon's voice quavered. '*You* don't want her. Or…is *that* it, Alastair? You fancy that huge dowry for yourself?'

Olivia's eyes had been half-open the entire time. Her drooping lids sprang open at Clevedon's words and her gaze flew to Hugo's face, a distinct question in her eyes, but he was beyond sending reassuring messages, his entire being now a mass of rigid, ice-cold fury. But he saw the instant that she dismissed Clevedon's accusation. She sent him a silent message…of reassurance…of intent… Then she dropped one lid in a wink and Hugo tensed.

Of a sudden, she surged upright and the shock caused Clevedon to momentarily loosen his hold on her neck. As Hugo leapt at them, Olivia jerked her elbow hard into Clevedon's gut and she twisted aside to allow Hugo to drive his fist into Clevedon's face—the solid thwack satisfying as knuckles connected with nose. He hauled Olivia clear as Clevedon sank to his knees.

The pounding of hooves penetrated the churning mix of fury and relief that still raged through him. He glanced back towards the town to see two horsemen galloping at top speed towards them. The Duke was in the lead, with Alex close behind—as soon as Olivia's note had been delivered to Alex, Hugo had guessed Clevedon was up to no good and had sent her brother to alert her father. Olivia, no doubt, would be relieved to be passed into her father's care while Hugo dealt with Clevedon.

The two horses skidded to a halt and first Cheriton, then Alex, jumped down.

'Hugo.'

He glanced down at Olivia's whispered plea. He still had hold of her arm, but one look at her—that handprint still livid on her cheek, stark against her ashen skin—and he forgot all about her father and her brother. She needed him. He released her elbow and opened his arms. She moved into his embrace and laid her head against his chest. As he folded his arms around her, holding her safe, he could feel the trembling of her entire body.

'Alastair—'

That one growled word of warning was cut short as Hugo's mother and Sir Horace hurried out from behind the barn.

'We came as quickly as we could,' said Mama breathlessly. She glared at Clevedon, who had regained his feet and was holding a blood-soaked handkerchief to his nose. 'You utter scoundrel!' She advanced on him, her small hands clenched into fists. 'If I were a man, I should call you out myself!' She poked him in the chest. 'You should be thoroughly ashamed, plotting to despoil such a lovely young lady in such a despicable way.'

Sir Horace hurried to Mama's side and gently urged her away. 'Allow Hugo and his Grace to deal with him, my love. Come, let us take charge of Lady Olivia. That is why Hugo asked us to follow him, after all.' He shot a look at Hugo. 'You were right. We asked the driver of the carriage waiting by the barn and he told us he was hired to drive a couple to London.'

As Hugo had suspected, Clevedon's plan had moved on from simply entrapping Olivia in a compromising situation. He had now planned to remove Olivia completely from the safety and security of her family until she was so thoroughly compromised there would be no way out other than for the couple to marry. Even a man as powerful as her father would have to concede defeat in those circumstances.

Mama came to Olivia and coaxed her from Hugo's embrace. He wanted to object, but Olivia was better off remaining ignorant of what would come next.

Mama smiled at him reassuringly. 'We will take her back to the house with us. She will be safe.'

He watched them move out of sight, then pivoted on his heel to face Clevedon.

'I shall see you, sir. Name your—'

'Alastair!' Cheriton's hand was on his arm. 'She is *my* daughter. I shall be the one to defend her honour.'

Hugo steeled himself against the imperious demand in that silvery gaze. 'You are too late, Duke. The challenge is issued.'

Fury flashed across Cheriton's face, but Hugo did not care. He thirsted for revenge. He would prefer to beat the man to a pulp, but it was decreed that a duel was the way by which gentlemen of their world settled their differences and he would not behave as other than a gentleman in this matter. Olivia deserved no less.

'Your second, sir?'

Clevedon swayed on his feet, shoulders slumped. 'Sudbury. Yours?'

Hugo raised a brow at Alex but, before he could respond, the Duke astonished him by saying, 'I'll stand as your second, Alastair. Least I can do.'

He crossed to Clevedon and gave him a shove in the direction of the barn. 'Take your bloody carriage and get out of my sight. Have Sudbury call on me at six tonight to make the arrangements.'

As Clevedon stumbled away, Cheriton rubbed at his eyes before facing Hugo and Alex.

'Now, will you two tell me what the *devil* has been going on?'

Alex took a letter from his pocket and handed it to his father. 'Livvy sent me this. I've been staying with Alastair at his house on Sir Horace's estate. It is further along that carriageway.' He pointed.

Cheriton nodded and then unfolded the sheet of paper and read it, his brow furrowed. His chest rose and fell, and he closed his eyes for a second before fixing them on Alex.

'You are in debt again? After everything…all the promises?' He sounded weary, almost defeated, and Hugo's heart went out to him. He might be one of the most powerful and wealthy men in the country, but the estrangement between him and his younger son—which Hugo knew existed, but still didn't fully understand—clearly mattered a great deal to him. 'That, I presume, is why you did not inform me you were staying near Brighton?'

Alex's face flamed. 'It's a damned lie! I owe Clevedon nothing and if Livvy had only had the sense to *ask* me instead of believing that bastard's lies, none of this would have happened.' The corners of his mouth turned down. 'That's typical. You always believe the worst of me.'

Cheriton's lips thinned. 'Then I apologise. I do try not to do so.' Hugo admired the Duke's control of the temper that simmered behind his eyes and the effort it must have taken to humble himself in such a way, especially in front of a virtual stranger. 'Please continue.'

'Tommy delivered the letter and he told us Livvy hadn't gone on the picnic ride with the rest of the family, but had then decided to catch them up. That sounded like a ruse to go and race Clevedon and Hugo here guessed that Clevedon had some plan to either compromise or abduct her.'

Those silver-grey eyes narrowed as the Duke's gaze shifted to Hugo.

'I was aware Clevedon was getting desperate and that he had set his sights on Olivia's dowry.'

'Olivia?'

Cheriton's growl stirred Hugo's temper. He was damned if he would cower in front of the man. If he wanted to call her by her given name, then he damn well would.

'I have been looking out for *Olivia* ever since you dismissed my warnings about the man.'

'Perhaps you should have tried harder. Told me exactly what Clevedon was capable of.'

'Perhaps I would have, had I known,' Hugo retorted.

Alex cleared his throat. 'Alastair,' he said pointedly, 'has just rescued my sister and your daughter, and he *has* been looking out for her *and* helping me while you have been distracted by other family concerns.'

Again, Hugo felt sympathy stir for Cheriton who, he knew, had been beleaguered by family affairs recently when his sister's half-Romany fiancé had been imprisoned at Newgate. Who could really blame the man for not realising what mischief was brewing in his young daughter's life?

'To continue,' said Alex. 'Tommy told me you hadn't ridden out with the rest of the family, so I rode to fetch you while Hugo headed over to the course to try to intercept them and stop Clevedon from whatever he planned. I don't know how come the Todmordens showed up, though.'

Hugo shrugged. 'That was luck. After Alex and I parted ways, I met Mama and Sir Horace coming back from town. When I explained matters, they told me they had seen a carriage waiting by the barn when they passed by earlier and I asked them to come with me to take charge of Olivia, to protect her reputation.'

Cheriton hauled in a breath. 'I appreciate your forethought and your consideration. I shall fetch Olivia now and take her home and I'll send you word once we have arranged where you will meet Clevedon.' His jaw firmed. Then he stepped forward and grasped Hugo's shoulder. 'Thank you.'

Chapter Twenty-One

Olivia held tight to her self-control until Lady Todmorden showed her into her private parlour and the butler had personally delivered a tea tray. But it took just one kind enquiry as to how she was feeling for her pent-up emotions to burst forth.

Her ladyship clucked sympathetically and sat beside Olivia, putting her arms around her to hold her as she cried. As the flood of tears subsided, she pressed a sensible, man-sized handkerchief into Olivia's hand and left her to mop up while she poured the tea.

'There now.' Lady Todmorden placed a teacup on the table beside Olivia. 'You no doubt feel better for a good cry. I know I always do. And a nice cup of tea will set everything right, I am sure. All's well that ends well, after all, my pet.'

Tears leaked again and Olivia dabbed her eyes with the now very damp handkerchief.

'It is all my own fault.' She gulped and then hiccupped. 'I was so certain I would be safe and win the race, and I thought I could save Alex.' She bowed her head as she twisted the handkerchief in her lap. 'Why didn't I listen? I am such a fool. A wicked, headstrong, conceited fool. Hugo warned me about C-Clevedon, but I thought… I th-thought…'

She felt the downward drag at the corners of her mouth as tears bubbled once again. She gritted her teeth hard and breathed strongly through her nose. She would not keep succumbing to bouts of weeping like some…some… silly milksop. But, oh, what a fool she had been indeed. When she thought about what could have happened… Sir Horace had pointed out the carriage that lurked unseen on the far side of the barn. She would never dare listen to that stupid, overly confident voice inside her head ever again.

How could she have made such a ridiculous mistake? How could she have, so mindlessly, taken such a stupid risk? No wonder Hugo wanted nothing to do with her. And on that thought, she promptly burst into tears again and Lady Todmorden once again took her in her arms.

'He thinks I am a s-s-silly little girl,' Olivia wailed. 'And he is right. I am a f-fool and he is quite right not to l-l-love me. But I—'

She stopped on a gasp as her brain caught up with her mouth and she recalled it was Hugo's mother whose shoulder she was drenching with her tears. She pulled away, the shock of having said such a thing out loud stemming her tears more effectively than any kind words.

'Now, now, my pet, I beg you not to work yourself into a lather over Hugo.' Lady Todmorden gathered Olivia's hands in hers. 'I assume that you are talking about that reprehensible son of mine?'

Olivia swallowed, willing her voice to remain steady. 'I am sorry. I should not have said that. I was distraught. Please, forgive—'

'Forgive you?' Through slightly blurred eyes, Olivia saw her ladyship tip her head to one side, a satisfied smile on her face as she scanned Olivia's face with her dark but bright eyes. 'There is nothing to forgive, my pet. Young love is—as I remember it—brutal and heartbreaking at times and then, at others—' her expression became wistful…nostalgic… '—it can make you feel as though you are soaring so effortlessly through the air your feet might never touch the ground again.'

Despite Aunt Cecily's constant reminders to Olivia to curb her curiosity, she could not help but ask, 'Was that with Lord Rothley, ma'am?'

Lady Todmorden started at her words and that wistful air dissipated.

'No. I am sorry to say that my father believed that girls should be biddable and marry whomever they were told to marry. *My* young love had no happy ending, my dear, and Rothley—my father's choice—was not a kind man, either to his young wife or to his sons. That is why, if you truly love him, I advise you to fight for Hugo. Your papa might disagree, but it is *your* life and you are the one who must live it.'

Lady Todmorden's spirit kindled Olivia's hopes until they were dashed all over again as she remembered the truth.

'It is hopeless. Hugo…' She gulped back another bout of tears. 'Hugo does not return my feelings.'

A dull, hollow ache filled her chest. Then she stared as Lady Todmorden laughed.

'Nonsense, my pet. Of course he returns your feelings. I have known that since I saw you both studiously avoiding one another's eye outside Gunter's Tea Room *weeks* ago.' She took Olivia's hand again, patting it. 'Let me tell you, my pet. I have *never* seen my Hugo put himself out so much for anyone other than for one of his own family. Do not despair. Although…' She paused and Olivia waited with bated breath. 'I pointed out Cedar Lodge as we passed, do you recall?'

Olivia nodded.

'Be very certain that you are prepared to live in such a modest house. Hugo is not a wealthy man and after getting into debt in the past, I know he is determined not to do so in the future. He stands to inherit Helmstone eventually— although I hope not for a very long time—but you must be absolutely sure your love is strong enough to live a much more modest life than that to which you are accustomed.'

'But I have a dowry—' She stopped speaking as her ladyship raised her hand.

'You have a very generous dowry, yes. I am aware of it. But my Hugo is a proud man and it can be difficult for such a man to accept a wife who both outranks him and is wealthier than him.'

'That did not stop Lord Clevedon from wanting to marry me. Although in his case it seems my dowry was the only lure.'

'Ah, but you see, my pet, Lord Clevedon is *not* an honourable man. But an unequal union…a disparity in wealth…*can* be most successful, even taking into account male pride. Only last year my niece—a wealthy peeress in her own right—wed the third son of an earl. Matthew had nothing of his own other than a business importing from the East and I have never known a couple happier and more content. Except for my Lucas and his Mary, of course.' She beamed with maternal pride.

Olivia pondered her ladyship's words as she sipped her tea and willed her tumultuous emotions to settle. Hope had once again been coaxed into life. This time, however, she would not allow it to run rampant, but she would keep it under control. She would not try to persuade Hugo to reveal his true feelings—although she prayed that her ladyship was right about them—but she would wait patiently for him to finally admit them to her. Then, and only then, would she do as Lady Todmorden advised and she would indeed fight with every fibre of her being to persuade Papa to accept Hugo as a suitable husband for his only daughter.

The sound of hooves outside brought both Olivia and Lady Todmorden to their feet.

'They will not bring Lord Clevedon here, will they?'

Olivia's stomach knotted—she did not know if she had the courage to face him, even if Hugo and Papa were both there.

'I am sure they will not bring him anywhere near you, my pet. But, just to make sure, I shall ask Sir Horace to check.'

She left the room and Olivia went to the window. Alex was outside, mounted on an unfamiliar horse, holding the reins of both Conqueror—Papa's horse—and Sprite. Olivia heard the low murmur of voices and then the door opened and she turned to face it. She had hoped Hugo might come, so that she might apologise to him and thank him again, but the doorway remained empty behind Papa and Lady Todmorden after they entered. Those treacherous tears threatened to erupt again, but she squared her shoulders and lifted her chin. She was a duke's daughter. She would take responsibility for her mistakes and stupidity, not attempt to avoid blame by crying.

'I am sorry, Papa.'

She felt she should say more but, really, she could find no words to excuse her actions. Papa shook his head at her and smiled ruefully. He opened his arms and she ran across the room and into his embrace, love for him flowing through her.

'Come on, minx. Let us get you home.' He pulled back and looked down at her. 'Are you up to riding, or shall I ask Sir Horace for his carriage?'

'No. I shall ride.' Olivia smiled at Lady Todmorden. 'Thank you—and I am sorry for all the trouble I have caused.'

'It was no trouble, my pet.' Lady Todmorden kissed her on the cheek and whispered, 'Courage, my dear. All will be well.'

They met no one else on their way out of the house. Papa lifted her on to Sprite and mounted Conqueror and then all three of them rode along the carriageway that led back to the Dyke road.

'I have everyone's agreement that the details of today will not be spread abroad,' said Papa. 'But I hope you have learned your lesson, young lady.'

'Yes, Papa.'

'You are not to go out without me or your stepmother, or your uncle and aunt, for the remainder of our stay in Brighton and I shall instruct two maids to watch you at all times. Is that clear? I will not have you take any further risks.'

His voice shook on those final words and guilt clawed at Olivia—she knew how he fretted over safety after what had happened to her mother, yet still she had put him through this.

'I understand, Papa.'

They rode in silence until they reached the neat brick house that Lady Todmorden had earlier pointed out to Olivia. It was set back from the carriageway in a forecourt bounded by stone piers and wrought-iron railings. A massive cedar tree dominated the neatly scythed lawn to the side of Cedar Lodge.

Hugo's home. Where was he? Why had he not come to her, to see that she was all right? That familiar ache swelled her throat again, but again she controlled her emotions.

'I shall leave you here.' Alex reined his horse close to Sprite and reached across to squeeze Olivia's shoulder.

'You're a troublesome brat, but I'm glad you're still here with us and not halfway to London with that bas—'

'Alexander!'

'Scoundrel,' he amended, with a wink at her. 'I'll come and see you tomorrow, Liv,' and with that he set his horse into a canter up the driveway to the Lodge.

Olivia scanned the windows, but the house was too far for her to see if Hugo was looking out. She swallowed, raised her chin and sent Sprite into a trot, back towards Brighton. Papa, seeming to sense her mood, trotted Conqueror alongside but, other than a few searching looks, he said nothing more until they arrived at the house. Thankfully, the rest of the family had not yet returned from their picnic ride—she was amazed that such a momentous event in her life had taken place in such a short time—and therefore had no idea of the drama that had taken place.

'I suggest—' said Papa, not unkindly '—that you go straight to your bedchamber and you remain there until the morning. That will back up your story that you were not well; the fewer people who know about this the better, even within the family. I shall ask Cook to send you a tray later on.'

Exhaustion and guilt and the need to just be alone robbed her of any argument or of any desire to question Papa about what had happened to Clevedon. She could not even think of him without a shudder. She climbed the stairs, pulled off her clothes and crawled into her bed, curling up into a tight ball.

There would be time to think later, when she was not so very, very weary.

Hugo paced the drawing room at Cedar Lodge, pausing only to look out of the window each time his circuit took him past it. Finally, he could see them: the Duke, Alex and

Olivia. She was riding Sprite and respect for her courage filled him anew. Most other women would be swooning on a sofa after such an ordeal, even without that vicious slap. Fury erupted again, but he tamped it down. He would get his chance tomorrow and, by God, it would give him the greatest satisfaction to put a ball in that bastard.

After Clevedon had gone, Hugo's first instinct had been to ride straight to Helmstone to assure himself that Olivia was all right. The Duke, however, had made it abundantly clear he must stay away—and the more he thought about *that* edict, and the way he had meekly submitted, the fiercer his resentment grew. At the time it had seemed best to give Cheriton the time to sort his family out, but now...

He turned as Alex sauntered into the room.

'Is she all right? Will your father punish her?'

Alex crossed to an armchair and flung himself into it. 'Don't know. Oh, she's all right—Livvy always bounces back—but m'father...' he scowled, thrusting both hands through his hair to sweep it back from his face '...he seems unnaturally calm. He'll probably wait until after you meet Clevedon...he won't want anything to distract you.' He slanted a look at Hugo. 'Or maybe he's hoping you'll both get shot and save him a job.'

Hugo passed his hand around the back of his neck, rubbing as he tilted his head back. So tense. He felt like...he wanted to...he must...

He anchored his thoughts in place as he sorted through them. The conclusion was—he could not bear to wait. He could not face Clevedon with this on his mind.

He swore out loud, softly and fluently. Alex flicked a brow. 'That's some inventive curse, my friend. Care to tell me what it's in aid of?'

Hugo strode for the door. 'I'm off to town. To talk to your father.'

* * *

An hour later—having first changed into fresh clothing—
Hugo rode into Brighton. At the house on Marine Parade
currently leased by the Duke of Cheriton he dismounted and
beckoned to a young boy on the opposite side of the road.

'Here.' Hugo tossed him a penny. 'Hold him, will you?
If I'm more than ten minutes, I shall pay you another.'

The boy's eyes brightened. 'Yessir.'

He was admitted without question and shown immediately to a back room.

'Lord Hugo Alastair, your Grace.'

The room—clearly in use as an office—was decorated
in a feminine, floral style that was completely at odds with
the furniture—a large mahogany desk set before the single window, several wooden chairs and a table piled with
papers, where Freddie sat. The Duke stood on the far side
of the desk with his back to the room, silhouetted by the
light coming through the window.

'Leave us, Freddie, will you, please? I shall send for
you when we are done.'

Freddie stood, tucked his crutch under his arm and
headed for the door. He raised his brows and smiled at
Hugo as he passed, but said nothing. Not until the door
clicked shut behind him did Cheriton turn around. He gestured at a chair on the far side of the desk to himself and
then settled himself in his own chair.

'You are here earlier than I anticipated.'

'I will not waste your time, Duke. I am here to ask for
your daughter's hand in marriage.'

Dark brows rose, but there was no surprise on Cheriton's face. Merely, it seemed, a weary kind of acceptance.
Hope germinated. He'd expected to be kicked out as soon
as he uttered those words.

'You need to know that I have not declared myself to

Olivia and she has no idea of the depth of my feelings for her, but I love her and I believe she loves me.'

Cheriton opened his mouth, but Hugo said, quickly, 'Please. Allow me to finish.'

The Duke inclined his head, and rose to his feet. 'Brandy?' At Hugo's nod, he crossed to a side table upon which there was a silver salver holding a crystal glass decanter and several glasses. 'Pray continue,' he said as he took the stopper from the decanter.

Hugo battened down a feeling of unreality. This interview was nothing like the one he had imagined as he had ridden into town. He gathered his thoughts and sucked in a steadying breath. He was determined to do this properly. Olivia deserved as much. After keeping her at arm's length for so long, the last thing he wanted was to raise her hopes only to have them dashed or—worse—for her to blame her father if he refused his consent.

'I know I cannot support her in the lifestyle she is used to, but I want to spend the rest of my life with her, if she'll have me.'

The Duke set a glass in front of Hugo, then rounded the desk to take his seat again. He took a sip and then placed his glass on the desk.

'Her dowry will go a long way to make up for any shortfall in her husband's income.'

The words were softly spoken, but there was a challenge in them, and in the silvery-grey gaze that pierced Hugo.

'I am not interested in her dowry. I will take her without any dowry, to prove my love is true. It is Olivia I want, not your money.'

His expression unreadable, Cheriton rose once again and turned to stare out of the window, his hands loosely clasped behind his back. Hugo waited. He had said his piece. Quite what he would do if the Duke refused his consent, he did not know.

'Are you prepared to wait for her?'

Here we go.

If her father refused his consent it would be three years before Olivia could wed without his permission. Unless they eloped. Hugo devoutly hoped it would not come to that. Now his decision was made—having denied his feelings for so long—he wanted no obstacles in his way.

'Yes. I will wait.'

Cheriton sat again, leaned his elbows on the desk and steepled his fingers in front of his face, his chin propped on his thumbs. He again scrutinised Hugo and then he sighed.

'Both Alex and Freddie have told me how you have helped and protected both Olivia and Alex over the past months, although they were both somewhat circumspect as to the exact details.'

Hugo sifted through his memories. They could not have told him about the necklace because neither of them knew about it. He doubted, therefore, that either of them would have told Cheriton about the visit to Vauxhall Gardens either. Having grown closer to Alex, Hugo now shared Olivia and Freddie's determination to help him achieve his dream of taking over Foxbourne.

'I shall embarrass neither of us by demanding those details from you,' Cheriton continued. 'Both my son and my daughter are—currently—safe and that is all that concerns me.'

He stood again and paced about the room. Hugo recognised that restless activity, the sign of a dilemma being grappled with. He waited until Cheriton sat again.

'I realise I owe you a great deal, Alastair, but that on

its own is not sufficient to support your union with my daughter. However, I also see in you an honourable man attempting to put his past behind him—I remember how you stepped up last year when your cousin, Lady Ashby, was in danger and I have seen how you have supported your mother and stepfather since their marriage. I also—' his perceptive gaze again pierced Hugo '—remember your father and what he was like.'

Again he paced the room and Hugo waited. A man such as Cheriton could not be pushed or cajoled and woe betide the man who attempted it. This time he did not sit again, but came to a standstill next to Hugo's chair. Hugo rose to his feet. It was one thing allowing the man time to come to a decision, quite another to have him towering above him as he delivered his verdict. Hugo met the Duke's gaze and raised a brow. A smile flickered across the Duke's features.

'You may call upon Olivia and, if you still wish to, you may offer for her with my blessing. I do, however, have two stipulations. Firstly, you are not to call upon her or communicate with her until after the duel. Olivia knows nothing about the meeting and she will not know anything until the affair is settled. Is that clear?'

Hugo nodded.

'My daughter, as you may have noticed, is somewhat headstrong. If she hears the slightest whisper of your meeting then she would, I am sure, find a way to be there.'

Hugo shuddered at the thought.

'Now, Olivia is but eighteen years old and so my second stipulation is that a formal betrothal is delayed until Christmas with the wedding to take place in the spring. I want you both—but in particular Olivia—to be absolutely certain that this is what you want. In the meantime, you are welcome to come and visit Olivia at Cheriton Abbey whenever you can be spared from Helmstone.' He raised his dark brows. 'Agreed?'

Hugo shook his proffered hand. 'Agreed.'

Chapter Twenty-Two

Dawn the following morning found Hugo and the Duke high up on the Downs that surrounded Brighton, awaiting the arrival of Clevedon and Sudbury. Lord Sudbury had called upon the Duke the previous evening, as agreed, to finalise the meeting place and weapons. And Hugo learned that Sudbury had passed on certain information that shed new light on Clevedon's situation and his subsequent behaviour.

Clevedon's debt to Bulbridge was huge, but it had not been entirely due to gambling. Sudbury told Cheriton that Bulbridge and his cousin, Douglas Randall, were the feared and despised owners of Diablo's—both the gambling club and the linked brothel that prided itself on catering for men of various and unusual desires. Clevedon's sexual preferences—which had come as no surprise to Cheriton, evidently—had rendered him a victim of blackmail by the unscrupulous pair who had layered demand after demand on the Earl, pushing him to the brink of despair and leading to him snatching Olivia in a desperate attempt to gain her dowry.

Hugo's nerves had completely disintegrated at that information. The relief that he could now delope with honour…that he did not have to actually kill Clevedon…was enormous. Sudbury had assured Cheriton that, if Clevedon survived, he planned to leave the country and escape Bulbridge once and for all.

In their need to keep the entire affair as quiet as possible, it was agreed that Sir Horace Todmorden would preside over the duel and he arranged for a discreet doctor friend to attend in case he was needed. Hugo and Clevedon paced the required distance and turned to face one another, but sideways on. They took aim, keeping one eye on the white handkerchief held aloft by Sir Horace. As it fluttered to the ground, Clevedon aimed his pistol into the air and fired. He then turned to fully face Hugo.

Hugo sited along the barrel of his own pistol and then, quite deliberately, he, too, aimed into the air and pulled the trigger. As the puff of smoke dissipated into the cool morning air, he lowered the pistol.

'Let us repair to the Old Ship for breakfast,' said Cheriton as they rode into the outskirts of Brighton a little later.

Sir Horace had declined an offer to join them and Clevedon, shamefaced, had come to them to confirm his plan to go overseas. Once they were settled in a private room at the inn, Hugo found himself undergoing such a thorough interrogation about his life that he was eventually goaded into saying, 'I wonder you will contemplate a man such as me for Olivia, sir.'

Cheriton, having eaten his fill, leaned back in his chair.

'Even six months ago, I would never have done so. But this Season has changed my attitude to love and marriage. It has been a momentous time for my family with not just me getting married after having vowed never to wed again, but now both my brother and my sister have found love in the most unlikely of circumstances. And if there is one thing I have learned it is this. We cannot dictate where love will find us but, when it does, we must grab it with both hands. I am no longer surprised that Olivia has followed in my generation's footsteps and I now find myself watching Avon with some trepidation. I almost expect him to turn up with an actress upon his arm.' He grinned. 'But I might then put my foot down very firmly.'

'And Alex?'

'Oh, I suspect Alex will confound us all and fall in love with a princess at the very least.'

Olivia bent her head to concentrate both on her embroidery and on keeping her simmering anger and fear from erupting into fury. She eyed the two maids who had dogged her footsteps from the moment she emerged from her bedchamber. They sat close to the parlour door, a basket of mending between them, but when Olivia left the room not ten minutes ago—saying she was going to relieve herself—*both* of them had accompanied her.

She swallowed her *hmmph* of disgust at Papa's lack of trust in her.

She was forbidden from leaving the house—his Grace's orders, the maids had said, apologetically—and she was therefore condemned to simply sit and wait for news as she had done since first thing that morning. She had risen early, driven by a nameless dread that lurked deep, deep inside, setting her insides in turmoil, only to find that Papa had already left the house…and a part of her knew what that meant. Alex had regaled her often enough with stories about duels—that peculiar method by which gentlemen settled insults and arguments—and she had always imagined them as dashing and romantic, with the clash of rapiers in the early morning mist or deadly pistols at dawn.

Until now.

There was nothing romantic about it when someone she loved might be involved.

Was there to be a duel? Or—looking at the clock— had there *been* a duel? And was it Papa who had challenged Clevedon? Or Hugo? She could not decide which was worse, but she was certain of one thing—the very worst thing was that it was her fault and if either of them were injured, she could never, ever forgive herself. Dread and self-recrimination mixed with her other emotions.

At a quarter past nine—before any of the rest of the family had even arisen—the parlour door opened and Alex sauntered in. Olivia threw down her embroidery and ran to him, grabbing his hands and tugging him over to the window, as far away from the door and the maids' ears as possible.

'What happened?' she hissed. 'Tell me, please.'

Alex's brows stitched together. 'You *know*?'

Those two words confirmed her worst fears. 'Who challenged him? Papa? Hugo?'

Alex growled, deep in his throat. 'You bloo—blasted menace, Liv. You *didn't* know.'

'Not for certain, but I guessed.' She clutched harder at Alex's hands. 'Please. Tell me the worst. Is anyone hurt? Have they been arrested?'

For that was another worry and one that had only just occurred to her. Duels were against the law. There had been enough stories over the years of men forced to flee the country to escape justice.

Alex glanced at the maids, then put his arm around Olivia's shoulders and manoeuvred them both so they stood with their backs to the room.

'Keep your voice down, do, Sis. The fewer people who know about this the better. Father will make sure the law doesn't become involved, never fear.'

'But why is Papa not home? He should be back by now.'

'Men never eat breakfast before they meet, Liv, so they've probably gone for a bite to eat. Devilish hungry work, staring death in the face as the sun comes up.'

'Did you not go to watch?'

'*Watch?* It is not a spectator sport, you silly gudgeon. It's serious business. Never fear. I'm sure Hugo'll come through all right—he's a tolerable shot, y'know.'

She swayed at his words, and he grabbed hold of her, supporting her. '*Hugo* challenged Clevedon?'

'Shhh. The last thing I want is for them pair to go gabbling to Father that I've been talking to you about this. You really have no idea of discretion, do you?'

'I will keep my voice down if you promise to tell me everything you know.'

'Such as?'

'Such as—did Hugo challenge Clevedon?'

'Well, of course he did. Haven't I just said so? Father was like fire that he got in his challenge first, but then he offered to stand as Hugo's second.' He hugged Olivia to him briefly before releasing her. 'Never fear, brat. Father would have been home long since had anything bad happened. They're having breakfast, you mark my words.'

Alex left soon afterwards and Olivia wore a track in the carpet, pacing around the parlour—terrified and furious in equal measures—as she kept her ears pricked for signs of arrival at the front door. Finally, she heard a murmur of voices in the hall and Grantham appeared in the doorway. First, intriguingly, he dismissed the two maids.

'There is a gentleman waiting to speak to you in the salon, milady.' He bowed, then favoured her with a rare smile. 'Lord Hugo Alastair.'

Olivia's heart skipped and jumped as she realised the implication of that announcement. But the fear and anger that had been brewing since she awoke still agitated deep inside her and Hugo needn't think she would simply fall into his arms because he had finally decided—presumably with her father's blessing—to make her an offer. Unless…

Her throat thickened. Did he feel it was his duty to offer for her, now she had tarnished her reputation? Had Papa put pressure on him and *forced* him to propose? She couldn't bear that. Resentment now mixed in with that volatile concoction of fear and anger.

She followed Grantham down the hall and he opened the salon door, standing aside for her to enter.

Her breath caught. Hugo stood on the far side of the room—utterly, mouthwateringly gorgeous—and, as Grantham shut the door behind her all that pent-up fear and emotion burst from her. She flew at him.

'You despicable cur!' She slapped at him, only for him to capture her wrist. 'You…you…misbegotten miscreant!' She aimed for his face with her other hand, but he caught that, too. Tears of pure frustration…and rage…and relief…flooded her eyes as she struggled to free herself. 'You swine! You…ch-churlish coxcomb!'

'You forgot sodden-witted lord.'

'Sodden-witted goat, more like. Why did you challenge him? *Why?* You could have been k-k-*killed.*'

'But I was not killed, was I, my sweet? Look at me. Nary a scratch.'

'But I did not know that! No one told me *anything.*' She fought again against his grip, but half-heartedly now as she gulped for air. Then the fight leached from her. 'Y-you didn't even come to see if I was all right,' she wailed.

And with that, he released her wrists to snake one arm around her waist, pulling her roughly, almost fiercely, to him. Her arms wound around his neck as their lips met with a savage intensity, his tongue plunging into her mouth. She returned his kiss with reckless abandon, meeting his tongue thrust for thrust until her lips were on fire, her body was throbbing with need and her lungs screamed for air.

She tore her lips from his. 'You could have been *killed.*' She could not let the thought go…she was compelled to say it again, to get him to understand how terrified she had been. She took his face between her palms and stared into his dark eyes, seeking his soul. 'Don't you *ever* do that to me again.'

She pressed her lips to his again but, as she did so, the realisation came from nowhere—this was *her* fault and, if they were to have a future together, she must find the courage to admit it. Again, she pulled away from their kiss and this time she wriggled free from his embrace. She inhaled and straightened.

'I am sorry.'

His brows knit together. 'Why are you sorry?'

'It is my fault you had to fight a duel. I should have listened to you. You only ever tried to help me, but I couldn't see further than what I wanted.'

His lips quirked. 'Which was?'

She bit her lips against her answering smile. 'You know the answer to that, Lord Hugo Alastair, but…very well— I shall pander to your ego. *You.* I wanted you. And now, because of my…my…stupidity—' she sucked in a shaky breath as she faced again the reality of the events she had set in motion and what could have happened '—you *could* have been killed.' She hauled in another breath, determined not to cry. 'I was mad with worry.'

'You were not *meant* to know anything about today. But… I find myself completely unsurprised that you do.' He opened his arms wide. 'Come here, Trouble.'

She walked into his embrace, the last vestiges of her

panic and her anger melting away as his arms folded around her, holding her close to his chest. She slid her own arms under his jacket and around his waist, hugging him tight as the steady, reassuring beat of his heart echoed through her and his spicy scent curled around her.

'Papa knows you are here now?'

His chest jerked a little as he huffed a laugh. 'Of course he knows.' He tilted her face to his, his eyes solemn as they searched hers, igniting a flame deep, deep inside her. 'I came here last night to ask his permission to pay my addresses to you.'

Her breath caught. 'And he *agreed*?'

He nodded. Then he stepped back and took her hands in his, smoothing his thumbs across her knuckles. And before she realised his intent, he was on one knee, looking up at her with such love and devotion in his ebony eyes that her own knees threatened to buckle.

'Lady Olivia Beauchamp…'

'Wait!'

His eyes crinkled in amusement. 'I might have guessed you would not allow this to go my way.'

Olivia huffed. 'I only want to know if you are *certain*. You are not here because you now feel *obliged* to offer for me? Or because Papa has *forced* you to make me an offer?'

He laughed. 'Trust me, sweetheart. No one—not even your father—can force me to do anything against my will. I am here because there is nowhere else I want to be and there is nothing else I would rather be doing than kneeling in front of you waiting for an opportunity to actually propose to you.'

'But…you do not love me.' Olivia searched his features. 'And…' A memory was struggling to the surface. She frowned, concentrating to fully recall words barely noticed at the time they were uttered, but that now stung.

'You told Clevedon to court me. He said so and you did not correct him.'

A rueful smile tugged at Hugo's mouth. '*That* was a grave error on my part. I was so intent on retrieving the necklace for you that the suggestion was made before I could think it through. I knew Clevedon was capable of trying to compromise you, but I persuaded him that—if he persisted in using your necklace against you, it would only turn you against him. I didn't understand at that point just how desperate he was, how far he would go to get what he wanted…'

'And I am not very experienced. You said so yourself.'

'Olivia…?'

'Yes, Hugo?'

'I love you to distraction. I love you to the moon and back. I think I have loved you ever since the moment I heard you haranguing those youths with insults from the Bard. Now, will you marry me? Please?'

Her heart swelled so much she thought it might explode. 'Oh, yes!' She dropped to her knees, took his dear face between her hands and claimed his lips in a searing kiss. 'Yes! Yes! A thousand times, yes!'

Epilogue

Cheriton Abbey, Devonshire—March 1813

Hugo grabbed Olivia by the hand and ran, towing her behind him.

'Hugo? Where are we going?'

She snatched up the flowing skirt of her wedding dress to avoid tripping on it. He did not slow until he reached the foot of the imposing polished oak staircase. He looked up the stairs and then returned his gaze to roam her face, raising shivers of awareness wherever it touched. His eyes glinted.

'Hugo.' Her breath hitched. 'We *can't*.'

He raised one brow in that arrogant way of his—the way she still could not emulate no matter how much she practised.

'Of course we can.' His deep voice sent shivers of awareness, need and pure excitement shimmering through her until every nerve ending felt alight.

'But…what will people say?'

She saw him bite back his smile. 'Is this the Lady Olivia Beauchamp I know and love? Fretting over what people will say? Surely not?'

She went up on tiptoes and pressed her mouth to his. The merest touch of their lips sent heat pulsing through her.

'Lady Olivia Alastair, if you don't mind.' She smiled against his mouth and felt his answering grin. 'Or have you so soon forgotten?'

She stifled a squeal as he swung her into his arms, cradling her against his chest. He began to climb the stairs.

'Hugo!'

'Olivia?' He did not pause but climbed relentlessly, one step after another.

'What will they *think*? My family…your family…they will *notice*.'

'They will think, my sweet—' they had reached the landing and Hugo turned in the direction of the best guest bedchamber. He paused, and kissed her, long, hard and hot. '—that I have been remarkably patient for all these months and that my patience has finally worn thin.' He started walking again and Olivia tightened her arms around his neck, peppering his jaw and cheek with tiny kisses. 'They will think, my darling wife, that I am making damned sure you are mine—at last—and that no man will ever come between us.'

She nipped his earlobe between her teeth.

'Ouch!' He tightened his grip on her. 'You'll pay for that, you little minx.'

She giggled and buried her face in his neck. They reached the bedchamber door and he paused again, waiting until she looked up into his beloved face. He pierced her with a look of such hot intent that her insides turned molten and her corset suddenly grew excruciatingly tight.

'They will think—' he pushed the door open '—my utterly gorgeous, desirable wife—' he kicked the door shut behind them '—that they are unlikely to set eyes on either one of us again until, at the very earliest, noon tomorrow.'

He laid her on the bed and followed her down, taking her mouth in a scorching kiss as his hands roamed freely.

It was full dark outside by the time she emerged from the sensual haze that Hugo—her irresistible, skilful, playful, *sexy* husband—had woven around her. She snuggled up to his warm, hard body, trailing her fingers through the soft hair that covered his chest, down over his flat belly to—

She bit back a smile at his groan.

'*Again?* Have a heart, my sweet. I'm out of practice.'

She kissed his nipple, then licked and, finally, softly, nipped at it.

'You owe me.'

She sensed he'd raised his head. '*Owe* you? What do I owe you?'

She wriggled to face him, draping her body across his, breast to chest, her nipples hardening at the rasp of his chest hair against them. She rested her arms on his chest and propped her chin upon her clasped hands.

'All these months and I had no idea what I was missing.' She shuffled, moving higher. 'All that time wasted. Why—' she bit gently at his chin '—didn't you tell me?' She licked delicately at his lower lip.

'Mmm...' His hum of appreciation sounded from somewhere deep in his throat.

She moved to straddle him and kissed him thoroughly. 'Well?'

His arms wrapped around her waist. 'You, madam, are insatiable,' he growled as he flipped her on to her back and covered her. 'A devious, manipulative minx. I didn't tell you because I know how curious and how persistent you are and I wanted our wedding night to be special.'

He bent his head to her breast, taking her aching nipple into his mouth. Olivia gave herself up to the sensation, smiling her satisfaction.

There were times when persistence most definitely paid off.

'I love you, Hugo.'

'I love you, too, Trouble.'

* * * * *

DARING TO LOVE
THE DUKE'S HEIR

To Lynn.

Thank you.

Chapter One

March 1817

Raindrops rattled on the roof of the carriage that carried Miss Liberty Lovejoy and her sister Hope through the dark, slick streets of a rain-drenched London.

'Liberty. I beg you…please do not do this. Gideon will never forgive you.'

Liberty wrenched her attention from the passing streets and resolutely swallowed down her own burgeoning doubt. She didn't want to do this, but she had to. *Someone* must save Gideon from himself.

'I have to do something, Hope. Gideon is running amok and it is all the fault of Lord Alexander Beauchamp. Gideon will be grateful to me for saving him from the results of his own folly. Eventually.'

'Well, I do not think you are fair to embroil me without warning,' said Hope tartly. 'You *said* we were going to Hookham's. I would never have agreed to accompany you if I knew you intended to visit Alexander's father, of all people. He is a *duke*, Liberty. People like us do not just call upon a duke.'

Hope's reaction did not surprise Liberty—she had

given up expecting support from either of her sisters when there was any unpleasantness to deal with. They had been so young when their parents had died within days of one another and they had come to rely on Liberty and her twin brother, Gideon—just nineteen at the time—to take charge. Uncle Eustace was worse than useless…far too selfish to stir himself, even though he had been appointed their guardian. It was no wonder her entire family took Liberty for granted.

'If you are afraid to come in, you may remain in the carriage while I speak to the Duke. *I* cannot afford the luxury of fear.' Oh, but how she wished she could order Bilk, their coachman, to turn the carriage around and drive back to their rented London house. 'It is my responsibility as the eldest—'

'You are the eldest by a mere five minutes, Liberty Louisa Lovejoy, and *Gideon* now happens to be an earl.'

'His conduct is more reminiscent of an overgrown schoolboy than a peer of the realm,' retorted Liberty.

Since Liberty's twin brother had unexpectedly acceded to the Earldom of Wendover last autumn his behaviour had grown increasingly exasperating. Was it really asking too much of him to help her to secure their sisters' futures instead of careening around town and frittering his newfound prosperity on wine, cards and horses and in the pursuit of females who were no better than they should be? Besides, she missed Gideon and how they had worked together to ensure the survival of their family.

'Well, I would say that being an earl makes him senior to you, do you not? Do not forget we are all reliant on his goodwill now if we do not wish to be banished back to Eversham with Uncle Eustace. I think it is very generous of Gideon to fund a Season for all three of us at the same time.'

Liberty clenched her jaw. If Hope only knew how much persuasion it had taken for Gideon to agree to his sisters coming to London in the first place...left to himself, she had no doubt her twin would have been content for his sisters to remain hidden away at Eversham for ever while he lived the high life to which he now felt entitled.

She stared out of the window, seeing neither the grey streets they passed nor the people hurrying along beneath their umbrellas, wrapped in coats and cloaks against the dreadful dark, cold and wet weather that had assailed the entire country for the past year. If it were not for Hope and Verity she would much prefer to still be at home, running the house for Uncle Eustace—her late mother's unmarried brother who had always made his home with the Lovejoys—and living in quiet obscurity.

But Hope and Verity, at one-and-twenty and nineteen respectively, deserved a chance to better themselves in life. After their parents' deaths there had been neither opportunity nor funds for the younger Lovejoy sisters to even dream of a come out, not until the unexpected death of a distant cousin and his two sons in a house fire and Gideon's sudden preferment.

'And do not forget what Mrs Mount said.' Hope's words broke into Liberty's train of thought. 'It is bad etiquette to call on your social superiors before *they* have left their card with *you*.'

Mrs Mount was the lady they had hired as duenna during their sojourn in London. The daughter of a viscount and now the widow of the younger son of an earl, she had many acquaintances within the *ton* and was thus perfectly placed to help steer the Lovejoy girls through the mysteries of polite society. Well, perfectly placed if Liberty chose to follow her advice. Which, in this instance, she did not.

'It is a certainty that the Duke of Cheriton is never likely to leave his card for us,' said Liberty, 'so I do not see that I have any choice if I am to persuade him to control his son's wild behaviour.'

'I cannot believe that a duke will take kindly to a country squire's daughter lecturing him on how he should control his son. Libby—it is not too late. Please, let us go home and I promise I will help you talk some sense into Gideon.'

'But we have tried that, Hope, many times, and he ignores us. I fear his new status has gone to his head and that he will never be the same again.'

She was not even certain she much liked the man her twin had become. He had become secretive and thoughtless, and the closeness that had bound the two of them together throughout their childhood now felt as though it hung by the most fragile of threads.

It breaks my heart, this distance between us.

Liberty slid one gloved hand inside her woollen cloak and pressed it to her upper chest, rubbing in a soothing, circular motion, but the familiar hollow ache remained, as it had for the five years since her childhood sweetheart, Bernard, died.

Being back in London had resurrected those dreadful memories and, with them, the guilt. If only she hadn't been so selfish by accepting the offer from her wealthy godmother to sponsor her through a London Season. If only she had stayed at home, Bernard and her parents might still be alive. At the very least she would have been able to say goodbye to her husband-to-be. A knot of disquiet had taken root in her stomach since their arrival in London…a nagging reminder of her selfishness and her failure.

Well, she would not fail Gideon, or the girls. And if it meant calling on a duke unannounced, then so be it.

In an unexpected gesture, Hope clasped Liberty's hand.

'You cannot protect all of us all the time, Liberty. Gideon is a grown man. I know you miss the old Gideon, but he will come to his senses, you'll see.'

'But what if he does not? What if I sit by and do nothing and he ends up destroying himself? And that's quite apart from the damage his wild behaviour will do to you and Verity.'

Their background would be hurdle enough without Gideon casting a deeper shadow over them. Papa had been a gentleman, but Mama had been the daughter of a coal merchant—that whiff of trade would be a difficult barrier to overcome, according to Mrs Mount.

The carriage rocked to a halt.

'This must be it,' Hope said, her voice awed. 'Goodness!'

Liberty was momentarily distracted as thunder growled in the distance, a stark reminder of the most terrible day in her life—the day she had learned that not only both her beloved parents, but also Bernard, had succumbed to the outbreak of cholera that swept through their village while Liberty had been enjoying dress fittings in London in preparation for her debut. She had not even glimpsed the inside of a ballroom before receiving that urgent summons to return home.

She thrust down the memory that still had the power to bring hot, stinging tears to her eyes and peered through the rain that streamed down the window. She gulped. *This* was Beauchamp House? It was huge. Mag-

nificent. Intimidating. It was not a house, but a mansion. Stretching for five wide bays, it would swallow
several houses such as their modest rented abode in
Green Street. A new surge of doubt as to her plan swept
over Liberty, but she had come this far and she wouldn't
allow herself to back away now. She gathered her courage, flung open the carriage door, grabbed her oilskin
umbrella and, opening it, thrust it out of the door into
the deluge. Lightning flickered and she braced herself
for the next rumble of thunder. Was the storm getting
closer? There were several seconds before the sound
reached her ears—it sounded more distant than before
and she released her pent-up breath. She gave herself
no time for further qualms. Bilk handed her down and
she hurried up the steps to the imposing front door of
Beauchamp House, which remained firmly shut.

She lifted the brass knocker—so highly polished it
gleamed even in the unnatural yellowish-grey afternoon
light—and let it fall. Then she waited, irritation clam-
bering over any nerves she felt at facing such a powerful nobleman. What was taking so long? 'Where—?'

'Might I be of assistance?'

She whipped around. A carriage was drawing away
from the front of the house, presumably after depos-
iting this man…her darting gaze settled on his face,
half-shielded by his own umbrella, and she gasped, her
stomach clenching with anger. She held fast to her courage and straightened her spine even though her knees
quaked. This close, she was only too conscious of Lord
Alexander Beauchamp's daunting presence—his height
and the width of his shoulders spoke of a powerful man.

'I have come to speak to your father about your
behaviour.'

He stiffened, his dark brows slashed into a forbidding frown. 'I *beg* your pardon?'

As she opened her mouth, he held up his hand, palm forward, effectively silencing her. 'Apart from the fact that you and I have never met, madam, I regret to inform you that the Duke is not in residence.' He brushed past her to the door.

'We may indeed never have met, my lord, but I know who you are.' Liberty set her jaw. She'd recognise Lord Alexander Beauchamp anywhere, even though she'd only ever glimpsed him in the distance as he gaily led her brother astray. 'The knocker is on the door.' She summoned her very haughtiest tone. 'That means the family is in residence.'

'A member of the family, maybe, but that member is not my father. Now, if you will excuse me? You might relish being out in such weather, but I can assure you I do not.' The door began to open. 'I suggest you put your grievance into writing. If you have it delivered here it will be forwarded on to my father for his attention, you have my word.'

The word of a rackety rakehell!

The door opened fully to reveal a liveried footman.

'Sorry, milord,' he said breathlessly. 'I was downstairs when I heard the knock.'

'No need for apologies, William. This—' Liberty stiffened, detecting the faint curl of his upper lip as His Lordship looked her up and down '—*person* wished to speak to my father. I have advised her to write to him.'

He handed his dripping umbrella to the servant and strode into the hall. Despair spread its tentacles through Liberty, squeezing her lungs. Coming here to confront the Duke had been a risk, but at least she would have had an opportunity to use her powers of persuasion. A

letter could be all too easily dismissed. It was true she
had never met Alexander, but perhaps if he knew who
she was…? If she could appeal to his better nature…?

'Lord Alexander! Please!' She tried to dodge around
the footman, who foiled her attempts using His Lordship's still-open umbrella. 'Wait, I beg of you.'

Once she succeeded in knocking aside that umbrella,
she could see His Lordship had stopped and now faced
her, a look of weary resignation on his face. Encouraged,
she discarded her own umbrella on the doorstep and
rushed towards him, darting around the still-protesting
footman.

'Please. May we talk? I am Gideon's sister.'

His brows snapped together, forming once again
a dark slash across his forehead. 'Gideon? Who is
Gideon?'

'Lord Wendover.'

'You have my sympathy.'

Liberty bridled. 'If you think so little of him, why
do you spend so much time together?'

He looked beyond her. 'William—take the lady's
coat and bonnet, if you please. Ask Mrs Himley to send
wine and cakes to the drawing room, and find a maid
to sit with us—' He looked Liberty up and down before fixing his gaze on her face. The chill in his light-
coloured eyes sent a shiver through her. 'For propriety's
sake,' he continued. '*You* might have no compunction
about calling upon your social superiors not only un-
invited but also unchaperoned, madam, but a man cannot be too careful.'

The nerve of him! 'My sister is in the carriage outside,' said Liberty, shedding her dripping cloak. 'She
was too afraid to come in and speak to your father.'

'Too afraid or too sensible? I suspect the latter. Perhaps you would be wise to pay more attention to your sister's instincts.' His bored tone sent Liberty's temper soaring. 'Invite her to join us, William, if you please. She cannot wait outside. But I shall still require a maid,' he called after the departing footman.

He eyed Liberty again, from head to toe, and she squirmed inside. She had donned her best Pomona-green bombazine afternoon dress for this visit to the Duke, but His Lordship's impassive inspection made her feel as though she was dressed in rags. It was not the height of fashion—she had been unable to reconcile herself to wasting money on new gowns when she had a trunk full of barely worn dresses and accessories from five years ago—but it was respectable.

'One cannot be too careful.'

He means for himself! He is not concerned with my *reputation, only that I might try to entrap him!*

Liberty squared her shoulders and elevated her chin. 'The drawing room, sir?' She was proud of the haughty tone she achieved.

Utterly unruffled, he strolled to a nearby door and opened it. 'This way, ma'am.' *His* tone conveyed bored amusement.

She swept through, head high. How dare he treat her as though she were of no consequence? Although, she had to admit it was humiliation that spurred her rage. Undoubtedly, to a duke's son, she *was* inconsequential. He followed her inside the elegantly furnished room with its vermilion-painted walls above white-painted wainscoting, its high ceiling with elaborately moulded cornice and three tall windows dressed with delicately sprigged floor-length curtains.

'You are suffering under a misapprehension.'

She started at the voice behind her. She halted her inspection of the room and turned to find him closer than she anticipated. Nerves fluttered deep in her belly as she got her first good look at his pale silvery-grey eyes and the utter confidence they conveyed. And why should they not? Not only was he the son of one of the most powerful Dukes in the land but he was sinfully, classically handsome with a straight nose, sharp cheekbones and a beautifully sculpted mouth above a determined chin. Those silvery eyes of his seemed to penetrate deep inside her and yet they were as opaque as a silver coin, revealing no hint of his thoughts.

She stepped back, dragging her gaze from his. His beautifully tied cravat—how Gideon would appreciate such skill in *his* valet!—sported a simple gold pin in the shape of a whip and his olive-green superfine coat hugged wide shoulders and well-muscled arms. Beneath that form-fitting coat he sported a grey-and-white-striped waistcoat that did nothing to hide the heavy muscles of his chest. Her eyes travelled further, skimming the powerful thighs encased in cream breeches. He had the look of a Corinthian…the name given to gentlemen who enjoyed and excelled at physical sports such as riding, boxing and fencing, according to Gideon.

The face of a Greek God, the body of a warrior and a duke's son. How could one man have so many advantages in life? Her gaze snapped back to his face, the sight of those powerful thighs imprinted on her brain. He was watching her. By the quirk of his lips, her perusal of his person amused him. Mortified at being caught studying him as a sculptor might study his subject, Liberty swallowed and then sucked in a deep breath. That did nothing to calm her nerves. Male and spicy, his scent filled her and those butterflies in her belly fluttered even more.

She forced a scowl to her face. This was Lord Alexander Beauchamp: the devil who was leading Gideon astray. She tilted her chin and looked down her nose at him, but the look that satisfactorily quelled the most persistent of tradesmen dunning for payment made no impression on His Lordship, judging by the arrogant lift of his eyebrows.

'Misapprehension, my lord?'

'Indeed.'

His deep cultured tones penetrated all the way inside her, stirring yet more fluttery sensations as she felt the full force of his attention.

'Allow me to introduce myself.' He bowed, the action somehow mocking. 'Avon, at your service. Miss…?'

His words jerked her from her irritation. 'What did you say? Who is Avon?'

'Alexander is my brother. My *younger* brother. I am the Marquess of Avon, hence Lord Avon.' His head tilted. 'Do you require an explanation of courtesy titles? I understand you and your brother were not raised in aristocratic circles.'

Liberty's face burned. Mrs Mount had warned them that their background would swiftly become common knowledge in the *ton*. No doubt His Lordship also knew her grandfather was a coal merchant. Without volition, her chin rose even higher than before.

'I am not ignorant of such matters, sir. If Gideon ever has a son, he will take Gideon's next highest title, Viscount Haxby, as a courtesy title to use as his own until Gideon's death, when he will become the Earl of Wendover.'

'I am relieved you have learned something since

your brother was elevated to the peerage. The fundamental etiquette of introductions appears to have passed you by, however. It is customary to introduce oneself in return.'

Infuriated that he was right, her face scorched even hotter. Lord Avon might resemble one of the marble statues she had admired at the British Museum last week, but he was as patronising and pompous as any man she had ever had the misfortune to meet.

She stiffened her spine and again looked down her nose. 'I am Miss Liberty Lovejoy.'

Chapter Two

Dominic bit back the sudden urge to laugh. Liberty Lovejoy? What parent would saddle their daughter with such a name? They had no choice over surname, to be sure—he was well aware Lovejoy was the family name of the Earls of Wendover—but what was wrong with naming their daughter Jane or Mary? Liberty Lovejoy— she sounded like some kind of actress. Or worse.

Still…he controlled his amusement and bowed. 'And to what do we owe the pleasure of your visit, Miss Lovejoy?'

He found himself scrutinised by a pair of intelligent, almond-shaped eyes. They were extraordinary and he found himself being drawn into their depths. They were the dark blue of the summer sky at midnight, with golden flecks in the irises and fringed with thick golden-brown lashes. Tawny brows drew together in a frown and her lips, soft pink and lush, compressed. He waited for her reply, controlling his visceral reaction to Miss Liberty Lovejoy. He was well practised in that art—his position as heir to a wealthy dukedom as well as his honour as a gentleman meant he simply did not indulge in idle flirtations.

'Your brother is tempting *my* brother into entirely inappropriate and wild behaviour and I came here to dem—*beg* your father to stop your brother from leading Gideon astray.'

Her velvety eyes glowed with fervour and he didn't doubt her genuine concern. His heart sank at the news that Alex might be falling back into his old, wild ways. He had already heard tales circulating about the newly ennobled Lord Wendover and his readiness to sample every entertainment available to a young, wealthy man about town, but Alex's name hadn't arisen in connection with them. The last he had heard, Alex was living at Foxbourne Manor in Berkshire and making a success of his horse breeding and training establishment—gaining a reputation for providing high-quality riding and carriage horses.

'Please be seated, Miss Lovejoy.' Dominic indicated a chair by the fireplace.

With a swish of her skirts, she settled on the sofa. Mentally, he shrugged. He would allow her that small victory. He studied his visitor as he strolled across to sit by her side—his scrutiny, his pace and his choice of seat specifically intended to ruffle her feathers. A man had to have some fun, after all.

Her gown looked new, but was outmoded by a few years, with its high neck and ruff of triple lace, and he couldn't help but notice how beautifully it clung to her curves. His pulse kicked, but Dominic controlled his surge of desire for this voluptuous woman. He prided himself on his self-control. In every area of his life. He sat, half-facing her, noting the crease of a frown between her tawny eyebrows and the tension in the lines around her mouth.

'I trust you have no objection to my sitting next to you?'

He allowed one corner of his mouth to quirk up and was rewarded by Liberty's subtle but unmistakable shift along the sofa, increasing the distance between them. The faint scent of roses drifted into his awareness—the scent of his late mother, remembered from his childhood—and all thought of teasing Miss Liberty Lovejoy vanished, swamped by a swirl of memories.

His mother had been on his mind more and more lately—ever since he had decided that this was the Season he would choose a wife. It was time to marry. Time to produce an heir. Time to fulfil the vow he had made all those years ago after his mother had died. He straightened, rolling his shoulders back. The sooner he addressed Miss Lovejoy's concerns, the sooner he could get on with compiling a list of candidates suitable for his bride.

'Tell me why you believe Alexander to be in any way responsible for your own brother's behaviour,' he said. 'Is he not his own man?'

She drew in a sharp breath but, before she could reply, William appeared in the open doorway.

'Miss Hope Lovejoy, milord,' he said.

Dominic stood. A young lady bearing a familial resemblance to Liberty Lovejoy entered the room, her cheeks blooming a becoming shade of pink. Out of habit, Dominic registered her appearance with one sweeping glance. Pretty. Golden-haired. Delicate features. Taller than her sister, with a trim figure, enhanced by the latest fashions. He couldn't resist glancing once again at Liberty and making comparisons. No. He wasn't mistaken. It would appear Liberty was a woman prepared to make personal sacrifices to ensure her younger sibling enjoyed every advantage. Was it that same trait that had driven her to come here and confront his father? That took some courage. His opinion of Liberty Lovejoy rose. Just a notch.

He bowed to Hope and directed his most charming smile at her, fully aware it would further vex the still-smouldering Liberty. 'I am pleased to make your acquaintance, Miss Lovejoy.'

Hope would prove popular with the gentlemen of the *ton*, he had no doubt. And she was fully aware of the effect of her beauty upon members of the opposite sex, he realised, as she rewarded him with a coquettish smile and a swift, appraising glance through her long lashes. A poorly stifled *hmmph* from Liberty reached Dominic's ears, stirring another urge to laugh which he manfully resisted.

'I am Avon. Please be seated.' He gestured to the place on the sofa he had recently vacated. 'Your sister and I were about to discuss the reason for this visit. Ah, Betty, Thomas, thank you.' A maid had come in with a dish of macaroons, followed by another footman carrying a tray bearing a bottle of Madeira and three glasses. 'Please be good enough to pour the wine, Thomas. Betty—will you sit by the window once you have served our visitors? You may remain until our visitors leave. Thank you.'

Liberty glowered at him, clearly irritated by the implication that her motives for this visit might differ from her stated reason. But, from a young age, Dominic had known his duty was to choose a suitable, well-brought-up lady as his future Duchess and it was now second nature to avoid any risk of getting trapped into an unsuitable alliance through carelessness.

Hope had now settled next to Liberty on the sofa and so Dominic moved to stand by the fireplace while he waited for the wine to be served.

'So. To continue with the reason for your visit, Miss Lovejoy—you lay the blame for your brother's wayward behaviour at the door of *my* brother?'

She raised her gaze from the contemplation of her glass. 'Yes.' She bit delicately into a macaroon.

Dominic frowned at her brusque reply.

'Why?' Two could play at that game.

The pink tip of her tongue as it rescued stray crumbs from her lips did strange things to Dominic's pulse rate. Irritated, he willed his body under control. Simple lust—not difficult for a man like him to resist. Yet he could not tear his gaze from her mouth as she chewed in a leisurely fashion, her fine tawny brows drawn together in a frown of concentration.

'Gideon has never been on the town before,' she said eventually. 'He is a...a...greenhead, I think is the word. He is being led astray by your brother, who appears intent on introducing him to every vice known to man.'

I sincerely hope not. Reading the earnestness of Liberty's expression, Dominic doubted she had the first idea of the full extent of the vices available in London to eager young bucks with money to burn. But he trusted Alex not to return to his past reckless behaviour. Didn't he? He made a mental note to check up on his brother's activities. If he felt Alex was in danger of sliding back into his old, wild ways, he would nip that in the bud before their father and stepmother came up to town.

'I am sure Alex is simply helping your brother to find his feet in town,' he said. 'I fail to understand why you feel he needs your protection. What would he say if he knew you had come here to speak to my father?'

Liberty's cheeks bloomed red. 'He would object, of course.'

She was honest, at least. His opinion lifted another degree.

'Then you will do well to allow him to determine his own path. No man would take kindly to his sister trying to control him. I presume you are older than him?'

'We are twins but, yes, I am the elder.'

'Twins? No wonder he objects to your interference. Heed my advice, Miss Lovejoy, and allow your brother to be his own man.'

Her lips parted as she inhaled. Her breasts rose, drawing Dominic's gaze like a lodestone. His pulse quickened and his cravat suddenly felt too tight. The room too warm. He swallowed down his reaction even as he acknowledged that Liberty Lovejoy's natural, curvaceous femininity was more attractive to him than any of the painstakingly elegant ladies of the *ton*. He could never act upon such attraction, however—as the sister of an earl and a lady, she was off limits other than for marriage. And she was definitely not marriageable material. Not for him.

He had sworn at his mother's death, when he was eight years old, that he would do his duty and make her proud of him.

Never forget, Avon—you will be the Duke one day. You must never bring your heritage into disrepute. Make me proud, my Son.

He'd spent his life striving to fulfil her expectations. He had never felt good enough for her while she was alive—other than that one hint of affection he had glimpsed from her, on the day she died—but now, this Season, he would finally prove to her that he was worthy. Besides, it was what was expected of a man in his position, and he owed his father that much, too. His bride must be perfect in every way: bloodlines, up-bringing, behaviour.

And Liberty Lovejoy fitted none of those requirements. Not one.

Unsettled and irritated by his visceral reaction to this woman Dominic lowered his gaze to where her hands were gripped together in her lap, her kid gloves stretched taut over her knuckles. He choked back his exasperation. It was not Liberty's fault he found her so…enticing. Her distress at her brother's behaviour was tangible and the urge to comfort her took him by surprise. He softened his tone.

'What your brother is doing is not so very unusual, Miss Lovejoy. Most young men on the town for the first time behave somewhat recklessly. But they soon settle down and I am convinced your brother will, too.'

'But I must stop him before he squanders his entire inheritance.'

'Are his debts so very ruinous?' He would have thought Wendover's estates were wealthy enough, even after the disaster of last year's harvest.

Liberty's lips pursed.

'*I* am certain you are right, my lord.' Hope smiled at Dominic and fluttered her lashes. 'As you might guess, my sister does have an unfortunate tendency to imagine the worst. We do not know the scale of his debts as Gideon, *quite rightly*—' she cast a quelling look at her sister '—refuses to discuss—'

'He is out until all hours and sometimes he does not come home at all.'

The words burst from Miss Lovejoy as she swept her hand through her hair, scattering hairpins and leaving bits of hair the hue of dark honey sticking out sideways from her scalp. Two locks unwound to drape unnoticed over her shoulder.

'And when he does, he is so…so distant. So *secretive*.' Her voice rang with despair. 'We have always shared everything, but he will not confide in me…the tradesmen haven't been paid…there is a stack of bills awaiting his attention, yet when I begged him to pay them, all he would say is that he must pay his gambling debts first as a matter of honour. He lost two hundred pounds at hazard last night. Two *hundred*!'

Her horror at such a loss was clear, but her words convinced Dominic that she was worrying over nothing. Her lack of understanding of the ways of the aristocracy was hardly surprising when she had not been raised in such circles.

'That does not sound so very bad to me.'

'Not so very bad? *Two hundred pounds?*'

He'd intended to reassure her. Instead she was looking at him as though he'd suddenly sprouted a second head.

'Well, no. The Earldom of Wendover is a wealthy one with properties in Buckinghamshire and Suffolk, if I remember rightly. It can stand a few losses at the gaming tables. I am convinced you are worrying over nothing, Miss Lovejoy. You will see. Your brother will eventually settle down.'

'But…the tradesmen. Gideon flatly refuses to pay them. He says they can wait. He never used to be so… so careless of other people, but whenever I remonstrate with him, all he will say is that is how everyone in society carries on.'

Dominic shrugged. 'Many do.'

He did not do that himself. Neither did his father. But he could not deny that many gentlemen considered tradesmen to be at the bottom of the list of debtors to be paid.

'It is your brother's prerogative to pay the tradesmen who supply your household as and when he chooses, just as it is the tradesmen's prerogative to cease supplying such late-paying customers if they choose. In my experience, most tradesmen elect to continue enjoying the patronage of their aristocratic clients for the prestige it brings them.'

'That is *appalling.*'

He agreed. It was one of the many habits of the higher echelons of society that he disliked, but he would not admit as much to Miss Liberty Lovejoy as she sat on his father's sofa passing judgement. She seemed determined to believe the worst of his world, including blaming *his* brother for *her* brother's misbehaviour.

'Can you not ask your brother to stop encouraging Gideon? *Please*, my lord.'

Dominic passed one hand around the back of his head, massaging the tight muscles at the top of his neck. 'Even if I were inclined to speak to him on this, I can assure you Alex would likely do the exact opposite of what I asked of him.'

And, now he came to think of it, that was no doubt the exact reason Gideon was behaving as Miss Lovejoy had described.

'Perhaps if you trusted your brother to make his own decisions instead of—how did you put it?— *remonstrating* with him, he would mend his ways that much sooner.'

Liberty surged to her feet.

'So it is *my* fault, is it, Lord Avon?'

Dominic didn't answer, distracted by her curvaceous

figure as she paced the room, her skirts swishing. She really was magnificent.

'*If* you would do me the courtesy of replying to my point?'

Her voice dripped sarcasm. Furious with himself for ogling her in such an ill-bred manner, Dominic blanked his expression and calmly met her glare. If looks could kill, or even maim, then he would be prostrate on the floor even now. The impulse to prod her further was irresistible. He raised one brow in deliberate provocation.

'You may have noticed, my dear Miss Lovejoy, that calmness, elegance and poise are three of the qualities most desired in the young ladies of our world. There is a very good reason for that and I would advise you to nurture such traits in your own behaviour.'

Her eyes narrowed. 'What do you mean?'

'Only that too much vigour and…er…*passion* are not the done thing, you know.'

He smiled kindly at her as she continued to look daggers at him.

'You, sir, are no gentleman.'

'I am merely trying to give you a hint as to how to go on in society, Miss Lovejoy.' He folded his arms across his chest, enjoying her chagrin. 'And, might I add, sarcasm does not become you. Am I correct in assuming that you and your sister will be making your debuts this coming Season?'

Liberty turned to her sister. 'Come, Hope. We are wasting our time expecting any assistance from His Lordship.' She glared again at Dominic. 'I shall write to your father, as you suggested, sir, in the hope that he possesses the conscience you so clearly lack.'

Hectic pink flushed Hope Lovejoy's cheeks as she shot a furious look at her sister. She stood and smoothed out her skirts, then dipped a curtsy as she smiled apologetically.

'Do please excuse us for invading your home, Lord Avon,' she said. 'Good afternoon.'

Dominic bowed. 'No apology is necessary. Good afternoon, Miss Hope Lovejoy.'

He then glanced at Liberty and guilt thumped him hard in the chest at the despair that dulled those extraordinary eyes. He stifled a sigh.

'I shall have a word with Alex and make sure he and Wendover are not getting in too deep, Miss Liberty Lovejoy—' and her name still made him want to smile '—but other than that there is little I can do. Alex will not take kindly to any attempt by me to tell him how to behave.'

Gratitude suffused her features.

'But I am still convinced you are worrying over nothing,' he added.

'I thank you nevertheless, my lord.'

Liberty's face lit with a more-generous smile than his offer warranted and, before he could stop himself, he found himself responding. He blanked his expression again and crossed to the bell pull. Liberty Lovejoy provoked strange emotions in him—emotions he did not care to examine too closely—but he was reassured by the knowledge their paths would rarely cross. Wendover, as a peer—even a hellraising peer—would find acceptance everywhere, but his sisters, raised in obscurity and with a grandfather in trade, would likely only frequent the fringes of society.

William, thankfully, answered his summons promptly.

'Please see the ladies out, William.'

He bowed again, avoiding eye contact with either

of his visitors, then stood stock still after they had
gone, staring unseeingly at the closed door, wondering how one voluptuous, sweet-smelling woman had
stirred such unaccustomed feelings within him. He
had always kept his emotions under strict control, as
behoved his father's heir. Alex and their younger sister, Olivia—before she had wed four years ago—had
always been the lively, mischievous ones of the family, but Dominic had grown up with the weight of expectation on his shoulders. It was his duty to make his
father proud, to uphold the family name and to always
behave as befitted a future duke.

Also, strangely, he felt compelled to protect his father—
a nonsensical-seeming notion when one considered how
powerful Father was. But Dominic recalled his mother's
death all too clearly, and how Father had suffered from
guilt. Dominic had seen and heard things no eight-year-
old boy should ever see and hear and, by shouldering the
responsibility of being the perfect son and the perfect heir,
he had vowed to shield his father from further distress.

He shook his head, as though he might dislodge those
memories and the thoughts they evoked, clicking his
tongue in irritation. He swung round to face the room.
Betty hovered not five feet from him, having been unable to get past him to the door as he stood there like a
mindless idiot, blocking her exit.

He frowned and moved aside, motioning for the maid
to leave, his promise to Miss Lovejoy—it *had* been a
promise, had it not?—nipping at him. He would speak
to Alex.

'Betty?'

'Yes, milord?'

'Is Lord Alexander currently in residence?'

Dominic did not live at Beauchamp House, preferring the privacy of his own town house when staying in London. He had travelled up to town yesterday from Cheriton Abbey and had merely called at Beauchamp House to warn the staff that his father's butler, Grantham, would be arriving shortly to prepare the house for the arrival of the Duke and Duchess and to find out what day his sister, Olivia, and his brother-in-law, Hugo, were due to arrive in London.

'No, milord.'

'Ask downstairs if anyone knows where he is staying in London, will you please?'

Betty nodded and then scurried past him out of the room.

Chapter Three

That glimpse of kindness in Lord Avon just before they left almost changed Liberty's impression of His Lordship. Almost, but not quite. That one final concession was simply not enough to wipe out the many black marks against him, and Liberty, crotchety and restless after that interview, was in no mood to forgive. She clambered into the carriage behind Hope and sat down before knocking on the roof with her umbrella as a signal to Bilk to drive on. As soon as the carriage was in motion, Hope swivelled on the bench to face Liberty.

'I was never more embarrassed,' she said. 'Do you *never* stop to think of the consequences of your actions on me and Verity? Lord Avon is the most eligible bachelor in the *ton* and Mrs Mount had grand hopes that one of us might catch his eye. She told me the family estates in Devonshire are *vast*, but now you have ruined our chances because you will *never* listen to *anybody*. You always think you know best. Oh! To think! I might have been a duchess.'

'A marchioness, Hope. Lord Avon's father is very much alive and well. And do please stop dramatising everything. That man would never seriously consider either you or Verity as suitable…he was utterly contemptuous about us not being raised with the expectations of moving in high society.'

'But we have our looks on our side. Why, Lord Redbridge called me an Incomparable the other day! And, oh, Liberty! Isn't Lord Avon the most handsome, well-set figure of a man you have ever seen?'

'Hmmph. A person might think that, if she cared for the Corinthian type, but he is also arrogant, haughty, conceited—'

Words failed her but, next to her, Hope unexpectedly giggled.

'He *has* made you cross, hasn't he, Liberty? Do you not realise all those words have the same meaning?'

Liberty pursed her lips. 'Unfeeling. Rude. Superior—'

'Superior means the same again,' crowed Hope.

'Well, we can't all have a way with words like you, Hope.'

Now Hope was relieved of the necessity to earn a little money by teaching in the local school, she either had her head buried in a novel, or was madly scribbling poetry and plays, while Verity was rarely seen without a sketchbook in her hands.

They were happy to leave the practicalities of running the family to Liberty—a responsibility she had taken on after their parents died, having promised her dying mother that she would look after the family and keep them safe.

'Well, it matters not what your opinion of His Lordship may be, Libby, for I am very certain he would not consider *you* as marriageable after the way you spoke to him.'

'I said no more than the situation warranted.' Liberty turned aside and stared pointedly through the win-

dow as she continued her diatribe against Lord Avon
inside her head.

*How dare he look down on us? Just because we
weren't raised in the lap of luxury it does not mean we
are worth less as people.*

She glanced down at her gown. Admittedly, it was
not today's fashion, but it had hardly been worn, and
surely it was wasteful not to make use of the gowns
made for her five years ago.

*At least His Precious Lordship can't fault Hope—
her gown is the very latest fashion!*

The carriage pulled up outside the Green Street town
house they currently called home. Lord Avon might
have tried to divert her by claiming the Wendover estates could stand such losses as two hundred pounds a
night—even thinking of such a loss made Liberty feel
quite faint—but Gideon's inheritance did not even include a house in London and his country house needed
complete rebuilding, which would cost a fortune, so
she was right to worry about money. Someone had to.
She'd wager Lord Avon had never had to worry about
money, with a father who was a wealthy duke. They
were clearly so vastly rich and so elevated on the social scale that ordinary people's fears simply did not
register with them.

Hope jumped from the carriage and scurried to the
door, leaving Liberty to follow. As she shrugged out
of her pelisse and handed it to Ethel, their housemaid,
Hope's tones of outrage floated down the stairs.

'And, *would you believe*, she dragged me to the house
of none other than the Duke of Cheriton to confront him
about his son's behaviour.'

Liberty sighed.

'Thank you, Ethel. Has Miss Hope ordered a tea tray?'

'Yes, miss.'

Liberty trod up the stairs, reluctance to face her sisters and Mrs Mount slowing her steps. Of course they would all three disapprove of what she had done, but what choice did she have?

She had kept to her word to Mama, working hard to help keep their small family estate solvent. Gideon—who had inherited the estate from Papa—had left university and thrown himself into the life of a country squire and farmer. He'd never complained. She'd thought he was content enough.

Gideon and she…they had been a true partnership through those hard years. But then, last year, summer had never materialised and harvests had failed the length and breadth of the country, leaving many in hardship and the poorest starving. Gideon had become morose and withdrawn, worrying about the survival of their family home. And then had come the most unexpected news of all. Lord Wendover and his entire family—distant family members they had never even met, so obscure was the connection—had perished, leaving Gideon as the nearest male relation and thus the new Earl of Wendover.

Gideon had changed. It had been as though he had been incarcerated in a prison, and freedom had taken him and turned him from a hard-working, considerate brother into…a stranger. That familiar hollow ache filled Liberty's chest and she rubbed at it absent-mindedly, tears burning behind her eyes. Her beloved brother. The other half of her. Her twin. They'd always shared a close bond but now…she feared he was lost to her for good.

What does Lord Avon know? Supercilious, over-privileged, condescending... He seemed to think this behaviour was normal. Well, Liberty knew Gideon as well as she knew herself and this was as far from normal for him as it was possible to be. It *had* to be the influence of Avon's wicked brother.

Head high, she walked into the drawing room and a deathly silence. Before she had taken a seat by the fire, however, all three occupants spoke at once.

Hope, accusing. 'I told them what you did.'

Mrs Mount, regretful. 'My dear—how could you possibly think that a wise course? If only you had sought my advice. You know how important it is for you all to get vouchers for Almack's—this sort of transgression will do nothing to help your cause.'

Verity, condemning. 'Isn't that just like you, Liberty—charging in without a thought as to how your actions will reflect upon the rest of us?'

Liberty sat down and arranged her skirts, then folded her hands in her lap.

'If you have all *quite* finished—I did what I thought needed to be done and I shall not apologise for it.'

She sensed the others exchanging glances, but she kept her attention on the flickering flames and concentrated on keeping any tell-tale tears at bay as she hoped Lord Avon would not spread the story of her visit far and wide. She had taken a risk, but she was growing desperate and she felt so alone. Where else could she turn for help? Even Godmama was gone now, having passed away last year. The alternative was to ignore Gideon's ever-wilder behaviour and simply pray he would come to his senses. Well, that approach might have been Mama and Papa's solution were they still alive—they had always put their total faith in God and the Bible—but Liberty had long ago stopped trusting in Divine intervention. Where had God been when first Bernard, then Papa, then Mama had all succumbed to the cholera, even though Liberty had spent the entire journey home from London in desperate prayer? Nowhere, that was where.

No. It had been worth the risk to visit the Duke, even though only his arrogant son had been in residence. Lord Avon had given his word to speak to Alexander, although his warning that his brother would be unlikely to pay any heed rang in her ears, reviving her feeling of utter hopelessness.

Ethel brought in the tea tray and Verity poured the cups and handed them round. Liberty accepted hers and sipped, relishing the slide of the hot tea as it soothed her paper-dry throat.

'What did the Duke say?' Mrs Mount's tentative enquiry broke into Liberty's circling thoughts.

'Ah.' Liberty placed her half-drunk cup carefully in its saucer. 'He is not in residence. We did, however, speak to his son, Lord Avon. Lord Alexander's older brother. Do you know him?'

'Yes, of course, although not as well as his father. He and I are of an age, you know—such a tragedy, his first wife dying like that...but there! That's all in the past now. Avon, now...he is a very different man to his brother—very serious and correct. And he is the most eligible bachelor in the *ton*.' Her reproving look scoured Liberty. 'I did harbour hopes he might develop a *tendre* for one of your sisters, but that is now a lost cause. Avon's behaviour is very proper. Beyond reproach. I dare say he was shocked at a young lady having the temerity to call upon him without prior introduction and unchaperoned to boot.'

Liberty shrugged. 'Firstly, I was not unchaperoned. Hope was there and there was a maid in the room, too.

And secondly, I should not care to even hazard a guess as to His Lordship's thoughts.'

She recalled the slide of his gaze over her figure— for a split second she had seen desire flare, before he masked his expression. The thought sent a quiver of heat chasing across her skin.

'Hope,' said Mrs Mount reprovingly, 'is not an adequate chaperon for you, nor you for her. And so the visit was a waste of time and a risk not worth taking?'

'Not entirely. He did offer to speak to his brother, but he did not give us much hope that Lord Alexander will pay him any heed.'

'Is the Duke coming to town? If anyone can control Lord Alexander, it will be him.'

'Lord Avon did not say. Maybe…should I speak to Lord Alexander myself?'

'Nooo!' three voices chorused.

Mrs Mount shushed Liberty's sisters with a wave of her hand before fixing Liberty with a stern look. 'You have done what you can, my dear. I really think you must allow Gideon to come to his senses in his own time. And he will. I am sure of it. In the meantime, we should concentrate on the upcoming Season and finding you three girls suitable husbands. Once you are married off and have families of your own, you will have more important matters to occupy your thoughts.' Her grey eyes raked Liberty. 'Are you *certain* I cannot persuade you to have a new gown or two made, my dear? That one does look sadly outmoded.'

'Mrs Mount is right, Liberty,' said Hope. 'Verity and I have had so much and you've barely spent a penny on yourself. You deserve something nice. Surely you can bring yourself to order one gown?'

Liberty recognised Hope's peace offering—their

family squabbles never lasted long, thank goodness. She recalled Lord Avon's initial perusal of her. Despite Gideon's assurance that he could *'stand the blunt'*, as he put it, Liberty had been unable to bring herself to squander even more money on herself. Now, however, she found herself eager to prove to His High-and-Mighty Lordship that the Lovejoys could be respectable.

'Very well. One evening gown,' she conceded. 'But not to catch a husband. I have told you. I shall never marry. Bernard was my one and only love and I shall remain true to his memory.'

The words were automatically spoken. When Bernard died, she had sworn never to look at another man, never to contemplate marriage. But over the past year she had come to accept the truth. She was lonely. Even with her entire family around her, she was lonely.

That hollow, aching feeling invaded her again and she rubbed absently at her upper chest.

But she was still afraid to admit her change of heart out loud…afraid to fully acknowledge that she dreamed of finding someone to love who would love her in return…afraid that no man could ever take Bernard's place. It was safer to keep that daydream locked inside. That way she would not have to face anyone's pity if she failed to meet such a man. That way, she could keep her pride.

'Still hiding behind the sainted Bernard, Sis? Isn't it time you looked to the future instead of forever harking back to the past?'

That careless drawl shot Liberty to her feet. 'Gideon!' She rushed to him and grabbed his upper arms, scanning him quickly: his drawn, pale features; the dark shadows beneath his eyes; the dishevelled evening clothes. The lingering smell of alcohol and…she wrinkled her nose…cheap perfume and—there was no other word for it—*bodies*. Activities she did not wish to think of. She released her brother and stepped back.

'You have been out all night.'

He quirked a brow and a faint smile lifted the corners of his mouth. 'I have indeed.'

'You need a bath.'

His eyes narrowed. 'So I do. And I have sent word for water to be heated. Not that it is polite for you to mention such a matter.'

'But—'

'But nothing, Liberty. You are not my keeper.' He moved past her. 'Good afternoon, Mrs Mount. Hope. Verity. I trust you are all well?'

All three returned his smile and his greeting but, before he left, Hope—after a sympathetic smile at Liberty—said, 'We do miss you when you stay out so very much, Gideon. Will you dine with us tonight? We have no invitations.'

In truth, invitations for the Lovejoy ladies to attend evening events were still a rarity. Mrs Mount had reassured the girls that the Season had barely begun and that once Easter was over many more families would come to town and the invitations would, hopefully, start to arrive. Currently only one invitation adorned their mantelpiece—to a rout at the home of Sir Gerald and Lady Trent, Sir Gerald being a cousin of Mrs Mount.

'Can't. Sorry.' Gideon turned to the door. 'A bath and a couple of hours' shut-eye, then I'm off to the theatre.'

'We could go with you,' said Liberty. 'We could hire a box.'

His look of dismay clawed at her, leaving her feeling raw and, somehow, exposed. 'I'm not going to the theatre with my *sisters*. Good God! Where's the fun in sitting in a box when I could be down in the pit where all the fun is? Tell you what, Sis—if you're that keen on seeing Mary the Maid of the Inn, I'll reserve a box for you another night. Just tell me when you want to go. You've got Mrs M. to chaperon you and you'll soon have beaux flocking around you if it's male company you're pining for.'

With that, Gideon marched out of the room, leaving the three sisters—and Mrs Mount—looking at one another in despair.

'I still say it's just the novelty of it all that has turned his head,' said Mrs Mount in a faint voice as the sound reached them of him bounding up the stairs. '*Surely* he will come to his senses?'

Liberty did not reply. She returned to her chair and stared at the fire, her mind awash with ideas as plans spiralled to the surface and then sank again as her common sense scuppered them. Finally, realising she was getting nowhere, she went to consult Mrs Taylor about dinner that evening. It went against the grain but, somehow, she must control her penchant for taking action and trust that Lord Avon would be true to his word and do something to curb his own brother's wild ways.

Chapter Four

The next day was dry but cold after the thunderstorm and Dominic, following a sparring session with Gentleman John Jackson in his saloon on Bond Street, strolled to White's for a glass of wine and a bite to eat. On arrival, he picked up *The Times* and appropriated a quiet table in the corner of the morning room, hoping the open newspaper would discourage anyone from joining him. He had important matters to attend to this Season, like selecting a wife—a well-bred young lady with the poise and the correct upbringing suitable for a marchioness, a society hostess and, one day, a duchess. His purpose in coming up to town in advance of the rest of the family was to make a decision about his bride-to-be and here was as good a place to plan his strategy as any.

After being served, he drank a little wine, took one bite of the cold beef and horseradish sandwich and then settled back into the chair, holding the paper but not actually reading. He'd written a list of names last night. Seven in all. He wasn't interested in a bride straight out of the schoolroom—his Marchioness would already have some town polish with, preferably, at least two

Seasons behind her. The highest families were in no hurry to marry off their daughters—they took their time and selected the very best husbands, usually with a view to allying with a powerful family. A huge dowry wasn't a prerequisite for his perfect bride; he was more concerned with their breeding and background as well as their conduct. These were essential qualities for a lady who would, at some time in the future, occupy the role of Duchess of Cheriton and give birth to the Eighth Duke.

Seven names were too many…he must cut his list to three or four ladies, then he could concentrate on making his final choice, but discreetly; it would not do to raise expectations in the ladies themselves or in society in general. He was under no illusion, imagining himself so perfect that any female would swoon at his feet. It was not conceit, but realism…any one of the ladies on his list would jump at the chance of marrying into the Beauchamps, one of the most powerful families in the land.

He lay down the paper, hooked one hand around the back of his neck and rubbed, sighing. He would be happy when it was all over and he could get on with his life. In his mind's eye he saw his future stretching ahead of him, and he felt…nothing. No excitement. No anticipation.

Unbidden, Liberty Lovejoy crept into his thoughts and he dismissed her with a silent oath. Wasn't it bad enough she had invaded his dreams last night…erotic, enchanting dreams that had him waking bathed in sweat and in a state of solid arousal? A woman such as Liberty Lovejoy had no place in his future—to marry well was his duty and his destiny, as it had been Father's. Dominic was fortunate that *he* had not been obliged to wed at eighteen as Father had done, when his own father was in failing health and worrying over the future of the Dukedom. *Father* had put aside any personal inclination by doing his duty and marrying Dominic's mother, the daughter of a marquess and the granddaughter of a duke. The current Duchess—his stepmother, Rosalind—might be the daughter of a soldier and the granddaughter of a silversmith, but that did not affect the aristocratic lineage of the Dukes of Cheriton.

At least Dominic was six and twenty and had some experience of life, but sometimes—although he would never admit as much, not to anyone—the responsibility lay heavy on his shoulders. Almost without conscious thought, he withdrew the list of names from his pocket, unfolded it and read the names. If he could cross off three names, that would make—

'Mind if I join you, old chap?'

Hurriedly, Dominic folded the list and shoved it back into his pocket. He looked up into the bright blue inquisitive gaze of Lord Redbridge and inwardly cursed. Of all men, it had to be Redbridge. One of Alex's friends, he was an inveterate gossip and Dominic could only hope he hadn't deciphered any of the names on his list. He smiled and gestured to the chair next to his, then reached for his sandwich and bit into it. His leisurely luncheon was about to change into a hurried repast.

Redbridge had no qualms in admitting he had recognised at least two of the names on that sheet of paper and proceeded to not only tease Dominic about its existence, but also badger him about the other names.

'There must have been half a dozen on there at least, Avon.' His eyes were alive with curiosity. 'You can tell me, you know. Soul of discretion and all that. It'd do you good to talk about it. Alex is always sayin' you're too buttoned up for your own good.'

Dominic knocked back what remained of his wine and stood up. 'Your imagination is running amok, as usual, Redbridge. Now, if you will excuse me…?'

Redbridge didn't take the hint. He stood, too, and exited the coffee room by Dominic's side. 'Are you thinking of getting leg-shackled then? Oh, my life— the ladies will be in a flutter! There'll be neither time nor attention for the rest of us poor sods once the word gets out…it'll all be about Lord Avon and his list!'

He nudged Dominic with a sharp elbow and grinned hugely. Dominic stifled the urge to grab his neckcloth and slowly choke the wretch. Instead, he halted and turned to face his companion. They were close to the front door of the club by now and Dominic was damned if he'd put up with the man's inane chatter all the way to his front door.

'I'll bid you good afternoon here, Redbridge. And I will repeat what I have already said—your conjecture over that list is entirely wrong. My sister arrives in town today and she asked me to list any ladies I can think of who came out in the past two Seasons, as she will not have made their acquaintance. The truth is as mundane as that. And if—' he thrust his face close to Redbridge's '—I happen to hear *any* rumours to the contrary, I shall know precisely whose door to knock upon. Are we clear?'

Redbridge's mouth drooped. 'Perfectly.'

Dominic pivoted on his heel and strode for the door, anger driving him to reach home in record time. He barged through the front door of his leased town house, his temper frayed and his nerves on edge. He knew better than to believe Redbridge would keep such a juicy morsel to himself. Half the *ton* thrived on gossip and this, he knew, would be avidly passed from mouth to mouth. He would have to tread very carefully indeed not to reveal any preference for any of the many eligible ladies in town, but at least there were now two names he could cross off his list—the two Redbridge had read. Dominic would avoid those two as he would avoid a rabid dog and concentrate his efforts on the remaining five.

'Brailsford?'

'My lord?'

His man, who fulfilled the roles of valet, butler and footman in his bachelor household, appeared like magic from the kitchen stairs.

'Send word to the mews for my curricle to be ready for three-thirty. I intend to drive in the Park.'

'Will you require Ted to accompany you, sir?'

'Yes.' He would need a groom up behind if any of the five ladies were in the Park: to hold the horses if he got out to walk or to add propriety if he took one into his curricle to drive her around the Park. He felt heavy…his heart a leaden weight in his chest. But this was his duty; his destiny. And he would not allow himself to shirk it.

At three-forty, Dominic steered his matched bays into the Park and sent them along the carriageway at a smart trot. Ted perched behind him on the back of the curricle, ready to take charge of Beau and Buck if needs be. As Dominic drove, he scanned the walkers they passed and the small knots of people who had gathered to exchange the latest on-dits. The Season was not fully underway and wouldn't be until after Easter, but many families were already in town to attend to essential dress fittings and other preparations. He eased his horses back to a walk as he spied Lady Caroline Warnock in a stationery barouche, next to her mother, the Marchioness of Druffield. A couple they had been talking to had just walked away as Dominic drew his curricle alongside and raised his hat.

'Good afternoon, ladies.'

'Good afternoon, sir.'

Lady Druffield honoured him with a regal smile as her daughter bowed her head, her own smile gentle and gracious.

'Good afternoon, Lord Avon,' Caroline said. 'A pleasant afternoon for a drive, is it not?'

'Very pleasant, following yesterday's thunderstorm.'

A delicate shudder passed through Caroline. 'I do not care for the loud bangs or the lightning.'

Lady Druffield patted Caroline's hand. 'Such things are bound to play havoc with your sensibilities, my dear. As they would with any lady.'

Unbidden, yet again, an image of Liberty Lovejoy surfaced. *She* had not been undone by a mere thunderstorm. He could not imagine Lady Caroline standing under a dripping umbrella, nor dodging around a determined footman. He bit back a smile at the memory and he couldn't resist a gentle challenge.

'But there is something delightfully elemental about a good storm, is there not?'

He raised an eyebrow at Caroline, whose serene expression did not waver.

'Of course, my lord. You are so right—a good storm can be most exciting.'

Lady Druffield nodded in approval at her daughter's response, but impatience already plagued Dominic. He was so easily bored by this sort of dance with words…

talking about nothing…being polite and mannerly… and females who hung upon and agreed with every word he uttered. But it was the game they all played, him included. And it was not Caroline's fault—she had been raised to be the perfect lady and that was what he wanted. Wasn't it?

'It is an age since we last met, sir,' Caroline said. 'Was it at…?'

She hesitated, her head tipped to one side, a smile hovering around her lips and her fine brows arched. Dominic complied readily with her hint…it would be unladylike for Caroline to admit she recalled their last meeting but he, as a gentleman, was expected to re-member the exact place and circumstances.

'It was at Lord Silverdale's house party in February, if memory serves me correctly, my lady.'

'Ah, yes, indeed.' Caroline settled her dark brown gaze on his face.

'I am delighted to renew our acquaintance,' said Dominic.

Caroline smiled and her lashes swept low as she cast her gaze to her lap, where her hands rested in tranquil repose. 'As am I.'

He might as well begin his campaign. 'Would you care to take a turn around the Park in my curricle, Lady Caroline? With your mother's permission, of course.'

Another gracious smile. Not once had she revealed her teeth. Nor had any of those smiles reached her eyes. He wondered if she might show a little more life out of earshot of Lady Druffield. Dominic directed his most charming smile at that lady.

'But of course. It will be perfectly proper with the groom up behind, Caroline. And I can trust His Lordship to remain in the Park…he will take every care of you, I make no doubt.'

Dominic tied off the reins while Ted ran to the horses' heads, enabling Dominic to climb from the curricle and assist Lady Caroline from the barouche and into his curricle. Then he leapt aboard.

'I will deliver her back to you safe and sound, my lady.' He gave Beau and Buck the office to proceed and they set off at a trot, the vehicle dipping as Ted sprang up behind.

The first person Dominic saw was Liberty Lovejoy. From the direction of her purposeful stride he could only surmise she had been heading straight for him, presumably with the intention of interrupting him despite the fact he was already engaged in conversation. He did not slow his horses. He had nothing to tell her, in any case, because—and guilt coiled in his gut—he had been putting off his promise to speak to Alex. He hadn't forgotten it—he hadn't been *able* to forget it because, since she had erupted precipitously into his life yesterday, he had been quite unable to banish Miss Liberty Lovejoy from his mind.

Liberty's accusing gaze pierced him as the curricle drew level with her and she raised her hand, as though to stop them. Dominic tipped his hat to her, but did not slow. There was nothing to say and he did not want to say it in front of Caroline.

'That lady looked as though she wanted to speak with you,' said Caroline, looking over her shoulder at Liberty. 'I do not believe I have made her acquaintance… is she someone?'

Someone. Dominic held back his snort. What did that even mean? Well, he knew what it meant, but it did not stop him disliking that too widely held presumption that only 'their' sort of people were anyone.

'She is the new Earl of Wendover's sister.'

'Oh. I see.' Those three words were sufficient to convey Caroline's opinion. 'Mama warned me to be wary of his sisters. She said they are not really our sort of people. How do you know her?'

'I do not know her.' Officially, her visit to Beauchamp House had never taken place and Dominic had never met either Liberty or her sister. Their transgression of the rules would not become common knowledge through him. 'I know her identity because my brother is friendly with Wendover.'

'I see.' Caroline folded her hands on her lap. 'I wonder what she wanted to speak to you about.'

'I doubt very much she wanted to speak to me. I am certain you are mistaken.'

'Yes, of course. That must be it.'

As luck would have it, two of the other ladies whose names were on Dominic's list—Lady Amelia Carstairs and Lady Georgiana Buckleigh—were promenading that afternoon so, after delivering Caroline back to her mother, he endured two further circuits of the Park. Not one of the three put a foot wrong or spoke a word out of place. He should be thrilled. Any one of them would be the perfect wife for him. There was little to distinguish between them so far and once he had also renewed his acquaintance with Lady Sarah Patcham and Lady Sybilla Gratton, he would decide which one of them to concentrate on. Then, as soon as his father arrived in London, Dominic would make his offer.

Two days later Liberty stood to one side of the Trents' crowded salon with Mrs Mount, and plied her fan, sipping from the wine glass in her other hand. Although the weather was chilly the number of people packed into the modestly sized room for the rout party, combined with the heat from dozens of candles, made the room insufferably hot and stuffy. And the tightness of her corset wasn't helping, she silently admitted. When she had dressed for the rout in the least outmoded of her evening gowns, it had proved a touch too snug across the bosom, and so she had donned her sturdiest corset and ordered Lizzie—the maid she shared with Hope and Verity—to lace it as tightly as she possibly could in order to ease the fit of the dress. Now the disadvantage of that was becoming clear as her breathing grew shallower.

To distract herself from her increasing discomfort, she focused her attention on her sisters—so charming and pretty, their golden hair shining with health—and she watched with pleasure as young gentlemen vied with one another for their attention. They weren't bad girls, just a little thoughtless at times, and she knew her tendency to take charge made it easy for them to leave any difficult or awkward matters to her.

Gideon, of course, had declined to escort them and his valet, Rudge, had confirmed his master's intention to visit the Sans Pareil Theatre once again, causing dismay to ripple through Liberty. She feared she knew the attraction of that particular theatre, recalling how Gideon had waxed lyrical over a certain actress called Camilla Trace.

She leaned towards their chaperon.

'I am hopeful the girls will both attract offers before the Season is out, Mrs Mount.'

'Dear Hope and Verity…their popularity is unmistakable,' said Mrs Mount, 'but I must implore you not to risk a scandal with any more ill-advised visits, Liberty. I saw Lord Avon a few minutes ago and it seemed to me that, when he noticed you, he deliberately avoided this area of the room.'

'Avon is here?'

Her pulse kicked—surely just at the prospect of finding out if he had kept his promise? She'd spied him only once since her visit to Beauchamp House, in Hyde Park. She'd tried to catch his eye but, although he acknowledged her, he had driven his curricle straight past her.

'I wonder if he has spoken to his brother yet?' She craned her neck to try to see over the throng of people, but it was impossible. 'I shall go and ask—'

'No!' Mrs Mount caught hold of Liberty's hand, restraining her. 'Did you not hear what I said? Or perhaps you misunderstand the meaning of his action? He *turned away* when he saw you. You *cannot* approach him. He is the most eligible bachelor in the *ton*. Eyes follow him wherever he goes and tongues will always find stories to spread about him. Merely to approach him is unthinkable and if he were to *cut* you…oh, my dear, the tales would spread like wildfire and they would scorch your sisters' reputations in the telling. The gossip columns in the newssheets would not spare your blushes— the upstart twin of the new Earl of Wendover making an overt play for the Marquess of Avon…oh, heavens!' She plied her own fan vigorously to ruddy cheeks. 'Do you not understand? Your situation renders it even more imperative that your conduct is above reproach.'

Anger smouldered inside Liberty, heating her still further, and she felt as though she had a furnace inside her. She drank more wine and then tugged discreetly at her neckline in a vain attempt to allow some cooling air to reach her skin. Each breath she drew seemed shallower than the one before.

'But I am not interested in Lord Avon in the way you imply,' she said. 'You know I am not. I am concerned only about Gideon and I wish to know if Avon has spoken to his rascally brother yet.'

'I know, my dear.' Mrs Mount patted Liberty's hand without loosening her grip upon it. 'But you can do nothing about it until he decides to tell you. And he will *not* do so here—he will no more risk awakening speculation by singling out an unattached female than he would strip off his jacket and cavort about in his shirtsleeves. Proper conduct is everything to His Lordship, particularly this Season, if that rumour is true.'

'Rumour? What rumour?' Despite her dire need for fresh air, or a chair to sit on, or both, Liberty was distracted by this titbit.

'It is said that he has compiled a shortlist of eligible young ladies who meet the standards he has set— breeding, upbringing, ladylike conduct—and that he will make his selection before the end of the Season.'

The hushed awe of Mrs Mount's words stirred resentment inside Liberty. No wonder Avon was so top-lofty with people hanging upon his every word and treating him like some kind of god.

'A shortlist? I presume you mean for a wife. Why on earth does he need a *shortlist*?'

'Avon's bride must possess the very best bloodlines, perfect manners and be of exemplary character. Only the best will do for a man in his position and to be the mother of a future duke.'

The suppressed excitement in Mrs Mount's voice irritated Liberty even more.

'You make the poor girl sound like a glorified brood mare,' she muttered.

Really! Had people nothing more to worry about? What about all the poverty in London? Children in rags living on the street while their so-called betters lived in luxury. People like Avon were in a position to help and yet, instead of helping those worse off than him, he put his time and effort into making pathetic *lists* in order that any bride he might choose was *worthy* of him.

'So you do see why it is imperative that you do not put a foot wrong in any further contact with His Lordship, do you not, Liberty?' Mrs Mount's anxious enquiry brought Liberty's attention back to her. 'Not so much for your sake, but for Hope and for Verity.'

'You are not suggesting that His Lordship might consider—'

'It is unlikely, my dear, but…one never can tell what might happen when a pretty girl catches a gentleman's eye. Avon is expected to look much higher for his bride—at the very *least* the daughter of an earl—and she will be a young lady who has been properly prepared from childhood for her role as the wife of a peer of the realm. But your sisters, especially dear Verity, are so very pretty—one never knows what might happen. A list may always be added to.'

Mrs Mount's voice appeared to fade. Goodness, it was so hot. Liberty plied her fan with renewed vigour as she stared at her chaperon's mouth, concentrating fiercely in order to make out her words.

'And the lucky young lady of his choice will be a future duchess. It is worth keeping our hopes alive for such high stakes.'

Liberty put a hand to her forehead. The room seemed

to sway and she was aware of Mrs Mount staring anxiously at her.

'Liberty? My dear? Are you quite well? Oh, dear.' Mrs Mount clutched at Liberty's arm. 'Are you sickening for something? Do you need to leave? Only, it would be such a shame...'

Liberty gritted her teeth in a desperate attempt to remain upright. She thrust her empty wine glass at Mrs Mount. 'I am not sickening for anything. I need air. Watch the girls, will you, Mrs Mount?' Desperate now to get out of the room, she headed in the direction of the door, weaving in and out of the chattering groups of strangers, until her way was blocked by a tall figure with a pair of wide shoulders in a dark blue swallowtail coat. To either side of those shoulders were people, pressed closely, clearly hanging on every word uttered by the gentleman. Liberty screwed her eyes shut, wafted her fan over her heated skin, sucked desperately at the stale air, then opened her eyes and prepared to negotiate her way around the group, for it was obvious she could not barge through the middle of them. She shuffled sideways until she spied a gap. Perspiration now dampened her forehead and she could feel it gather on her chest and trickle into the valley between her breasts. She frowned, concentrating on placing one foot in front of the other as she edged through that gap. She was close to the door now—she could see it above people's heads—and she blindly aimed for it, desperate now to get away from this crush of people.

'Well! Of all the—'

'I say! That was my foot!'

'I'm sorry.' The words came on a gasp. 'I cannot—' Horror filled her as her knees buckled.

A strong arm encircled her waist from behind. A deep voice barked, 'Stand aside. She's swooned.'

She desperately wanted to deny it—she had never swooned in her life—but all she could manage was to turn into that embrace, her head tipping forward until her forehead rested against a solid chest. She breathed in a clean smell of soap and starch, mixed with a pleasing masculine scent.

Then she knew no more.

Chapter Five

Dominic stared in disbelief at the swooning woman in his arms, her head tipped into his chest. How in hell had this happened? He tightened his hold around her as she sagged. There was no other word for it—her head lolled back on her neck and he was certain her legs were no longer supporting her. He tightened his arms again, instinctively taking note of her womanly curves and her soft flesh.

He peered down into her face and recognition speared him. Miss Liberty Lovejoy. Her eyes were closed, her golden lashes a feathery fan against her creamy skin; her cheeks were flushed pink; her lips... plump and rosy...parted to reveal small, white, even teeth. And the urge to press his mouth to hers took him completely by surprise.

He tore his gaze away and scanned the faces that surrounded the two of them, noting the various expressions.

Eager—they were the gossips! Disgruntled—the young ladies who aspired to his hand. Envious—the rakes and...well, more or less every male within touching distance, damn them. As if he would relinquish her to *their* tender mercies. Speculative—he would soon put a stop to *that*! And concerned...

He focused on the nearest of those faces. Lady Jane Colebrooke, whom Dominic had known since childhood. Jane's family were neighbours of the Beauchamps in Devonshire—she was a kind girl with not a spiteful bone in her body.

'Lady Jane, would you come with me, please? I shall need your assistance.'

He bent down and slid one arm behind Miss Lovejoy's knees and hefted her up into his arms, cradling her like a baby. He felt something inside his chest shift as her rose scent curled through his senses and his exasperation melted away. However much she had defied the conventions when she had called on him, he knew it was from love for her brother. His own family were large and loving and he could not condemn a woman who put her family first.

'Yes, of course, my lord.' Jane bent to scoop Liberty's reticule and fan from the floor.

Dominic headed for the door, slicing through the crowd which parted before him—like the Red Sea before Moses, he thought sardonically. Through the door and out on to the landing—the fingers of his left hand curving possessively around the soft warmth of her thigh. Jane kept pace with him and thankfully refrained from bombarding him with inane comments or pointless conjectures. Then the pitter-patter of footsteps behind them prompted a glance over his shoulder.

Just perfect!

Not the lady—presumably the Lovejoy girls' chaperon—he had seen Liberty with earlier, nor either of her sisters. Any one of those would be welcome at this moment. No, they were being pursued by two determined-looking young ladies, both of whom happened to be in Dominic's final five. He had little doubt that their reasons for following him had everything to do with currying his favour and absolutely nothing to do with a desire to help a stricken fellow guest. In fact, he had overheard Lady Amelia being particularly scathing about 'those common Lovejoy girls' earlier that evening.

At least with them here as well as Jane, I cannot be accused of compromising anyone.

A servant directed them to a small parlour.

'Send a maid to assist, if you please,' said Dominic, 'and tell her to bring a glass of water and smelling salts.'

He gently deposited Liberty on a sofa and Jane snatched an embroidered cushion from a nearby chair to tuck under her head while the other two hung back and stared, doing absolutely nothing to help.

'Lady Sarah!'

The Earl's daughter started. 'Y-yes, my lord?'

'If you have come to assist us, be so good as to fan Miss Lovejoy's face. She appears to have been overcome by the heat.'

Lady Sarah moved forward, but thrust her fan into Jane's hand. With a wry flick of her eyebrows at Dominic, Jane wafted the fan, the breeze lifting the curls on Liberty's forehead. Her colour was already less hectic, but Dominic's hand still twitched with the urge to touch her forehead and check her temperature. He curled his fingers into his palm and stepped back, yet he could not tear his gaze from her luscious figure. The fabric of her gown—the colour of spring leaves—moulded softly to every curve and hollow, revealing far more than it should: her rounded thighs; the soft swell of her belly; the narrow waist above generous hips; and above that…good Lord…those gorgeous, bountiful breasts…

Dominic quickly shifted his gaze to Liberty's face, uncomfortably aware of both Lady Sarah and Lady Amelia watching him closely.

Liberty's lashes fluttered and her lids slowly lifted to reveal two dazed eyes that gazed in confusion into his before flying open in horror. She struggled to sit and Dominic instinctively pressed her back down. Her skin was like warm silk, smooth and baby soft and he longed to caress…to explore…to taste… The hairs on his arms stirred as his nerve endings tingled and saliva flooded his mouth. Good God…how he wanted to—he buried that thought before it could surface.

'Lie still!'

She collapsed back at his barked command, eyes wide, and he snatched his hands away.

'Who should I request to attend to you, Miss Love-joy?'

'Mrs Mount.' Their eyes met and his heart thudded in his chest as his throat constricted. 'She is our chaperon. Thank you.'

She half-raised her hand and he began to reach for it before recalling their surroundings. Their witnesses.

'My Lord Avon, you may safely leave Miss Love-joy in our care.' Lady Amelia inserted herself grace-fully between Dominic and the sofa. 'This is no place for a gentleman.'

Our care?

He controlled his snort of derision—he'd seen pre-cious little care from either Amelia or Sarah—but he knew she was right. This was no place for him and Liberty *would* be safe in Jane's hands, he knew. Jane, still gently fanning, caught his eye and again flicked her brows at him, clearly sharing his cynical reaction.

'I have hartshorn here.' Lady Sarah, on his other side, reached into her reticule.

'Good. Good,' he said, retreating. 'Make sure she remains lying down. I shall send a footman to alert Mrs Mount. Jane, is there anything else you need?'

Both Amelia and Sarah shot resentful glances at Jane. Mentally, he scratched their names from his list although he would still pay them some attention, if only to divert the gossips from identifying the three names that remained.

'No, thank you,' said Jane. 'I am sure Miss Lovejoy will soon recover.'

Dominic strode for the door, every step between himself and all that temptation lifting a weight from his shoulders. He had purposely avoided her tonight. He had seen her across the room with a spare-framed woman in her mid-forties and he'd taken care to keep his distance—partly for propriety's sake, when they had not, officially, been introduced, and partly through guilt because he still had not fulfilled his promise to speak to Alex. And the reason for that, he knew, was because his innate cautiousness was screaming at him to keep his distance from Liberty Lovejoy. But, try as he might, he had been unable to entirely banish her from his thoughts and he knew he must remedy his failure as soon as possible.

For the first time he wondered if she had seen him, too, and had purposely swooned to force him to catch her. He cast a look over his shoulder. Eyes like midnight-blue velvet followed his progress from the room. No. He did not believe her swoon was faked—she hadn't even glanced his way as she stumbled blindly through the group that surrounded him and, if he was absolutely honest with himself, there had been half-a-dozen fellows closer to her than him, any one of whom could have caught her when she swooned.

Except… His jaw clenched as he reviewed his actions. He might not have consciously recognised her but, by the time she collapsed, his feet had already moved him to her side, putting *him* in the perfect position to catch her.

He paused outside the room, still thinking. His head began to throb. *Good grief…*he rubbed his temples. He hadn't even known she existed three days ago, but she'd been on his mind ever since and now here he was—the instant he saw her again—playing the hero like an eager young pup in the throes of first love. He scowled as he scanned the landing. All his life he had avoided any behaviour that might give rise to gossip or speculation. He had always been far too conscious of his position as his father's heir and the expectations he placed on himself.

He beckoned to the same footman he had spoken to before.

'Please find Mrs Mount and ask her to attend Miss Lovejoy in the parlour at her earliest convenience.'

He was damned if he'd take the message himself—the more distance he kept between himself and the Lovejoys the better.

The sooner I make good my promise and speak to Alex about her dratted brother, the better.

His enquiry as to Alex's whereabouts had elicited not only the information that his younger brother had taken a set of rooms at Albany, St James's, but also that he often frequented the Sans Pareil Theatre, on the Strand, in the company of a group of young noblemen, the new Earl of Wendover among them. He felt a twinge of envy at Alex's ability to make friends so easily—a trait that had somehow always eluded Dominic.

He returned to the salon. He had no particular urge to rejoin his earlier companions, but he must—he could not allow the other guests' last sight of him to be of him carrying a swooning female from the room. He made polite conversation for twenty minutes or so and, once he was confident enough people had noted his return, he took his leave.

Too restless to go home and prompted by the events of the evening, he headed for Sans Pareil in search of Alex, determined to discharge his promise to Liberty as soon as he possibly could. From the floor of the theatre he scanned the boxes, finally spotting his father's close friend, Lord Stanton and his wife, Felicity, Dominic's second cousin. He ran up the stairs and slid into a vacant seat behind them.

'Mind if I join you?'

Felicity's head whipped round and a huge smile lit her face. 'Dominic! Of course. We're delighted to see you. But you have missed the play, you know. There is only the farce left.' Her eyes twinkled. She knew very well that most people preferred the farce to the serious drama, which was why the theatres always showed the farce last in the programme.

'I'm not here to watch either—I'm looking for Alex. Have you seen him?'

Stanton leant forward, searching the pit below. He pointed. 'There he is,' he said, 'with Wolfe and Wendover.'

Felicity also leant forward. 'Wendover? Is that the new Earl? Oh, yes. I see—the man with the golden hair? I've never seen him before, although I have, of course, heard the gossip.' She settled back into her seat. 'Such a dreadful thing to happen—the previous Lord Wendover and his entire family perishing in that fire.' She shuddered. 'It's frightening.'

Stanton took her hand. 'Try not to think about it, Felicity Joy. You mustn't upset yourself.' Then he twisted in his seat to face Dominic and lowered his voice. 'The entire house was gutted, I hear. It is beyond repair. Wendover will have to rebuild.'

Was that why Liberty was so anxious about money? The knowledge that the family seat would need to be completely rebuilt?

'Have you heard how the fire started?'

'The bed hangings in the main bedchamber caught fire. Wendover and his lady were in bed. They didn't stand a chance—the house went up like a rocket, with all those dry old timbers to feed the flames.'

Dominic suppressed his own shudder. Fire…it was a terrifying prospect, and an ever-present danger with candles and lanterns supplying light and with open fires where an unwary soul might find their clothes catching alight and going up in flames. There were new innovations, with gas lighting now more common in London streets, but there was widespread distrust at the idea of employing the new technology in private homes.

Felicity looked at them, frowning. 'What are you two whispering about?' She narrowed her eyes at Stanton and shook her head. 'You should know better than to try to hide unpalatable truths from me, Richard.'

Her husband laughed. 'I wouldn't dare,' he said, with a wink at Dominic. 'But this is not hiding. It is *protecting*. You know the tragedy that occurred, but you do *not* need to know the details, my sweet.'

Felicity pouted, then smiled. 'You are right. As you so often are, my darling husband.'

A laugh rumbled in Richard's chest. 'If you believe that last remark, Dom, my boy, you do not know women. Or, more particularly, wives. We men might hold the titles, property and wealth, but, in a marriage, it is the wife who holds the power.' He captured Felicity's hands and kissed first one palm, then the other. 'My heart. Your hands.'

His smile confirmed his happiness at being in such thrall to Felicity and Dominic was happy for them. He was very fond of Felicity—they had worked together closely for years, supporting and funding Westfield, a school and asylum for orphans and destitute children— and he remembered only too well the traumas of the early months of Richard and Felicity's arranged marriage. Would he be so fortunate in his marriage of convenience? He mentally ran through his shortlist and doubts erupted. Not one of them, from his observations, had Felicity's kind heart and sincerity. He shifted uneasily in his seat and tried to quash those doubts.

I'm not looking for love. Nor for a comfortable wife. I want a lady suited to the position of a marchioness; someone with the perfect qualities to be a duchess in the future and capable of raising a son who will one day be a duke. Someone of whom my mother would approve and a daughter-in-law to make my father proud.

That had always been his destiny. From a young age, his mother had drummed into him his responsibility as his father's heir and his duty to marry a lady worthy of the future position as the Duchess of Cheriton. It was the price one paid when one was firstborn.

His situation was entirely different to that of the Stantons.

He dragged his thoughts away from his future marriage to concentrate on the reason he had come to the theatre. If he could set Miss Lovejoy's mind at rest about her brother, then hopefully he could move on with his plan without distraction.

Liberty's brother was easy to pick out in the auditorium below, with his hair the same shade as Hope's—a golden-blond colour, two shades lighter and much brighter than Liberty's dark honey hue. Dominic watched him. He was behaving much as every other young buck in the pit—whistling and calling at the hapless performers and, during those times the on-stage drama failed to hold his attention, boldly ogling the theatre boxes and any halfway pretty occupants. So far, no different to how most young men behaved when they were out with other young men and without the civilising influence of ladies to curtail their antics.

Alex, Dominic was interested to see, was more subdued—indeed, he looked almost bored, gazing in a desultory fashion at the surrounding boxes. He gave every impression of wishing he was anywhere but where he was. Whatever jinks the three young men were up to, Alex was not the ringleader.

Dominic leaned forward. 'What do you know of Wendover, Stan?'

'Not a great deal,' Stanton replied. 'A gentleman's son, but his mother was some sort of merchant's daughter. He attended Eton, but left Oxford early after his father died. He has three sisters and I've heard it was a financial struggle for them after their father's death. He's a lucky man, inheriting so unexpectedly. Why do you ask?'

'He and Alex were pally at Eton and I've been told that Alex is encouraging Wendover in some wild behaviour. I'm worried Alex will slip back into his old ways.'

'How old is Alex now?'

'Five and twenty. Old enough to know better.'

Alex had always been a difficult youth, but Dominic, and the rest of the family, had believed the worst of his wildness was in the past.

'I didn't even know Alex was in town,' said Stanton. 'I heard Wendover's new-found fortune has gone to his head and, looking at them now, I should say he is the instigator, not Alex or Wolfe. It is Wendover's first time on the town—he's bound to kick out. I shouldn't worry too much, Dominic.'

How perfect if Stanton was right and it was Gideon trying to lead Alex and Neville astray. Dominic would enjoy putting Liberty straight...although...there was still the effect of Wendover's behaviour on his sisters' reputations—they would face enough of a struggle to be accepted in society, with their maternal grandfather being in trade, without a rackety brother to further taint the family.

He stood. 'I'll go and talk to him, nevertheless. I think you are right, but it won't hurt to make certain.' He shook Stanton's outstretched hand and bent to kiss Felicity on the cheek.

Down on the floor of the theatre, he stood at the back until the end of the play, keeping a close watch on Alex, Neville and Wendover. As the audience began to leave, he moved to meet the three men.

Alex's eyes met his. A smile was swiftly masked.

'Dominic.' Alex nodded casually.

'Alex.' Dominic kept his nod just as casual. 'Why did you not let me know you were in town?'

He cringed inwardly as soon as he said the words. There was nothing he could have said more likely to provoke Alex into a fit of the sullens, as their aunt Cecily used to call them.

Alex shrugged. 'I don't need your permission to have some fun in my life, do I?'

Dominic bit back the urge to cuff his brother's ear as he might have done when they were lads.

'No, of course not. But if I'd known I could have let you know Olivia, Hugo and the twins arrived yesterday.'

They'd been due to arrive the day he'd met Liberty at Beauchamp House, but had delayed their journey a couple of days when one of the twins was poorly.

Alex's eyes lit up. 'Are they staying in Grosvenor Square?' Dominic nodded. 'Good. I'll call on them to-morrow.'

Dominic then turned to Neville Wolfe, a friend of Alex's since boyhood.

'Wolfe. How do you do? Are your family well?'

Neville grinned and shook Dominic's hand. 'Very well, Avon. Very well.'

Dominic shifted his attention to Gideon, Lord Wendover. Miss Liberty Lovejoy's twin brother. The family resemblance was strong—the same stubborn chin and the same blue eyes. He wondered idly if Wendover's irises were likewise flecked with gold before jerking back to the realisation that he was staring mindlessly at the man. He thrust out his hand.

'I don't believe we've met. I'm Avon… Alex's brother.'

Gideon shook Dominic's hand. 'Wendover. Good to meet you, Avon, but… I beg you will excuse me—I'm due backstage.'

His words slurred and Dominic could smell the gin on his breath, but at least neither Alex nor Wolfe appeared foxed. Gideon was quickly absorbed into the throng of people slowly shuffling out of the theatre.

Alex muttered a curse. 'I'll call on you tomorrow, Dom. I have to go now. C'mon, Nev.'

He followed Gideon but, as Neville began to move, Dominic grabbed his arm.

'Hold hard there, Wolfe.'

Neville halted, but looked pointedly at Dominic's hand on his sleeve. Dominic released his grip.

'Give me a moment,' he said. 'I just want to be sure he's safe.'

Understanding dawned on Neville's face. He'd been friends with Alex for a long time and had stood by him through difficult times and wild behaviour. 'There's nothing going on that need trouble you, Avon. We're tryin' to watch out for Gid, that's all. He's got the bit between his teeth—taken a fancy to Camilla Trace and we're trying to stop him doing anything stupid like promise to marry her when he's in his cups!'

Camilla Trace was a beautiful and popular actress currently appearing at the Sans Pareil.

'Is Alex in danger of following Wendover's path?' At Neville's startled expression, Dominic elaborated. 'I don't mean falling in love with an actress. I heard Wendover's getting in deep and I'm worried Alex might get drawn back into high-stakes games.'

'Don't worry, Alex won't lose sight of what's important to him—he values his horses too much to put his business in jeopardy.' Neville clapped Dominic on the shoulder. 'Leave it to me to watch him.'

Dominic watched the other man go, his brows knit in a frown. Neville Wolfe and Alex had been partners in crime throughout their youth—what if they *both* slipped back into their old ways? With neither Father nor Uncle Vernon in town, it was up to Dominic to keep Alex safe. So, while Alex and Neville watched over Gideon,

Dominic would watch over his brother. From a distance. Because one thing was certain—if Alex got wind of what Dominic was up to, he would just as likely dive headlong into any and every vice that presented itself to him. Simply to prove he was his own man.

Dominic sighed and made his way to the door into the backstage area. He entered and immediately spied a cloaked and hooded figure lurking in a doorway up ahead. He adjusted his grip on his ebony cane, which handily concealed a sword, but the figure did not move as he passed.

He'd taken two steps past before the scent of roses reached him, sending the hair on the back of his neck on end. He pivoted round to face...Miss Liberty Lovejoy.

Chapter Six

Liberty gasped as a vice-like grip encircled her upper arm. The thick wool of the cloak she wore did little to disguise the strength in those fingers. Heart pumping with fear, she raised her eyes to her assailant and the breath whooshed from her lungs.

'You scared me half to death. What are you doing here?'

Dominic did not answer. His fingers tightened, then he was dragging her with him, opening doors at random, muttering apologies, until he found an empty room. He whisked her inside and released her, pushing her to the far side of the small, cluttered space. A lamp illuminated the interior, revealing clothing strewn over a chair and brushes and pots of face powder and rouge scattered upon a table with a mirror fixed on the wall behind it—a mirror that reflected Dominic's furious expression as he glared at the back of Liberty's head.

She squared her shoulders and pivoted to face him. 'How dare you manhandle me?'

She strode for the door, but his hand covered hers on the handle before she could open it. She tugged her hand free and turned to face him, her back to the door.

He was close. Too close. And his expression had, some-how, transformed from fury into... Stillness. Focus. Like a cat waiting to pounce. Heat shimmered in those silvery eyes.

Liberty swallowed—hard—as her pulse hammered. His body was against hers, all unyielding muscle and spicy, musky, masculinity. Her stomach fluttered and liquid heat pooled in her core. She could not tear her gaze from his as he propped his hands against the door, one either side of her shoulders, pinning her. His scent surrounded her, sending waves of pure longing crash-ing through her—a feeling she hadn't experienced since Bernard had died. And just like that, she broke free of his spell. She shoved at his chest, ducked beneath one of his arms and stalked to the furthest corner of the room. Her breathing steadied the more distance she put between them...he remained by the door and did not follow her.

'What are you doing here?' He growled the ques-tion out.

Liberty elevated her nose. 'I asked you first.'

No doubt he is here to visit his amour. That's what gentlemen do, is it not? Keep company with lightskirts and actresses and the like?

And that's exactly what she feared Gideon was doing here now. Wasting his time and his money on an actress when he should be thinking about securing his new po-sition as a peer. He would need an heir. He wouldn't meet a suitable wife backstage at a theatre!

'I am a man. I can do as I please. My reputation is not at stake.'

'And *my* reputation matters not when it comes to my brother's well-being.'

His narrowed gaze pierced her. '*Your* reputation

might be of little consequence to you, but what about your sisters' reputations?'

'What of them?'

'If you are seen, not only will *you* suffer, but your sisters will be irretrievably tainted. Is that really what you want?'

Her bravado was shrinking fast. She had been unable to settle after their return from the rout, so worried was she about what Gideon was up to. She had taken a calculated risk in coming here tonight, sneaking out of the house, persuading Bilk, their coachman, to drive her to the theatre by telling him that Gideon had asked her to meet him there, and entering such a place unescorted. A scandalously improper way for a lady to behave, but she had persuaded herself she would not be noticed.

Now, though, she was well and truly caught, and her disgrace would rebound on Hope and Verity if Lord Avon chose to reveal it.

But she refused to beg for his help again, not when he had failed to keep his earlier promise.

'Well, I *have* been seen now, so I have nothing left to lose, have I?' She dipped a curtsy, intending the gesture to be ironic. 'If it is your intention to expose my conduct, I cannot stop you. If it is not, then please allow me to leave so I can find Gideon.'

His lips firmed. 'You asked why I am here. I shall tell you. I have come to see what your brother is up to and to ensure that his bad example does not corrupt my own brother.'

'Oh! That is outrageous! It is *your* brother leading mine astray.'

He raised one brow, making her itch to slap him. Smug, superior know-it-all.

'I hate to contradict a lady, but my observations thus far indicate the exact opposite.'

Their gazes remained locked for several fraught seconds until Dominic's shoulders relaxed and one corner of his lips—his beautifully shaped mobile, enticing lips—lifted.

'Liberty—'

She opened her mouth to object, but held her silence when he raised his hand, palm forward.

'It is shocking for me to call you Liberty, but acceptable for you to wander alone backstage at a theatre?'

His lips twitched. They really were fascinating lips. What would it be like to kiss him? To feel his lips moving over hers? His tongue in her mouth, sliding against hers?

Oh, dear God. Forget scandalous. I am utterly depraved.

She moistened her dry lips. His eyes darkened. A pulse in her neck fluttered wildly and, without volition, she pressed shaking fingers to it. A vain attempt to suppress it? Then his gaze lowered and her nipples peaked in immediate response. She swallowed again and tugged at the edges of her cloak, pulling it across her chest in a defensive gesture.

Dominic hauled in an audible breath, his broad chest swelling and then deflating again as he released his breath.

'Let us begin again, Miss Lovejoy.'

His tone meant business. His very stance meant business. Despite herself, Liberty paid attention. This was not a man to defy, not in this mood.

'I am here at this theatre to see what *both* of our brothers are up to.'

Despite herself, she rather liked that—it was nice to

have someone on her side, someone to rely on, if only for a short while. Although she would die before she admitted it to him.

'How did you know they would be here?'

'I asked the servants. They tend to know everything, you know—they seem to have their own methods of finding things out and of spreading the word. You would do well to remember that.'

Her thoughts flew to Bilk. She had sworn him to secrecy, but could she trust him? Liberty bit back her doubts. It was too late now. Unconsciously, she raised her chin.

'Continue,' she said.

Drat him. There was that barely concealed smirk again.

'I have spoken with all three of them—my own brother and Mr Wolfe are watching over your brother to ensure he does nothing...stupid.'

'Stupid? Like...what?'

'Like making rash promises.'

Liberty pondered his words. 'Promises? To whom?' They were in a theatre...that must mean... 'As in... promises of marriage? Offers? Oh, dear God.'

She rushed for the door, but Dominic grabbed her arm as she brushed past him. Liberty struggled to free herself.

'Let me go! You mean one of these floozies, don't you? A common actress. I have to stop him.'

A tug unbalanced her and suddenly she was in his arms, held for the second time that night against the solid comfort of his chest. She felt herself relax into him, despite her panic over Gideon. It felt good, to feel a man's arms around her, to feel protected, even if for a split second.

'You can do nothing.' His voice rumbled in his chest, vibrating through her. He gripped her shoulders and set her away from him, gazing down at her. 'Gideon will heed his friends' advice and opinions more readily than that of his sister. Leave it to us.'

'Leave it to the men, you mean. You think because I am a female that my opinions count for nothing.'

That infuriating brow rose once again. 'I think that because you are his sister, your opinions will simply drive him into contrary behaviour. Take my advice, Miss Lovejoy. Use your time wisely and channel your energies into finding respectable husbands for yourself and your sisters.'

'I do not seek a husband for myself,' she muttered. Pride would not allow her to admit her private dream of finding love again. Especially to him.

'Then concentrate on your sisters' futures, if that is the case. Leave your brother to me. It is all under control.'

She raised her gaze to his. Those silvery eyes shone like polished steel. She could see herself reflected in them, but she could read nothing of the man within. They were like a mirror. What secrets did he hide? Or maybe he had none. Maybe he was exactly what he appeared to be—a handsome, straitlaced nobleman who never succumbed to spontaneity and always behaved with utmost propriety, as Mrs Mount had said.

'Why should I put my trust in you? What do *you* care what Gideon does?'

'I shall keep my eye on your brother simply to ensure Alex does not follow him into reckless behaviour and harmful habits.'

'But you are not watching him now. You are here with me.'

'That is true, but I happen to know both Alex and Mr Wolfe are with Gideon so he is in no imminent danger of making a complete cake of himself. Now, will you allow me to escort you home, Miss Lovejoy?'

'There is no need. I shall take a hackney.'

Earlier, she'd had no qualms about how she would get home, anticipating that Gideon would feel honour-bound to escort her. Now, for the first time, she realised her predicament, but pride, again, forbade her from admitting as much to His Lordship.

His eyes narrowed. 'Refusal is not an option. *That* was not a question.'

'It sounded exactly like a question to me.'

A muscle leapt at the side of his jaw. 'I was being polite.'

'Be that as it may, I am in no need of your escort. Just think how your reputation will suffer if we are seen together.'

He sighed. 'I told you before that sarcasm does not become you, Miss Lovejoy. Your choice is twofold. Either you allow me to take you home. Now. Or you and I shall go and find your brother and see what he has to say about his twin sister snooping around the nether regions of a theatre. The choice is yours.'

'My lord… I have no wish to sound ungrateful, but you cannot simply order me around. Besides, I have no wish to disrupt your evening further than I already have.'

His sensual lips thinned into a firm line. He spun to face the door, grabbing Liberty's right hand as he did so. He drew it firmly between his left arm and his ribcage and then crooked his elbow, clamping her arm in place. He strode for the door and she found herself stumbling in his wake, unable to resist his strength.

'My lord… Avon! Stop!'

'No.' The word was gritted out. 'No more talk. Pull up your hood.' They left the room and he slammed to a halt. 'Do it,' he growled, 'or I'll do it for you. Unless you *want* to be recognised?'

The sight of a figure emerging from a nearby door spurred her to obey. She pulled up her hood, tugging it forward to cover her face and, without another word, Avon headed towards the rear of the theatre, towing Liberty behind him. She kept her gaze to the floor, avoiding eye contact with anyone they passed, then they were out of the door, into the chill night air, with rain-drops pitter-pattering on her hood and, when she risked glancing up, her face.

'Keep moving and don't look at anyone,' Dominic muttered. 'Maiden Lane is no place for a lady.'

He walked briskly, rounded a corner and then an-other, and she recognised the Strand and the front of the theatre, where a town coach and pair waited, a coach-man at the horses' heads. The waiting man whisked sacking from the horses' backs as Liberty found herself bundled unceremoniously into the vehicle. Avon leaned inside as she perched on the edge of the seat.

'Where do you live?'

'Green Street.'

He withdrew and she heard him call, 'Webster. Green Street, please.'

The carriage dipped as Dominic climbed inside. He stripped off his gloves and hat and cast them on to the opposite seat before settling next to her, his hip and thigh touching hers. She inched away from him, until her own hip was pressed against the padded side of the coach, still stiffly upright, wondering how it had hap-pened that she had been removed from the theatre with-out catching even one glimpse of Gideon or discovering what he was up to. And how she was now in a carriage, alone with a man she barely knew.

'I presume you have fully recovered from your swoon earlier tonight?'

'Yes, thank you.' It infuriated her that he'd seen her behave in such a feeble way. 'I do not make a habit of swooning. It was excessively stuffy in that room.'

'It was.' His amused tone set her hackles to rise. 'I did not, however, notice any other ladies swoon.'

She had no answer to that. It was true. And the episode had undermined her determination to have only one new gown made. She had no choice now. She would need more. She only hoped Gideon could afford it.

'How can I be sure Gideon is safe?'

'You cannot be sure. Not completely. But you have to understand there is nothing you can do. You are a female. You simply *cannot* follow him around to spy on him. Perhaps you should instead learn to trust him? And besides—' Dominic swivelled on the seat to face her '—tell me truthfully. What exactly did you intend to do if you caught Gideon behaving recklessly?'

'I… I do not know, for certain. I suppose I would try to persuade him to leave and to return home with me.'

'I see.'

The simple scepticism in those two words spoke volumes. In the silence that followed Liberty began to realise the futility of her plan—what *had* she thought she might achieve?

'And your chance of success would be?'

Liberty slumped back against the squabs.

'Very well. You are right. He would refuse. We would argue.'

'And the result would be that the distance you spoke of between you and your brother would widen further.'

That was the last thing she wanted. She missed sharing things...*life*...with Gideon; missed having him to lean on; she missed his company. And she was terrified he would make some drastic mistake and blight his life. She rubbed at her aching chest while the guilt lay heavy in her stomach. She had failed Bernard and her parents. She could not fail Gideon, too.

Dominic faced forward again, folding his arms across his chest. Liberty waited for the 'I told you so' or 'How could you be so stupid?', but no recriminations were forthcoming. After several excruciating minutes of silent self-recrimination, she exhaled sharply.

'I am sorry.'

He cocked his head. 'Sorry for what?'

'My behaviour. I know it is not what is expected of a lady, but I—I could not go to bed and sleep without trying to do *something*.'

'I do understand. Gideon is your brother and your worry for him overrode everything else.' A long, quiet sigh escaped him. 'Lest you forget, I have a brother, too, and, although he is not as wild as he used to be, he is still not an easy man to understand or even, sometimes, to like.' He leaned forward, his forearms propped on his knees and his gaze on the floor. 'Our sister has been known to get herself into some difficult scrapes in an effort to protect Alex—often without regard for the consequences. In that respect you remind me of her.'

He looked at her. 'For the Beauchamps all that is in the past and Olivia is a respectable married lady now. If you will take my advice—concentrate your efforts on your sisters even if you have no wish for marriage yourself. I meant what I said earlier—if you bring disgrace upon yourself, your sisters will suffer. They will be tainted for life. You already start from a lowly position in society and there will be many who will relish any disgrace as it will reinforce their view that inferior breeding will out.'

Liberty bristled at being lectured. 'A view you yourself agree with, I am given to understand. I've heard you have a list of perfect ladies suitable for a future duke and that breeding comes right at the top of your requirements.'

'Only insofar as it affects my choice of bride,' he retorted. 'It is my duty as my father's heir to marry well, but I do not hold such views in general.'

'Because everyone below you is so far beneath your notice?'

She felt the full force of his stare. 'Not at all,' he said, stiffly. 'As it happens, I'm involved—'

Liberty waited, but he did not continue. 'You're involved…?'

'It is of no matter.'

He faced forward again and they lapsed into silence. Within a short time, Liberty felt shame creep through her. She had been unfair, needling him in that way. For all he was infuriating, he *had* been trying to help her.

She swivelled slightly so she could study him. She could just about make out his profile in the gloomy interior of the coach. As they passed the occasional street lamp, she could make out lines of strain running from his nose to his mouth.

'Do you really believe your brother can be trusted to bring Gideon back to his senses, my lord?'

He hooked one hand behind his neck, further obscuring her view of him. At first she thought he would not answer her, but then he abruptly released his neck and lowered his arm, shooting her a sidelong look.

'I believe so.' He twisted to face her then, and

touched her hand. '*You* may trust *me*, however. I shall keep an eye on both Alex *and* Gideon.'

And she did trust his word.

'Thank you. You are more generous than perhaps I deserve.'

His eyes glittered as they passed another street lamp. 'Generous?' He reached out, and touched her face with one finger, tracing her cheekbone, raising a shiver in its wake before he withdrew it. 'You needed help and I have been in a position to provide it.' His teeth gleamed as he smiled and her heart tumbled over. 'Twice. As I said, you remind me of my sister…oh, not in the way you look, but in that stubborn determination to make sure the people you love are safe. How could I not help?' He leaned forward, gazing out of the window. 'We are here. Green Street. Which house is it?'

'A little further along, on the left-hand side.'

She felt dazed. What had happened to the pompous lord she had met at Beauchamp House? Dominic rapped on the carriage ceiling and it halted. He climbed out, then turned to hand her out.

'Pull your hood up again,' he whispered. 'I will watch to see you safely inside the house, but I won't escort you to the door in case we are seen. I hope we are now agreed that your reputation is important, if only for the sake of your sisters.'

'Yes. Thank you again.'

His eyes gleamed briefly, then he raised her hand to his lips. 'You are most welcome, Miss Liberty Lovejoy.'

Chapter Seven

A sense of urgency—of events slipping out of his grasp—drove Dominic to head straight for home and for his sitting room.

'I shan't need you again tonight, Brailsford,' he said to his man. 'You get off to bed.'

'Can I fetch you something to eat before I go, milord?'

Dominic consulted his gut. 'No. I'm not hungry.' Actually, he felt a little nauseous…sort of uneasy…a churning, unsettling sensation. Apprehension, that was it. Well, it was hardly surprising when he was about to make such a momentous decision. 'But you may pour me a brandy before you go, if you would.'

Dominic crossed the room to his writing desk and, opening a drawer, he extracted a sheet of paper. He had no real need of the list—the names that remained were indelibly inscribed into his memory. There was no chance he would forget any of them. But he nevertheless carried the list over to his favourite chair—a deeply buttoned green-leather-upholstered wing chair—and waited while Brailsford poured a glass of brandy, set it on the small table next to his chair and stirred the slumbering fire into life before refuelling it. Dominic did not look at the list until the door had shut behind Brailsford, then he scanned the names before steadily working his way through them again, from the first name to the fifth. Amelia and Sarah, of course, he had taken against, leaving three. For each name—Caroline, Georgiana and Sybilla—he conjured forth a mental image of the lady in question, mentally reviewing what he knew of each one: her family connections, her qualities, her conduct. Any one of them would be suitable for the Marchioness of Avon, and for the future Duchess of Cheriton, although he hoped that last would not be for a very long time. No one lady stood out among the others, but Georgiana was, he knew, afraid of horses. Did he want a wife who was afraid of horses? And Sybilla wasn't even in town yet.

'Lady Caroline Warnock.'

He closed his eyes, recalling the sweet sound of her singing at a musical recital last Season. Her voice had raised the hairs on his arms. He opened his eyes again and mentally shrugged. She had a beautiful singing voice. It was as good a reason as any. Her attitude towards Liberty the other day had irritated him, but it was, he knew, no different to the attitude of many in the *ton* to those whom they considered of inferior breeding and upbringing. That was settled, then. Although no one but he would know—he would pay equal attention to all five original names but, as soon as Father came up from Devonshire, Dominic would make his offer. He did not doubt Caroline would welcome an offer from him—she had been raised with a view to taking her place as the wife of a high-ranking aristocrat.

The sound of the door opening disturbed his thoughts.

'I told Brailsford to leave me to find my own way.'

Alex sauntered across to the brandy decanter and poured himself a generous glassful. 'You don't mind, do you?' He raised the glass as he wandered across to the fireplace and sat in the matching wing-back chair set on the opposite side to Dominic's.

'Be my guest. Oh. Wait. You already have.' Dominic reached for his own glass, raised it in a silent toast to his brother, drank, then returned it to the side table. He placed his list next to the glass before eyeing Alex. 'I didn't expect to see you again tonight. To what do I owe this pleasure?'

'My insatiable curiosity. Saw you leaving the back door of the theatre with a woman and, if my eyes weren't deceiving me, it was Wendover's twin sister—the interfering and irritating Liberty.'

Dominic frowned. 'I didn't think you'd seen us. And I didn't know the two of you had even met.'

'We haven't…but I've seen her from afar and I recognised her, before she pulled up her hood. That description, by the by, is verbatim from her ever-loving brother.'

Sympathy for Liberty bloomed in Dominic's chest. He drank some brandy then shifted in his chair, unsettled, staring into his glass as he swirled the amber liquid around. He'd come in here determined to finalise his future and to forget Miss Liberty Lovejoy and now here was Alex, stirring up her presence all over again.

'So I was right. It was her.'

The softly spoken comment jerked Dominic from his thoughts. He looked up to find Alex watching him with a knowing look.

'Is she the reason you came to the theatre? What were the pair of you doing backstage?'

Dominic tilted his glass and drank again, considering. Then he set his glass down again and steepled his fingers in front of his mouth, his joined forefingers resting against his lips.

'It was coincidence. But I do know she is worried about her brother. I saw her there and I persuaded her to leave. That is it.' This subject needed changing. 'More importantly, what are you up to with Wendover? You're not slipping back into old habits, are you?'

'No.' Alex sipped his brandy. 'Lucky for you it was me that saw you.'

Silently damning his brother's tenacity, Dominic asked, 'What d'you mean?'

Alex's eyes gleamed, crinkling at the corners. He was unmistakably a Beauchamp, but he was the only one of the three children who had inherited their late mother's colouring—thick mahogany brown hair and golden-brown eyes that always reminded Dominic of a tiger he had seen at the Exeter Exchange when he was a boy. Now, those eyes mocked Dominic, whose jaw clenched.

'Careful you don't get caught, that's all,' Alex drawled. 'I doubt the luscious Liberty would tick many of the qualities on the list of the perfect bride for the perfect heir.'

Alex left his chair in one fluid motion and, before Dominic realised his intention, he snatched the list from the table. Dominic surged to his feet.

'Alex!'

Alex spun away and scanned the names. Then he thrust the paper at Dominic and subsided back into his chair. Gritting his teeth, Dominic folded the list and put it in his pocket before sitting back down, steeling himself for the ribbing he sensed was coming his way.

'I was hoping the existence of that list was a daft rumour.' Alex recited the five names, his voice soft and almost sorrowful. '*Really*, Dom? They're the best you can conjure up?'

'What are you talking about, you numbskull? They come from the very best families in England and every one of them has been properly raised and educated to take her place in society and to be the perfect choice for a nobleman's wife.'

Alex drained his glass and went to refill it, and topped up Dominic's while he was up.

'There's not one of 'em with an ounce of warmth or spark,' he said once he regained his seat. 'Yes, they're perfect ladies, but they're so icy and correct they can freeze a fellow with just one look.'

'Alex…you know I have always planned to marry a lady worthy of being a future duchess. I need to choose my bride carefully.'

Alex simply held Dominic's gaze.

Goaded, Dominic said, 'I never took *you* for a romantic. I should have thought you would approve of marriages of convenience.'

'This isn't about me. It's about you.' Alex scrubbed his hand through his hair, a slight flush washing across his cheeks. 'You always seem so…alone, somehow. I don't want to see you alone in your marriage as well,' he added, his voice gruff.

Dominic stared at his brother. How unlike Alex to trouble himself over someone else, even a member of the family. That thought unsettled him far more than Alex's words and he shifted uncomfortably in his chair.

'Do you remember Liv and I used to call you Lord Earnest after…after…?'

'I remember.' Dominic knew he meant after their mother's death, but they never talked about it. Ever.

He supposed they'd been too young to fully understand what had happened at the time and it had become something of an unwritten rule. He couldn't even remember his father or Aunt Cecily really mentioning it, except as a fact. They had never *talked* about it. 'Someone had to be the responsible one. I am the eldest…it was my duty to help keep you and Livvy out of trouble, as it is my duty to marry well.'

'You take care that sense of duty don't choke you, Brother.' Alex sipped again at his brandy. 'I look at you sometimes, Dom, and all I see is the perfect heir to the Duke of Cheriton—the man you present to the world. And I wonder about the man inside and about *his* dreams and desires.'

Dominic's heart pounded uncomfortably. 'You're talking utter rubbish.'

His brother might be a year his junior—and he might have spent his youth bouncing from one scrape to another—but there were times when he appeared much, much older than his years. It was all right for Alex…*he* wasn't burdened by the weight of duty and expectation. *He* wasn't the heir.

Dominic had never questioned that duty—it was the way of their world. He was destined to follow the example set by his father, when he had married their mother for the good of the Dukedom.

'The family have it all wrong, Dom. They've spent years fretting about me, watching over me. But it's *you* they should be worrying about. I don't believe any of those women will make you happy. You are allowed to be happy, you know.'

Dominic stared at his brother as those words sank in, stirring unfamiliar feelings that, somehow, tightened his throat until it felt as though he had tried to swallow a lump of dry bread. He was not used to this sombre and, somehow, sorrowful version of Alex; where was his devil-may-care brother who took mockery to new heights?

He thrust down the unfamiliar surge of emotion and unclenched his jaw. Never would he reveal how that simple comment had reached deep inside him and wrenched at his soul. He drew in a deep breath before forcing a hearty laugh.

'All this is an excellent ruse, Alex, but you won't divert me that easily.'

Alex shrugged. 'Not trying to divert anyone. Just telling it as I see it.'

Dominic straightened his spine, now thoroughly irritated with himself for succumbing to Alex's mood and allowing him to raise doubts in his mind. 'I spoke to Wolfe earlier.'

Alex's eyes narrowed. 'He said.'

'What's your game with Wendover? Tell me you're not getting in too deep. Is everything truly all right?'

'Why wouldn't it be?'

'Alex...'

Alex's eyes glittered. He tossed back his brandy and rose to his feet. 'Worry about your own future. Not mine. *One* day maybe my family will see me as something other than a boy looking for trouble. 'Night, Avon.'

Dominic sat for a long time after Alexander left, that same nervy apprehension churning his stomach relentlessly even as he reassured himself that Alex didn't have a damned clue what he was talking about.

The following morning, Dominic called at Beauchamp House, to take his brother-in-law, Hugo, to Jackson's boxing saloon for a sparring session. It was Olivia and Hugo's first visit to London for the Season since the birth of their two-year-old twins, Julius and Daisy, and he found them waiting for him in the first-floor salon. After greeting Olivia with a kiss, Dominic said, 'Ready to go, Hugo? We'll soon get you back in condition.' He jabbed at Hugo's abdomen. 'Seems to me you've gone soft since you married.'

Hugo laughed, but Olivia leapt to his defence. 'He has not gone soft, Dominic! I'll have you know—'

She stopped as the door opened again and Alex strolled in. Dominic's heart sank as their eyes met. Their conversation of the night before was unfinished and Alex, he knew, would have no hesitation in raising the subject in front of Olivia and Hugo.

'Alex!' Olivia flew across the room to embrace him. 'Oh, I am so happy to see you! *Why* have you not been to visit us for such an age?'

'Hey! Steady on, Sis! You near to knocked me flying— you're no slip of a girl nowadays, are you?' Alex held her away from him and looked her up and down, mischief glimmering in his eyes. 'But still as much a hoyden as ever.'

'Oh, do stop teasing, Alex.' She reached up to tidy her black hair, re-pinning it haphazardly. 'I'm a respectable matron now, don't you know.'

He grinned. 'I'll accept matron, but respectable?'

She punched his arm. 'I am a mother! Of course I am respectable!'

Alex kissed her cheek, then greeted Hugo and Dominic, who took the opportunity to suggest to Hugo it was time they left.

'Something I said, Brother?' said Alex. 'Or something I *might* say?'

Dominic shrugged. 'I thought you and Livvy would appreciate the chance to catch up.'

'Oh, we'll have plenty to talk about,' drawled Alex, casting himself down on the sofa. 'See you later, Dom. Don't take out *all* your frustrations on Hugo, will you?'

Dominic didn't trust himself to answer—not without causing an argument. He strode from the room and waited until he saw Hugo's tall form descending the stairs before he left the house and climbed into his carriage. Hugo settled by his side and the carriage moved off.

'Well?' he said eventually, unable to stomach the continuing silence. 'I suppose Alex told you?'

Hugo raised one dark eyebrow. 'That you intend to select a bride this Season? Yes, he did. Congratulations.'

'You might say that like you mean it.'

Hugo huffed a laugh. 'As if you care for my opinion. I warn you, though, Livvy is hell-bent on meeting the ladies on your list.'

He'd been afraid of that.

'I've warned her not to interfere, but I have no doubt you'll know her verdict once she's met them all.'

'No doubt.'

Silence fell, and Dominic gazed from the window as the carriage turned into New Bond Street, idly watching the people they passed. Then he stiffened as he caught sight of Ma Prinks, shabbily dressed as ever, carrying a wailing toddler. Dominic rapped on the ceiling and the carriage halted.

'What is it?' Hugo leaned over to peer out of the window.

'I know that woman and I know her game.'

Dominic leapt from the carriage and strode back towards Prinks, who halted the minute she saw Dominic, her scowl morphing into an ingratiating simper.

'You're a long way from your usual haunts, Ma. What are you up to?'

'Not up to nuffin, milor'. Just takin' my young nipper for a walk, see?'

Dominic studied the child, pale-skinned and red-haired, with puffed-up eyes and snot trailing from its nostrils, and then eyed Prinks's dark hair and swarthy face.

'Yours, is it?' It was impossible to tell the sex of the child.

'His pa was ginger.'

'I don't believe you, Ma. Are you up to your old tricks again?' He glanced at Hugo, standing by his side. 'Ma Prinks here has a talent for "finding" young 'uns and using them to gain sympathy and money from passers-by.'

'You never cease to amaze me by the company you keep, Avon,' drawled Hugo.

Dominic frowned as he noticed the interest of people passing them by. Fortunately, it was still before noon and most of the *haut ton* had not yet started to shop, but he had no wish to continue drawing attention.

'Did you think Bond Street might give you easy pickings, Ma?'

The woman snorted. 'So it would if certain nobs would keep their conks out of poor folks' business.'

'Did you steal him?'

'No! I never! 'Is ma's dead, in't she, and 'is father's nowhere to be found. I'm doin' him a favour, see? At least wi' me he'll get fed.'

Dominic held out his arms. 'Give him to me, Ma. I'll make sure he's cared for.'

'You got no right—'

'Hand him over, or I'll hand *you* over to the constables. I'm sure the magistrates will be even more interested than me to hear how you came by the boy.'

She thrust the child at Dominic, not even waiting until he had him securely before releasing him. 'Tek 'im,' she snarled. 'Plenty more where 'e came from.'

By the time Dominic had the boy in a secure hold, Ma Prinks was striding away. He sighed.

'She's right,' he said to Hugo. 'We do our bit at Westfield, but it simply isn't enough. There are just too many children.'

He led the way back to the carriage and, once inside, he looked down into the infant's face. Two blue eyes stared back. Then Dominic checked his limbs. Two arms. Two legs.

'At least this one appears unharmed. The last one she had was blind.' His heart clenched at the memory. '*Deliberately* blinded, to gain more sympathy and thus more alms. It's a filthy business.'

'That…' Hugo's voice choked. He cleared his throat. 'That is atrocious. He looks the same age as our twins. When I think…' Again, his voice failed him and he cleared his throat again. 'What now?'

'I'll take him straight out to Westfield. The Whittakers will take him in and then Peter will make enquiries just in case anyone *is* missing their child. I don't hold out much hope, though.' He smiled wryly at Hugo. 'Sorry. It looks like we'll have to postpone our session. But we can drop you off at Jackson's if you wish. I'm sure someone there will spar with you.'

'No.' Hugo's voice was thoughtful. 'I'd rather come with you, if you've no objection. I have a sudden urge to discover what it is you do at this school of yours.'

* * *

Three days later, Liberty sat with Mrs Mount at one end of Lord and Lady Twyford's ballroom, absorbing the gowns and the jewels, the elegant dancing and the smiling faces, tapping her foot in time to the music from the quartet sitting on the dais at the far end of the room and just…just…*enjoying* being there.

This was the first truly prestigious ball she and her sisters had been invited to attend, courtesy of the un-flagging efforts of Mrs Mount to inveigle invitations for the Lovejoy sisters who were indeed viewed as upstarts by many members of the *haut ton*. Liberty hoped and prayed this ball would be the first of many. It was her sisters' first opportunity to mingle with the highest in society and they had already proved a draw for several eligible gentlemen eager for introductions. Hope—her blue eyes shining with excitement—had been led out for the first dance by the youthful Lord Walsall and Verity's card was also full although Liberty would have preferred a less…seedy-looking partner for her youngest sister's first dance. The gentleman, who had been intro-duced by Lord Twyford himself as Lord Bridlington, looked forty if he looked a day and there was a gleam in his sleepy-lidded eyes as he leisurely inspected Ver-ity's person that Liberty could not quite like. Still, she consoled herself…it was just one dance.

Gideon and Lord Alexander Beauchamp were also gracing the ball with their presence which meant Lib-erty could relax and enjoy herself rather than fretting over what her twin was up to. The rules that governed high society, she had decided, were hopeless as far as females were concerned. Even *she* hesitated to follow Gideon to some of the haunts he frequented. But she had found an unlikely ally in Gideon's valet, who was as determined as Liberty to prevent his master from committing social suicide, and Rudge was proving a satisfactory spy, informing Liberty of Gideon's intended destination every evening. But every time Liberty was tempted to throw caution to the winds and follow Gideon, Dominic's words would echo in her memory.

It is your sisters who will suffer. They will be tainted for life.

She was infuriated at finding herself controlled by his words even in his absence but, because she knew him to be right, she could not disregard his warning. Nor had she found it easy to banish Dominic himself from her thoughts. For the first time since Bernard's death she was attracted to a man but, in a hopeless twist of fate, it was to a man who—although she could see he found her attractive in return—would never in a million years act upon that attraction. He was not only heir to a powerful duke, but he had set out a list of essential qualities for his perfect bride to help him make his choice. Liberty suppressed a snort. His choice, indeed. As if he just needed to snap his fingers and any female he selected would simply fall at his feet.

She banished Lord Avon from her thoughts. It was Lord Alexander she must apply herself to for, as far as she could see, his bad influence on Gideon continued unabated despite what Dominic claimed. Now she had seen him at close quarters Liberty wondered how she had ever mistaken Dominic for his brother. Their facial characteristics were similar, to be sure, but Alex was nowhere near as intimidating as his brother. Not quite as tall, not as solid, nor as *dark*…as brooding.

Nor is he as handsome.

The latter observation whispered through her thoughts before she could prevent it. She swatted it away and distracted herself by watching Gideon as he partnered one of Lord Twyford's daughters. Her hand rose to her chest, as though to fill the hole there…the void that yawned deeper and darker the more her twin seemed to reject her.

Again, she gathered her scattering thoughts and re-directed them to Alex, who was also dancing. Gideon had already declined to introduce her to him, but she was determined to find somebody who would. Maybe a direct appeal to him might work after all? She wouldn't know until she tried. Lord knew, she'd made no prog-ress in bringing Gideon to his senses over the past week and although she'd seen Lord Avon a few times, driving or riding in the Park, he had done no more than tip his hat to her so she had no way of knowing if he had kept to his promise to watch over their respective brothers.

She scanned the Twyfords' ballroom for the ump-teenth time, searching for *anyone* who might introduce her to Lord Alexander Beauchamp. Of a sudden, her pulse kicked. Across the floor, through a gap in the dancers, she spied a face she recognised—Lady Jane Colebrooke, standing with a beautiful young woman with shining black hair and a tall, dark gentleman.

Chapter Eight

'Mrs Mount.' Liberty leaned towards their chaperon. 'Lady Jane Colebrooke is over there—I should like to renew my acquaintance with her and to thank her again for her kindness. I shan't be gone long.'

Mrs Mount nodded and smiled, then resumed her conversation with the matron sitting on her other side. Liberty stood and shook out the skirts of her new violet gown—one of three she'd had made after the disaster at the Trents' rout—before making her way around the edge of the room. She slowed as she reached Lady Jane and her companions and, as she hoped, Lady Jane noticed her.

'Miss Lovejoy! How do you do?'

'Why, Lady Jane. What a happy coincidence. I had hoped I might see you, to thank you again for your kindness.'

Lady Jane blushed. 'Oh, it was my pleasure. Might I introduce you to Lord Hugo Alastair and his wife, Lady Olivia? Miss Lovejoy is Lord Wendover's sister,' she said to Lady Olivia. 'We met when she was overcome by the heat at a party last week—I merely leant my assistance when requested by your brother, Avon.'

Brother? Liberty's breath seized as cool silvery-grey

eyes—the mirror of Avon's—slowly assessed her. Of all the rotten luck—she could hardly beg an introduction to Lord Alexander when his sister was within earshot. Liberty curtsied again, this time a little deeper. Lady Olivia, after all, was the daughter of a duke and would no doubt expect her due. And Lord Hugo must be the son of a high-ranking aristocrat, she realised, as he bowed with a charming smile.

Mrs Mount's efforts to drum lessons of aristocratic precedence into the three Lovejoy sisters had not been for nothing because Liberty now knew that only the sons of marquesses and dukes had the courtesy title of 'Lord' affixed to their Christian names, so Lord Hugo must at least be the son of a marquess. Or marquis as some of them chose to be known. But Liberty still couldn't quite fathom why sons of earls were not called 'Lord' when their sisters were afforded the title of 'Lady'. This world was still a confused muddle of rules and details that had never touched upon her or her life before, but to which she must now conform.

Lady Olivia's gaze fixed on Lady Jane. 'I am all agog, Jane. What happened? And how came Dominic to be involved?'

'Livvy.' There was a note of warning in Lord Hugo's voice. He smiled at Liberty. 'I apologise for my wife's inquisitiveness, Miss Lovejoy.'

'Oh, *pfft*, Hugo. Jane knows me too well to take offence and I am sure Miss Lovejoy will forgive my curiosity about what my brother gets up to when I'm not around to keep an eye on him.' Lady Olivia grinned at Liberty. 'Jane's family estate adjoins our father's in Devonshire. We grew up together and dear Jane is well accustomed to the Beauchamps' ways, are you not, Jane?'

It struck Liberty that, for all their high birth, these aristocrats seemed less stuffy than many of the lower ranks of the peerage she had encountered since their arrival in London. *They* did not appear to view her as a person not fit to associate with.

Jane smiled. 'I am. As to the other night, all I recall is seeing Miss Lovejoy walking towards the door and then she seemed to stumble over someone's foot before…well, her knees simply buckled. And Dominic… he was quite the hero. He must have been quick to notice something amiss because, even though he was on the far side of our group, he was the first to reach Miss Lovejoy and he caught her before she could fall to the floor.'

Liberty kept her attention on Jane although she felt the weight of Lady Olivia's silver-eyed stare. Nerves quaked in her stomach. Would she think it had been a deliberate ploy on Liberty's part? A trick to attract Avon's attention? That particular rumour had already reached the Lovejoys' ears, but Liberty knew any attempt at denial would sound like too much protestation.

'And he asked you to go with him to protect Miss Lovejoy's reputation?'

'I believe it was with a view of protecting his own reputation.' The tart words blurted from Liberty's lips before she could stop them. Horrified, she clapped her hand to her mouth but, to her amazement, Olivia laughed.

'That sounds just like Dominic—his behaviour must always be above reproach. Does your brother attend this evening, Miss Lovejoy? I do not believe I have ever met him—this is our first time in town for over two years.'

'Yes. He is dancing in the same set as your brother Alexander…the man with the golden hair.'

'Oh, he is very handsome, is he not? I can see many

girls losing their hearts over that head of hair!' Olivia grinned. 'Do you envy him? Oh! I do beg your pardon. I did not mean to be rude. Your hair is very pretty, but it is not quite so...um...eye-catching, is it?'

Liberty smiled back. 'I take no offence. I am used to my brother garnering all the attention. We are twins and when we were children people would stop and exclaim at his angelic appearance—'

'*Twins?*'

'Why, yes.'

'Hugo!' Olivia nudged her husband. 'Did you hear that? Miss Lovejoy and her brother are *twins.*'

Lord Hugo smiled indulgently. 'I heard her say so, my love.'

'Miss Lovejoy! Will you do me the honour of calling on me at Beauchamp House tomorrow? I should deem it a great favour.' Olivia's eyes shone with excitement. 'We have two-year-old twins—a boy and a girl also. I should appreciate hearing from you direct what it is like to grow up as a twin.'

Liberty was happy to accept. She liked what she had seen so far of Lady Olivia and who knew what advantages Hope and Verity might gain if Liberty and Olivia were to become friends?

'I shall be happy to call upon you, but you must realise I have no experience of growing up *not* a twin so I am not sure I can be of much help.'

'Oh, I am sure you can. Shall we say two o'clock? You must come, too, Jane. I long to hear how things are at home.'

'I am sorry, Livvy, but I cannot. Stepmama wishes me to remain at home every single afternoon in case of gentlemen callers.' She sighed, sending a rueful smile Liberty's way. 'She is determined to see me married this year, before my stepsister makes her debut next Season.' She lowered her voice. 'Unfortunately the only gentleman who ever calls on me is Sir Denzil Pikeford and my fear of displeasing Stepmama is not yet as great as my fear of marrying a drunkard with scant manners and even less conversation.'

Olivia pulled a face. 'Pikeford? You have my sympathies!'

The music stopped and the dance ended, and Liberty was happy to see Lord Alexander heading in their direction. This would save her from having to beg an introduction. As he neared, he was joined by Lord Avon and Liberty's heart performed a lazy somersault as his gaze swept over her. What would he think, finding her here with his sister and brother-in-law after their last encounter at the theatre? His impassive features gave nothing of his thoughts away and, without volition, Liberty plucked at the low, round neckline of her new violet ball gown—a neckline that exposed rather more of her décolletage, shoulders and back than she was used to. She stopped that nervy fidgeting as soon as she realised what she was doing, but she was grateful she had given in to Mrs Mount's persuasion and had some new gowns made, even though the cost had set her nerves jangling. They jangled again now, but for a completely different reason, as the Beauchamp brothers neared.

Liberty watched Olivia greet both of her brothers with a kiss…she really was very different from so many members of the *ton* with their painfully correct behaviour. Liberty found herself looking forward to her visit the next day.

Olivia drew Liberty forward. 'You have already met my brother Dominic, of course, Miss Lovejoy.'

Avon's eyes met hers and the question in their silver-grey depths prompted Liberty to elaborate. 'Jane has been regaling your sister with the story of how she and I met, my lord.'

'Ah, yes. I trust you are fully recovered, Miss Love-joy?'

'Thank you, sir. I am.'

'And have you met my other brother, Alexander?' Olivia said. 'Alex, this is Miss Lovejoy.'

Liberty found herself the object of a quizzing stare from Alex's tawny eyes before he inclined his head. 'Miss Lovejoy. We have not formally met, but I am acquainted with your brother, Wendover.'

'I am aware of it, my lord.'

She knew her tone was a touch terse and a frown flicked between his brows, but he did not respond. Instead, his eyes moved on to his older brother, his gaze mocking. 'I'm surprised you're wasting your time with us, Dom. Haven't you an agenda to follow? Important decisions to make?'

Avon's eyes narrowed. 'Not here, Alex.'

'Your list is an open secret, Brother. No need for coyness. Did you know about it, Jane?' Jane nodded, somewhat reluctantly it appeared to Liberty. 'Have you heard of it, Miss Lovejoy? Lord Avon's list?'

Finding herself the centre of attention, Liberty swallowed, suddenly as nervous as Jane had looked. 'I have heard a mention of it,' she admitted.

Alex shrugged. 'Common knowledge, Dom. They're taking bets at White's.'

'In that case...' Dominic straightened the cuffs of his black swallowtail coat '... I shall go and attend to my...er...*agenda*, as you so elegantly phrase it, Alex.'

'No! Wait!' Olivia clutched at Dominic's sleeve.

'Don't do anything hasty, Dominic. I should like to at least meet these girls before you decide.'

A smile curled Avon's lips, but there was no humour in it. 'You wish to inspect my choice of potential bride, Sis?' He swept the room with a searching glance. 'You wish me to introduce you?' He crooked his arm. 'Come, then. Let us proceed.'

Liberty watched the byplay, fascinated by this glimpse into the undercurrents that swirled around the Beauchamps. The hint of sarcasm in Dominic's tone had brought fire flashing into his sister's eyes and Liberty was aware of Lord Hugo watching intently, with the focus of a cat waiting to pounce. She didn't doubt he would intervene to protect his wife if needed. Alex, on the other hand, now stood back. It was as though, having lit the fuse, he was waiting to enjoy the fireworks.

Liberty had always imagined other families were calm and polite in their dealings with each other. It appeared she was wrong. Maybe the Lovejoy family wasn't so different after all, with their petty squabbles. But there was no denying the strong bond between the Beauchamps and she prayed the bond between her and Gideon would prove resilient enough to be repaired.

'I have no wish to meet them in a noisy ballroom,' Olivia snapped. 'How can I talk to them properly or get to know their characters?'

'Their characters are none of your concern, Olivia. It will be my decision. Not yours.'

'*Pfft!* You know what I mean, Dominic.' She bit her lip, then stepped closer to him, putting her hand on his arm, her voice softer. Pleading. 'Of *course* it is your decision, Dom, but I want to help. Let me help. Please.'

A muscle ticked in his jaw. 'Very well. I shall drive you in the Park tomorrow and make the introductions.'

'Perfect! Are they all in town?'

Olivia was all smiles again and Lord Hugo relaxed. Alex, strangely, also looked satisfied, although Liberty would have sworn he had deliberately stirred trouble between his brother and sister in order to enjoy the ensuing argument.

'Yes, they are all here. And will no doubt be on parade in the Park at the fashionable hour,' he added in a cynical undertone.

'You never know, I might find you another lady to add to your list.' A frown darkened Dominic's brow, which Olivia blithely ignored. 'You may call for me at four o'clock. Miss Lovejoy is calling at two to meet Julius and Daisy. Did you know she and Wendover are twins as well?'

'I did know, but I don't understand why you should believe that has any relevance, Liv. Neither your two nor Miss Lovejoy and her brother are identical twins and—from the behaviour of the twins I have observed at Westfield—the non-identical twins appear to be much like any other family members who are close in age— they bicker much of the time and yet woe betide anyone who dares to upset the other.'

'Pooh! You cannot compare Julius and Daisy to the children at Westfield—heaven knows what traumas those poor mites have been through. Besides, Liberty *wants* to meet the twins, don't you, Liberty?'

'I…' Liberty—busy puzzling over Dominic's comments about children and Westfield—was caught unawares by the sudden direct appeal to her. 'I…of course, Lady Olivia. I should love to meet them.'

'Olivia! You must call me Olivia, for I foresee that we shall be great friends.' Olivia turned a triumphant smile on her brother. 'There, Dominic. See?'

Dominic shook his head at her. 'I see you are as manipulative as ever, minx.' He grinned at his brother-in-law. 'Thank God she is your responsibility now, Hugo. You should get a medal.'

Hugo grinned back. 'It's as well I thank God every day she's mine as well, then, is it not? Come on, Trouble—dare you be unfashionable and dance with your husband?' He led his beaming wife on to the dance floor.

Liberty felt it the second Dominic switched his attention back to her. 'So…you are to be interrogated about what it is like to be a twin, are you? Poor Olivia. She will go to any lengths, so determined is she to be a good mother.'

Alex smirked and Liberty stiffened.

'*Any* lengths? That includes, I collect, fraternising with someone like me?'

Dominic's lips quirked, but his voice was deadly serious. 'That is not what I meant at all, Miss Lovejoy. You really ought not to belittle yourself in such a way. There was no hidden meaning in my words—I meant exactly what I said. Olivia is determined to be the perfect mother and she drives herself relentlessly. I only hope the twins will not end up spoilt brats.'

'Like their mother,' Alex murmured, earning him a frown from his brother. 'Well, you can't deny she's always been wilful, Dom.'

'And you, my dear brother, should remember her good heart. She helped you out of more scrapes than I care to remember.'

'And led me into enough, too,' grumbled Alex, before straightening, his attention caught by something behind Dominic. Liberty followed his gaze and saw a group of young ladies heading in their direction, their collective attention firmly fixed on Dominic.

'Oh, lord,' Alex muttered. 'Pack alert. I'm off.'

Dominic glanced round at the approaching pack, as Alex had called them. It was an apt description, Liberty thought—like a pack of wolves with tasty prey in their sight. Beyond the tightening of his jaw, however, Dominic did not react.

'Janey...' Alex bowed '...would you do me the honour, etcetera, etcetera?'

'Alex! That is hardly the way to invite—'

'Oh, Janey don't mind, do you?' Alex grabbed Jane's hand. 'She knows me too well—she don't expect me to do the pretty with her! C'mon, let's dance.'

He tugged Jane on to the floor, leaving Liberty with Dominic. They were very soon surrounded by the young ladies, simpering and making eyes at Dominic, who appeared to effortlessly don the guise of the perfect gentleman as he responded with consummate gallantry. Liberty, although she was acknowledged, soon found herself deftly cut out. She stood, irresolute, for a moment but, as she made up her mind to walk away, Dominic raised his voice.

'Miss Lovejoy—pray tell me you have not forgotten our dance?'

She was torn between irritation at being an excuse to escape his coterie of admirers—and how was that different to how Alex had used Jane?—and admiration of his adroit handling of his dilemma. At least he waited for her reply rather than taking her acquiescence for granted as Alex had done with Jane.

She dipped a slight curtsy. 'Of course I have not forgotten, my lord.'

He sent his charming smile around his admirers. 'Please do excuse us, ladies.' He extended his hand. The girls parted and Liberty stepped towards him, trying to ignore the poisonous glances sent her way. She put her hand in his and their eyes met. She felt the jolt way down inside, in the pit of her belly, and heat washed across the entire surface of her skin, including her cheeks which she was certain were scarlet. His eyes darkened and she felt her lips part in response as her tongue darted out to moisten her unexpectedly dry lips. He dragged his gaze from hers.

'Come, Miss Lovejoy.'

His expression blank, his tone was one of world-weary boredom. But Liberty recognised it for the act it was. He led her into the set and she found herself the object of many more envious and a few disapproving looks.

'Are you sure your reputation will survive a dance with me?'

He cocked a brow and his lips twitched. 'Oh, I am tolerably sure it will remain intact.' He placed her next to Olivia in the line of dancers and, before retreating to stand with the gentlemen, he bent his head close to her ear and murmured, 'But please do not swoon again. *That* might take some explanation.'

His breath whispered across her neck, raising shivers in its wake. She smiled, reading it as a teasing remark rather than a reproof. When they first met she'd thought him superior and pompous, but was revising her opinion after he had spoken so movingly about his sister and now upon seeing him with Olivia and with Alex. A man who cared that much for his family couldn't be all bad. She only wished Gideon would demonstrate the same caring attitude.

Among the dancers taking their places for the next dance Liberty saw Hope and Verity and she experienced a tiny glow of triumph at her sisters' shocked and envious expressions when they noticed Liberty's partner.

Now dare to tell me I've ruined your chances!

It could only help their standing in society to be accepted by the Beauchamps, but she found herself hoping their acquaintance would prosper for her own sake. She had thoroughly enjoyed being included in their circle this evening and it made her realise quite how isolated she had become since Bernard's death, when she had withdrawn into the cocoon of her family.

She still found it difficult to accept that she deserved happiness. If she hadn't come to London five years ago, might she have spotted the symptoms earlier? She might have nursed them better. Saved them. The only way to make her guilt bearable had been to care for and protect the family she had left. But how could she protect Gideon...save him...when every time she tried to talk to him she ended up pushing him further away?

The music began. It was another country dance—one with which Liberty was familiar—and while she performed the steps mechanically she set her mind to wondering how might she use the Beauchamp connection to further her sisters' chances of meeting eligible men. If she could only persuade Dominic to stand up with both Hope *and* Verity, that would be a real coup. She had realised, since their first encounter, just how many of his peers looked up to Lord Avon, mainly due to his sporting prowess, and neither could she help but notice how many ladies—both young and not so young—fluttered around him, vying for attention. She understood their interest. Not only was he heir to a wealthy duke but he was handsome, he cut a fine, manly figure and he was intelligent.

'Miss Lovejoy? Liberty!'

Startled, she met Dominic's gaze, his silvery eyes like mirrors, as ever—reflecting the world back rather than allowing the light through to his soul.

'It is customary to make at least some pretence of interest in your partner's conversation.'

'Sorry. I was… I was…'

Chapter Nine

The movement of the dance separated them before Liberty finished her excuse, leaving Dominic even more time to regret not following his instinct to avoid them when he had first seen Liberty Lovejoy with Hugo and Olivia. But then Alex had headed in their direction and he had seen Liberty's eyes light up. Her expressions were utterly transparent—a window to her inner thoughts and feelings—and Dominic's feet had carried him over to the group without a second thought. Who knew what mischief Alex might stir if he felt unjustly accused of leading Gideon astray; his tongue could be sharp and—quite why, he did not know—Dominic felt this compulsion to stay close rather than to walk away.

He'd almost forgotten she was a virtual stranger as he relaxed among his family and fell to bickering with Olivia, as they had in the old days before she had wed. But he had not forgotten Liberty's *presence*. He was viscerally aware of her the entire time, sensitive to the slightest change in her expression and the strange sensations she conjured within him. He could not shake the feeling—no, the certainty—that, somehow, he *knew* her, understood her, could feel her deepest emotions. And he felt...happy. Content.

Until those girls had surrounded them, isolating Liberty as effectively as a well trained sheepdog would cut a single sheep from a flock. Dominic had felt the cloak of his public image fall into place as he became the Marquess of Avon and unaccustomed resentment at those girls had bubbled under his skin when he saw Liberty hesitate, then turn to walk away. Before he could consider the consequences, he was asking her to dance, when nothing had been further from his thoughts or intention. But the pleasure that radiated throughout his body as she placed her hand in his banished his doubts as to the wisdom of his action. Why should he not dance with his sister's friend? Nobody else could see how Liberty Lovejoy fascinated him. As far as anyone else was concerned, it was no different to him standing up with Jane.

But the minute the dance began, those insidious doubts wormed their way once again into his thoughts, fuelled by those memories of his mother, who had been more and more on his mind since his decision that this would be the Season he chose his bride.

Make me proud, my Son. Society will watch your every move. Never disgrace your position as heir.

His attempts to quash his mother's voice were not helped by the fact that the innocuous remarks he addressed to his partner were roundly ignored. Liberty appeared more interested in her sisters than in her own partner and he questioned again why he hadn't just left her to Alex's tender mercies. As the steps brought them together again, his irritation got the better of him.

'Well? Have you a reason for ignoring me?'

Even as the words left his mouth he regretted them.

It was hardly Liberty's fault he found her so maddeningly irresistible.

Her eyes flashed and her lips thinned. 'I was debating which of those charming young misses were on that list of yours, Lord Avon.'

They parted company, then the steps brought them together again, but before Dominic could speak, Liberty continued, 'I am certain any one of them would make the perfect Marchioness—as long as they possess the requisite bloodlines, of course.'

Her words stung and he retaliated instinctively. 'None of them, for your information. My future wife will not be a female who makes her intentions so very obvious. Discretion and poise—they are the attributes I seek.'

He cringed inside at how very pompous he sounded, but the words were out there and he was damned if he'd humble himself by retracting them.

'As well as *calmness* and *elegance*, if my recollection is correct.' Hectic flags of colour painted her cheeks. 'And now *discretion* to add to your list of requirements.'

'Do not forget poise, Miss Lovejoy.'

'I have not forgotten it, sir, but I am well aware that elegance and poise are one and the same. Did you think me uneducated as well as ill-bred?'

The words hissed out at him from under her breath. The movement of the dance parted them again and he cautioned himself not to further fuel the flame of her temper with any attempt to defend his position. Liberty— as he might have guessed—had no such compunction. She continued as soon as they were close enough for him to hear her. He supposed he should be grateful she waited until none of the neighbouring couples would be able to overhear her tirade.

'I am sorry to disappoint you—although I make no doubt that well-educated is not an essential quality for your ideal wife. I also happen to have an excellent memory. Not this time for the attributes necessary for the perfect Marchioness, but for the *undesirable* traits.'

Again they moved apart and again they came back together.

'Now…let me see…it was most *definitely* no vigour or passion. I can see, however, that none of those insipid young misses would disappoint you in that regard!'

He clamped his jaw tight as the movement of the dance parted them again. What the hell was he doing dancing with Liberty Lovejoy and allowing her to provoke him? All five of the ladies on his original list, together with their families, were present tonight. He would dance with them all, even though Caroline was currently his first choice. That would keep the gossips busy and it would be a far better use of his time.

He and Liberty circled one another, with no opportunity for speech before they parted company yet again. A glance across the ballroom brought Lady Caroline into his line of sight. She was elegant and cool as she performed the steps, smiling serenely as she responded to her partner's comments. He switched his gaze to Liberty—her eyes bright with accusation, her skin flushed, her lips parted and plump, her breasts…*glorious*. His loins tightened. He could not even summon any anger towards her because every word she had said was true. But it didn't change the fact that his bride must be the perfect lady, despite the yearning of every fibre of his being for a woman who was palpably *not* the perfect lady.

Never had he felt so very enticed by any female at a society event. Or by any female anywhere.

He found himself executing a figure of eight with Olivia.

'Are you and Miss Lovejoy *quarrelling*, Dominic?'

Caution whispered through him. If Olivia had noticed, others might, too.

'Don't be absurd!'

Olivia smiled impishly as she circled around him and rejoined Hugo. Dominic and Liberty came together again and this time, before she could speak, Dominic squeezed her hand.

'I apologise unreservedly. Tell me how I might make amends.'

It stole the next wave of invective from her tongue, but the gleam in her eyes warned him that she would take full advantage of his peace offering.

'Will you dance with my sisters, my lord? Please?'

'Your *sisters*?'

Her worry was plain as she sought her sisters among the dancers before directing her gold-flecked midnight-blue gaze back to him.

'Surely that would help us to be more fully accepted?'

He could not bring himself to refuse such a simple, direct request. 'Very well. I shall dance with each of them tonight. But please do not ask me to make a habit of it.'

Her grateful smile caressed him and he cursed the fact that his list was common knowledge. If it were not, he might have delayed finding a wife until next year. But he could not, with honour, back away now speculation over his choice was rife. Or, rather, he *would not* back away. It was one of the standards he set himself as a gentleman—to be true to his word. He knew there could never be more than friendship between him and

Liberty, but he might have been better able to relax and enjoy that friendship had the eyes of the *ton* not been watching his every move for a hint as to his intentions.

'I am relieved they have achieved *some* success,' Liberty continued, 'but I cannot help worrying.' She frowned and bit into her plump lower lip, sending sparks sizzling through him. 'I know we are not fully accepted everywhere and I'm afraid that can only get worse if Gideon continues in his reckless ways. If only he would come to his senses...he still won't listen to me.'

'But he is here tonight and behaving impeccably. He looks in a fair way to being smitten with Twyford's eldest girl. That must surely please you?'

She released her lip and smiled again, her eyes crinkling—a smile that was balm to his soul. He kept his expression impassive, again conscious of too many eyes watching.

'Yes, it does. Anyone would be preferable to that actress—I pray he has given her up entirely! And thank you for agreeing to partner Hope and Verity after having danced with me. It is very kind of you.'

'It will help some people to accept you more readily, as will your friendship with Olivia if that continues.'

The dance ended and Liberty took Dominic's proffered arm as they left the floor.

'As I said at the outset, your brother is simply finding his feet in town. I've talked to Alex and I've kept an eye on the pair of them—I have seen nothing for you to worry about.'

Liberty smiled with such trust in her eyes that his heart clenched. How could she affect him so, with just one look? Again, he blanked his expression, delivering her back to Mrs Mount with a wash of relief. Resolutely, he walked away. He would approach her sisters later, after dancing with other partners...partners whose name was not Lovejoy. And, as he had already put Caroline Warnock to the head of the queue, where better than to start with her?

'Good evening, Lord Avon.' Lady Caroline dipped a graceful curtsy.

'Good evening, my lady.' Dominic bowed. 'May I say how very charming you look this evening?'

'You are too kind, my lord.' Caroline raised her fan and fluttered it, her dark brown gaze clinging to Dominic's face.

'Dare I hope you have a dance available this evening, Lady Caroline?'

'I do, my lord. It is the supper dance, if that is acceptable?'

Dominic was aware of Lady Druffield watching them from her nearby chair with a gleam of satisfaction. Lady Georgiana's mother sat with the Marchioness and was also watching Dominic and Caroline, her expression revealing no hint of her feelings, yet Dominic knew she would be loathing every second of her rival's triumph.

'That is most acceptable,' he said to Caroline. 'Now, if you will excuse me...?'

He did not wait for her response, but headed straight for Lady Amelia and Lady Sarah and secured their hands for dances. Then he scanned the room for Lady Georgiana. His gaze collided with that of Liberty, accusation burning in her eyes. Her thoughts were as plain as if she had shouted them across the ballroom—*You promised to dance with Hope and Verity.* Although such transparency of feelings was frowned upon by most members of the *ton*, Dominic was charmed and entertained by them. And by her. As long as he took care not to single her out—*or to annoy her while we are dancing! I've learned my lesson there!*—he could still amuse himself by teasing her.

He cocked his brow and had the satisfaction of seeing that blatant accusation darken into a glower. He would approach her sisters in his own good time—he would not march to Liberty Lovejoy's command. He caught sight of Lady Georgiana and made his way across the room to discover she was free for the next dance. He led her on to the floor, only to find they were next to Liberty and her current partner, Stephen Damerel, damn his eyes. The man was older than Dominic and the second son of Lord Rushock. He was a decent enough man, but he was a scholar and far too staid for a lively woman such as Liberty.

'My lord? My *lord*!'

Georgiana's petulant tone grabbed his attention. He pushed Liberty and Damerel from his thoughts to concentrate on his own partner, but the dance seemed never ending and, despite his best intentions, he found his gaze straying to Liberty on several occasions. By the time he'd seen her smiling at Damerel in that open, guileless way of hers he was ready to punch something. Or someone. But through it all, he chatted with Georgiana and, at the end of the dance, he felt sure she would have no cause to label him as an inattentive partner.

One ticked off. Three more to go. Plus Hope and Verity, of course.

He didn't dare to question himself as to why he was keen to get his duty dances out of the way. He just knew he was. He had no partner for the next and, spying Hope close to where Mrs Mount sat, he grabbed a glass of champagne from a footman carrying a tray, drained it in one and headed in their direction. He arrived at the same moment as Liberty, her hand on Damerel's arm. Dominic nodded at the other man, who returned his nod, bowed to the ladies and then sauntered away.

Dominic turned to Hope. 'Would you care to dance, Miss Lovejoy? If your card is not already full?'

She glanced at Liberty before replying, 'Thank you, my lord. I am engaged for the next two, but the first after supper is free.'

'Perfect. And I believe the one after *that* is a waltz, so...' He captured Liberty's gaze. 'Would you do me the honour of waltzing with me, Miss Lovejoy?'

Her brow creased, puzzlement in her eyes. If she could have asked him what he was about—which she could not with Mrs Mount and Hope in earshot—he would not be able to tell her because he had no idea himself. What the devil had prompted him to ask her to waltz, of all things? He must enjoy being tortured. And, quite apart from that, he must now make very sure to engage his other partners for a second dance—ever since he had first been on the town he had made a point of never dancing more than once with any lady at a ball. He suppressed a sigh. How did this one woman manage to provoke him into such uncharacteristic behaviour? And why did he have to meet her this Season of all Seasons? He couldn't stop thinking about her, but it would not, could not, change the future he had mapped out.

Liberty parted her lips to reply but, before she could speak, Alex joined them, slapping Dominic on the shoulder as Hope's next partner arrived and led her on to the floor.

'Just the people I need to speak to,' said Alex. 'And both in the same place as well. Am I not the fortunate one?'

Liberty's eyebrows flicked high.

'Miss Liberty Lovejoy.' Alex bowed. 'Would you kindly do me the honour of saving the supper dance for me?'

A silent growl vibrated in Dominic's throat, not helped by the impish smile Alex directed at him.

'Why. Yes. Thank you. Both of you.' Liberty looked from one of them to the other, clearly as confused as Dominic. 'You are most kind.'

'Oh, think nothing of it,' said Alex airily. 'Livvy wanted me to ask you, so we can eat supper with her and Hugo.'

'Oh. Well...will Jane not expect—?'

She fell silent as Alex laughed. 'Lord, no. We're just friends and, besides, her stepmother has promised the supper dance to Pikeford on her behalf.' He grinned at Dominic. 'It makes you thankful we didn't end up with her as our stepmother, don't it? Thank the Lord we've got Rosalind. So, Dom...who've you bagged for supper? Livvy said I was to ask you to join us, too, but— just a hint, you understand, Brother—when Olivia said *ask* she meant *tell*.'

Dominic closed his eyes briefly, shaking his head as he suppressed a smile. Life had been dull the past few years without Alex and Olivia and their irrepressible antics to brighten his life.

'I think I might legitimately dodge that particular invitation. I'm promised to Lady Caroline and I should imagine she will wish to remain with her particular friends.'

'On your head be it, Brother. Only Olivia did say, most particularly, that she wanted us all together for supper because, believe it or not, she has missed us.'

'Oh, very well. I'll see what I can do.'

'Good man! I'll leave you two in peace.'

With a wink, Alex wandered away. Dominic had already spent too much time with Liberty that evening but, somehow, he could not tear himself away. Not yet.

'Do you not have a partner for this dance, my lord?'

'No. I do not care to dance every dance. What about you?'

'Alas, no gentleman requested my hand for this dance.' Her full lips pursed slightly, then twitched into a half-smile. 'But I *am* engaged for a waltz after supper and I am looking forward to that exceedingly.'

'In order that you may tear me off another couple of strips?'

'Avon! That is *most* ungentlemanly of you.' Her eyes sparkled, drawing him in, and it was with an effort he tore his gaze from hers, blanked his expression and cast a bored look over the dancers. 'You did admit I was sorely provoked.'

He couldn't resist another sideways glance at her, a glance that revealed twinkling eyes above pouting lips that drew his gaze like a magnet. Good grief. They were in a crowded ballroom and all he could think about was sweeping her into his arms and kissing her. His hand rubbed at the back of his neck as his inner voice of caution screamed at him to walk away. But still he lingered.

The trouble was…his interest in her wasn't confined to lust. He just enjoyed being with her, even when they were bickering. Especially when they were bickering, in fact, because she treated him like an ordinary man. Every other female—apart from his family—treated him as 'the heir'. And damned if he wasn't complicit in that…he had occupied that public position for so much of his life it had become second nature.

'As I recall,' he adopted a light, teasing tone, 'I offered you an apology without admitting fault. It is called being gallant.'

'Very well.' She sighed dramatically. 'If you are intent on making me shoulder the blame, there is nothing more I can say. But I must tell you how grateful I am that you kept your promise and are engaged to stand up with Hope.'

He read the question in her expression.

'I have not asked Verity yet, but I shall. Which reminds me—I saw her dancing with Bridlington earlier. You may not be aware, but he has a somewhat disreputable reputation—an unsuitable partner for any young innocent.'

She changed instantly from a teasing, flirting girl into a serious woman. 'Thank you for the warning. I confess I thought him rather old for her and I have noticed he seeks her out between dances, too. I shall speak to Mrs Mount.'

'Would you like me to have a word with him?'

'N-no. I do not think so. I think it is Gideon's place to do so, don't you?'

'You're probably right. But if you wish me to intervene, just let me know.'

'Thank you. I will.' They watched the dancing in silence for a few minutes. 'My lord…may I ask you something?'

'If you must.'

'Oh! You wound me. How grudging you sound.'

'I sound that way because such a request from you usually means trouble.'

She laughed. 'You barely know me and you have deduced that already? You cut me to the quick, sir.' Then she sobered. 'I realise it may be an impertinent question, but what is Westfield?'

'Westfield?'

He was happy to be a patron of the school and to help the children with their lessons and find positions for the older children in households and as apprentices but he was uncomfortable talking about it—it smacked too much of puffing off his own good deeds. He did what he did for the children, not to bolster his reputation.

'Yes. You spoke of it earlier, when we were with your sister.'

'It is an orphan asylum supported by my second cousin, Lady Stanton. I merely help her out occasionally.'

'I was intrigued by how knowledgeable you seemed about the children. And about twins.'

He shrugged, keeping his attention away from her and on the dancers. 'Much of what I said is common sense. The rest I have gleaned from Felicity...Lady Stanton, that is.' The introduction of this subject gave him the impetus he needed to tear himself away from her. 'Now, if you will excuse me, Miss Lovejoy, I ought to circulate.' He bowed. 'I expect I shall see you at supper.'

He walked away without giving her a chance to respond. He knew, from when he had first started supporting Westfield, that it elicited more questions from others than he cared to answer. Questions as to why he, a wealthy and privileged aristocrat, should concern himself with orphans and other destitute children. But to answer those inevitably led to questions about his mother and her death...and he had no wish to resurrect those memories, or to share them. With anyone. He strolled on, stopping and chatting to acquaintances on occasion, but all the time he was conscious that none of these people were really his friends. The people he wanted to be with were his family. He was looking forward to his father's arrival and that of his aunts and uncles.

He paused and scanned the ballroom, his restless gaze settling as it found Liberty. She was talking, animatedly, with her brother, who was glowering at her. Why would she not take his advice? Could she not see that the more she badgered Wendover the more likely he was to rebel?

'Keeping an eye on the luscious Liberty again?'

He gritted his teeth as Alex joined him. 'I don't know what you are talking about.'

'Come on, Dom…best to keep moving, or the wolves'll be circling again.' Alex linked his arm through Dominic's and they strolled on. 'And you know precisely what I'm talking about. I haven't seen you pay this much attention to a woman for…well, for ever, actually. What I don't understand is why you left her standing just now. I gave you privacy and you threw the opportunity away.'

'It makes no difference—I might find her attractive and enjoy her company, but you know as well as I do that she is totally unsuitable to be a future duchess.'

'Do I? How so? Her brother's an earl; you give every impression of enjoying her company.' He leaned in closer. 'And you can't tell me you don't want to—'

'Enough!' Dominic snatched his arm from Alex's. 'How about you and I meet for a sparring session at Jackson's tomorrow?'

It would give him huge satisfaction to punch that knowing smirk off his brother's face, but he could hardly plant him a facer at the Twyfords' ball.

Alex grinned. 'Not on your life, Brother. I ain't that stupid.'

'Despite appearances to the contrary!'

'Ouch! Take care! That wit of yours is sharp enough to cause real damage to a fellow.'

'Good. You deserve it.'

'Aw, come on, Dom. It's just a bit of gentle ribbing… you know I don't mean anything by it.'

Dominic scanned Alex's expression of innocence. He sighed. 'I know it's hard for you, but try to respect the fact that I am simply not in the mood for your peculiar sense of humour. Not today.'

Alex nudged him. 'We'll talk again tomorrow, then.'

He winked and strolled away, leaving Dominic to inwardly seethe. The music was drawing to a close, which meant the supper dance would be next. Battening down his exasperation, he set off to find a drink before it was time to seek out Lady Caroline Warnock—his next partner and, very possibly, his future wife.

Chapter Ten

Dominic's warning about Lord Bridlington had brought Liberty's protective instincts rushing to the surface. She watched His Lordship as he sniffed around Verity—really, there was no other way to describe it—and her disquiet grew. He reminded her of nothing more than a street dog on the hunt for a casual coupling. Liberty crossed the ballroom to her sister and drew her aside.

'Lord Bridlington is very attentive, Verity. Has he put his name down for a second dance?'

Verity flushed. 'Yes. The supper dance.'

Liberty frowned at her sister's subdued tone. 'Do you like him?'

'Not…not really. But Mrs Mount told us we must never refuse a gentleman if he asks us to dance. And, if we do, we cannot then dance with *any* gentleman. And she told me I should be flattered by his attention because he is an earl and…and he would be a suitable match.'

'Well, *I* think it would be an appalling match—*if* his intentions are honourable, which I beg to doubt. I'll ask Gideon to warn him off, shall I?'

'You mean you won't go storming up to him yourself

and harangue him?' There was a teasing note in Verity's tone, but Liberty recognised the kernel of truth in her question and felt her skin heat.

'No, I shall not. That,' she added, with a wink, 'is not how a lady should behave. You see… I *am* learning.'

But Gideon, when she caught up with him, was less than amenable to her suggestion that he pull rank as Verity's brother and partner her for the supper dance, ousting Bridlington.

'Don't see there's anything I can do if she's already agreed to have supper with the fellow,' he said, stretching his neck to peer over the sea of heads in the ballroom. 'I'm engaged myself for the supper dance, as it happens. To Lady Emily.' His wrapt expression as he said her name spoke volumes. 'In fact…there she is! I must go, Sis. Look, don't worry—nothing's going to happen to Verity in a crowded ballroom. I'll speak to Bridlington later.'

Liberty bit back her frustration as Gideon hurried away. Was it really too much to ask him to take an interest in his sister and to protect her?

'Libby.' A flustered-looking Hope grabbed her arm. 'My flounce is torn.' She pivoted and indicated the damaged lace at her hem, at the back of her dress. 'Will you come and help me fix it? Only I needs must make haste because it is the supper dance next and I am promised to Lord Whiteley.'

'Of course.' Liberty couldn't mistake Hope's suppressed excitement. It seemed she was as happy with her supper partner as Gideon was, unlike poor Verity. 'Come, we'll go to the withdrawing room and pin it up. It won't take long.'

As they headed upstairs, Hope said, 'Are you quite well, Lib? You look a little out of sorts. Was it…was it something Lord Avon said?' She glanced around, then drew Liberty to one side of the landing to sit on a window seat. 'I saw you with him earlier and I cannot help but notice how you seem to…to…gravitate towards one another.' She clutched Liberty's hand. 'Oh! Would it not be exciting if he fell in love with you?'

Liberty wrenched her hand free and stood up. 'What nonsense you talk at times, Hope. No, it was nothing to do with Lord Avon. It was Gideon.'

'Oh, *Liberty*! Have you been harrying him again? Why can't you *trust* him?'

Liberty bit her tongue, hurt that Hope assumed she was interfering when all she was trying to do was to protect Verity.

'Come.' She recalled she was due to partner Alex and that Dominic might join them for supper. Perhaps she would take him up on his offer after all, if Gideon was so blind to his brotherly duty. 'I have a packet of pins in my pocket so we shall have that tear mended in a trice and you can return to your Lord Whiteley.'

They went into the room set aside for the female guests. A maid was on duty, ready to assist any ladies who needed help, but Liberty waved her away. It would be a matter of moments to pin the flounce and then they could return to the ball. They went behind a screen placed across the room to afford privacy and Hope stepped up on to a low stool while Liberty knelt behind her. She barely registered the sound of the door opening until a haughty female voice said, 'Have you seen that lumpy Lovejoy creature positively *throwing* herself at Avon?'

Liberty froze as a spiteful titter sounded from the other side of the screen. She settled back on to her heels and looked up at Hope, who was peering over the top of the screen. Seeing her sister's mouth come open, Liberty wrapped her fingers around her ankle and squeezed a warning. Hope glanced down and Liberty shook her head, putting one finger to her lips. Hope grimaced back and held three fingers aloft.

'I declare, I don't know how he remains civil to her.' It was the same voice, one she did not recognise, but one that clearly denoted the aristocratic heritage of its owner. 'I heard that she swooned right into his arms at the Trents' rout party and, even before that, I saw her for myself in the Park, attempting to waylay him while he was driving *me* in his curricle.'

Lady Caroline!

Mrs Mount had identified Lady Caroline Warnock as Dominic's passenger in the Park that day and, since then, Liberty had increasingly heard her name touted as the front runner in the race to become the Marchioness of Avon. It was hard to reconcile this malicious-sounding female with the butter-wouldn't-melt-in-her-mouth young lady Liberty had seen in public.

'But there…what else is to be expected of such a family?' the hateful voice continued. 'The Earl of Wendover, indeed! The grandson of a coal merchant! Better they allowed the title to slip into abeyance than let such people be elevated above their station.'

'Did Avon mention her? I saw you talking with him.' A different voice this time.

'No, he did not. And quite rightly, too. She is far beneath his notice, although for some unfathomable reason his sister appears to be encouraging an acquaintance with the woman. No, Avon was too intent on engaging me for the supper dance.'

Caroline's smug self-satisfaction made Liberty long to slap her. A third voice joined in the conversation.

'Well, *I* saw Avon dancing with her and they talked together afterwards, too. They looked positively *intimate.*'

'Such a comment is beneath you, Elizabeth—' Caroline again, her voice sharp now '—and I suggest you do not repeat it, for it makes you appear a bad loser. I have not heard anyone whisper *your* name in connection with Lord Avon's list. But, then…a mere baronet's daughter…hardly a fitting background for a duchess, is it, Pamela?'

'Oh, no. Most unfitting, I agree.' The breathless adoration in Pamela's reply raised Liberty's hackles and presumably had the same effect on the invisible Elizabeth, for a soft *hmmph* reached the listeners' ears. 'My brother is certain you will win him, Caro. Oh, to think! A marchioness! Vincent told me he has a hundred guineas riding on you, so you'd better make sure you win.'

'Oh, I shall. I made sure to drop him a hint about poor Georgiana's shocking piano playing. I don't see *her* usurping me as favourite…and rumour has it Avon was less than impressed by Sarah and Amelia scuttling after him when Lumpy Liberty staged her swoon. But… let us not linger, or we shall miss the start of the supper dance. Did I mention that I am promised to Avon?'

The door opened and closed and they heard a muttered 'Yes. More than once' from Elizabeth before she, too, left the room.

'Well!' Hope's voice rang with indignation. 'How *dare*—?'

'Yes, yes. I agree, Hope, but let me finishing pinning your lace or we shall be late for the dance. We will complain bitterly about those arrogant madams later.'

'Very well. But you will take note that I am not the

only person who noticed that you and Avon seemed somewhat...friendly.'

There was little she could say to that, so Liberty finished the repair and they hurried down to the ballroom, reaching the door just as the first strains of the dance sounded. Both of their partners were standing with Mrs Mount. Lord Whiteley's face showed nothing but relief at the sight of Hope. Alex's showed...nothing at all as their eyes met and Liberty's courage wavered as she walked forward to take his hand. No doubt here was another one who disapproved of her and the thought of sharing supper with that spiteful cat, Caroline, set her stomach churning. How would she resist retaliating if Caroline was as nasty to her face as she had been in the withdrawing room?

To her surprise, however, Alex was the perfect gentleman and at no point did his inoffensive conversation cause Liberty even the slightest discomfort. Once the dance was over, he escorted her into the second supper room where he had arranged to meet Olivia and Hugo. It was one of the smallest tables, set for six, and they were the first to sit down, shortly followed by Olivia and Hugo.

'Well!' Olivia's attention was fixed on the doorway as footmen served the dishes for a hot supper. 'I know you asked Dominic to join us, Alex, for he told me so himself. And he promised he would do so. Where can he be?' She spooned up some white soup from the bowl set in front of her. 'This is delicious! Oh! Look! *There* they are...and...is that not one of your sisters, Liberty?'

Liberty looked up at the doorway to see Dominic walk into the room with Verity on one arm and Caroline—sporting a sour expression quite unlike her usual ladylike mien—on the other. Dominic looked...impassive.

But the slight compression of his lips told her he was angry. Verity looked... Liberty pushed back her chair, ready to rush to her distressed sister's aid, but a strong hand closed around her wrist, preventing her from rising.

'Don't draw attention,' Alex muttered. 'You'll find out soon enough.'

Dominic paused by a footman and murmured something, indicating their table with a nod of his head. The footman hurried away, and Dominic guided Verity and Caroline to their table. He seated Verity first, next to Liberty, and then a pursed-lipped Caroline next to Hugo. The footman brought another chair, which he placed between Verity and Caroline, and another man arrived with porcelain and silverware to set a place for Dominic. No one uttered a word until the servants were out of earshot, but Liberty could see Verity's hands gripped tightly in her lap and her chest rose and fell as though she were out of breath.

'What happened?'

Liberty's question was directed at Dominic. He saw her grope for Verity's hands and cover them, folding her fingers around them.

'Bridlington became a little over-enthusiastic,' he replied. 'Fortunately, Caroline and I happened to see what he was about and I...er...persuaded him to think again.'

Alex gestured at Dominic's hand—he saw a smear of blood on his knuckle and slipped his hand beneath the table, out of sight.

'Lord Avon was quite the hero,' said Caroline. 'Goodness knows what the outcome might have been for your dear sister, Miss Lovejoy, had he not intervened.'

She smiled warmly at Dominic, surprising him. When they first saw Bridlington trying to manoeuvre

Verity into a side room, Caroline had tried to persuade Dominic not to get involved, more concerned about her own and Dominic's reputations than about what was happening to Verity. Maybe he should excuse her immediate reaction. After all, most gently born ladies would surely prefer to avoid any sort of altercation.

'I confess the entire event has shaken my nerves alarmingly.' She reached for her glass with a visibly trembling hand. 'I dare say I do not stem from such robust stock as the Lovejoys.'

Liberty's eyes glinted dangerously and her mouth opened.

'I am sure no one was unaffected, Lady Caroline,' Dominic interjected, quick to forestall Liberty. 'But now I suggest we all settle down and enjoy this delicious supper and forget all about it. Lord Bridlington has left the ball now so there is no need to dwell upon what happened.'

'But I want to know—'

'You do know, Miss Lovejoy. I have told you.'

'I should like to know as well,' said Olivia. 'Did you *punch* him, Dom? We've all seen the blood on your hand, so you needn't bother to hide it.' She leaned across the table. 'Are you *sure* you are all right, Miss Lovejoy?'

'I am all right now, thank you. I am exceedingly grateful to your brother, however.' Verity smiled at him. 'He is right…can we please forget this and enjoy our supper?'

Olivia's intervention had given Liberty time to subside, but Dominic could tell her blood was still simmering and he had no doubt he would be questioned thoroughly during their waltz. His pulse kicked at the thought of holding her even as he again mentally slated himself for taking the risk of dancing with her twice.

'Indeed. I suggest we forget all about that unfortunate occurrence.' Caroline raised her spoon to her mouth, and swallowed. 'This white soup really is excellent, do you not agree?'

'Excellent indeed. How fortunate it is not *lumpy*, Lady Caroline,' said Liberty in a kindly manner. 'That, I am persuaded, would quite spoil your enjoyment.'

Dominic frowned and he saw Olivia shoot Liberty a questioning look, but Caroline seemed not to notice Liberty's overtly sweet tone.

'Indeed it would, Miss Lovejoy.'

Her smile was all graciousness. Did she have any clue that Liberty's smile wasn't genuine? It didn't take Dominic long to realise that she did not. It was increasingly clear that none of Liberty's comments or opinions mattered to Caroline because she quite clearly viewed Liberty—and Verity, too, although she barely joined the conversation—as utterly beneath her notice. She was polite and respectful—even delightful—in her dealings with Dominic, Alex, Olivia and Hugo, however.

It took the duration of that one supper for Dominic to change his mind about his list. A beautiful singing voice was no compensation for such arrogance. And how, he wondered, would someone such as Caroline respond to the spouses of his father, uncle and aunt? Rosalind, his stepmother, might be a duchess now, but her father was a simple soldier and her grandfather a silversmith. Thea, Uncle Vernon's wife, was the daughter of a glassmaker, and Zach, Aunt Cecily's husband—who refused to allow anyone to call him uncle—had a Romany mother. Dominic would never risk introducing discord into his beloved family.

He was still hesitant about Georgiana and her fear of horses, which left him with Lady Sybilla Gratton.

As they finished their supper, Gideon appeared behind Liberty and Verity.

'I thought you said Verity was having supper with Bridlington, Liberty?' he said, accusingly. 'I've been searching everywhere for them... Mrs Mount didn't seem to know where they were and neither did Hope and now, after worrying the life out of me, I find she's been with you the whole time!'

Liberty's cheeks flushed. 'If you had done your duty as I asked, you would have known precisely where she was.'

Verity jumped to her feet. 'You are being unfair, Gideon.' She grasped his arm, and lowered her voice. 'I was due to have supper with him, but...but...'

She cast an anxious look around the table, then put her lips to her brother's ear. As she whispered, Gideon's face leached of colour and his gaze sought Dominic's as one hand came to rest on Liberty's shoulder.

'I am sorry, Sis. I shouldn't have sounded off at you... I was worried when I couldn't find them. And I am grateful to you, Avon. You can be sure I'll have something to say to Bridlington next time our paths cross.' He put his arm around Verity and hugged her. 'Are you all right? Do you want to go home? I'll take you, if you do.'

'No.' Verity raised her chin and Dominic recognised the family resemblance with Liberty in that defiant gesture. 'I shall not allow that...that...*scoundrel*...to spoil my enjoyment of my first-ever ball.'

Alert to the nuances of Liberty's expression, Dominic saw her pride at her sister's strength and then, as her gaze met and held that of her twin, love shone from her eyes. Then a tut and a sigh sounded from behind him and he sensed movement. Caroline, her lips thinly disapproving, was preparing to leave the table. He stood up and pulled her chair back.

'Allow me.'

'Thank you, my lord.'

She smiled at him and held out her hand. Dominic helped her to rise and then she placed her hand on his sleeve, clearly expecting his escort back to the ballroom. He breathed a sigh of relief when he returned her to her mother and then sought out Hope, his next partner. But throughout the dance he was distracted, watching Liberty, who was dancing with Redbridge—that incorrigible tattletale—and laughing up at him.

'You are dancing with Liberty next, I believe, my lord?'

The question jerked his attention away from Liberty and back to Hope, who was studying him with something like speculation in her eyes. Drat the girl.

'I am. I apologise for neglecting you, Miss Lovejoy. Seeing your sister with Lord Redbridge reminded me of a matter I must discuss with him, but that is no excuse for ignoring my partner.'

He set himself to entertaining Hope and, by the end of the dance, he thought his distraction a success. They reached Mrs Mount at the same time as Redbridge and Liberty, who was beaming all over her face. Hadn't anyone ever told her it was unladylike to exhibit an excess of emotion? He could not tear his gaze from her as he wondered who had conjured up such a ridiculous rule. And, more importantly, why?

He bit down his irritation at Redbridge for encouraging Liberty and then had to bite it back even harder when he noticed Hope looking from him to Liberty and back again. He didn't try to interpret her expression, he just concentrated on blanking his own.

It was a relief when it was time for the next dance and he could lead Liberty on to the dance floor.

'Why did you ask me to waltz?'

Liberty gazed up at Dominic, her eyes smiling although her lips were serious. Dominic's fingers flexed on her waist, holding her more securely as they entered their first turn. The truthful answer was that he did not know. The words had slipped from his lips before his brain could stop them. But he didn't regret his impulse—she felt so right in his arms. If only... He quashed that wish before it could fully form. There was no *if only*. Not for him. He knew his duty to the Dukedom. To his father. To his mother.

As ever, the thought of his mother conjured forth that feeling of never quite being good enough. If she had lived, what would she think of the man he had become? *Would* she, finally, be proud? His chest tightened as he recalled the last time he had seen his mother— the only time in his eight years he could remember any spontaneous gesture of affection from her. It was her custom to walk around the lake every day when she was at home at the Abbey and, that day, Dominic had asked if he might go with her. Rather than the brusque refusal he expected, she had smiled at him and patted his cheek.

'Mr Brockley will be waiting for you, Dominic, but—if you are good and pay attention in your lessons— maybe we can go out again later.'

Later had never come. He had never seen his mother again and the memory of that last encounter had, over the years, helped to fuel his determination to fulfil his destiny.

He wrenched his thoughts out of the past—Liberty awaited his answer…why *had* he asked her to waltz? He gazed into her midnight-blue eyes, breathed in the scent of roses…now not solely his mother's preserve, but that of Liberty Lovejoy as well. Mother wouldn't approve of Liberty, that was for sure. But it was only one waltz.

'Why not?' he countered.

'Well, now. Let me see. Maybe because this is the cautious Lord Avon who is intent on selecting the perfect bride to complete his perfect life and who appears to conduct his entire life with the sole purpose of protecting his reputation?'

He strove to keep his expression blank at her succinct summation of his life.

'So cautious, in fact,' she continued, 'that I have heard it whispered that he never dances twice with the same young lady. And yet this is our second dance this evening.'

He hid his surprise. 'You will note, however, that I have engaged several young ladies to dance with me twice this evening.'

Their gazes fused, her blue eyes knowing. 'I *also* noted that the other engagements followed mine as you sought to divert attention from your uncharacteristic slip.'

'Slip?'

'You masked it well, my lord, but I saw the shock in your eyes in the split second after you asked me to waltz. Were I a more generous person, I would have refused that impulsive offer, but I could not resist accepting, if only to see how you would manage your mistake.'

'It was no mistake. I did and I *do* want to waltz with you, Liberty Lovejoy.'

He heard her quick intake of breath and, without volition, his hand tightened on hers and his other hand slid further around her waist, drawing her closer. Caution clamoured through his brain, but he ignored it.

'You...' Her voice sounded breathless. 'You are unused to acting on impulse, I would guess.'

'A man in my position cannot afford to act on impulse.'

She stayed silent and a quick glance down revealed a wrinkled forehead.

'You are puzzled?'

Her head snapped up. 'No. Not puzzled. Sad.'

'Sad?'

He felt her shrug. 'It must be an uncomfortable existence, to be forever on your guard, wary of how you appear to others.'

Her words came close to his earlier thoughts about ridiculous rules, but they were a fact of life. His life, in any case. 'That is the world we live in. That is what it means to be part of the *haut ton*. But, to return to your original question, I asked you to waltz because it is a chance to talk uninterrupted. With no risk of being overheard.'

Her eyebrows arched. 'You wanted the opportunity to talk to me without being overheard? Why, Lord Avon...' she batted her eyelashes at him '...what can you possibly have to say to me that ought not to be overheard?' She tilted her head, her lips closer to his ear. 'Will I be shocked?'

Her breath on his skin raised the hairs at his nape. He was playing with fire. His common sense warned him to keep his distance. But something deep inside him—something older, baser, more primeval—now challenged the innate caution that had been part of his character for as long as he could remember...challenged it square on, with raised fists and a desire to knock it out. But, he reasoned, as long as he managed to keep that challenger under control, there was no reason why he could not indulge in a little flirtation.

'It depends, Miss Lovejoy, on how easily you are shocked.'

His voice sounded husky. Deep. And he felt Liberty's reaction. He *had* intended to shock her and it seemed he was successful.

She cleared her throat. 'Tell me what happened with Verity and Lord Bridlington.'

Dominic bit back a smile. For all her boldness a moment ago, that change of subject revealed much about Liberty's true character, even though she might flirt a little and take risks.

'You know what happened. I told you.'

'You punched him? Did he hit you back?'

'No. He knew he was in the wrong. He was caught before any damage was done and he will accept he has lost.'

She frowned. 'Should I be worried? Will he target Verity again?'

'I doubt it. He is an opportunist. He viewed Verity as easy prey with no father to protect her and a brother who appeared not to care less. He knows differently now. He will turn his attention to someone less well protected, especially after Gideon speaks to him, as he promised he will.'

She shivered. 'I did not realise there are such men in the *ton*, masquerading as gentlemen.'

'I am afraid there are such men in all walks of life.'

'I am so grateful you saw him and stopped him.'

'It was my pleasure.'

Her smile did strange things to him. It was the trem-ble of her lip—it was not artifice, he was certain—and it was the hint of vulnerability in her eyes, the deep breath she often took before replying to a comment, as if steeling herself. The truth hit him like a lightning strike. She acted and spoke boldly, but it was not bold-ness but bravery. She found the courage from some-where to stand up for those she loved and for what she believed in.

He didn't want to admire her. Wasn't the ever-present lust enough for him to fight against? It felt as though his well-ordered, meticulously planned life was spinning out of control. He clenched his jaw, set her at the cor-rect distance from him and concentrated on the steps of the waltz even as the scent of roses wove magic through his veins.

Chapter Eleven

The following afternoon Liberty was about to set out on the short walk to Grosvenor Square when Gideon descended the staircase. She took a minute to admire him—he was so handsome and he looked a proper gentleman in his blue superfine coat, cream breeches and polished Hessians. She frowned. She had grown accustomed to him staying out until dawn and then sleeping most of the day away. Since their arrival in London it seemed that the only times she'd seen him this early in the day he had been unshaven and wearing a dressing robe and slippers. But last night he had escorted his sisters home and, it would appear, gone straight to bed.

'You look very smart, Gideon.'

A faint flag of colour washed over his cheeks. 'I intend to call on Lady Twyford, to pay my respects and to thank her for last night's entertainment.'

'Ah.' Of course. Gideon had spent much of his time in a group of young men surrounding Lady Emily Crighton, Lord Twyford's eldest daughter. And joined her for supper. 'Please extend my gratitude as well—it was kind of them to invite us.'

'Well, I have no doubt the invitations will roll in

apace, now you've established yourself as part of the Beauchamps' inner circle.'

Stung by the implication she was a social climber, Liberty finished pulling on her second glove before she trusted herself to answer him.

'I hope you know me better than to think I would pretend friendship with someone simply for advancement.'

She held her twin's gaze, hating that he might think that of her. Particularly when her sole reason for approaching Jane last night had been to inveigle an introduction to Alex and the reason for *that* was standing in front of her looking positively angelic.

Gideon looked away first.

'No. Of course you would not. And I'm sorry, again, for not listening when you warned me about Bridlington. I'll be sure to speak to him when I next see him, but I trust Avon when he said Verity isn't in any danger now. But enough of that. Where are you off to? And where are the others? You're not...' His eyes narrowed. 'Tell me you are not going out *alone*?'

That was exactly what she had intended. It was such a short walk to Beauchamp House—just around the corner, really—that she hadn't even considered the impropriety until Gideon asked his question. Dominic's words whispered through her brain: *If you bring disgrace upon yourself, it is your sisters who will suffer.*

She put her nose in the air. 'Of course I am not going out alone, Gideon. I was on the brink of sending for one of the maids to accompany me but, as you are here now, you may escort me yourself.'

Gideon scowled. 'I ain't going *shopping* with you, if that's where you're off to. I told you. I'm calling on E— Lady Twyford.'

'Well, for your information, I am not going shopping. I have been invited to Beauchamp House to meet Lady Olivia's children.' Liberty snaked her arm around Gideon's and headed for the door, towing him with her. 'It is barely out of your way at all.'

'Very well.'

They were soon strolling in the direction of Grosvenor Square.

'Gideon.' It was rare lately that she had the chance to speak to him privately. She could not pass up the opportunity and, for once, he was not suffering the consequences of either overindulgence or lack of sleep. 'I *have* been worried about you.'

'I know. You've made that very clear.'

'That actress…'

He halted and frowned down at her. 'What,' he said, menacingly, 'do you know about her?'

'I am not a fool! I know you haven't been haunting the Sans Pareil for the quality of the performances.'

He growled, deep in his throat, then continued to walk. 'I cannot believe I am having this conversation with my sister. Listen, Liberty—you must stop thinking you can dictate where I go or what I do.'

'I am not trying to dictate to you. I—I just want you—all of you—to be safe. And happy.'

Gideon slipped his arm around her waist and gave her a quick squeeze. 'Lib. Listen to me. It wasn't your fault they died.'

Her heart clenched. 'I—I know.'

'And it doesn't mean it is your responsibility to protect all of us. I am a grown man and I can look after myself.'

'I know that, too.'

He raised his brows. 'Do you? Look…yes, I visit the

theatre, but…it is just a bit of fun. I am at no risk. You say you are not a fool. Well, neither am I—I am a peer now and I'm aware of my obligations. And before you complain again about me frittering my fortune away, believe me when I tell you I can afford a few losses at the gaming tables.'

If only she could fully believe him. It seemed the habit of protecting her family, especially her beloved twin, would not be satisfied *that* easily. Wisely, she did not say so.

Gideon sighed and slanted a smile at her, his blue eyes glinting. 'I *also* admit it will not help Hope and Verity to find decent husbands if I continue to set the gossips' tongues alight. So, I shall henceforth be the soul of discretion—I shall still have fun and enjoy myself, but I shall do so well away from the public gaze.'

They had arrived at Beauchamp House and the door opened before Gideon could knock, giving Liberty no chance to reply. A haughty-looking butler peered out, looking down his long nose at her.

'Miss Lovejoy. Lady Olivia is expecting me.'

The butler's gaze slid to Gideon, perused him from head to toe, then stood back and bowed.

'Please come in, Miss Lovejoy; my Lord Wendover.'

'Oh, I'm not coming in—just wanted to see my sister safely delivered. I'll see you at dinner, Lib.'

Liberty watched Gideon walk away, whistling a jaunty tune, leaving Liberty to enter alone. She paused on the threshold, remembering the last time she had called at this house, and a smile tugged at her lips as she recalled her efforts to dodge the footman.

'Ahem.'

The butler raised one brow and Liberty wiped any

hint of amusement from her features before entering the hall.

'Lady Olivia is expecting you, Miss Lovejoy. Please follow me.'

He led the way up the magnificent marble staircase to a parlour on the first floor—a cosy and informal room and not nearly as grand as the room into which Dominic had shown her. Olivia was sitting on a sofa, her legs tucked up under her, reading. She looked up, smiled and set her book aside.

'I am so pleased to see you, Liberty. Thank you for coming. Grantham, please inform Mrs Himley that my guest has arrived and she may send up refreshments. Now—' as the butler left the room '—come and sit by me... I asked Ruth to bring the twins down after we have drunk our tea—lively two-year-olds and cups of hot liquid are a poor combination.'

Liberty did as she was bid.

'I'm sorry to receive you in here,' Olivia went on, 'but the servants are working so hard to prepare the house for Papa's arrival that I could not in all conscience receive you in the salon, not when the twins will be joining us.' She grinned. 'They have the ability to reduce any room to utter chaos without even trying. Grantham was mortified when he discovered I intended to receive a guest in the family parlour, but I made sure you would not object.'

'Of course I don't object. Is Grantham your father's butler?'

'He is. He arrived in London yesterday.'

'I am rather pleased he was not here when I called—' Liberty snapped her mouth shut as her cheeks burned.

Olivia tilted her head. 'When you called...? You have been here before?'

'No. Yes. Oh, heavens…my wretched tongue! I…'

But hadn't Dominic told her Olivia had always been protective of Alex? Surely she would understand? She told Olivia of the reason for her visit to Beauchamp House and how she had mistaken Dominic for Alex. Olivia's eyes danced with merriment.

'What fun! That takes me back to my debut year— I tied myself in tangles trying to protect Alex from the consequences of his actions…but we both survived and I met my beloved Hugo, and all turned out for the best. In the end. But…forgive me, but Wendover does not seem near as wild or as…*self-destructive*…as Alex used to be. I noticed nothing out of the way in his behaviour last night. Indeed, he appeared the perfect gentleman.'

'I believe…I *hope*…that may be because he has developed a *tendre* for a certain young lady. It appears there is nothing as likely to persuade a man to behave himself as the presence of watchful parents.'

Olivia sighed. 'Oh, how I wish Alex would develop a fancy for a nice girl. I fear he will never wed—his temperament is too unpredictable.' She caught Liberty's eye and smiled ruefully. 'You and I seem very alike. As do our families. Ought I to apologise for our family squabbling last night? It's odd. Here I am, married for four years and the mother of twins, yet as soon as I am with Dominic and Alex the years seem to drop away and we slip back into the same old relationship. With me as their little sister,' she added in a disgusted tone. 'I keep meaning to resist, but it seems impossible—that role is so natural to me, it happens quite without any intent on my part.' Olivia sent Liberty a rueful smile. 'I don't know! Brothers! They spend half their life tormenting and teasing you—pretending they are so very superior simply because they are male—and the rest of the time they appear hell-bent on ruining their lives. You cannot help but try to protect them from their own folly.'

Liberty frowned. 'But…surely… Lord Avon…he, at least, is all that is proper and gentlemanly. *He* cannot give you cause for concern.'

A maid came in at that moment, with a tea tray and cakes. The butler had opened the door for her and he lingered, waiting until the maid had poured the tea and handed Olivia and Liberty their cups.

'Thank you, Betty,' said Olivia. The maid flashed a smile, then hurried towards the waiting butler and the still-open door.

'The poor things don't know what's hit them since Grantham arrived—heaven forfend Papa should find a speck of dust or a picture unaligned when he arrives.' Olivia gurgled a laugh.

'H-he sounds quite intimidating,' said Liberty.

'Oh, pooh. He gives himself airs and graces, but underneath it all he's an old softy.'

Liberty stared at Olivia, open-mouthed. Olivia returned her quizzical look, then burst out laughing. 'I meant Grantham, silly! Not Papa! Not that he's intimidating either…well, he might appear so at times, but he is not. Not really. Grantham could give any duke lessons on how to be pompous and unbending.'

Silence reigned as they sipped their tea and nibbled at slices of moist fruit cake.

'Speaking of Lord Avon—' Liberty could contain her curiosity no longer '—I was intrigued by your conversation about Westfield last night. For a bachelor, your brother appears strangely knowledgeable about twins and children in general, but when I asked him about it, he seemed to…well, to withdraw somehow.'

'Oh, Dom is never one to puff off his good deeds.

Or anything about his life, in actual fact. He is quite private. But Westfield—he's been a patron for…ooh, seven years now—since he was nineteen. It is a school and orphan asylum in Islington.'

'That seems a strange thing for such a young man to get involved with.'

'Maybe to outsiders,' said Olivia, 'but not when you know Dominic. Lady Stanton, who is one of our cousins—second or third, or some such—was already a patron, even before she married, and when she told Dominic about it he decided to help. He knows how hard it was to lose Mother and *we* still had Papa. He said at the time he could not bear to imagine how much worse it would be if your family was poor and you lost both parents. He wanted to help give those children a future other than crime and begging.'

'I remember how hard it was to lose both *our* parents and I was nineteen.'

Liberty tried, and failed, to imagine how dreadful it must be for a very young child to suddenly find itself all alone in the world. Her respect for Dominic increased— he did not have to help those children, but he chose to.

'Westfield is not just for orphans, but for abandoned children, too. There are more of those than you would care to know about. Why, just a few days ago he recognised a beggar woman on the street with a child that wasn't hers and rescued it. My Hugo was with him, or I'd never have known about it, of course. Hugo is taking me to visit Westfield soon—he went there with Dominic and he told me it is hopelessly overcrowded. He thought we might set up an establishment in Sussex, near to where we live, to take some of the children.'

'That is a kind thought.'

'I'm ashamed to admit I've never been there before,'

Olivia said. 'That makes me rather thought*less*, doesn't it?' She chewed at her lip, staring down at her hands in her lap. 'I've never considered getting involved myself, even though I know how hard it is to lose a parent. And I had every advantage in life, because of who Papa is, and we had my aunt and my uncle, too.'

'What was your mother like?'

'I don't remember her very well. All I remember is rejection and impatience. I was only five, of course, when she died—I've no doubt I *was* a constant nuisance—but try as I might I can never remember approval or affection. I will never know if that would have changed as I grew up...never know if she would finally approve of me and be proud of me.' She raised her eyes and Liberty was concerned to see tears sheening them. On impulse, she took Olivia's hand and squeezed. Olivia emitted a sound, half-laugh, half-sniff. 'Hark at me, getting all maudlin. But at least now you understand why I am so determined to be a good mother to my twins.'

'I am sure you could never be a bad mother, Olivia. You have proved how much you care and all children need is to know they are loved.'

'They know how much their papa and I dote on them, but I am still curious about them being twins and interested in how, if at all, it might make them different from other children. Will you tell me about your childhood? Were you and your brother always close? Was your relationship with him different to your relationship with your sisters?'

They chatted for several minutes about twins in particular and brothers and sisters in general—although Liberty didn't feel she offered Olivia any special insight into being a twin. She and Gideon had naturally bonded more as children, but she believed that was due more to the age difference between them and their younger sisters than simply because they happened to be born at the same time. It was hard to accept the bond she had believed unbreakable had frayed so badly, although there was more hope in her heart after their talk on the way to Beauchamp House. The time flew by, until the door opened and a nursemaid entered, ushering two infants into the room. They were followed by a footman carrying a large wooden ship which he set down on the rug in front of the fireplace. The children stood stock still upon spying Liberty, their eyes huge, thumbs jammed into their mouths.

'Ruth,' said Olivia to the nursemaid, her silver eyes brimming with laughter, 'this pair can't possibly be Julius and Daisy—I do believe you have switched them for imposters. *They* are never this quiet.' She held out her arms then. 'Come to Mama, sweeties, and meet Mama's friend.'

Before too long, Julius, still somewhat shy, was perched comfortably on Liberty's knee, patting and stroking her hair and face, while Olivia had joined her daughter on the floor to play with a splendid ark and a collection of carved wooden animals.

Julius was so soft and huggable. Liberty's arms closed around the little boy and that familiar hollow ached in her chest. She no longer doubted that she was ready to find love again, but the only man she had ever come close to having feelings for was Dominic. And he was so far out of her reach it was futile to even daydream about it.

'Liberty? *Liberty!*'

She was jerked out of her thoughts by Olivia's persistent calling of her name. Then Julius stiffened in her lap before wriggling free of her arms and sliding down to the floor.

'Well, young Julius,' drawled a deep, familiar voice, 'I see you have started young with the ladies.'

Heat scorched Liberty's cheeks as she realised Dominic must have been watching them for some minutes before being noticed. She quickly tidied her hair. Her heart, from being an aching void, bloomed with joy as his mouth curved in an irresistible smile and mischief twinkled in his eyes and she struggled to keep her feelings hidden—she could not bear it if he realised how she was beginning to care for him. How utterly mortifying that would be. She smiled a cool greeting as the twins rushed to him and he gathered them both up and kissed their cheeks soundly, blowing air against their skin to make loud noises and sending them into fits of giggles.

With blinding clarity she saw he was two different men. There was the public Lord Avon, with his proper behaviour and his correct manners—the Lord Avon who was familiar to the *haut ton* and who had attended to Lady Caroline at supper last night—and then there was the Dominic who emerged when his family were around him. His family…and her. Liberty Lovejoy. Because somehow, without even trying, Liberty had been admitted into the inner circle of people with whom Dominic felt able to relax and to reveal more of the real man inside.

But did that simply mean her opinion was unimportant to him?

A lump swelled in her throat as she watched him with Olivia's children. He would make a wonderful father… and he was a man who *cared*. How many nineteen-year-old wealthy and privileged young men would bother themselves with the plight of orphans? Not Gideon, even now he was almost five-and-twenty. Dominic was clearly a man who trod his own path, regardless of what his peers expected of a man in his position.

He was so much more than she had first believed, when all she had seen was a wealthy but shallow aristocrat who knew and cared nothing for the plight of others. Not only did he take practical steps to help those less fortunate, but his selflessness was not in order to enhance his own reputation. He was well-known in society, and often talked about, but Liberty had not heard the slightest hint of his charity work.

Her thoughts whirled with what she had learned… was learning…about him. Olivia's revelations about her childhood and the mother who had never given her the unconditional love she craved prompted Liberty to wonder about Dominic and his relationship with that same mother.

'Dominic!' Olivia regained her feet and shook out her skirts. 'You are early! We agreed four o'clock, did we not, and it is only just gone three.'

'I wanted to spend a little uninterrupted time with my niece and nephew while I have the chance.'

He hugged them both into his chest again before setting them down on the floor and strolling further into the room.

'Good afternoon, Miss Lovejoy.' He bowed. 'I do hope you will not object to my disturbing your time with Livvy? I can always go up to the nursery with the twins if I am *de trop* and you wish to gossip unhindered.'

'Now, Dom, you know very well we would not gossip in front of the children…not that we do gossip, of course,' Olivia added hastily.

'Of course,' Dominic agreed smoothly as the twins tugged at him to play with their toys. He sighed. 'Very well, scamps, but allow me to remove my coat first—

Brailsford will never forgive me if I soil my coat *before* I display my elegance in the Park.'

'Dominic! Miss Lovejoy is my guest. You cannot cavort before her in shirt sleeves!'

Liberty found herself the object of a penetrating look from Dominic. A look that set off a delicious fluttering deep in her abdomen.

'Will I offend your sensibilities, Miss Lovejoy?' He arched one brow. 'I know it is not quite the done thing, but surely we may relax a few of the conventions after our recent…er…slightly *un*conventional encounters?'

'You need not be coy, Dominic—Liberty has told me how she called here to beard Papa in his den and mistook you for Alex.' Olivia giggled as she sat next to Liberty on the sofa and nudged her. 'You should be honoured— he only ever teases people he likes and they're mostly family. Oh! I know! You can be our honorary sister. I always wanted a sister!'

Chapter Twelve

Dominic tried to ignore the tension swirling in his gut. This had seemed a good idea at the time—an opportunity to spend a little time with Julius and Daisy before Father and Stepmother arrived, when his half-sister and half-brother, Christabel and Sebastian, would also demand his attention. Besides, he adored spending time with the little monkeys.

That Liberty Lovejoy would be here was entirely incidental. Wasn't it? She tempted him like no other woman of his acquaintance and—if he was wise, which he clearly wasn't—he should do all he could to avoid her. Yet here he was, concentrating on steadying his breathing as the subtle note of her perfume weaved through his senses. That picture of her with young Julius on her lap—her pensive, wistful expression—was now seared into his brain. His heart had twitched with longing as he took in the sight and, try as he might to replace her image with any of the ladies on that original shortlist, he simply could not imagine any of them dandling a child on their knee and allowing it to fiddle with their hair.

Mother, certainly, would never have tolerated such behaviour. She had been goddess-like to her three children—

a goddess they had all worshipped and done their utmost to please, forever seeking her praise. He thrust down those memories and the weight of duty, responsibility and expectation they evoked.

'Olivia.'

'Dominic?'

'By my calculations I have now spoken to Miss Lovejoy twice since entering this room, including asking her a number of direct questions, and she has yet to reply to any of them because you have rushed in to speak for her.'

He welcomed the familiar spark in his sister's eyes. 'Well, that is entirely your fault, Brother dear, for asking her such awkward questions in the first place! *I* am Liberty's hostess and it is my duty to protect her from feeling uncomfortable. You forget, she is not used to your teasing ways, Dom.'

'Good Lord, you haven't changed, Livvy! Four years wed and you are still the fiery brat you always were.'

Olivia's cheekbones sported two bright flags of colour and he regretted the words as soon as they were spoken. What was he? Sixteen years old again? Of course Olivia was still the same spirited girl and he prayed she always would be—she would not be the little sister he loved and cherished if marriage and motherhood changed her too much.

'Liv... I'm sorry! We do seem to slip back into that same old relationship when we get together, don't we?'

The colour in her cheeks faded and she grinned. 'I was saying much the same thing before the twins came down, wasn't I, Liberty?'

'You were indeed, Olivia.' Liberty's response was calm, with just the right touch of light amusement. 'And in answer to your query about your jacket, sir, please do so. I pledge myself to remain utterly unoffended by such an action.'

Dominic saw that their little spat had given Liberty a chance to collect herself. When she first became aware of him, a soft pink blush had washed across her skin and her velvety-blue eyes had widened and darkened as her lush lips parted. Her unguarded reaction had lasted a bare second, but her joyful expression had drawn a similar happy response from him. Then her expression had shuttered and it was apparent that the woman he had first met, whose feelings shone in her expressions, had changed in the time he had known her. Her features were no longer a window into her soul. He could not blame her—society and the *ton* were enough to make even the toughest-skinned person wary—but, damn it, he hated that he could no longer read her every thought.

Olivia's words resounded through his head. *An honorary sister*, indeed. Nothing could be further from the way he felt about Liberty Lovejoy. But he could, and must, view her as a family friend, such as Jane Colebrooke was—although he had never lusted after Jane in his entire life. He could cope with thinking of Liberty as a friend…just. But in no way could he view her as his sister.

He shrugged out of his jacket and joined the twins on the rug. He was soon lost in their game, pairing up the animals and marching them up the ramp into the ark, the faint murmur of conversation fading into the background, until he realised Liberty was standing up, clearly preparing to take her leave. He jumped to his feet and collected his jacket from the chair where he had laid it.

'Did a maid accompany you, Miss Lovejoy?'

She probably came alone. I wouldn't put it past her.

'No. My brother escorted me, sir. I wonder if a maid might walk with me back to Green Street, Olivia?'

She caught Dominic's eye and raised one challenging brow as if to say, *See? I can behave like a lady when I choose to.*

He bit back a grin. 'There's no need to bother one of the maids—might I offer to drive you home?' He batted away the inner warning that he was, again, playing with fire. He was merely being practical. Being a gentleman. 'I ordered my curricle brought round for four but, unless Olivia has changed the habits of a lifetime, I cannot see her being dressed and ready to go by then as it is already three minutes to the hour. Unless, of course, you no longer wish to drive in the Park this afternoon, Liv?'

'Heavens! Is that the time? Oh, I have enjoyed our time together this afternoon, Liberty…do say you will come again.

'And of course I still want to go to the Park, Dom. How else am I to properly meet your young ladies without calling upon them…and that would never do, would it?'

'No. It would not.'

A shudder racked Dominic at the very idea. As soon as any member of his family showed marked attention to any one of the names that were thought to be on his shortlist, the news would be on every gossipmonger's lips and he would soon find himself in a corner and honour-bound to make an offer. At least any attention he paid to Liberty was unlikely to be misconstrued, firstly because of her friendship with Olivia but, more importantly, because no one in the *ton* would imagine for one moment that such an unsuitable female would ever be included on his list.

'Well, Miss Lovejoy? Are you happy to accept my offer of escort?'

'Indeed I am, my lord. Thank you.'

Olivia said nothing but, at the gleam in her eyes as she looked from Dominic to Liberty and back again, a warning trickled down his spine. His sister was no fool—he must work even harder at masking his growing feelings for Liberty. As Olivia, Ruth and the twins headed upstairs after saying goodbye to Liberty, Dominic walked with her to the front door where Grantham waited.

'Your curricle arrived two minutes ago, my lord.' The butler opened the door.

'Thank you, Grantham.'

'They are a beautiful pair.' Liberty surprised Dominic by heading straight to the horses, being held by his groom, Ted. She looked them over with clear appreciation, then removed her glove and held her hand to each horse's nose in turn to allow them to snuffle at her palm and take in her scent. 'Very well matched. What are their names?'

'Thank you. Beau and Buck—they are a pleasure to drive. Very responsive.' He was proud of his bays, which he had purchased last year. 'Alex bred and trained them. Do you drive, Miss Lovejoy?'

She smiled up at him, and his heart soared. 'I have never driven anything other than our old cob at home. But I have a lovely riding mare.' Then she frowned. 'At least, she *is* lovely, but she is also now quite old. We left her behind in Sussex.'

With one accord they returned to the curricle. Dominic took Liberty's hand to help her into the vehicle, his fingers closing around hers. She hadn't replaced her glove and Dominic had not yet drawn his on and, as he registered the warmth of her smooth, soft skin his breath seized and he had to stifle the urge to haul her into his arms. He swallowed and released her hand as soon as she was in the curricle. He pulled on his gloves, willing his heartbeat and his body under control as he climbed up next to her.

Liberty nudged into him with her shoulder—the slightest of movements, but his heart lurched again at that contact. He looked down into her innocent expression. One golden brow arched.

'Do not forget to order your groom to jump up behind,' she whispered. Her lips curved into a delicious, teasing smile. 'You have your reputation to protect.'

His throat ached with suppressed longing, but he refused to yield to his base desires. Duty was what mattered, not physical needs. He smiled back. 'With what you already know of me, Berty, you cannot possibly imagine I would overlook such a crucial matter.'

'Berty?' She sounded outraged, but her eyes twinkled.

'Liberty is such a mouthful.' His loins instantly reacted to his unintentional double entendre.

'What is wrong with Libby?' She stared up at him, innocently, clearly having missed the meaning. 'Or Lib? That is what my family call me sometimes.'

'Oh, I couldn't possibly,' Dominic murmured. 'They are far too easily confused with Livvy and Liv, and I most definitely do *not* think of you as another sister, despite what Olivia said.'

Her cheeks bloomed pink. The curricle dipped as Ted climbed up behind and Dominic flicked the reins. They set off on the short drive to Green Street.

'Maybe I should be relieved that we cannot now talk without being overheard.'

Another teasing smile filled him with the urge to simply touch her mouth. With one fingertip. To test whether her lips were as soft and luscious as they looked....to trace their fullness...to slip his finger into that hot, moist... Blood flooded his groin and different urges took him in their hold. He wrenched his gaze from her mouth to her eyes, full of teasing laughter, battling to keep his expression blank.

'A good groom knows when to turn a deaf ear,' he said. 'Is that not right, Ted?'

'Beg pardon, milord? Were you speakin' to me? I didn' quite catch what you said.'

Liberty laughed, a delightful gurgling sound of pleasure. 'Oh, that is famous! Lord Avon, you, sir, are such a contradiction—the perfect lord whose servants are as well trained as his horses.'

'I prefer to describe my staff as loyal rather than well trained.'

'Loyal, indeed. What else, I wonder, have your servants failed to notice over the years, for fear of sullying your reputation?'

Their eyes met. And held. And the naked look of... *longing* in those velvety-blue eyes matched exactly what was in his heart. His voice when he answered her was husky.

'I wish I could lay claim to a wild, exciting parallel existence to this life but, alas, what you see before you is the whole.'

'What? No hidden depths? You disappoint me, sir.'

And the thought of disappointing her wrenched at him. He cleared his throat and, this time, his words emerged light and airy. Nonchalant. Exactly as they should sound.

'Nary a one, I'm afraid.'

Liberty fell silent. A sideways glance revealed a blush on her cheeks and her golden eyebrows drawn into a frown. Had she, like him, recognised the dangerous territory into which they had strayed? He drove around the corner into Green Street and the relief that flooded him took him by surprise. He had intended a light flirtation. He enjoyed Liberty's company, but this…this flirtatious repartee… It was dangerous. *Here* were the depths his life had so far lacked and his inner voice of caution was screaming at him to take care and not to venture so far that he could not return to the shallows.

He offered a change of subject and her relief was palpable. 'I am pleased you and Olivia seem destined to be friends.'

'I like her very much. I… I have not had many friends my own age. Gideon and the girls were always enough.'

That comment alone explained much about Liberty— she had devoted her life to her family. Was that why she fretted so about Gideon? The huge change in their lives must be as unsettling for her as it was for her brother. Their lives would never be the same again.

He reined Beau and Buck to a halt outside the Love-joys' house. 'Here we are.'

Ted ran to the horses' heads and Dominic leapt to the pavement to hand Liberty down. She placed her hand— gloved this time—into his. Without volition, his fingers closed around hers, pressing. Another blush coloured her cheeks and Dominic cursed himself for a weak-minded fool. What the hell was he playing at? Whenever he was in Liberty Lovejoy's presence he seemed to lose all vestige of self-control.

The second she reached the ground he released her hand as though it were red-hot. He knocked on the door and, as soon as it opened, he bowed.

'Thank you for driving me home, my lord.'

'It was my pleasure, Miss Lovejoy.'

And he meant it. He really did. It had been—it had always been—a pleasure to spend time in her company. But he must take care to avoid such tête-à-têtes in future. It was simply too dangerous and it would be Liberty's reputation that suffered. Not his.

Liberty removed her pelisse and bonnet and handed them to Ethel, her thoughts in turmoil, matching the bubbling confusion in her belly. Did it mean anything that Dominic had come early to Beauchamp House, knowing she would be there? Or was her presence neither here nor there and he had told the absolute truth—that the only reason he called earlier than expected was to spend time with the twins? Was her imagination running away with her—envisaging a happy ever after where there could never be one, simply because she had discovered that he was the man who stirred her blood like no other—even Bernard? Because she had found that, in addition to all his other attributes, Lord Avon was also a kind and charitable gentleman?

Why, then, had he insisted on driving her home? Had he been flirting with her, or was she naïve in thinking there was a special warmth in his voice when he spoke to her? He had called her Berty and the memory kindled a glow inside her. He found her attractive, she knew, but was his behaviour with her mere practised flirtation from a gentleman or did his feelings go deeper? He enjoyed her company, and he was relaxed and informal with her in a way she never saw him behave with any of the ladies on his shortlist, but did *any* of that amount to anything other than wishful thinking on her part?

She could not decide. But, increasingly, she knew what she would like the answer to be.

'Mrs Mount is in the drawing room, miss,' said Ethel.

Liberty headed upstairs to the drawing room where she found Mrs Mount having a quiet doze in a chair by the fire. She awoke with a start as Liberty entered the room.

'Where are Hope and Verity?'

'They are riding in the Park. With Lord Wendover.'

'Gideon?' Liberty sat in the opposite chair. 'Do my ears deceive me? Do you mean to tell me he came back home after calling on Lady Twyford?'

She had been certain that was the last any of them would see of her brother until dinner that evening.

'Yes. He returned in a rush to inform us he had hired two horses from the livery stables and that your sisters were to get changed and be ready to ride out with him. He was most insistent. Verity believes he had arranged to meet up with Lady Emily in the Park and Hope and Verity will provide him with the perfect excuse to ride with her.'

'Oh, that is wonderful news. Lady Emily would be a splendid match—'

'Stop!' Mrs Mount leaned forward. 'I beg your pardon, my dear, but please do not get carried away. Gideon only met Lady Emily last night and he is still young.'

Liberty sighed. 'You are right. I cannot help but be happy she is distracting him from that horrid actress, though.'

Mrs Mount relaxed back with a relieved sigh. 'Now.

What about you, my dear? You must count yourself fortunate that Lady Olivia has taken a shine to you.'

'Fortunate? How so?'

'So there will be no repercussions from your… um…*unusual* encounters with Lord Avon, of course. He could scarcely cut his sister's friend—he is far too much the gentleman—and, to think, he not only danced with you last night, but with Hope and Verity, too! I always prayed they might catch his eye.'

She beamed with satisfaction and Liberty bit her tongue against telling her the real reason Dominic had danced with her sisters.

'Well, I do not see what is so very special about His Lordship,' she muttered, even though she knew exactly what was so very special about Dominic. But she would be mortified if anyone had the slightest suspicion of her growing feelings for him.

'And that attitude, miss, will get you nowhere in society.'

A blush heated Liberty's cheeks at Mrs Mount's reprimand. She had been hired to help Liberty and her sisters learn how to behave as well-brought-up young ladies should and Liberty was aware of the flaw in her own personality that prompted her to rebel against such strict mores.

'Whether you approve or not, Liberty, the heir to a dukedom will always command respect and be fêted and courted by those lower in precedence.' Mrs Mount's voice softened. 'Now, tell me all about your visit—did you meet the twins?'

'Oh, they are delightful! Olivia is besotted with them, but I cannot think I have helped her understand how raising twins is different to raising other children. She is so determined to be the perfect mother to them.'

'Well, I hope for their sake she is a better mother than her own proved to be.'

'Olivia's mother? Why?' Olivia's confidences about her childhood had piqued Liberty's interest. 'What was she like? Did you know her well?'

'The first Duchess? Why, yes, my dear. We were close in age and we made our debut together. She was three years older than Cheriton, you know. Oh, she was as selfish as they come and utterly arrogant, especially after becoming a duchess. She had not a thought for anyone or anything beyond her own selfish pleasures. Poor Cheriton. He married young…far too young…and all *she* wanted was the glamour and acclaim of the title. She had no interest in those poor children—she spent as much time as possible in London after Olivia was born. She could not bear to be "buried in the depths of the countryside" as she used to put it.' Mrs Mount huffed a laugh. 'Ironic, really, when you consider that's where she ended up—buried at Cheriton Abbey.'

'What happened?' Liberty could not help her curiosity. 'Did she die in childbirth?' That tragic fate befell so many women it seemed a reasonable assumption. Then a shiver chased across her skin as she recalled her parents and Bernard. 'Did she fall ill?'

'No, my dear.' Mrs Mount lowered her voice. 'She was *murdered.*'

'Murdered?' That was the last thing she expected to hear. A duchess, murdered? 'But…how?'

'No one knows, my dear. They say it was probably a passing vagrant. And, much as it pains me to speak ill of the dead, it was probably a blessing for those poor children and their father. Their aunt, Lady Cecily, raised them after that and it's a wonder they have all turned out as well as they have. Well, apart from Lord Alexander…he was ever a wild youth, but it does seem he has settled at long last.

'Now, tell me all about today, my dear. Has the Duke arrived yet?'

'Not yet—only Lady Olivia and her family are in residence at the moment but the staff are all bustling about preparing the house, so the Duke and Duchess and their children must be expected soon. And Lord Avon called while I was there.' She hadn't meant to mention him, but his name slipped past her lips quite without intention. 'He had arranged to drive Olivia in the Park, but came early to spend some time with the twins.'

'The Park?' Mrs Mount clapped her hands together. 'How wonderful… I do hope he will acknowledge your sisters! He is sure to do so after dancing with them last night. Oh, I do hope Gideon has chosen their mounts wisely, to show them off to best advantage!'

'Mrs Mount!'

'Yes, my dear?'

'I do not believe you. You criticise me for getting carried away with the possibilities for Gideon and yet you insist on imagining castles in the clouds when it comes to Hope and Verity's prospects.'

'It does not hurt to have ambition, my dear Liberty. Who knows what might happen should a man like Avon lose his heart? And your sisters are exceptionally pretty.'

Liberty ground her teeth in frustration. 'He drove me home this afternoon. Lord Avon, that is. In his curricle.'

And, again, she hadn't meant to say such a thing, but the words, and his name, were battering the inside of her head, desperate to be spoken. She held her breath, awaiting Mrs Mount's response.

'*Avon* drove you home? Good gracious…such condescension! Although you are, of course, his sister's friend so no doubt he felt under some obligation. But, still, what a feather in your cap, my dear—to be singled out and driven by such a notable whip.' Then her eyes narrowed and a slow smile stretched her lips. 'Especially after such a sought-after gentleman singled you out last night, to dance. Twice! And you had supper together!' Mrs Mount's voice shrilled with excitement. 'Oh!' She lowered her voice into a conspiratorial whisper. 'Has he *said* anything to you, my dear? Has he passed any hints?'

Exasperated, because she really wished she could say yes, Liberty said, 'No. He has said nothing. And I had supper with his brother, not him. As you quite rightly said, ma'am, I am his sister's friend and both Avon and Lord Alex were merely acting the gentleman. You told me yourself about Avon's list and Lord Alexander mentioned it last night…it appears to be common knowledge and Avon did not deny its existence.

'In fact, that is precisely the reason he is driving Olivia in the Park as we speak, because she insisted she wants to meet the ladies concerned before he makes his decision.'

A surge of energy sent Liberty to her feet. She crossed to the window, which overlooked the street, and peered out.

Who in their right mind would have a list of candidates for a wife? What about the heart? What of love? That emotion clearly had no place in Dominic's plans. She thought of the time he had compared her to Olivia… that protective care each of them held for their family. That was love…a different sort of love, maybe, but Dominic clearly did not completely dismiss the emotion. Could such a clinical choice of partner ever lead to happiness? It hadn't for his father, so it seemed.

She returned to her chair. 'You said Olivia's father married too young, Mrs Mount. Why did he do so? Did he fall in love?'

'Oh, no, my dear. Many more marriages back then were arranged affairs, you know. He was only eighteen and he married to please his ailing father. Margaret was three years his senior, but she was the daughter of a marquess—very suitable in that respect. She was one of the most selfish creatures I have ever met, although she put on a good show for Cheriton and, at eighteen, I dare say he did not know enough about human nature to see the danger signs.' She shook her head. 'She had affairs. Many affairs. And not always discreetly. She even played him false with his own cousin, although I'm not sure he ever knew about that.'

She sounded an awful woman. Poor Dominic, to have such a mother.

'What about the present Duchess? Olivia seems fond of her.'

'I do not know her well, but they say it was a love match and that the Duke is very happy, even though she was only a soldier's daughter. They wed five years ago now.' She sighed. 'Now *that* was a year for romance— first the Duke, then his brother Vernon and lastly their sister, Cecily. All in the same year, all love matches and all with unexpected and, some would say, unsuitable partners.' She studied Liberty, who felt a blush heat her skin. 'I wonder…?'

Liberty leapt to her feet again. She could not allow Mrs Mount to speculate. That way lay heartache, she knew, because if someone else began to think the un- thinkable she just knew that her hopes would mushroom out of control. And she could not bear that. Lord Avon had his shortlist and her name was not on it. She did not possess the qualities he looked for in a bride and to hope he might change his criteria for a woman he only met for the first time less than a fortnight ago was stretching believability a little too far, even for her.

'Please excuse me, Mrs Mount. I must consult with Mrs Taylor on dinner tonight.'

She fled the room before she could be tempted to stay and hear what Mrs Mount was going to say.

Chapter Thirteen

Bond Street, as usual, was busy with members of the *ton* shopping, Liberty, her sisters and Mrs Mount among them. Liberty's heart was not really engaged in finding the perfect hat to go with Hope's new walking dress, but she'd realised that staying at home brooding over Dominic would be even worse than being forced to exclaim at each and every hat Hope tried on, only for her to then discard it as being not *precisely* what she wanted.

As they exited the third milliner's shop, however, her attention was grabbed by a high-pitched yelp and, half-hidden in a doorway, she caught sight of a burly man, wearing a bloodied apron, who had a squirming dog tight by the scruff of his neck as he raised his other arm. The thin stick in his hand swished audibly through the air and landed on the dog's back with a resounding crack. A scream split the air, and a bloodied welt appeared in the dog's pale golden fur.

Rage surged though Liberty. She raced to the man's side, grabbing his arm as he raised it once more.

'Stop that, you rogue!'

The man paused and eyed her with astonishment.

'Get your hands off me,' he growled. 'The dog's a thief and I'll learn him a lesson if it's the last thing I do.'

He wrenched his arm from her grip and lifted it again. The dog cringed, fear in its eyes.

'Liberty! Come away. Please.' Mrs Mount took Liberty's arm and tugged her from the doorway, away from the man and the cowering dog. 'Don't get involved,' she hissed. 'People are watching.'

The whistle of the stick cut through the air once more and the dog's scream this time was even more desperate. Gorge rose to clog Liberty's throat. She snatched her arm from Mrs Mount and rounded again on the brute. He was tall and wide, his face showing no emotion as he prepared to hit the dog again. She couldn't bear it. She didn't care who saw her. She thrust herself between man and dog and shoved at his chest with all her strength.

'Stop!' Fear and rage in equal measures sent her voice soaring a couple of octaves. 'You *will not* beat that poor animal!'

'An' 'oo are you to tell me what I may and may not do? That's my livelihood, that is.'

He gestured to the ground, to a half-mangled joint of meat. 'I chased that mangy runt from my shop an' now I've got 'im bang to rights. He won't be nabbin' meat off anyone again. Not when I've finished with 'im.'

He shoved Liberty aside and she stumbled back, her shoulder and arm colliding painfully with the hard edge of the door recess. The man raised his arm again and she pushed her hands against the brickwork and propelled herself forward, again putting her body between the two in a desperate effort to spare the dog.

'I wonder what's going on over there?'

Hugo paused outside the doorway to Angelo's Fencing Academy and drew Dominic's attention to a crowd gathering further along the street. Dominic shrugged.

'Some altercation or other, it looks like. Nothing that need—'

He stopped speaking as he recognised Hope and Verity clutching one another on the periphery of the crowd. He didn't know, not for certain, but something told him Liberty was in there, somewhere. In the thick of it.

'I'll join you directly,' he called over his shoulder as he set off at a run towards the crowd. He hadn't even covered half the distance when he realised Hugo was by his side.

'You don't get to have *all* the fun, Dom,' he panted, with a grin.

Dominic shouldered through the crowd in time to see a huge brute of a fellow shove Liberty against a wall and raise a stick high. He took in the scene in an instant—the pain and shock on Liberty's face as she collided with the brickwork and the cowering, bloodied dog, its neck held fast by a huge hand. He recognised her utter determination as she thrust herself away from the wall. Rage boiled and he leapt forward even as Liberty pushed herself between the dog and that stick. He thrust his arm over Liberty's shoulder and grabbed the stick just as it began a downward trajectory.

The brute struggled, trying desperately to free the stick from Dominic's grip, as he glared down at Liberty and the dog she shielded. He hadn't even spared a glance at Dominic, he was so intent on his target. He didn't even appear to realise that, if he continued, he would hit Liberty.

'Leggo!' Spittle flew from his lips as he roared his rage.

Seeing the other man's uncontrolled fury just made Dominic more determined to control his own temper.

'I will take that.' The man's gaze snapped to Dominic. 'Or is it your intention to hit a lady in broad daylight, in front of witnesses?'

The man paled and gulped, and his grip on the stick loosened. Dominic took it from him and handed it to Hugo, standing to one side of him. Then he stepped in front of the bastard who had dared to threaten Liberty and he bunched his lapels in his fists. 'Don't you *ever*...' he spoke softly, '...let me see you again. Or the pain that dog suffered will be nothing to what I inflict upon you. Do you understand?'

The man's mouth twisted. 'It *stole* from me, m'lord. A man has to make a living.'

He felt a hand tug at his arm.

'Leave this to me, Miss Lovejoy.'

She took no notice, though. Almost before the words had left his lips she was nudging him aside so she could confront the brute.

'You are a despicable specimen of a human being.' She glared up at him. 'But even disgusting types like you need to make a living. Here.' She cast a handful of coins at his feet. 'The meat is paid for. Now, give me the dog.'

Dominic released his lapels and the man, with a snarl, thrust the pitiful dog at Liberty, scrabbled for the coins and then disappeared into the slowly dispersing crowd. In the absence of any means of holding the dog, Liberty grabbed its scruff, crooning to it in a low voice. Dominic placed a hand on her shoulder.

'He's gone, Miss Lovejoy. You can leave it now.'

She looked up at him, her eyes swimming. 'Look at him. The poor creature. He is skin and bone. I *cannot* leave him to fend for himself.'

'But what do you mean to do with it? It is filthy and no doubt riddled with fleas.'

'It really is not your concern, is it, my lord?' She regained her feet, but had to remain half-bent in order to keep hold of the animal, twisting her head to look up at him. 'I am grateful for your help in seeing off that scoundrel, but if I choose to keep this sweet little dog then I shall. I do need some way of securing him, though.'

She gazed around, then her eyes lit up.

'Be pleased to hold him a minute, sir, if you will.' She thrust the dog at Dominic, who had little choice but to comply. Next thing, she had removed her bonnet and was pulling at a ribbon that was threaded through her lustrous hair. 'This will do nicely, I believe.' She smiled happily as she thrust it at Dominic. 'Would you be so good as to tie it around his neck while I put my bonnet back on?'

Dominic registered the sound of a muffled snort and he relieved his feelings by glaring at his brother-in-law. But he did tie the blue ribbon around the dog's neck. It left a very short length with which to lead the dog, however. Liberty frowned as she studied the dog.

'Liberty.' Her chaperon, Mrs Mount, took Liberty by the elbow. 'We *cannot* take that filthy creature home with us.'

'Of course we can, my dear ma'am. Why ever not? Once he is bathed and his coat brushed, he will be quite respectable and he really does have the sweetest expression, do you not agree?'

'My lord?' Mrs Mount gazed at Dominic beseechingly.

Dominic looked down at the dog, who returned his look with a curl of his lip and an ingratiating grin. Then he looked at Liberty, taking in her outward bluster of confidence, but that same hint of vulnerability in her eyes that unmanned him every time he saw it.

'I cannot see what harm it will do.' Liberty's smile was his reward. 'Allow me to hail a hackney—that will make it easier to get the animal home. Hold him, will you, Hugo?' He thrust the short length of ribbon at his brother-in-law, who grinned and stuck his hands behind his back.

'*I* shall hail a cab,' he said. 'You're doing such a fine job there, Dom. I should hate to let the little ru—*darling* slip!'

After they had deposited the Lovejoy sisters and their chaperon at their home, Dominic and Hugo elected to walk together back to Beauchamp House. Dominic was soon aware of Hugo's amused scrutiny.

'Something on your mind, Hugo?'

'Just wonderin' where the lovely Liberty fits into your future plans, Dom.'

'Nowhere.'

Hugo shrugged, strolling on without further comment, swinging his cane.

'I admire the way she takes a stand for what is right,' Dominic said eventually, goaded by his brother-in-law's continuing silence and his mildly sceptical expression.

'Rushing in where angels fear to tread?'

'Not at all! She reminds me of Olivia, as it happens.'

Hugo cocked an eyebrow and his lips curved. 'Quite.'

'Are you calling your wife a fool?'

'Far from it—but you have to admit she used to act first and worry about the consequences afterwards. She has…er…mellowed somewhat in that regard. Since the twins. But she has *always* had her family's backs and still does.'

'That is what I admire about Miss Lovejoy.'

'But that, my dear Dominic, was a stray dog.'

'It is to her credit she did not ignore the suffering of a fellow creature, as so many others do.'

'Something like you and your orphans?'

Dominic's stomach clenched in warning. Oh, Hugo was a sly one…he could see exactly where this conversation was leading. He knew his brother-in-law well enough to know he would not continue to badger Dominic once he had replied to that initial question about Liberty, not like Olivia or Alexander might—questions that would inevitably lead to an argument. Hugo was far more subtle, skirting around the same subject until a less cautious man might let too much information slip. Well, he'd have no luck here.

'*Nothing* like that.'

Hugo smiled and Dominic promised himself he'd make him suffer next time they sparred at Jackson's.

They reached Beauchamp House and Dominic accepted Hugo's invitation to come in to visit Olivia. He very soon wished he hadn't, although at least Olivia didn't plague him about Liberty Lovejoy. No. *She* was far more interested in his blasted list…and how he wished he had never written the damned thing! Or at least had taken more care that nobody but he ever set eyes on it.

'Have you thought about Miss Whitlow? Why is she not on your list?'

'Unsuitable. Her father's a reckless gambler.'

'And only a viscount,' Hugo pointed out.

'Lady Elisa Critchlow? Oh! I know! Lady Frederica Sutton.'

'No and no. You're like a dog with a bone, Livvy,'

Dominic growled. 'Why can't you accept this is my business and my decision?'

'Talkin' of dogs—'

'Hu-u-u-u-go…'

Hugo opened his eyes wide at Dominic's growled warning. 'I merely thought the tale might distract my wife and stop her throwing an endless succession of names at you. It was, after all, merely a diverting interlude of little importance.' He arched his brows. 'Was it not?'

'You know it was.' But Hugo had a point…it *would* divert Olivia from the subject of his damned list. 'Your friend Miss Lovejoy rescued a dog that was being beaten. It was nothing. Over almost before it began.'

'With your intervention,' said Hugo.

'I shall ask Liberty to tell me all about it,' said Olivia, somewhat absently. 'Now, Dominic. What about Miss Fothergill?' She frowned, tapping one finger to her lips, then sat bolt upright. 'Of course! Jane Colebrooke! She would be perfect! So sweet-natured!'

'Good God, no! It would be like marrying my sister! And that thought, at this moment in time, fills me with abject horror. Olivia…if you do *not* stop pestering me I shall never call on you again. Or are you *trying* to drive me away?'

Olivia leapt up from the sofa to perch on the arm of Dominic's chair. She ruffled his hair and he jerked his head away. What did she think he was? A small boy to be humoured? He was the eldest, dammit. *He* had always been the sensible one; the one they listened to. Her arm slid behind his neck and she hugged him to her.

'I'm sorry. I don't mean to plague you. But I'm worried, Dom. I can't picture any of those women in among us. The rest of the family, I mean. I know Papa is a duke, but the thought of how some of them might behave with Aunt Thea, or with Zach, sends shivers right through me.' Her voice betrayed the strength of her feelings. 'We Beauchamps always stick together—I couldn't *bear* the thought that anyone might drive a wedge between us.'

'You're being overdramatic, Liv.'

But his anger dissipated at her words—he knew how much the family meant to Olivia. And to him, too. But that would not stop him doing his duty as he saw it and as he had promised Mother. *Make me proud, my Son.* The memories, as ever, weighted him down.

Duty. Expectation. Responsibility.

Except recently they had also brought doubts creeping into his thoughts. Undermining his determination. And he shied away from examining those doubts too closely, for fear of what they might reveal.

'You know me better than to think I would marry anyone likely to upset any member of the family. That is the reason I am taking my decision so seriously.'

'But what is so wrong with marrying for love? We did. Uncle Vernon and Aunt Cecily did. Even *Papa* did.'

'Father only married for love because the succession was already secure through his marriage to our mother.'

Olivia pouted. 'I suppose I cannot argue with that, but I still think you are making a mistake. When do you think you will decide?'

'Soon.' His spirits dipped as he said the words: 'I shall speak to Father when he arrives and, as long as he has no objection to her family, that will be it.'

His life sorted. It was what he wanted. It was what he had always planned.

* * *

'Romeo!'

A sleek head emerged from behind the floor-length curtain that, a moment ago, was being shaken with vigour, accompanied by ferocious growls. Liberty marched across the room and took her new pet by the collar. It was the day after she had rescued him and already she doubted her wisdom in keeping him. Not that she would admit that to the rest of the family, or to Mrs Mount, who were all extremely vocal in their condemnation of both her actions yesterday and her stubbornness in bringing him home. It had taken her two hours to bathe him and, by the time she had finished, the kitchen was in uproar and Mrs Taylor was prostrate on a chair in the corner, her apron over her face. It did little to muffle her shrieks. They had dined on cold meat, bread and cheese last night.

The name, Romeo, had popped into her head when Gideon asked what the dog's name was and the resulting hilarity from her entire family had been enough to stop Liberty changing her mind. Even though the name, she silently agreed, did not suit him in the slightest. He was a rascal. Up to every kind of mischief, having already chewed a rug, one of Gideon's slippers and now attacking the curtains.

Romeo gazed up at her, his brown eyes innocent and full of adoration, his head, with its two permanently upright ears, cocked to one side and his tail, tightly curled over his back, waggling his entire bottom. Liberty's heart melted. She dropped to her knees and hugged his thin body close. And then, without warning, she was crying into his soft golden coat; sobbing, her arms tightening around him as he wriggled, trying to reach her face and lick the tears from her cheeks.

'I must be cursed, Romeo. Bernard died and now there's Dominic—so far out of my reach he might as well be a prince.'

She hugged the dog closer, as the agony of unrequited love clawed at her. Twice she had loved and twice lost. And now she felt she was losing Gideon as well.

'I miss him, Romeo. I thought nothing could weaken the bond we shared, but now I don't know how to mend it. I *hate* London.' She'd been content before they came here. Numb, but content. 'I wish we'd never come here.'

'Liberty?'

She froze and desperately gulped back her sorrow as Gideon came into the room and sat on the floor next to her. He handed her his handkerchief and put his arms around her, pulling her close.

'Don't cry, Sis. You *never* cry.' She hid her face against his chest and hot tears flowed anew. 'I heard what you said. This is my fault.'

She shook her head, but he took no notice. 'Please don't cry. I know I've been selfish. I'm so sorry—I never thought how it must bring it all back to you, being in London again. Look.' He tilted her face up, his expression serious. 'I don't deny all this went to my head at first, but I will behave better. I promise. Our bond is not broken. It will never break, but it *will* change. It is inevitable. You do see that, don't you?'

Liberty nodded, then dried her face on his handkerchief.

'And I'll say no more about the dog. I promise. I can always buy new slippers and I'll make sure the others know he's welcome to stay.'

'Th-thank you.'

She bit her lip against the confession that her tears were not entirely about Gideon and not at all about the arguments over Romeo. It was no use admitting the real cause, because no one could help her and her family's pity would be far more painful than enduring her heartbreak alone.

Gideon handed Liberty a sealed note. 'Lady Olivia has sent a message—her footman is waiting for your reply.'

'Thank you.'

Liberty broke the seal.

'Olivia has asked if I would care to join her to promenade in the Park this afternoon,' she told Gideon.

'Shall you go?'

'Yes.'

Her spirits lifted even as anticipation and hopelessness warred in her mind—Dominic was likely to be in the Park at that hour, too, but he would no doubt be discreetly courting one, or more, of his contenders. Anticipation won that battle. Any glimpse, any contact, was better than none. And she did enjoy Olivia's company—she would help keep Liberty from chasing impossible dreams.

'I'll escort you there if you like,' said Gideon.

'You are not riding today?' Liberty asked as she headed for the small writing desk to reply to Olivia.

'Not today.'

'Then I accept. Thank you.' Liberty penned a quick acceptance to Olivia, agreeing to meet her in the Park at four o'clock.

'Maybe we could ride in the Park together one afternoon soon?'

Liberty laughed. 'Only if you can hire me a better beast than the ones Hope and Verity ended up with. They told me all about it.'

'I'll see what I can do,' Gideon said. 'They *were* a

poor couple of plodders…bad enough for our sisters, but hardly suited to a rider of your ability.' Gideon held out his hand. 'I'll take that to Lady Olivia's man for you.'

Pleasure at his compliment warmed Liberty as she handed over the folded note. 'Thank you.'

An hour later, Liberty walked to the Park with Gideon and met Olivia, as arranged, just inside the gates.

'I thought you might have brought your new dog,' Olivia said with a smile as they strolled among the crowds. 'Hugo told me all about it and how you rescued him from that cruel brute.'

Liberty gazed around. Some ladies did indeed have dogs on leads, or in their carriages.

'I am not certain Romeo is quite respectable enough for promenading in the Park,' she said.

'Romeo? Is that his name? Oh, I cannot wait to meet him. And don't worry whether he's respectable enough. You have every right to walk your dog here. It doesn't matter what anyone else thinks.'

Spoken like a true duke's daughter.

'Maybe I shall.'

A few paces further on they met Dominic, Lady Sybilla on his arm. Liberty's heart sank and jealousy clawed her. She curtsied, Dominic bowed and Olivia and Sybilla inclined their heads graciously.

'Such a pleasant afternoon for a walk,' said Sybilla.

'Indeed,' Olivia responded.

'Mama and I had the intention of driving around the carriageway, but Lord Avon persuaded me to walk with him instead and Mama gave her permission. Is Lord Hugo not accompanying you this afternoon, Lady Olivia?'

'As you see, he is not,' Olivia replied gravely. 'He is otherwise engaged, I am afraid.'

'That is regrettable.' A slight smile touched Lady Sybilla's lips. 'However, one cannot expect one's husband to dance attendance upon one *all* of the time, can one?'

Liberty risked a glance at Dominic. His face was impassive, but his silver eyes betrayed a hint of resignation.

'No, indeed,' Olivia agreed.

'We ought perhaps to keep moving, Lady Sybilla,' said Dominic. 'It would not do to catch a chill.'

'Good heavens, no.' She tinkled a laugh. 'That would indeed be unfortunate this early in the Season.' She inclined her head again. 'Good afternoon to you both, Lady Olivia; Miss Lovejoy.'

'Oh, dear.' Olivia tucked her arm through Liberty's as they strolled away. 'Although my brother is nothing but discreet, I do fear he is now angling towards Sybilla Gratton as first choice.'

Dominic's list was the very last thing Liberty wished to dwell on, but at the same time the subject drew her back like a magnet.

'I thought his preference was for Lady Caroline?'

'Her attitude after that business between your sister and Bridlington at the Twyfords' ball changed his mind, I believe.'

'I see.' Liberty was glad Dominic had seen through Caroline, but she knew very little about Lady Sybilla other than she was the eldest daughter of the Duke of Wragby and she always appeared perfectly poised and calm. In other words, perfect for Dominic's bride. 'You do not approve?'

'I do not. She is like a…like a statue carved out of

ice.' Olivia huffed in disgust. 'I have never seen a natural expression on her face nor heard an unconsidered word leave her lips. Not that I have known her long, for her family were late coming up to town, but still... Poor Dominic will be frozen out of bed by that one.' She gasped and clapped her hand over her mouth. 'Oops. I apologise. I should not talk to you like that. I keep forgetting you are unmarried.'

Liberty couldn't help but laugh. 'I am not so easily shocked, Olivia. But you cannot deny she meets all of your brother's requirements. She's the daughter of a duke and her upbringing, manners and behaviour are impeccable.'

'She is...oh, I don't know! She is so false, somehow. I wonder if she even knows what joy is? How will she ever make him happy?'

'I don't believe his own happiness features very highly on your brother's list of requirements.'

'But it *should*. Oh, Liberty... I don't how I shall do it but, somehow, I must find a way to persuade him to think again, even though I know very well he will not listen to me.' Olivia swished her closed parasol in a gesture of frustration. 'Not one of them is right for him, but he is so stubborn and he will not listen to sense...he just accuses me of meddling! But all I want is for him to be happy, as I am with my Hugo. But it is like Alex says...once Dominic has set his mind on a course of action he is the very devil to divert from it.'

'But...' Liberty ignored her inner voice that shrieked at her to change the subject. 'But...what if he, say, met someone and fell in love?'

'Hah! You don't know my brother and his...his... *blinkered*ness! He believes the wife of a future duke should be chosen with the head, not the heart. He will marry for the sake of the Dukedom, not for himself.'

'Could your father not talk to him, if you ask him to?'

'I doubt Papa will interfere,' said Olivia gloomily. 'His whole life, Dominic has done his utmost to be the perfect son and the perfect heir—constantly aware of his responsibility as Papa's heir. If Papa was to say *Don't marry Lady X, marry Lady Y*, Dominic would do just that to please Papa. *That's* not choosing with his heart. And Papa knows he would do it, too. So he won't risk interfering. Oh…how I wish Aunt Cecily were here. *She* might talk some sense into Dom, but she and Zach aren't coming for another three weeks at least. It'll be too late by then.

'No. I don't know how I shall contrive it, but I must try. *Someone* has to do *something*.' She lapsed into a brooding silence before adding, 'Oh, and talking of Dominic… Hugo and I are going to visit Westfield to-morrow. Would you care to join us?'

'I would love to—as long as your brother will not object to my accompanying you?'

'Why should he? Hugo is happy for you to accompany us and I don't suppose Dominic will even be there. He'll be too busy courting his blasted list of perfect brides.'

Chapter Fourteen

The following afternoon, Dominic entered the schoolroom at Westfield where Mrs Whittaker was supervising the children at their lessons. He pulled up a low chair next to Tommy, who he knew struggled with his reading. Westfield prided itself on teaching both letters and numbers to the children in its care—not to make scholars of them, but to prepare them to become useful members of society, able to earn their living. And that was where Dominic and Felicity were invaluable, in helping to place the older children in positions with tradesmen or in households where they had the opportunity to better themselves with hard work. But Dominic also loved to spend time helping the individual children when he could—and, just at this moment, it was exactly what he needed to take his mind off his dilemma.

The past few days had been thoroughly dispiriting. He had spent time with all five ladies from his original list and the only thing he was certain of was that he was less sure of his ultimate decision now than he had been a week ago. But speculation in society was rife and he would look a dithering fool if he did not proceed when the talk was of nothing else. And yet he still hesitated over making that final, irreversible decision.

Make me proud, my Son. You were born to be the Duke...never disgrace your position in society...the eyes of the world will be on you. Judging you. Never let them see weakness.

His mother's strictures when he was a boy. The demands he had striven to obey as a boy, desperate for her love and approval...the same demands that had driven him to follow his duty all his life, ever conscious of his responsibility to his heritage, his mother's memory and to the family name.

But, also, the gentleman in him rebelled against insulting the ladies on his list with the implication that not one of them was up to his standards. He was eager to set up his nursery—that was the one bright, hopeful thing in this mess—and he knew he'd be in a worse position if he delayed until later in the year, or even until next Season. The same names would be on any list he drew up, only now they would be aware of his reluctance. And the name he longed to include—Liberty Lovejoy—would still not be on his list. Her maternal grandfather would still be a coal merchant.

You are the Marquess of Avon. You will be Duke of Cheriton one day, and your son and your son's son. That is your destiny. Do not allow the weakness of base desires to contaminate the bloodline—it is your duty to keep it pure.

His father would arrive in town within a fortnight. By then, the decision *would* be made. That had been his plan from the beginning of the Season when he had been keen to get on with his selection and to start his own family. But now he simply felt numb as his well-ordered plans appeared to fragment around him.

He pushed his worries aside and pointed to the word *apple* written on the slate.

'Try again,' he said.

Tommy scowled down at the slate. He'd not long been at Westfield, having been referred by the magistrates' court after being arrested as a pickpocket...his first offence.

'Sound out each letter...you know the sounds they make, Tommy. Come on. You can do this. I have faith in you.'

He barely registered the sound of the door opening until he heard Peter Whittaker—who owned and ran Westfield with his wife, Jane—say, 'And this is the schoolroom.'

Dominic glanced around, then shot to his feet as he saw Liberty, her eyes huge and riveted on him. He felt the colour build in his face and he gritted his teeth as he struggled to control his suddenly erratic breathing and to keep the smile in his heart from reaching his lips.

'Good afternoon, Miss Lovejoy.' He bowed. 'It is a pleasure to see you again.'

He nodded at Hugo and Olivia—whom he had expected—and who followed Liberty into the room.

'I invited Liberty to come with us.' Olivia smiled happily. 'I knew you would not object and she is very interested in Westfield.'

Is she indeed?

He was somewhat gratified to see Liberty's blush. At least it wasn't just him who felt awkward. But he also caught a glint of surprise in her eyes...she hadn't expected him to be here? Or was her surprise that he was helping teach the children?

'Why should I object?'

Olivia crossed the room to him. 'Well, you are so very close-chested about this sort of thing, Dom, you know you are. Does Lady Sybilla know of your connection with Westfield?'

Beyond Olivia, he could see Hugo questioning Peter as Liberty listened intently.

'Why would I mention it to Lady Sybilla?' How did Olivia know Sybilla had been his favourite until his current state of indecision? He'd taken such care not to single out any one lady more than another. 'Or to anyone else, come to that?'

'Why indeed? Your Lady Sybilla has about as much compassion in her as that statue of Venus in the British Museum—I cannot see her ever sharing your interest in the welfare of these poor children, Dom.'

Dominic bit back his frustration.

'Shouldn't you go and listen to Mr Whittaker, Livvy? I thought Hugo brought you here to find out about Westfield, didn't he? Not to plague me about that dam—dratted list.'

'Of course he did, silly! I didn't even know you would be here. I'll see you later.'

With a quick smile, she returned to the others, where Peter was explaining the workings of the school and what they hoped to achieve for their children. Dominic returned his attention to Tommy and his reading.

Finally, realising Tommy's concentration was drifting, Dominic stood up and realised, with a start of surprise, that although Peter's voice had long since fallen silent and he had assumed the entire group had left the schoolroom, Liberty was still there, crouching by the side of another, younger, lad, and helping him with *his* reading. His heart lurched as she smiled up at him.

'Little Ronnie here is doing very well, Lord Avon, but I think he is growing a little weary. Would you mind…?'

She reached out to him and he took her dainty hand in his. He helped her to rise, stifling the urge to press his lips to her palm, and released it the second she gained her feet.

'Thank you. I am grateful you are here, for my legs had grown quite stiff with crouching down like that and I feared a most inelegant lurch to my feet.'

Her smile twinkled in her eyes.

'I was unaware you were still in the room.'

'Mr Whittaker offered Hugo and Olivia a tour of the place, but I preferred to remain here, with the children.' She hesitated. Then touched his arm. 'This is admirable…that both you and Lady Stanton have been involved in this place for so long. I…' She paused before continuing, 'It's not what I would ever have expected of…'

'Of a man like me?' He didn't wait for her reply. A glance at the room showed the children paying more attention to them than to their lessons. 'Come. Let us leave Mrs Whittaker to teach in peace. We are disrupting her lesson.' He sent a smile across the room to Peter's wife, then ushered Liberty out into a passage and towards the entrance hall, where the afternoon sun sent beams of coloured light through the stained-glass windows either side of the front door. 'We can wait here for the others—or we can go and find them if you prefer?'

'No.' She stared at him, a light of calculation in those beautiful midnight-blue eyes of hers. Her throat rippled as she swallowed. 'There is something I should like to say to you.'

So serious. A shiver of disquiet rippled across the skin of his back.

'I… I…'

He moved closer, breathing in her scent. Roses—they no longer exclusively recalled his childhood and his mother but, increasingly, brought the image of Liberty Lovejoy into his thoughts.

'It is not like you to be hesitant, Berty. I thought you were unafraid of any subject, or any man.'

She sucked in a breath. 'It is about your list.'

He felt his forehead bunch. 'What about it?'

'I…' She paused. Gold-flecked midnight-blue eyes searched his and then her lips set in a determined line. 'I am worried about the…the…singlemindedness of your plan.'

'My plan is actually none of your concern.' He heard the finality in his tone, sensed the barrier rise up between them. 'Do you not believe me capable of making the right decision?'

'I just feel… I am worried…' A frustrated growl rattled in her throat. 'Surely by sticking so rigidly to this list of yours, you are limiting your choice of bride?'

'But that is the idea. It is all about finding the perfect bride.'

She frowned at him. A puzzled frown, not angry. 'But why not just choose the lady you like best?'

He set his jaw, feeling his own frown deepen. 'What do you mean?'

Liberty sighed, a gust of exasperation. 'Exactly what I say. Who—do—you—like—best?'

He tensed. 'That is neither here nor there. Personal taste doesn't come into it.'

She didn't understand. How could she possibly understand? This was his destiny. His duty. He was the Duke's heir.

'But…it is madness! The lady you choose… Dominic…you will be bound to her. For ever. Surely you want to be happy?'

'That is not how our world works. Many people marry for convenience.'

'Olivia and Hugo did not. Nor did the rest of your family, from what Olivia has said.'

A suspicion seized him. 'Did my sister put you up to this?'

'No! No, of course not. Although I do know she is worried about you, too.'

'No one needs to worry about me. My life is under control. *My* control.'

Then why haven't you decided yet? Why do you still hunger after what you cannot have?

He thrust down that inner voice.

'And in answer to your question, the rest of my family are not in my shoes. *I* am my father's heir. He married my mother for the future of the Dukedom, to keep it secure for the generations to come. It is my destiny…my *duty*…to do the same. Happiness does not come into it.'

'But that is so sad. It sounds a lonely life to me.'

He shrugged and could see his indifference infuriated her. But it really did not matter to him—any one of those ladies on his list would do.

'What do you actually want from this marriage, Dominic?'

'Me?' He paused, pondering her question. 'I want to do my duty. To do what is right for the title and for my father. And I am ready to start a family. I want my children to grow up close in age to Olivia's twins and to my father's second family and my little cousins.'

'So you will choose duty over happiness?'

'There is no reason for me to be unhappy once I make my choice.'

'Dominic…' his name on her lips and the hand she rested on his chest as she gazed up at him sent his silly heart tumbling '…please…at least consider other young ladies in addition to your shortlist.'

'Like you?' His voice rasped. The unfairness of that question shocked him, but that did not stop the rest of it from spilling out. 'Or maybe you still harbour hopes for your sisters?'

She snatched her hand away and stepped back, hurt in her eyes. 'That is not what I thought for one moment. I know only too well that neither I nor my sisters match your requirements. Dominic… I am speaking to you now as your *friend*. At least, I hope we are friends?'

He raised his hand to the back of his neck and rubbed. He craved more than friendship with this woman. But it could never be. And he should have known better than to accuse her of self-interest. He had seen her passion for protecting those she cared about, from her brother to a stray dog. And she cared for *him*, too. She felt that same connection between them that he was trying so hard to resist.

Of course she would want to protect him from making what she saw as a mistake. He should expect no less.

'I apologise. That accusation was unjustified. Yes, we are friends and I value it.'

'Then, as your friend, *please* think again about your choice of bride. I don't believe any of those on your shortlist will make you a comfortable wife.'

'Comfortable?' He huffed a laugh. 'I do not seek a comfortable wife, Liberty. I seek a suitable wife. There is a world of difference.'

'And there is a world of difference between a suitable match on paper and the reality of marriage to that same person.' She laid her hand upon his sleeve. 'Please reconsider. There is nowhere as lonely as a poor marriage. Make certain you have at least something in common with your bride.'

'We'll have the most important thing in common,' he growled. 'Breeding.'

She shook her head and sighed. 'I can say no more.'

A door opened at the far end of the hall and Hugo and Olivia emerged.

'Do you go to the Attwoods' ball tonight?' Liberty asked Dominic as the others joined them.

The evening was mild for April. Afterwards, Liberty used that as an excuse for what happened at the Attwoods' ball. If it had been cool, she would never have ventured alone on to the terrace instead of going to supper. There were a few others out there, taking the air, but she did not approach them, preferring her own company. One by one, they returned inside, but she had no wish to indulge in more polite conversation. She sighed, propped her hands on the stone balustrade and gazed up at the stars. Somewhere, up there, Bernard was watching her, wishing her well. She was sure of it even though, with every year that passed, his memory faded—his features more indistinct; his voice more silent; his touch… She shivered, pushing that memory away. But that old guilt persisted. That nagging feeling she might have saved them, if only she had done more.

His scent alerted her to his presence and she turned. His features were in shadow as he stood close. Almost too close.

'I neglected to ask you earlier. How is that dog?'

'Romeo? He is—'

She fell silent as he erupted into laughter. 'Romeo?

You could not give that mongrel a more inappropriate name if you tried!'

Still shaky after her memories of Bernard, she shoved at his chest. 'Do *not* mock me!' She pushed past him, heading for the French window and the ballroom beyond. As she reached for the handle, Dominic grabbed her wrist, bringing her to an abrupt halt.

'Don't go!'

She would not look at him. 'Why not?'

He tugged her to the side, away from the window and out of the patch of light that spilled on to the terrace and into the shadow of the house wall. He turned her to face him and, his free hand on her shoulder, he backed her against the wall. The bricks were hard and cool through the silk of her gown, but she was anything but cold as her stomach flipped and heat spiralled through her. He towered above her—dark, strong, masculine—the trace of his spicy cologne mingling with the scent of wine and brandy on his breath. He moved closer, his body against hers, all that hard, solid muscle…all that strength…all that power… Her breathing hitched and her lips parted as she desperately sucked in a new breath.

His head bent towards her as his hands slid lower to settle on her hips. It was too dark to decipher his expression, but his tattered breathing punctuated the silence of the night air and his thudding heartbeat vibrated through her.

'Liberty…'

Warm breath feathered across her face and the ache in his voice tore into her heart. She reached up to touch his mouth…those fascinating, sensual lips she had fantasised about kissing. Her forefinger traced his bottom lip and she craved…oh, she craved… Her fingers splayed and her hand slipped up and around his cheek, learning the shape of that sculpted cheekbone, tracing the curve of his ear and pushing into the thick softness of his midnight-dark hair.

With a tortured groan, he slid his hands around her, hauling her away from the harsh unyielding bricks at her back, crushing her against his sculptured heat, his hands cupping her bottom, lifting. His lips captured hers, demanding as his tongue plunged into her mouth. Helpless to resist, she returned thrust for thrust, relishing every moment of that stormy kiss. Her arms wrapped around him, clinging, as that initial passionate desperation eased, as the movement of their lips slowed and gentled, as their murmurs of appreciation mingled in the night air...until the sound of the musicians resuming play in the ballroom ended their kiss.

Dominic's tight embrace eased, his hands gliding soothingly up her back as she regained her balance. He rested his forehead against hers, his chest heaving even as Liberty, too, struggled to catch her breath. Eventually, he raised his head and she caught the glitter of his silver-grey eyes as their gazes met. And held.

Frustration tangled her stomach into knots. Nothing had changed. Nothing *could* change. Not unless *Dominic* changed and turned away from what he had grown up to believe was his duty. And, unless that miracle happened, Liberty could never be more to him than...

'Just friends?'

'Friends.' His eyes bored into hers, sending waves of longing crashing through her. 'It is all we can ever be.'

Regret coloured his tone, but also resolve. Could she accept his decision, even though it broke her heart?

'I... I should not have kissed you.' His fingers brushed her cheek. 'It was self-indulgent and I am sorry.'

'I am also at fault.' The blame was equally theirs.

They were both grown-ups. He had not forced her. 'We shall forget it happened.'

She gathered every vestige of strength she could find and stepped aside, away from his warmth and his strength. She turned from him and returned to the ballroom.

She had survived worse, although it would be hell watching him with another woman. Especially when she fully believed he was heading towards disaster. Without volition, her eyes swept the ballroom until she had seen each one of his shortlist, but her worried gaze lingered on Lady Sybilla. Olivia believed she was now his preferred option—*option! How cold that sounds*—and of all of them, she was the one Liberty knew the least about. Oh, she knew the public guise, but of the woman beneath that ice-cool exterior she knew nothing. Did Dominic know any more than she did, or had he, too, only ever seen what the lady chose to reveal?

There was little she could do other than hope he came to his senses in time, but if she wanted to protect herself... her heart...she should not risk being alone with him again.

Heavens! The entire surface of her body heated at the memory of that kiss and her stomach swirled with unspent restless energy. How had she become entangled in the web of desire so quickly? So fiercely? And now, if she allowed herself to, she could easily succumb to misery, knowing there could be no happy ending. But she would not indulge herself. She had known him but a few weeks. Passion would fade. It couldn't be anything more...meaningful.

It couldn't be love.

Could it?

With Bernard there had been a slow, sweet build to love and desire over the years they had known one another. There had never been that sudden violence of passion that had held her in its thrall on the terrace.

It *couldn't* be love.

'Miss Lovejoy.' Lord Silverdale, an attractive man in his middle thirties, bowed before her. 'If you lack a partner, may I request the pleasure of this dance?'

The distraction welcome, she accepted, smiling up at the Earl. As he led her into the set, she caught sight of Dominic, with Lady Sarah as his partner. Their gazes fused and a shiver chased across her skin, desire pulsing at her core. She tore her eyes from his and directed her attention to Lord Silverdale, pushing all thought of Dominic from her mind.

Afterwards, she stayed close to Olivia and Hugo when possible and occupied herself by watching Gideon as he danced attendance on Lady Emily Crighton, and her sisters, both happy, both contented, partnered by a succession of good-looking, handsome and eligible bachelors.

'You are not still worried about your brother, are you?' Olivia asked later.

'No. He and I…we had a talk—' she would never admit to Olivia that Gideon had found her weeping '—and he has allayed my fears.'

Olivia's silvery gaze swept the room, settling on Dominic and Alex, deep in conversation. 'I wish I could say the same about my brothers. I fear Alex will never change and Dominic is still determined to select his bride before Father arrives.'

Liberty did not want to talk, or even think, about Dominic and his future wife and she soon took her leave of Olivia and wandered around the perimeter of the ballroom, trying not to catch any gentleman's eye.

She really was not in the mood for dancing. She spied an empty chair in an alcove and settled gratefully into in, partially shielded from the floor by a floral arrangement on a pedestal. She relaxed, closing her eyes, trying to dismiss that kiss from her mind and her heart and yet reliving every second of it, and relishing it. Her heart sang—he had kissed her as though he meant it—and it ached, because that kiss could never lead to what she now admitted she wanted above all else.

Him. And her. Together.

'Why are you hiding away?' Her eyes flew open at Dominic's question. 'Are you unwell?' He stood two paces away, worry creasing his brow. He lowered his voice, but came no nearer. 'Are you upset about what happened?'

Her throat ached. This was torment. Did she have the strength to see him, talk to him, to pretend that kiss had not pierced her heart?

'I am not upset, merely enjoying a little peace.'

'I cannot leave you sitting in here all alone—who knows what manner of undesirable men might corner you?' His smile slipped, becoming crooked, and she longed to soothe it. To soothe him. 'Will you allow me to escort you to Mrs Mount or to Olivia?'

Dominic held out his hand and, as she placed her hand in his, he murmured, 'Are you certain nothing is troubling you, Berty?'

The strength of his fingers as they closed around hers, and his use of her private nickname, stirred all sorts of warm feelings deep inside. They were still friends and, if she could expect nothing more from him, she would settle for that.

As she rose to her feet, she said, 'I am certain.'

Chapter Fifteen

Liberty stepped towards Dominic, her hand still enclosed in his, her midnight-blue gaze open and honest. The silky fabric of her blue gown clung to her curves, her décolletage enticingly framed by her low, lace-trimmed neckline. Her honey-blonde hair was piled on her head, leaving tendrils to frame her face and brush her bare shoulders.

His hands twitched with the longing to stroke. To caress.

His back was to the ballroom, blocking her from view and, without volition, his forefinger trailed down her arm, from the lace that trimmed her short sleeve to the edge of her elbow-length glove. Her skin was warm satin and his eyes charted the shiver that followed in the wake of his touch.

He was playing with fire. Again. He clenched his jaw and locked his feelings inside, placing her hand on his sleeve as he turned to face the room and escort her to Mrs Mount.

'I am engaged with Lady Sybilla for the next,' he said. 'But I hope to see you in the Park tomorrow afternoon.'

Her face lit and her soft gasp whispered past his ears, but the glow in her blue eyes quickly dimmed. Her tawny brows gathered in a frown.

'Why?' Her whisper was fierce.

'Why what?'

'You kiss me. You say we can never be more than friends. Yet still you stroked my arm and now you "hope to see me in the Park". What is it you want from me, Dominic?'

He wanted *her*, that was the truth. And she was right to rebuke him. He was being unfair and he would take greater care from now on. But tomorrow…he was almost tempted to tell her the reason he mentioned the Park and to reveal the secret Alex had told him earlier. But it was not his secret to tell. And although he would be wise to stay away, he could not wait to see her face. Was it so wrong to indulge himself?

He told her none of that. 'I am sorry.'

He bowed, leaving Liberty with Mrs Mount, swallowing past the emotion that thickened his throat as he walked away. He had struggled to keep away from her after that kiss, knowing that all he wanted was to kiss her again. And again. But he must protect her reputation and so he had kept his distance. Until Alex had let slip that it was Gideon and Liberty's birthday the next day and that Gideon and her sisters had planned a surprise for Liberty. In the Park.

And because Dominic would never have the right to give Liberty a gift of any kind, he could not resist the chance to see, and to share in, her joy and excitement when Gideon revealed his present to her.

He did his utmost to push Liberty from his thoughts as he danced with Lady Sybilla, but it proved impossible. Sybilla was utter perfection in her looks: a beautiful brunette with burnished locks and porcelain skin. Her serene expression rarely altered and her behaviour was correct in every way: she never displayed a vulgar excess of emotion; she agreed amenably with every opinion he uttered; she, quite properly, revealed little knowledge about any subject under discussion. Dominic had spent enough time with her in the past week or so to know she was polite to servants, but never overly familiar, and that she never appeared to look down on anyone she might deem beneath her because of their more lowly birth. In short, she was the perfect bride. She was exactly the lady he had set out to find at the start of the Season.

And he was already bored. She was simply *too* perfect. Try as he might, he couldn't imagine her having fun, teasing him, cuddling a child, rescuing a dog, crouching beside a child to help it read until her legs were so stiff she couldn't rise without help. The entire time he danced with Sybilla, it was Liberty's face he saw in his mind's eye. Liberty's lips he could still taste. His head ached with the constant inner battles that plagued his thoughts and, lately, kept him awake at night.

What would it matter if you changed your mind? Why not follow your heart? Others have and the world did not end.

But what of my promise to Mother? And how can I abandon my duty to the succession and to the family name?

He had spent his boyhood trying to live up to his mother's expectations...trying to be good enough...determined to be worthy of that approval he had glimpsed just before she died. And still he chased that image of duty and responsibility that was part of the expectations of society as well as his own expectations of himself.

Still he strove to conform.

He escorted Sybilla back to her mother, the Duchess of Wragby, the arguments still raging inside his head, which was starting to throb.

'Well, Avon?' The Duchess looked him up and down with approval. 'Do you have news of your father's arrival in town?'

'Indeed, Your Grace. He and my stepmother arrive next week.'

Time is running out.

That thought had clawed at him for days now. The time was coming when he must announce his decision and his future would be set in stone. His stomach clenched with nerves. He had always been decisive, but now he dithered, unable to take that final, irrecoverable step. And his indecision, he knew, was because, in his heart of hearts, he simply didn't care *who* he wed, unless it was Liberty.

And as soon as any such thought arose, an image of a coal merchant would materialise in his head...a man such as Liberty's grandfather.

'Never allow your base desires to contaminate the bloodline, my Son. Keep it pure. Make me proud.'

Not one whisper of his inner turmoil was allowed to surface, however. His behaviour was as correct as it had ever been. No one would suspect the whirlwind of indecision that plagued his thoughts. If Lady Sybilla was the perfect lady, *he* had always taken care to present himself to the world as the perfect gentleman.

He had only ever allowed himself to relax that perfection when he was safe among his family.

And with Liberty.

He shrugged that thought away. If he was a different man beneath the gentlemanly exterior, then Sybilla, too, might be different.

But different how? In a good way or a bad way?

He could stand no more. He felt as though he rode a runaway steed, the reins slipping through his useless fingers. He bowed abruptly to the Duchess and Sybilla. 'If you will excuse me, ladies?'

Not by a flicker did either lady reveal any disappointment in his departure. He really could not read either of them. He was sick of puzzling over his dilemma. He would speak to Alex and Gideon and check on the arrangements for tomorrow, then go to his club and banish that blasted list from his mind for a few hours.

The following afternoon Dominic met Gideon and Alex as arranged, at three o'clock by the Park gates. Gideon looked as giddy as a schoolboy, his blue eyes dancing with excitement, as he sat on his black gelding, holding a pretty chestnut mare by her reins. This was his surprise… Bella. A new horse for Liberty's birthday— one with outstanding conformation and, Alex had assured him, perfect manners. And Alex should know, because he had bred and trained Bella, using one of his stable lads to help accustom her to the side-saddle.

Alex was astride his huge grey, standing up in his stirrups, scanning the crowds for their first sight of Liberty. Hope and Verity had pledged to be in the Park by three and to bring Liberty with them.

'I do hope she doesn't suspect anything,' Gideon said for the umpteenth time.

Dominic was on foot. He wished he felt half as lively as Gideon, but his head still thumped from his late night at White's, when he had imbibed rather too freely of the brandy, and another restless night. He massaged his temples and closed his eyes briefly.

'I see her.' Alex lowered himself into his saddle. 'She's with your sisters, but they've got that dog with them.'

'I heard Liberty say she planned to walk it in the Park today,' said Gideon, 'and I *told* Hope on no account were they to bring him along. Why do sisters *never* listen?'

'I'll go and meet them,' said Dominic. 'I can steer them towards a less crowded spot, in case Bella should start to fidget.'

Gideon glanced at the mare. 'She seems calm enough—I just hope she doesn't object to dogs.'

'Indeed,' said Alex, with a wink. 'Or you'll be left holding Romeo, Dom. That won't do your image as a suave man about town any good at all.'

Dominic didn't dignify that remark with a reply. He set off through the throng of walkers and, before too long, he came across Liberty, Hope and Verity. Romeo, tongue lolling, was prancing by Liberty's side, exhibiting a showy action that would not be out of place on one of Alex's specially bred high-stepping carriage horses. His upright ears were even more highly pricked than ever, and his tail curled tightly over his back.

Dominic bowed, taking in Liberty's blushing cheeks and the hint of self-consciousness in her eyes. Her periwinkle-blue walking dress fitted her like a glove, moulding to her breasts, and the memory of their fullness softly pressing against his chest last night sent the blood surging to his groin.

He conjured up Sybilla's serene half-smile and his lust subsided.

'Good afternoon, ladies. May I wish you a happy birthday, Miss Lovejoy?'

'Good afternoon, sir, and thank you.' Liberty's lips curved in a smile as all three ladies curtsied, but her smile was strained.

'Good afternoon, Lord Avon,' Hope and Verity chorused.

Hope caught his eye, raising her brows, a question in her blue eyes, and Dominic gave her a brief nod. Yes. Gideon *was* at the Park with Liberty's gift.

'And Romeo...' Dominic continued smoothly, eyeing the hound, who eyed him back, a definite hint of arrogance in his stance. 'Well, he appears to have fully recovered from his ordeal. Anyone would think he was born to parade in the Park at the promenade hour.'

'We did try to persuade Liberty to leave him at home, my lord,' said Hope, 'but she would not listen.'

'Well, as it is your sister's birthday, I think she might be allowed a little indulgence.' He patted Romeo, who tolerated it. Gone was the cringing, fawning animal of only a few days ago. 'May I walk with you a short way, ladies?'

'We would be honoured, my lord.' Liberty was all graciousness, but, as they fell into step, she whispered, 'Your sister suggested I should walk Romeo here, but is it *really* acceptable?'

Her disquiet was unmistakable.

'Are you actually *asking* my advice? Is this the Liberty Lovejoy I... I first met on my father's doorstep?' He maintained his teasing tone, but flinched at the words he had so nearly uttered. *The Liberty Lovejoy I know and love.* It might be trite and a cliché, but those words had come from somewhere.

From the heart.

Nonsense. Friends. She agreed with me. It's lust on my part. That's all.

'I am sure it could not be anything *other* than acceptable now *I* have lent you countenance by walking with you,' he said, using his haughtiest tone.

He was rewarded with a gurgled laugh and a light slap on the arm.

It was a relief to see Gideon and Alex riding towards them. Dominic clasped Liberty's elbow and drew her to a halt. She looked at him, an enquiring frown hovering. He nodded to the carriageway ahead. Her eyes widened and her mouth fell open. Dominic removed Romeo's lead from her slack hold and nudged her forward.

Gideon slid from his horse's back and waited, a huge grin on his face, as Liberty walked towards him.

'Lib, meet Bella. Happy birthday.' He handed her the lead rein.

As Dominic watched Liberty's joy and excitement a previously unknown emotion raked his insides. It took him a moment to realise he was jealous of Gideon. *He* wanted to give her things. *He* wanted to be the recipient of that joyous smile and that unrestrained hug. For the first time in his life he cursed that he was a duke's son. The heir. He longed to break free of the shackles and expectations of society.

He concentrated on keeping all trace of emotion from his face until, with relief, he spied his cousin and friend, Felicity Stanton, driving her pony pair, Nutmeg and Spice, at a spanking trot towards him. He thrust Romeo's lead at Verity and flagged Felicity to stop, which she did with a flourish.

'Dominic! How lovely to see you... I was at Westfield this morning and Peter told me all about your visit yesterday. And what splendid news, that Lord Hugo and

Olivia are going to become patrons. Do you know any more of their plans?'

'Take me up and I will tell you all I know,' he said.

Gideon, Liberty and her sisters were all preoccupied examining Bella. They wouldn't even notice Dominic had gone. He caught Alex's eye, raised his hand in salute and then climbed in next to Felicity.

His destiny was ordained and it did not include Liberty Lovejoy, the granddaughter of a coal merchant. The time until his father arrived would pass quickly and as long as he kept reminding himself that he and Liberty were only friends all would be well.

He filled those days with activity: visits to Westfield, where he again helped the older children with their lessons; boxing and fencing sessions; visits to his clubs, where he partook in several lively political debates; and daily rides in Hyde Park, where he had yet to see Liberty out on Bella. He both longed for and dreaded seeing her, knowing his resolve would not be strong enough to refrain from riding by her side, even if the most he could hope for would be polite chit-chat.

Friends.

The evenings were trickier, but he was proud of his demeanour. He remained totally in control and even Olivia and Alexander had stopped badgering him about his damned list, although Olivia couldn't quite disguise her anxiety whenever she thought he wasn't looking.

No one, he was certain, would suspect the knot that had taken up residence in his guts and that inexorably tightened with each day that passed.

He danced with every lady on his shortlist and a few more besides, keeping up a flow of frivolous conversation. If Liberty were present, he danced with her, too, his stomach muscles rigid with the effort required to maintain his mask of light friendship. Not by a word or a look did either of them refer to that kiss.

In short, he presented the same Lord Avon to the *ton* that he had presented for the past nine years, since he first came to town at seventeen years of age.

On the day of Father's arrival it brought him no relief to realise that this strange charade was near its end and so he awarded himself one last indulgence. Olivia and Hugo were to ride in the Park with Liberty. Dominic made sure to join them.

The days since their kiss had provided a salutary lesson for Liberty.

Dominic had proved time after time that their kiss meant nothing to him even though that same kiss haunted her dreams. He was the same suave, sophisticated gentleman he had always been. Any observer would claim he behaved no differently to her, but she knew there was a faint but discernible detachment in the way he acted around her. He avoided any situation where they might speak privately and, when they danced, he no longer teased her, but merely kept up the same light, inconsequential conversation he maintained with all his partners.

She ought to be pleased at his caution, but she missed him and she missed their friendship and his teasing. Her heart sank whenever she saw him with one of the ladies on his list, especially Sybilla following Olivia's suspicion that she was now Dominic's choice.

On the day Olivia's father was due to arrive in town, she and Hugo arranged to meet Liberty for a ride in the Park. Gideon rode with Liberty and waited with her by the Park gate until Hugo and Olivia arrived. Liberty tried to ignore the silly way her heart leapt at the sight of Dominic accompanying them, telling herself his presence meant nothing. She marshalled her courage and smiled serenely as he greeted her, but no sooner had they started to walk their horses along the carriageway than they appeared to fall naturally into two pairs: Hugo and Olivia, followed by Dominic and Liberty.

'I hope you do not object to my joining you this afternoon?' Dominic said, after they had exchanged comments on the weather—which was dry but still unseasonably cold.

He grinned at her. Totally relaxed and utterly gorgeous. No hint of self-consciousness over that kiss. No tinge of regret either. It was as though it had never happened.

'Why should I?' She was pleased with the light nonchalance of her reply.

'I have been wondering how you were getting on with Bella. Do you like her?'

Liberty smoothed one gloved hand along Bella's silken mane. 'Oh, yes. She is perfect. It was a lovely surprise.' She narrowed her eyes at him. 'I collect you knew all about it at the Attwoods' ball, when you said you hoped to see me in the Park the following day?'

'I did—and now you see why I could not tell you the reason for my question. You were a tad irritated with me at the time, as I recall.'

She *had* been irritated and still was—but by his ability to sweep the memory of that kiss...of her...away. She must have tensed because Bella threw her head up and danced sideways. Liberty forced her hands to relax on the rein and settled her with a hand to her neck and a soothing word. Dominic watched her and she caught a glint of admiration in his silver gaze.

She didn't want his admiration. It made everything so much harder to bear.

'You are well aware, my Lord Avon, that was not the only reason for my irritation,' she snapped.

Her mood only appeared to amuse him and a teasing smile stretched his lips.

'Ah. So you *were* upset because I kissed you.'

His remark riled her still further, until she realised he was being deliberately provocative and that she was rising to it. She reined in her temper and aimed for a similar kind of teasing banter.

'I was not. It was merely a kiss.' She stuck her nose in the air, but kept her tone light. 'It was hardly my first! It was your subsequent behaviour that I found so objectionable, sir.'

'*Sir* is it now? You *are* in a huff with me!' He laughed. 'Very well. I apologise for taking advantage of you by stroking your naked arm.' His choice of words set her pulse racing. 'But, really, Berty…what do you expect of a red-blooded man when you present him with such temptation in a secluded alcove? If you will take my advice, you will remain close to your chaperon in future and not run the risk of leading random gentlemen astray.'

'Why, thank you so much for those words of wisdom, Lord Avon. Truly…' she placed her hand over her heart and fluttered her eyelashes at him '…I do not know how we weak females would manage without such penetrating male insight to guide us. Perhaps I should clothe myself in a nun's habit for future balls, if one expanse of bare skin can have such an undesirable effect on so-called gentlemen.'

She saw the effort it took him to bite back his grin.

'Now, now, Berty. I have told you before, sarcasm does not suit you.'

'And pontificating about the blinking obvious does not suit you, Dominic.'

'Touché,' he murmured.

They drifted into an amicable silence as they rode on, but the question that had plagued her for days bubbled in her brain, foiling her efforts to ignore it. She had to know the worst. She had to prepare herself.

'I have something I wish to ask you.'

His features blanked, a hint of wariness in his eyes. 'Go on.'

'Have you made your choice?'

He would know what she meant, no need to elaborate further. She burned to know *who* and *when*, so she could be ready to stand by and smile benignly even though she was still convinced he was heading for a cold and miserable future.

His eyebrows met in a dark slash. 'I have.'

Her heart tumbled and nausea rose to choke her. She swallowed hard. 'Is the young lady aware of her good fortune?'

His lips firmed and a muscle leapt in his cheek.

'Not as yet. You are the first to know.' He paused, the groove between his eyebrows deepening. 'I shall ask Lady Sybilla to be my wife,' he said eventually.

Her throat thickened. She had asked and now she knew. Olivia had been right. Sybilla was exquisitely polite to Liberty if ever their paths met, but she had never caught the slightest glimpse of the real woman beneath that emotionless façade. And now Liberty would be forced to smile and congratulate the happy couple.

How will he be happy with Sybilla? He'll end

up lonely and embittered...he needs a woman with warmth and kindness to bring joy into his life, not an ice maiden.

Sybilla was cold enough to freeze a stream of lava in mid-flow.

'And when shall you offer for her?'

His silver gaze roamed restlessly around the Park.

'Father arrived today and the family will all dine at Beauchamp House tonight. I shall inform them of my decision then.'

'So you will tell your family before you speak to Lady Sybilla?'

'Of course.' His chest swelled as he inhaled. He switched his gaze to Liberty. Then the air left his lungs in a rush. 'You know very well this is a practical arrangement. I want my family's blessing before I make any commitment. Once I make my offer there will be no going back.'

She knew that. Knew that his gentleman's honour, let alone his obsession with *duty*, would never allow him to behave otherwise. And her heart ached for him. From everything she had learned from Mrs Mount and from Olivia, the members of his extended family were all happily married—every one of them a love match. But even with those examples, Dominic still steered resolutely on his chosen course.

'And if your father gives his approval?' She knew it was his father's approval that was crucial. The rest of the family were important, but the Duke's opinion was the one that mattered.

'Then I shall call on the Duke of Wragby in the morning.'

She had pushed him far enough. There was a finality in his tone that warned her to stop. She swallowed again and concentrated on maintaining her posture in the saddle even though she longed to slump in defeat.

'I wish you well.'

'Thank you.'

They rode on in silence.

Chapter Sixteen

Dominic felt no relief at announcing his decision. What he didn't tell Liberty was that, until the moment she asked, he had still not made his final choice—wavering from one name to the other and back again until he was in a state of utter confusion—even though he still planned to tell the rest of the family tonight. Her question had pushed him into the final decision, but the words in his head had felt alien and they felt even worse coming from his mouth. But he said them none the less, that promise to his mother still on his mind…his promise and her expectations…he had vowed to prove to her that he was worthy. And he also wanted to please his father; he surely deserved at least one trouble-free son.

Dominic had spent his life conforming to what was expected of a man of his birthright precisely in order to protect his father from pain and anxiety. He was not about to change now.

Besides. He glanced over at Liberty. All that 'follow your heart' nonsense was just that. Nonsense. Pure, honest-to-goodness lust was the driving force behind his craving for Liberty Lovejoy. Without volition, his gaze slid over her, lingering on her full breasts, outlined by the snug fit of her dove-grey riding habit. Everything about her sent desire racing through his bloodstream, but he could rise above that visceral response. He'd done it before, often and often.

He'd made his choice. Lady Sybilla. She was twenty-one years old—no green girl on the town for the first time. He'd met her many times, during the Season and at house parties out of season, and she had never put an elegantly shod foot out of place. She was beautiful, reserved, well-mannered, a graceful dancer and an accomplished rider and she deferred to a man's opinion just as she ought.

He frowned, sneaking another sideways look at Liberty. No one could ever accuse her of deferring to a man's opinion simply because of his sex. If she thought her opinion was right, she had absolutely no compunction in voicing it. Much like the rest of the females in his family, he mused, except, maybe, Aunt Cecily...until she met Zach and had changed from the quiet, compliant lady Dominic had always known. He frowned. Aunt Cecily, it turned out, had not been truly happy all those years when she was raising her brother's children. She'd been content, but not happy. Not fulfilled. But she had never said so.

Would Liberty end up the same? A maiden aunt, quashing her own desires and deferring to her brother and sisters? He shook those thoughts away. It was her decision...there was nothing to stop her marrying if she chose to, even though the thought of her with another man sent anger spiking through his veins.

'Why do you care about my choice? Or when I intend to make my offer?'

He thrust down the voice that reminded him that she

had kissed him. Passionately. Of course she cared. Probably more than she should and more than he deserved.

'You are my friend. I *care* about you… I want you to be happy.'

'I shall be happy.' His reply came by rote.

She shook her head at him, then smiled. Her pearly teeth sent waves of longing crashing through him and he wrenched his gaze from hers with a silent snarl at his rampant lust.

'We *have* become serious,' she said. 'Come. Let us enjoy our time together for, once you make your announcement, I make no doubt you will be far too busy with your betrothed to spend time riding in the Park with me.' Was it his imagination, or did her voice hitch, just a little? 'The ride is less crowded here,' she continued gaily. 'Let us canter.'

She didn't wait for his reply, but set off and, after a moment's hesitation, Dominic sent Vulcan in her wake.

Beauchamp House was alight with chatter and laughter when Dominic arrived at six that evening. He entered the salon and paused, unnoticed for a few moments, just taking in his family…the smiles on their faces as they caught up with one another's news. The children, too, were there, together with their nursemaids who would whisk them away once dinner was announced. His two-year-old half-brother, Sebastian, was the first to see him.

'Dominic!'

He scurried across the room, closely pursued by his older sister, Christabel. Dominic swung Sebastian up and around, the boy's dress flaring out, his chubby legs kicking in delight as he giggled. Dominic planted a kiss on his cheek, then settled him under one arm as he scooped up Christabel with the other. Her arms wound around his neck and she pressed her hot cheek against his.

'I love you, Dominic. You're my *bestest* brother.'

'I love you, too, sweetie-pie!' Dominic hugged her close for a minute, then groaned theatrically and staggered. 'Help! Help me! I... I... I can't hold these monsters any longer!'

The conversation had paused as everyone watched the byplay then, accompanied by more laughter, Father strode forward and plucked Christabel from Dominic's arms.

'I *told* you not to eat so much, Christy—you've reduced your big brother to a quivering wreck.'

He cradled her in one arm and freed his other to tickle her. She shrieked and squirmed.

'Papa! No! Mama! Help!'

Dominic's stepmother, Rosalind, came up with a smile. As he kissed her in greeting, she said, 'I might have known you would reduce our ordered gathering to chaos as soon as you arrived, Dominic. It is good to see you, though.' She turned to Father. 'Let me take her, Leo, or Penny will complain they're too excited to sleep.'

'Yes, Your Grace.' Leo handed his daughter over to Rosalind and gave her a mock salute.

Dominic's adopted sister, Susie—now thirteen and growing up into a serious, studious girl—came over to take charge of Sebastian and order reigned once more.

'How are you, my Son?' Father's silver gaze—so like Dominic's—scanned him. 'Are these rumours I've heard true?'

Trust Father to know what was going on in advance

and to have no compunction in raising the matter. He always seemed to be two steps ahead of everyone else.

Dominic forced a nonchalant shrug. 'There are always rumours. Have you taken to listening to gossip now, Father?'

Tell him! Get it over with!

'Ah, well. I dare say I have it wrong.'

His tone suggested otherwise, but Father merely slung his arm across Dominic's shoulders and they joined the rest of the family. Dominic sought out Olivia, Hugo and Alex one by one and sent each of them a look of warning. This was his business—it was not their place to pre-empt him. Not that Alex was likely to, as he rarely voluntarily spoke to Father, but Olivia...she was a very different matter. She returned his look with an innocent lift of her eyebrows, but Dominic thought she would stay silent, not least because she had made it clear she did not approve of any of the ladies on his shortlist.

He stood to one side of the room, drinking, and he watched his family, paying particular attention to Rosalind and Olivia as they interacted with their children and their husbands, trying to picture Sybilla in that role. Then he tried to imagine her fitting in with his family as they chattered together, laughing and teasing. But he could not imagine her behaving with such informality, even in a family setting. Liberty, though...

He thrust her image away, clenching his jaw. Perhaps one of the others would be a better choice? After all, nobody knew he had selected Sybilla. Apart from Liberty and she would not tell anyone. He tried to put any one of those ladies into this scenario, but the only face that surfaced in his imagination was Liberty Lovejoy's.

'Things on your mind, Dom?'

'No.'

'Have you made your choice yet? Have you been picturing her here in the bosom of our family?'

It was too close to the truth. Dominic drained his wine glass. 'Don't be ridiculous.'

Alex leaned closer. 'Father knows. Look at him. He's waiting for you to broach the subject.'

'He told you that, did he?' Irritation with Alex prompted him to add, 'Or did you somehow let it slip during one of your cosy father-and-son chats?'

One corner of Alex's mouth lifted in a half-smile that roused Dominic's guilt. He was normally careful not to enflame his brother's hostility towards their father.

'Unworthy, Brother. You should know by now the Duke doesn't need to be told things...he just knows.'

Again, Dominic was conscious of his father's gaze on him even though he carefully avoided looking in his direction. He signalled to William, who crossed the room to fill his glass again. As soon as the footman was out of earshot, Alex turned serious.

'Dom. Listen to me. Don't tie yourself to any of 'em. Not yet. Any fool can see your heart isn't in it—'

'The heart is irrelevant, Alexander. I make decisions with my head. With logic and planning.'

'You're a damned stubborn fool once you get an idea in that head of yours, that's for certain,' Alex growled. 'Tell me, once and for all. Are you going to tell Father tonight or not?'

Dominic's clenched jaw ached as he battled with his answer. Yes? Or no? One simple word. That's all it needed.

'No,' he said finally and the relief when his decision emerged washed over him like a tidal wave, sweeping all tension and friction from him. 'No. I will not tell him tonight. There is no hurry.'

Alex grinned and slapped Dominic on the back. 'Best news I've heard in an age. There'll be a lot of anxious punters at White's, wondering what the verdict will be, mind.' He leaned in again and lowered his voice. 'I know you won't take my advice, but I shall say what I think nevertheless. Scrap that list and think again.' He walked away before Dominic could reply.

How easy it was for Alex to say that and to believe it.

He was not the heir.

He didn't have the weight of expectation on his shoulders.

He was not bound by duty.

Dominic's chest ached and his throat constricted. He had never felt so alone, even though his family were all around him. He rubbed at his chest and the action brought Liberty bouncing into his head. How many times had he noticed her doing the exact same thing? He scowled down into his glass. How many times would he continue to allow her to invade his head and upset his carefully laid plans? No matter how many times he caught himself wishing to share a joke with her, or to point out a beautiful flower or an interesting cloud formation in the sky, nothing could change the fact that the granddaughter of a coal merchant was unsuited to the position of Marchioness of Avon, let alone the future Duchess of Cheriton.

The children were shortly packed off to the nursery and dinner was served. Throughout the meal, even as the conversation ebbed and flowed, Dominic was conscious of his father's eyes resting on him from time to time, a crease between his dark brows. He didn't doubt his father knew all about the list…the question was, would he speak to Dominic about it or would he wait for Dominic to approach him? Somehow, Dominic thought he would wait. The relief he had felt had been temporary. Tension still wound his gut, robbing him of his appetite. He picked at his food.

'Are you quite well, Dominic?' Rosalind spoke softly. 'You are hardly eating a thing and you are very quiet. And drinking more than usual. Is…is something troubling you? Your father has noticed…he looks concerned.'

'I am perfectly well, thank you. I made the mistake of eating at my club earlier—I must have eaten more than I intended for I am simply not hungry now.'

The excuse slid readily from his tongue, but her face was still etched with worry. He raised his wine glass in a toast.

'Good health.'

Sarcasm laced his words and Rosalind, after another long, level look, turned her attention from him. He thrust away the guilt that stabbed at him—it was unfair to take his mood out on his stepmother, but he didn't want to talk. Not about anything. He just wanted this damned Season to be over with…for all decisions to be made and irreversible. Surely, then, he would stop this nonsensical yearning after a woman he could never have?

If that's how you feel, why not make the announcement now? This minute? The decision would be made then.

He stared blindly at his plate, unaccustomed rage battering at his chest. It was the pain from his jaw— again clenched so tightly his teeth hurt, too—that pulled him back from the brink. He concentrated on breathing steadily until he was back in control. He would not be goaded into a hasty announcement, not even by his own inner voice. He slipped on the cloak of urbanity that he wore in public and joined the conversation, but he was rattled by his uncharacteristic gibe at Rosalind. His father's frown revealed it had not gone unnoticed, but he had not mentioned it.

Yet.

But Dominic was sure it would come and he was in no fit state to verbally spar with the man who had never lost a match yet.

I cannot cope with much more of this.

He craved solitude. As soon as it was polite, Dominic made his excuses to leave Beauchamp House and Alex, to no one's surprise but to Dominic's exasperation, elected to leave with him. Dominic wanted to be alone to think through his future. Yet again. Did he need to rethink his strategy? He couldn't deny his doubts about choosing a wife from his shortlist all stemmed from his feelings for Liberty. But that didn't make her any more suitable. He could not get away from that. So, in that case, wasn't one shortlist much like another?

'Come on, Dom. A few hands of whist will shake you out of the doldrums.'

They had reached the corner of his road and Dominic glanced towards his house, further along, on the opposite side. A flash of pale skin by the area steps caught his attention and all his senses went on to high alert. He halted.

'Thanks, Alex, but not tonight.' He clapped his brother's shoulder. 'You go on. I'm for my bed. I've a session booked at Angelo's in the morning.'

And after he'd honed his fencing skills with Henry, he might very well call in next door to Jackson's—

maybe a sparring session would work off some of his bottled-up energy. Or—and his grip tightened on his ebony cane—maybe whoever was lurking near his front door might provide him with that opportunity right now.

'Oh, well.' Alex shrugged. 'I'll be off then—I arranged to meet Nev and Gid once I'd done the family duty bit. G'night, Dom!'

'Goodnight, Alex.'

Dominic watched his brother saunter away before he crossed the road and strolled along the pavement towards his house, swinging his cane nonchalantly. If it was a thief lying in wait for an unwary passer-by, he would get more than he bargained for. Dominic was in just the mood for some physical action. Something to work out his frustrations.

As he drew level with the steps that led down to the basement kitchens, a movement flickered in the corner of his eye. He gripped his cane, unsheathing the sword in one smooth movement. Then the scent reached him, curling through his senses, bringing with it a sense of peace…and a desperate longing.

Roses.

Liberty gasped as a steel blade flashed in the light from the nearby street lamp.

'It's me,' she hissed.

His face was in shadow, but she saw from the way he squared his shoulders that he was annoyed.

Of course he's annoyed! What am I doing, lying in wait for him like this?

But she had to try, one last time, to save him from himself. If she failed…well, if she failed she would at least know she had left no stone unturned and, once she returned to Eversham, she would probably never see him again. The melancholy thought weighed heavy on her, her heart aching with loneliness. She rubbed at her chest.

'What the devil are you *doing*?' He growled the question. 'Do you *want* to cause a scandal?'

He still stood on the pavement. She still stood on the steps, her face at the level of his groin. She felt her skin heat as she remembered the things Bernard had told her a man and a woman could do together. Things with mouths and…

She swallowed. Such shocking thoughts—she would never be a lady. Dominic was right not to even consider her. Although Bernard had not taken her innocence, they *had* kissed and been intimate—hardly the behaviour suitable for a society lady—and she was familiar with a man's anatomy and what it could do. She had seen and recognised Dominic's physical reaction to her more than once—and she'd felt his arousal that time they kissed. He wanted her as a man wants a woman.

And she…God help her…wanted him. She could not deny it. She was five-and-twenty now…would probably never marry…and Dominic haunted her dreams.

And though she knew she could never have him, she still wanted him to be happy. She couldn't bear to think of him unhappy. She had failed to save one man she loved, Bernard, and now she was here to try to save Dominic from this huge mistake. She wasn't entirely sure what lay in his heart, but she was damned certain it was not Lady Sybilla Gratton. So she would try, one last time, to open his eyes and his heart to the truth… to show him the difference between what he wanted and what he needed.

'Of course not.' She kept her voice to a whisper as she answered him, conscious that any member of his staff could see them if they happened to look out of the window behind her. 'But I cannot stand by and watch you make a mistake you will live to regret.'

'How can you possibly know I would regret it? And, besides, how does it concern you?'

'You asked me that this afternoon. My answer is the same. You are my friend. I want you to be happy.'

'And you think my choosing a suitable wife will make me *un*happy?' His head snapped round and he stared along the street. 'You cannot stay there. How did you get here?'

'I walked.'

'Walked? Alone? Good God, Berty…anything could have happened. You know it's unsafe for a lady to walk alone, especially at night.'

She might as well admit the worst, because he would see for himself soon enough. She sucked in a shaky breath and stepped back, away from the wall. Dominic craned his neck over the railings. She heard his spluttered laugh and, offended, she rammed Gideon's best beaver hat back on her head. It slid down to rest atop her ears, the brim half-covering her eyes.

'There is a reason females do not wear trousers.' He was using his superior voice and it set Liberty's hackles rising. 'They are entirely the wrong shape for them. At least…*you* are entirely the wrong shape.'

She didn't think she looked that dreadful…although, admittedly, her hips and legs *were* curvier than Gideon's and the pantaloons *were* stretched somewhat more thinly than they were designed for. She *hmmph*ed quietly even as she registered the change in Dominic's voice. It had turned, somehow, caressing. He couldn't hold on to all that anger, she knew he couldn't. She stared up at him.

'Did you tell them?'

He shook his head. 'No.'

The knot in her stomach loosened, just a little. She wasn't too late. If only—

'I want to talk to you. Please.'

'But I know what you are going to say and it will make no difference. Besides, we cannot stand here much longer without attracting all sorts of the wrong attention.'

'Please?'

He tipped his head back and stared up at the house. 'Stay there and keep quiet.'

He disappeared from her sight and she heard the sound of a key in a lock followed by the murmur of masculine voices and the quiet sound of a door closing. She waited…and she had just begun to think he had abandoned her there as a joke or a punishment when the door opened, spilling light on to the pavement.

'Be quick.'

Liberty ran up the remaining steps and in through the front door as quickly as she could. Contrary to what Dominic thought, she really did have no desire to be seen dressed in men's clothing and loitering outside his door. It had taken all her courage to come here, but she had come nevertheless—scurrying through the streets with her head down—because she simply couldn't bear the thought of the future that awaited him. She'd come prepared for a lengthy wait—not knowing what time he might arrive home—and had almost cried with relief when she had seen him turn the corner into his street.

Dominic ushered her into a very masculine, but comfortable sitting room. A fire blazed in the hearth. A cold repast was laid out on a side table next to a silver salver with two glasses and a full decanter. The door closed behind Liberty with a soft click and she wheeled around to face Dominic.

Chapter Seventeen

Liberty's heart tumbled in her chest, her breathing quickened and her pulse leapt, heat flushing her skin.

Dear heavens, he is gorgeous. If only…

She batted away that errant thought. There were no 'if onlys'. She clung tight to that knowledge. She would not fool herself…she loved Dominic. And she knew he…what? He liked her, certainly. They were friends. They enjoyed one another's company, they made one another laugh. But she also knew that caring for him… loving him…meant wanting what was best for him. And that was *not* to burden him with a wife who was so far removed from his ideal that she might as well be a duck.

This was not about persuading him to throw away the principles he held dear and to marry her regardless. It was about persuading him he deserved to find a suitable lady for his wife who would make him *happy*.

'Do take off that preposterous hat, Berty,' Dominic drawled as he crossed to the table and poured two glasses of wine.

She removed it with relief. Her ears were already sore from the brim chafing them. Dominic handed her the glass and gestured to the fire, bracketed by a pair of green-leather wing-back chairs. Liberty sat and sipped her wine.

'Let me have it, then, Berty.'

Dominic moved to stand in front of her, his glass in one long-fingered hand. His reflection in the gilt-framed mirror above the mantelpiece revealed a muscle bunching in his jaw as he clenched it. The firelight played across his skin, making it glow and highlighting the dark hairs that dusted the back of his hand. There was strength and beauty in that hand and she itched to just reach out and touch it.

'Best we get this out of the way. I'm tired and I need my bed.'

His bored tone didn't fool Liberty for one second. He was as tense as she'd ever seen him. She mulled over how to start.

'You do realise how preposterous your behaviour is?' he drawled. 'And what would happen if someone caught us in here? Like this?'

She jumped to her feet at that. 'You know that is not why I have come.' She couldn't bear him to even suspect she might try to entrap him. 'I would never behave in such a low, sneaky, despicable way.'

A mirthless smile stretched his lips. 'I do know it. You are doing what you always do...risking yourself for those you...those you *care* for. You are a good, kind-hearted woman, Liberty Lovejoy, but you must allow other people to tread their own path, even if you believe they are making a monumental mistake.' He raised his glass in a mock salute and downed it in one again, before eyeing his empty glass in disgust. 'I need something stronger than this.' He wheeled away and went to a side table, returning with two glasses in one hand and a bottle in the other. 'Brandy?'

Her wine glass was empty. She nodded and watched him pour amber liquid into the glasses, her eyes following him as he bent to set the bottle down on the hearth, took Liberty's empty glass from her hand and passed her the new one. She sipped. It was good brandy— the fiery spirit slipped down a treat. She'd occasionally enjoyed a glass in the evening with Bernard. They'd shared a glass the night before she left for London. It had been the last time she ever saw him.

Without warning, her eyes brimmed. She should never have gone to London. She should never have left Gideon... Mama... Papa... The guilt scoured her.

'Liberty?' The gentleness of Dominic's tone was nearly her undoing, but she blinked furiously and swallowed back her tears before facing him again, chin up.

'I am sorry. It is nothing...a memory caught me unawares, that is all.'

'Your intended?'

She nodded, rubbing at the lonely ache in her chest as she stared into the flames. What was she doing here? *Could* she ever persuade Dominic to think again?

'How do you know about Bernard...my intended?'

'Was that his name? Gideon told Alex who told Olivia. I just happened to be present.' Dominic steered Liberty back to her chair. He sat opposite and fixed her with an unwavering silver gaze. 'Will you tell me about him?'

And she did. How they had grown up as neighbours, always knowing they were destined to be married.

'You were childhood sweethearts, then?'

'Yes.'

'And no other man will ever usurp the sainted Bernard in your affections?'

She frowned. 'That is how Gideon always refers to

Bernard. It's not true. He was no saint and I never set him up on a pedestal to worship.'

'I meant no disrespect. To either of you.'

Liberty pushed her fingers through her hair and stood up. 'I am too hot.' She unwound her roughly tied neckcloth and then began to shrug out of Gideon's coat. 'Do you mind if I take this off?'

'Be my guest.'

He pushed himself out of his chair and came behind her to help, for which she was grateful. She'd had enough of a struggle getting the tailored coat on in the first place. Removing it was even more difficult. As Dominic grasped the collar his fingers brushed Liberty's neck and she gasped as tingles radiated through her body. Her arms free, she then felt him lift one lock of hair, just behind her ear. His breathing in her ear was erratic, almost harsh. Their reflections in the mirror above the mantelpiece showed his attention transfixed by that tendril as he allowed it to slip through his fingers to drape over her shoulder.

She stepped away. 'Thank you. No wonder you gentlemen need valets.'

She sat down again, avoiding eye contact, conscious of that visceral attraction between them, careful not to tempt fate. Liberty Lovejoy was still Liberty Lovejoy. Not a suitable future duchess.

Dominic placed the coat on a wooden chair near the door and then flung himself into the other fireside chair.

'So…when did you get betrothed to the s—to Bernard?'

'Two days before I left for London to make my debut. He urged me to go…to take advantage of my godmother's offer to sponsor me.' She swallowed. 'He fell ill two weeks after I left…'

In a halting voice, she told Dominic about the message that had reached her…the worst day of her life… that terrible dash back to Sussex, urging the post boys to go ever faster.

'The worst thing,' she said, at the end of her tale, 'is the guilt that I was not there. At least I saw my parents again and helped to nurse them. But not Bernard… I never said goodbye and I can barely picture his face any more.'

'There is no portrait?'

'No. He promised to have a miniature painted for me, but he never did.'

Again her throat ached with the memory, but the sorrow was distant now…almost as though it had happened to another person. Slowly, the thought surfaced that she had never felt for Bernard what she now felt for Dominic. She had loved him, but it had been a quieter love… steadier. Passion had kindled, when he had kissed her, and touched her…but it had been a slow burn. It had never been this all-encompassing fire that consumed her whenever she thought of Dominic. Whenever she was near him.

'I suppose I am fortunate that there is a portrait of my mother at the Abbey.' Dominic was staring into the fire, the orange flames reflected in his eyes. 'And I still had my father and my aunt and uncle. You suffered a dreadful blow, losing your parents at the same time, too. It must have been so hard for all of you.'

There was no answer to that other than *Yes.* Liberty sipped her brandy as she, too, contemplated the flames.

'How old were you when your mother died?'

'Eight. And she didn't just die. She was *murdered.*'

His bitterness shouldn't shock her, but it did. He sounded so…angry. 'Did they ever find out who did it?'

'No. Alex found her body. He was only seven. He didn't speak for a year and he was never quite the same afterwards.'

'Oh, poor little boy. That must have been dreadful for him…for all of you. And for your father, too, to lose his wife that way.'

His eyes glittered. 'The memories of that time are hazy now…as though a veil covers the details. I just remember feeling…disbelief, I suppose. I was upset but, looking back, I doubt I fully understood I would never see her again.' He sank his head into his hands, elbows propped on his knees. 'As a family, we never talk about it. We were too young when it happened and I suppose we all just got used to not discussing it. The past is the past and we move forward into the future.'

'And is that how you feel inside? That it's all in the past? That it cannot affect you…any of you…now?'

'Yes. No.' He scrubbed his hands through his hair. 'I don't know.'

Liberty said nothing, waiting for him to go on—sensing his battle between wanting to unburden himself and family loyalty.

'I do know it affected Father for a long time.' His words came quietly. 'He had refused to allow her to go to London. He told her she must spend more time with us. Her children. And a week later she was dead. I know he felt guilty for failing to protect her.'

She knew that feeling…the guilt of failing to protect. Dominic stared down at the rug.

'We were never enough for her.' His voice was raw. 'She used to say she was proud of "her boys"—particularly me, as I was the heir—but they were just words to her. They had no meaning—there was never any pleasing her. And poor Olivia never got *any* maternal attention or affection from her.

'My memories are those of a child—at the time I overheard things that made little sense, but as I got older I understood. Probably more than I cared to.' He huffed a mirthless laugh. 'I know she married Father for his wealth and for the prestige of being a duchess. She was never happy at the Abbey—she craved the excitement of London and the adulation of her admirers even though we all tried hard to behave well and to be worthy of her attention and her approval.

'But we knew no different—she was our mother, and we worshipped her, constantly seeking approval. Now…when I look back… I compare Cecily and how she loved us all and I can see that all we ever got from Mother was coldness and rejection.'

The pain in his voice wrenched at Liberty's heartstrings, and she ached for those children.

'She wanted to be adored by us all, but she gave nothing…apart from one time…' Dominic faltered, then he cleared his throat and dashed one hand across his eyes. His voice hardened. 'She gave us nothing in return. Certainly not love.'

Liberty stared at him. 'But…you…'

He met her gaze, his eyes glittering. 'But…? I…?'

His tone mocked. She tried to gather her thoughts, frowning. It made no sense.

'I do not understand. Why are you so set on fulfilling a promise to your mother if she was as cold as you say? Surely you owe her nothing?'

'I don't…' He emptied his glass and set it down. He leaned forward, his head bowed, his eyes screwed shut. His elbow propped on the armrest and his splayed hand covered his face, all four fingertips pressed to his forehead, his thumb digging into his cheek. 'I don't know...' he said, his voice muffled. Aching. 'Just before she died, I hoped she might...' He shook his head. 'I suppose I still want to prove I am worthy of her and to make her proud of me.'

Liberty longed to take him in her arms and soothe away his pain.

'You were eight years old, Dominic. You should not feel bound by such an oath.'

His head jerked up. 'I shouldn't be talking to you like this. Besides, there's my father to think of. He suffered, too, and Alex... Alex... Well, I don't understand, but Alex and Father will never be close. I am his heir... I cannot let him down.' His voice broke. '*He* did not shirk his duty. I want to make him proud.'

'Oh, Dominic.' Liberty went to him, sank on to her knees on the floor and cradled his face in her hands. 'I have not met your father, but how could he not be proud of you? And the rest of your family love you— that is obvious. Do you really think they wish you to be unhappy?'

He jerked his head from between her hands at that, lowering the hand that shielded his eyes. For the flash of a second, Liberty saw his vulnerability before his silvery eyes shuttered.

'Why should I be unhappy? My marriage will be no different to hundreds of others—it is the norm in our world.'

'It is not the norm in your family, from what I have been told. What is your stepmother like? Does she make your father happy?'

Dominic's eyes warmed. 'Oh, yes. She is perfect for him. We all love her.'

'And can you picture Lady Sybilla in the bosom of your family? Will she fit in?'

His gaze slid from hers. 'Why should she not?'

Liberty's hands were on his knees. Her thighs and belly pressed against his shins. A knot of emotion lodged in her throat as she struggled to find the arguments to get through to him…the words that would help him to see what a huge mistake he was about to make.

'Can you not see, though?' She slid her hands up his thighs, the muscles rock hard beneath her fingers. She captured his gaze. 'If you marry a woman like Lady Sybilla, you are asking for history to repeat itself.' Her hands moved further, up his flat belly to his chest, his silk waistcoat smooth and warm to her touch. His eyes darkened and a thrill spiralled through her. 'Is that truly what you want? Look around you, Dominic. Look at your father and your stepmother, your uncles and aunts, Olivia and Hugo. They all have love matches and are happy and content.' Olivia had told Liberty all about the Beauchamps. 'Is that not what you want for yourself?' She reached his neck and curved her fingers around his jaw, his dark stubble scratching her skin.

'Dominic…is that not what you want for *your* children?'

All her altruistic notions fled as she gazed deep into those silvery-grey eyes that were no longer cold mirrors, but deep, white-hot furnaces that blazed, sending bolts of pure energy and need sizzling through her. He needed a woman with warmth and curves and love to bring happiness to his life. He needed—if only he could see it—Liberty Lovejoy. But could she persuade him before it was too late?

She pressed closer and his knees parted as his hands

gripped her sides and lifted, pulling her almost roughly to him. For what seemed an eternity their eyes locked and held as blood rampaged through her veins like a river in flood and the heat of desire pooled between her thighs. She fancied a question formed deep in his silvery gaze—and she knew her answer.

With a sigh of pleasure, she slipped her fingers into the heavy silk of his hair and she pressed her mouth to his.

Neither the frantic attempts by his controlling inner voice nor the stridency of the warning bells that reverberated inside his head could stop him. The groan vibrated deep, deep inside Dominic's chest as he wrapped his arms around Liberty Lovejoy and gloried in the caress of her mouth. He had no strength to fight the strongest impulse he had ever known: the impulse to take, to enjoy, to wallow. To simply *feel* and not to plan…or to control…or to consider any implications. His mind might clamour all it liked for him to resist, but his body would not…could not…obey. This was what he had craved since the day he'd met her. The dam of his self-control had burst and this was what he wanted.

Right here. Right now. Regardless.

His hands plunged into her hair, shaking it loose, the heavy tresses spilling down her back as her soft body moulded to his. Her breasts—glorious, abundant, wonderful—pressed between them. Her scent curled around him, through him, drugging him…roses…no longer a smell to awaken regret and failure, but a smell to conjure forth hope and possibility. With another heartfelt groan, one hand at the small of her back, the other between her shoulder blades, he slithered from the chair, holding her carefully until they were on their

knees on the rug before the fire, caressing her sweet
mouth that tasted of honey. His tongue traced the soft
fullness of her lips and, as they parted, swept inside,
his lips sliding over hers, kissing her with a hunger
that set his entire being on fire. Gently, he eased her
back and he half-covered her—exactly where he had
fantasised having her ever since the day she had burst
into his life.

He explored her mouth at first with dreamy intimacy—
lingering, savouring every moment…a kiss for his tired
soul to melt into. He shifted to ease the fullness in his
groin and angled his head, deepening the kiss, his tongue
thrusting now with more urgency, his fingers curling into
her silken tresses, holding her head still as he plundered
her mouth. Her hands skimmed his back restlessly as a
low moan sounded in her throat and her body arched beneath him. He forced his mouth from hers, raising himself on one elbow to look his fill, his heart pounding in
his chest.

Heavy lids half-covered slumberous midnight-blue
eyes. Her sweet-scented skin was flushed and her lips…
oh, her lips, were softly sheening and succulent. Her
breasts rose and fell with every fragmented breath, the
sound intensely, intoxicatingly feminine.

'Dominic…'

Her voice low and husky, she reached for him again,
her fingers insistent as they clutched at his shoulders.
He brushed her hair back from her temple and took
her lips again in a slow, intoxicating kiss that made
his senses swim and every nerve ending pulse with
life. Every thought that tried to intrude was ruthlessly
quashed.

She was all that mattered. All he wanted. She…*this*…
was what he needed.

Her arms wound around his neck and her fingers tangled again in his hair. His fingertips skimmed down the side of her face to her neck and lingered over the sensitive skin by her ear as a delicate shudder racked her. He deepened the kiss, plunging his tongue again and again, and she responded—each sensual stroke ensnaring him deeper in her spell. He stroked her neck, inside the open collar of the shirt she wore, tracing the delicate skin over her collarbone, then moving lower, seeking…he bit back a groan as his hand closed possessively around her breast, only the fine fabric of her chemise between his hand and the heat of her skin, her nipple a hard bud against his palm.

He dragged his mouth from hers and nuzzled her neck, searching for her pulse, laving it as it hammered beneath his tongue. His own heart pounded, sending hot blood surging through his veins, around his body, flooding his groin.

How long had he dreamed of her breasts? Conscious thought played no part in him tugging both shirt and chemise free from her waistband. He pushed both garments high, then reared back to gaze his fill at her beautiful, full breasts, the nipples and areoles a dusky pink. Each firm globe more than filled his hands. She shivered, a low moan escaping her lips as he teased her nipples into hard peaks, rubbing and tugging.

Her hands were on his jacket, pushing it open. On the buttons of his waistcoat. Again he reared back and shrugged out of both garments. She watched him, her eyes glinting.

'Your shirt,' she whispered. 'I want to see.'

He didn't think he could get any harder, but he did as he pulled his shirt over his head and saw her reaction. She reached up, and stroked her hands up his belly and across his chest, then down each arm to his hands.

'Help me.'

She sat up, took hold of her shirt and began to pull. He needed no further encouragement and the feeling of those wonderful breasts as they brushed against his chest was torture. He dipped his head and she gasped as he paid homage to them, licking, sucking and nipping to his heart's content while she explored his arms and torso—seemingly fascinated with the dark hair that covered his chest. He didn't know who initiated it, but before long they were on their feet, ripping off the rest of their clothes.

He stilled, feasting his eyes on all that glorious, naked flesh and gently, reverently, he cupped her upper arms, willing his body to be patient even as slender fingers wrapped around his length, squeezing and stroking. He removed her hand and pulled her towards him, kissing her long and deep as her body softened, moulding into his, and she moaned her pleasure.

He wanted nothing more than to lay her full length on the floor and to plunge his aching arousal into her heat, but he wouldn't rush this. He would make it good for her. So he laid her down and followed her. He took his time, worshipping her with his touch and his mouth, listening to her sighs and her gasps of pleasure, learning her, feeling her body arch beneath him, her nails digging into his shoulders, the impatient tilt of her hips, her husky 'Dominic...please...'

And when her fingers clutched harder and her head moved restlessly from side to side, when she was hot and wet and ready for him, he moved between her open thighs, positioned his throbbing shaft at her entrance, reached again for the pearl hidden in her secret folds and he pressed.

She screamed his name as she reached her zenith and, as her body shuddered with ecstasy, he thrust inside her. It took only a few thrusts for him to reach fulfilment, but he was happy. Her pleasure was his pleasure, her ecstasy, his ecstasy.

He gathered her close and settled down with her in his arms.

Chapter Eighteen

She felt so right in his arms, nestled into his chest, her hair tickling his chin.

But…

Those warnings he had successfully kept at bay came clamouring into his brain. The head-banging, gut-churning reasons why he could not even dream of marrying Liberty Lovejoy, even though his soul cried out for her. Even though he had, tentatively, begun to believe dreams might come true.

'Make me proud, my Son.'

His mother's words…uttered in that cold, demanding voice…the one all three of her children had striven to obey, desperate to win words of praise and approval. A taunting reminder of the past. Those insidious words—sneaking around his head, prying into the corners where hope had dared to germinate, marshalling his embryonic dreams together and, mockingly, dismissing them as the unworthy fantasies of a child.

'Never forget your duty—you were born to be the Duke. Never disgrace your position in society—the eyes of the world will be on you. Judging you. Never let them see weakness. You are not the same as other

*men, driven by base desires. You are the Marquess of
Avon. You will be Duke of Cheriton one day, and your
son, and your son's son, and countless generations to
follow will also fulfil that role. Do not allow your weakness to contaminate the bloodline—it is your destiny to
keep it pure. Choose your wife with care and with pride
and, above all, with your intelligence.'*

Nausea and a deep, throbbing dread filled him. He
tightened his embrace and breathed in her sweet, subtle essence—mixed now with the scent of their love-
making. Honour whispered he must offer for Liberty.
His heart craved nothing more than to spend his life
with her. But duty and cold hard reasoning dictated
otherwise.

He scrambled to his feet and grabbed his clothes,
pulling them on hastily and haphazardly, the battle between heart and mind filling his head.

'Dominic…?'

Low, pained, questioning…her voice grabbed at
his emotions and twisted. Hard. There was Liberty
to think of…*her* feelings. Her future. And that tipped
the balance of the scales in favour of his honour and
his heart.

'I'm sorry. That shouldn't have happened…would
never have happened had you not…had I not…' He was
gabbling…his words sounded cold. Heartless.

'Never forget your duty, my Son.'

The scales tilted the opposite way. But he could not
abandon Liberty. Not now.

'I will apply for a special licence in the morning. Get
dressed. I will escort you home.'

'What?'

He looked at her then—sitting before the fire, the
flames bronzing her skin, highlighting the honey and

gold of her hair, her brother's shirt clutched to her breasts, her midnight-blue eyes with those glinting gold flecks, huge…searching…uncertain.

What more could he say? He could not reassure her, not properly. How could he when he barely knew which way was up? How could he, with his head churning with such conflict? Everything was in turmoil…his carefully laid plans…he barely knew what to think, let alone what to say or do. For once in his well-ordered, meticulously planned life, he was lost. The path he had followed from childhood had not only forked, it had vanished, leaving him frantically searching with no clue which way to turn.

A childhood memory surfaced of tumbling out of a tree, scrabbling at the branches, trying desperately to slow his fall. He felt the same sensation now—as though he were tumbling, ever faster, out of control.

His heart twisted in his chest at her beloved face, her doubt. The last thing he wanted was to hurt her, but he couldn't find the right words, not when he was still reeling. He needed space and time to get his thoughts straight. But he *would* make it right—explain properly— later. He just needed time to think.

He softened his voice. 'Get dressed, Liberty. I will call on you in the morning and we will put this right.'

Her eyes flashed and she bounced to her feet.

That shouldn't have happened…would never have happened had you not…

He hadn't needed to finish that thought… Liberty could read between those lines. What he meant was: it would never have happened had she not defied all the rules of proper behaviour and come here clandes- tinely, and then compounded her offence by drawing him out about his mother and resurrecting all those painful memories for him.

Humiliation burned through her as she tugged Gideon's shirt over her head and pulled on his pantaloons, wriggling to fit them past her hips.

'A licence will not be necessary, Dominic.'

Her gamble had failed. She had hoped—stupid, forlorn, immature hope—that by loving him…by showing him what he *could* have in his life…he would finally open his eyes and his heart to the truth. He did love her—he had proved that with every kiss, every caress, every touch. He had proved it every time he looked at her with his heart in his eyes.

But that was not enough. If he was only offering for her under duress—from some stuffy, ridiculous sense of honour—she could never accept, no matter how much she loved him. He might love her now, but she feared that love would never survive if he was ashamed of her. And his reaction…his words…confirmed that fear.

'I have taken your innocence. We *must* be wed.'

'You did not take my innocence.' God help her, she lied. She had been intimate with Bernard, but they had never actually made love. But the act had not hurt as she had thought it might. It had been wonderful…swept along on a tide of passion…the slightest of discomforts when he first entered her…but she had been wet, and so ready for him, longing for him. There had been no pain. 'Bernard and I…'

She had no need to finish; she read his comprehension in his eyes. And was that a tinge of relief? Her heart tore…not even in two, but into shreds. Too numerous to count.

'You need not concern yourself with me. Just promise me you will think twice before pledging yourself to

Lady Sybilla.' She couldn't help herself. She couldn't bear to think of the cold, lonely life that awaited him. She went to him, touched his arm. 'Please. You deserve better than her, whatever her pedigree might say.'

'You must marry me!' His silver gaze pierced her, filling her with sudden hope. Hope that was dashed with his next words. 'What if you are with child?'

Liberty swallowed hard. 'And what if I am not? Marriage is for a lifetime and my grandfather was still a lowly coal merchant.'

Please. Argue with me. Tell me you've reconsidered. Anything!

Dominic passed one hand around the back of his neck, then picked up his discarded coat, shrugging into it. 'We will talk about this tomorrow. But…' he paused, and she saw his throat move as he swallowed 'if you find there are consequences you must let me know.' He avoided her gaze. 'I will see you want for nothing… I will pay you an allowance. Buy you a—'

She shoved him. He staggered back a pace, taken unawares. Liberty followed him, thrusting her face close to his. *'I do not want your money.'*

She cast an eye around the room. Boots. She grabbed them and easily pulled them on as they were many sizes too big for her. Jacket. She snatched it from the chair, passed it wordlessly to Dominic. He held it for her while she wriggled into it. Hat. She bundled her hair into a rope, piled it on top of her head and rammed the hat down hard, relishing the pain as the brim folded her ears and trapped them. Any pain was preferable to what she felt inside.

She reached for the door. 'And I do not need your escort.'

He reached past her and held the door shut. 'I will not allow you to walk the streets alone.'

'I got here without mishap. I can get home.'

He released the pressure on the door and Liberty marched into the hall and out of the front door, crossing the street to make her way home. There were a few people about, but most were in carriages. She kept her eyes fixed firmly on the pavement in front of her and walked as quickly as she could. As she reached the corner, a movement caught her eye.

Dominic. Five paces behind her.

'Berty!'

She ignored his whisper and increased her pace to a trot, a stitch forming in her side at the unaccustomed exertion. He made no attempt to catch her up. Good. The less she had to do with that stubborn numbskull in the future, the better she would like it! Lord Arrogant could ride to hell backwards on a donkey for all she cared! He didn't deserve her!

As they turned into Green Street, however, he caught her up and grabbed her arm, forcing her to a stop.

'What are you doing? Someone might see us,' she hissed.

They were close to a street lamp and Dominic manoeuvred her so her face was in shadow. She supposed she should be grateful for that. She wasn't so enamoured of the lift of one dark eyebrow and the quirk of his lips that she could now see quite clearly, with the lamplight illuminating his features.

'They might indeed. But that doesn't matter because we *will* be married, Liberty. I will call on you tomorrow at noon and I shall request a private interview.'

She thought quickly. If he did that, there would be no doubt in her sisters' or Mrs Mount's minds that he intended to propose to her. Her heart quailed at the thought of trying to convince them she would refuse… they had all noticed how friendly the two of them were and her sisters had both, laughingly, accused her of carrying a torch for Lord Avon.

'Come at two,' she said. They had arranged to pay visits tomorrow afternoon…she could easily excuse herself.

His eyes narrowed. 'Are you up to something, Berty? Because, I warn you, I expect you to be at home. Or I shall come looking for you.'

She suppressed the shiver his softly spoken words aroused. 'I will be there.'

He tilted her chin with one long finger and for one wild moment she thought he might kiss her. But he merely said, 'Good.'

Anger sustained her as she crept indoors and upstairs. Safely back in her bedchamber, she struggled out of Gideon's coat—hearing an ominous rip in the process—then shed the remainder of his clothes and shoved them beneath her bed, out of sight. She would deal with them in the morning. She had the rest of her life to deal with them. She burrowed under the bedclothes and, finally, she gave way to her misery.

After Mrs Mount and her sisters left the house the following afternoon, Liberty paced around the small salon feeling like a caged animal. She didn't fool herself Dominic would give up easily—he would consider himself honour-bound to marry her even though it had been her decision to visit him and they had been swept away on a mutual tide of passion. Her stomach swooped and her skin tingled at the memory of his touch, his whispers, the caress of his lips…and of *him*. The spicy, musky scent of aroused male; the salty tang of his skin; the texture of his hair-roughened skin beneath her questing fingertips; the slide of skin over his hot, hard length as she stroked. His weight on her, between her thighs… her belly tightened at those memories and hot, sweet need pooled at her core.

They had both lost control, that was the honest truth, and she did not shy away from her own culpability—it was more her fault than his. *She* had gone to *him* with the genuine aim of stopping him from making a dreadful mistake. Had she truly believed he would suddenly discard his belief in his duty? A belief that had lasted a lifetime. How utterly foolish, to think that she—Liberty Lovejoy—could ever influence a man like the Marquess of Avon.

But then, once they were alone together…when he told her about his mother…oh, then her heart yearned to heal him. And she had wantonly indulged her own desire to make love with the man who haunted her dreams, knowing she might never again have the chance.

And because it was more her fault than his, she would save him from another mistake and protect him from marrying her out of a misguided sense of honour. It was a marriage she was afraid he would come to regret and she could not bear that he would grow to rue the day he met her.

If she allowed herself to, she could sink into a swamp of despair. But a thought had surfaced…the faintest glimmer of a hope. There was no doubt that Dominic would try by any means to persuade her to accept his offer today. And she could not, would not, accept.

But…if the possibility of a child were removed… what then? What if, by some miracle, Dominic *did* change his mind? What if her gamble had borne fruit and opened his mind to the possibility of another way... of a marriage for love instead of duty?

It was a fragile hope, but it was all she had to cling to. If, of course, he *did* love her. Last night, she had been convinced. Now, in the clear light of day, she was not so sure.

All she could do, for now, was to remain steadfast in her refusal of him. For both their sakes.

And pray she was not with child.

She was so lost in thought she jumped when Ethel opened the salon door to announce Lord Avon. Her heart hammered and it felt as though every muscle in her body turned to jelly. She hauled in a steadying breath and smoothed her palms down the skirt of her gown.

'Show him in, please, Ethel.'

She took advantage of the few minutes it would take him to come upstairs to check her reflection in the mirror on the wall by the door. Her cheeks were flushed, her eyes somewhat wild and there was a quiver in her lower lip she could not quell without taking it between her teeth and biting down on it. She patted her hair into place, then hurried to stand before the window, feeling more confident with the light at her back.

'Lord Avon, miss. Would you like me to stay?'

Just one look at him set her heart skipping and jumping—his tall, broad frame, his dark good looks, his crooked smile revealing his uncertainty over the action he intended to take.

Liberty switched her attention to the maid. 'No, Ethel. That will not be necessary. His Lordship will not remain above five minutes.'

As soon as they were alone, Dominic strode across the room and reached for her hands. She tucked them behind her back. He frowned, but he took the hint and stepped back.

'Liberty…look…' He swept a hand through his hair. 'I am aware I made a complete mull of it last night after…after we…well. I am sorry. Truly I am… I didn't think what I was saying before I blurted it out.'

'You voiced your immediate thoughts, Dominic. It is quite all right. I understand.'

'No. It is not all right.'

He moved closer again and his spicy cologne weaved through her senses as he cupped her shoulders. The warm, steady strength of his hands was nearly her undoing. How simple it would be to bow to the inevitable… to fold into his embrace, to lean into his solid frame and allow him to take control, to accept him and to worry about any consequences later. She blanked her expression and forced herself to remain rigidly upright.

'Accept me and I shall leave here and arrange the licence straight away. We can be wed by the end of next week.' He put his lips to her ear. 'We will be happy together.'

His breath tickled, but she gritted her teeth, determined not to squirm. Was he trying to convince himself as much as persuade her? It was not hard to believe and it made her even more determined to stick to her plan.

'No, Dominic. I will not marry you. You are only offering for me out of guilt, but there is no need. I am an adult, not some green girl who did not know what she was doing. There is no need to ruin both our lives.'

'*Both* our lives?' His grip tightened. 'What are you saying…that you do not care for me after all? Are you in the habit of giving yourself to random men you have no feelings for?'

She tore herself from his grasp and paced across

the room before whirling to face him. 'I care for you too much to saddle you with a wife you are marrying out of duty.'

He visibly flinched. '*Duty?* It is duty that resulted in that damned shortlist. It is my honour that dictates I make an honest woman of you.'

She stared at him, holding his gaze without wavering, willing him to say more…to speak of what was in his heart. Did he love her? Or was last night purely about lust after all? If she accepted him like this, she might never know. But of one thing she was certain— if he did not love her and he was offering purely with his honour, then he would soon grow to resent and even hate her.

She had faced heartbreak before and survived. She would do so again.

'No. You are free to continue with your perfect, dutiful life, my lord. You are under no obligation to me.'

'And if you are with child?'

She had done the calculations. It would not be long before she knew. A matter of days only.

'If I am, we will talk again.' She moved to the door and opened it. 'I hope we may remain friends, when we meet?'

He searched her face, then nodded.

'Then I shall bid you good afternoon, Lord Avon.'

If she thought he would give up that easily, she could think again. Dominic strode up Green Street, fury at her stubbornness biting at his gut. The clip-clop of hooves behind him reminded him that he had driven his curricle to her house. He gestured at Ted to stay back and he kept walking.

Who does she think she is? Doesn't she realise the honour I've—?

His whirling thoughts steadied and he lopped off his diatribe before he could finish it, recognising his sheer arrogance to even think such a thing. As his thoughts slowed down so did his pace and his tumbling emotions, and his churning gut.

Why are you so damned furious?

He halted on the corner of the street, staring blindly at the houses opposite as he strove to untangle his thoughts from his feelings.

Why *was* he so furious? Madly, rigidly, agonisingly furious?

He had what he wanted. He'd told himself, time and again, that it was lust driving his obsession with Liberty Lovejoy. He should be rejoicing. He'd had her. She'd set him free. Free to have what he wanted—the perfect Lady Sybilla Gratton as his wife. His Marchioness. The mother of his children. The future Duchess of Cheriton.

He paced onwards, his steps slow and measured, his gaze on the pavement.

And slowly the truth emerged out of that muddle of emotions and he finally accepted it with a clear head. The idea of having Liberty Lovejoy as his wife had taken hold in his brain and it felt right. He could not dislodge that image. It grew stronger and brighter with every second, every minute that passed. He didn't only want Liberty Lovejoy, he *needed* her. In his life. Always.

On the brink of spinning around to march back to Green Street, he halted.

She had refused him. And he—the perfect, gentlemanly Marquess of Avon—had managed to both insult and infuriate the woman he loved. If he returned to her now and prostrated himself at her feet, she would no doubt laugh him out of the house. And he wouldn't blame her. He'd made an utter mess of the entire thing.

He walked on.

He would make a plan.

I'll court her properly... I'll make her change her mind.

He halted at the next corner and waited for Ted to bring up his curricle. He felt a burning need to work off his frustration. A visit to Jackson's would help.

The next few days tried his patience to the limit. A new and different Liberty Lovejoy had emerged—coolly correct in everything she did and said. She smiled graciously. She danced with precision and with elegance. She smiled at him, but with her lips closed. And she refused to rise to any provocation, merely agreeing with every word he said. She had encased her heart and her soul in an exquisitely polite but impenetrable shell and nothing he said or did could pierce it.

If she should get with child, though, it will change everything. She won't refuse me then.

A part of him understood he was clutching at that thought in the hope it would solve this impasse for him. But that was all he had to cling to.

Chapter Nineteen

A mere six days after *that night*—the night when Liberty had gambled the highest stakes of all and lost—Lord and Lady Stanton threw a ball at their mansion in Cavendish Square. The Lovejoys, along with most of the *ton*, were invited and Liberty waited with bated breath and with a thudding heart for Dominic to make an appearance. She had a very important message for him.

At every ball since *that night* Dominic asked Liberty to dance. And, if she had a dance free, she accepted. But she avoided any hint of personal conversation, talking only of inconsequential matters and agreeing with every single one of Dominic's opinions, which grew increasingly outrageous as the days passed. He was being deliberately provocative, she knew, but she refused to lower her guard for one single second. He wanted a perfect lady? Well, she might have missed out on the strictly correct upbringing of Lady Sybilla and her ilk, but she would show him she could be a lady when necessary.

As far as the rest of the *ton* were concerned, his behaviour was still impeccable. He partnered several perfectly eligible young ladies, including Sybilla, at every ball but the announcement everyone was waiting for never came.

And Liberty knew why. And tonight she would set his mind at rest. If he was *still* determined to marry the perfect Lady Sybilla, he could now do so with a clear conscience. This morning her prayers had been answered and tonight she would reassure His Lordship that there had been no unwanted consequences from *that night* and that he was free to continue with the life he'd mapped out from a young boy.

And she was free to continue with hers. She rubbed absently at her chest. This hollow feeling was one she must grow accustomed to…unless this final, desperate gamble of hers bore fruit. But the decision must be his. She would give him no encouragement. And if *this* gamble paid off, she would *know* he loved her, even if he never actually said those words.

She gazed around the room despondently. Olivia and Hugo were absent tonight as Olivia was suffering from a slight head cold and Liberty could garner no interest in joining Mrs Mount and the chattering chaperons. A nagging ache low in her belly was a constant reminder of her news for Dominic. How would he react? She didn't fool herself that he would suddenly throw himself at her feet and declare his undying love for her, but would he…*could* he…reconsider his plans?

She was confident she had been right to refuse Dominic's offer. Although offer wasn't the right word—it had been more of a statement.

This is what we will do. I have decided. You will comply.

Her heart still ached for him. Her body still craved him. But, most disconcerting of all, she missed him— just talking to him, laughing with him, teasing him.

Being teased in return.

No one but he called her Berty.

The heart of her uncertainty was that she knew he liked her and cared for her and was attracted to her. She was almost certain he loved her.

But did he love her *enough*?

And would he give himself the chance to find out, or was he so committed to his lifelong vision of his future that he would continue along that path without considering the alternative? Without considering her?

A flurry of activity at the ballroom door grabbed her attention as all activity seemed to freeze for an instant before conversations restarted, seemingly brighter and more animated than before. Liberty knew without looking what that meant. She had become accustomed to the phenomenon since Dominic's father had arrived in town—he had that effect whenever he walked into an event.

Liberty had never been introduced to the Duke, but he did not appear to be the sort of man who would welcome someone like Liberty Lovejoy as the wife of his son and heir. As Dominic had said, on *that night*, his father had not shirked *his* duty—his first wife, Dominic's mother, had been the daughter of a marquess and the granddaughter of a duke. The aristocratic heritage of the Dukedom was intact, even though the current Duchess's grandfather was a simple silversmith. And that also confirmed Liberty had been right to refuse Dominic because, unless she knew without a shadow of doubt that he loved her and, more importantly, unless *Dominic* knew and admitted it, she was convinced he would grow to regret their union and become ashamed of her.

Only love, in all its strength and glory, would give

a union between them the chance to stand strong and withstand other people's opinions.

So. Had Dominic arrived with the Duke and Duchess or would Liberty have to be patient a little longer? She tiptoed up to peer towards the door. She could not see. There were too many people in the way.

'What are you up to, Sis?'

She smiled up at Gideon as he slipped his arm around her waist. 'Looking for Hope and Verity,' she lied.

Since Gideon had caught her crying he had become a calmer, nicer person. Lady Emily, too, had influenced him in a positive way although he still stayed out late with his friends. Liberty, however, no longer fretted about him quite so much and, surprisingly, the less she worried about him, the closer they had grown.

'You're a proper mother hen, aren't you, Sis? Don't worry about them—that's what Mrs Mount is for. You should be looking to your own future.' His blue eyes searched hers, suddenly serious. 'It's been five years, Liberty. It's time you began to live your life again. Bernard would want you to.'

Tears prickled at the back of her eyes. 'I know he would.'

It was the first time she had admitted to any member of her family that she might be ready to find love again. Until now it had felt as though she were laying her soul bare to be trampled over but, somehow, this time in London had helped all of the Lovejoys to change. They had grown closer as a family, although her sisters still complained bitterly when Romeo got up to mischief.

'You deserve to be happy again, Lib. And you will be. I can feel it in my bones. I'm on my way to make sure Verity is all right. Bridlington is here. I had a word with him, but it's best to be sure. I'll see you later.'

Gideon hugged her closer before releasing her and she watched as he made his way across the room.

'Is he still causing you concern?' The deep voice sent tingles racing through her.

It was the same whenever they met.

Whenever they spoke.

Whenever they danced—the touch of his hand pure agony with the wanting of him. And, if he could, he always picked a waltz—her hand on his shoulder, his hand on her waist, the helpless longing in her heart and the aching void of loneliness in her chest. That void had begun to fill. Before. Now, it gaped wider and blacker than ever.

She stretched her lips in a cool smile and turned to Dominic.

'No. He is doing his duty as an older brother. It seems Bridlington is here tonight. He has already spoken to him and now he is checking on Verity.'

'I'm pleased to hear it.'

A swift scan of him showed he was on edge, as he had been ever since *that night*. He disguised it well, but she could read his moods where other, more casual, observers would see nothing. It was time to put him out of his misery. And time to take that chance…to destroy that last tie that bound them together, that final strand that had been keeping her fragile hopes alive. And to hope Dominic would reach into his heart and see that the power was in his hands to forge a deeper, stronger link that could join them for ever.

'Have you a dance free this evening, Liberty?'

'I am afraid I do not dance this evening, my lord.' She would go home early, with a headache as an excuse. 'But I have news for you.'

Their gazes fused, his as opaque as it ever had been, his face impassive.

'I can confirm there were no c-c-consequences.' Try as she might, she could not control the wobble in her voice. Anguish scorched every fibre of her being. 'You need delay your betrothal no longer.'

She bobbed a curtsy and turned away, but Dominic grabbed her elbow, stopping her. 'Liberty!' His voice was low. Urgent. 'We need to talk.'

She pivoted to face him. '*We* need do nothing. *You* are free now to make your choice—and you know as well as I that not one unattached lady in this room tonight would refuse an offer from you. The choice is up to you.'

She stared up into those silvery eyes, but all she could see was her own image, reflected in them.

'Not one, Dominic,' she added softly. 'Your choice.'

She tugged her arm free and hurried away through the crowd to where Mrs Mount sat with the other chaperons. She looked up at Liberty enquiringly, her look changing to one of concern.

'You were right, dear ma'am,' said Liberty. 'I should have remained at home this evening.'

She laid her hand briefly to her lower belly and Mrs Mount gave her an understanding smile. She knew Liberty's courses had begun. She would not think it odd for Liberty to leave.

'There is no need for concern,' Liberty continued. 'I shall ask Gideon to escort me home and he will be back before you know it.'

Dominic watched as Liberty was absorbed into the crowd. He should feel released. He felt the opposite—as though prison walls were closing in on him. Ever since that night—the most glorious, wonderful night of his entire life—he had been as though held in limbo. He saw an insect trapped in amber once, at the British Museum, and that is exactly how he had felt since *that night*. But he had made a complete mull of it afterwards…talking of them marrying by special licence, speaking of *consequences*. Offering her *money*.

She was rightly disgusted with him, but no more disgusted than he was with himself. What had happened to his famed manners? His powers of address? They appeared to have deserted him at the time he most desperately needed them. He had tried everything to recover their friendship as a prelude to courting Liberty Lovejoy properly. To prove to her that he loved her. Only her. And to prove he could not give a damn whether she was the daughter of a duke or the daughter of a ditch-digger. But how could he do that when she kept him at arm's length with her perfect lady image and her exquisitely correct manners? His heart yearned for the old Liberty back…the real Liberty.

Dominic snagged a glass of champagne from a passing footman, swallowed one mouthful and then stilled.

It was not only his life that had been in limbo since *that night*. His thinking, it seemed, had been suspended, too. The family had noticed—he'd seen them watching him with concern when they thought he wouldn't notice—but none of them had mentioned his list.

Except Father.

'You may feel you have backed yourself into a corner, Dom, but there is absolutely no need to make any decisions this year. It will wait. What is your hurry?'

And he could not bring himself to admit that the hurry was the fear he might lose Liberty for good. And neither could he admit he had fallen in love. Not to Father, because he would then move heaven and earth to put things right for Dominic.

But this was *his* mess. He was a grown man and it was up to him to sort it out.

He tipped the remainder of the champagne into a nearby urn of flowers—with a silent apology to Felicity—and cursed himself for even more of a fool.

He had been waiting…hoping…that circumstance would intervene and that Liberty would find herself with child and she would *have* to marry him. A coward's hope. Her words tonight had shattered that dream, but now, picking through the wreckage of the plan that had not even been a plan but a weak, vague hope that everything would turn out all right, he understood that Liberty's news was a blessing.

Now, she had provided him with the perfect way to prove he loved her. If she had been with child, she would never believe he *wanted* to marry her. She would always fear he had been, in effect, trapped into it. Now…*now* he was free to prove to her that he loved her and only her.

With renewed vigour, he turned on his heel and went to find his stepmother. He had plans to make. Proper plans this time.

Chapter Twenty

It would be *the* ball of the Season. Everybody who was anybody would be there.

'But you *must* attend, Liberty. Tell her, Hope.' Verity looked from one of her sisters to the other. 'It is the first ball the Duke of Cheriton has hosted since Lady Olivia made her debut *five years ago!*'

The ball had been announced just four days before, much to the consternation of those members of the *ton* who already had evening events arranged for tomorrow night. They had bowed to the inevitable and many events had been cancelled amid speculation as to whether there might be a specific purpose to the ball... whether a *special announcement* was imminent.

And people had nudged one another and cast surreptitious looks at the Marquess of Avon as they did so, convinced that he had finally chosen his bride and that the ball was to celebrate their betrothal. But not even the most incorrigible tittle-tattles could pretend they had an inkling of his choice. His Lordship went about his daily life as inscrutably as ever and not one of the young ladies believed to feature on his shortlist gave the smallest indication that she harboured a grand secret.

Liberty had no more idea than anyone else. Dominic had continued to be friendly whenever their paths crossed and he continued to dance with her as well as with many other young ladies, including those on his shortlist. His provocative teasing had stopped, however, much to Liberty's mingled consternation and relief.

His behaviour to her was that of the consummate gentleman and hers to him was that of the perfect lady.

Not even Olivia had let any information about the ball slip, although that, Liberty was fairly sure, was because even *she* did not why the ball had been arranged with such haste. All she knew, she had told Liberty crossly, was that her stepmother was rushing around like a whirlwind—for, as the lady of the house, the ball was under her jurisdiction—and that Grantham was being impossibly officious. Her father, she added, had brought in an army of additional servants to help get the ball ready on time.

But Liberty's entire family appeared unable to accept that she was happy not to attend the ball. Ever since the Stantons' ball she had steeled herself for the announcement of Dominic's betrothal and now, having been forewarned it was likely to happen tomorrow night, she would be a fool to put herself through such a trial in such a public setting.

'You *must* attend.' Hope added her voice to Verity's. 'Think how dreadful it would be for us to miss it.'

'*You* do not have to miss it.' Liberty put her arms around Romeo—seated beside her on the sofa—and kissed his head. 'Mrs Mount and Gideon will be there. Nobody will even notice or care about my absence.'

'Lady Olivia will be offended if you do not attend,' said Hope. 'You are friends—why on earth do you not want to go to her stepmother's ball?'

Really! Can they not see my heart is breaking?

No sooner had that very unfair thought surfaced than it was swept aside by the reassurance that no one actually *knew* Liberty's heart was shattered or that her life was over. She hadn't felt pain like this since Bernard died. She simply could not summon the strength to stand there and smile and look happy for Dominic and the flawless Lady Sybilla and, even worse, to congratulate them and wish them happy together.

She couldn't do it.

'I have no suitable gown to wear.'

It was no lie. Liberty had worn each of her three new ball gowns at least twice and the *ball of the Season* surely warranted a new gown.

'That is no excuse!' Hope grabbed Liberty's hand, forcing her to pay attention. 'Gideon, Verity and I decided it was time to show you our appreciation for everything you have done for us and we ordered a new gown. Cinderella *shall* go to the ball!'

Despite her dejection, Liberty could not help but laugh. 'Does that make you two the Ugly Sisters?' Then she sobered. 'But the ball is tomorrow night. There is no time. I shall send a note to Olivia explaining I am indisposed. The dress will come for another night... perhaps the Derhams' ball next week?'

Hope pouted. 'I think you are being very mean, Liberty. What have you got against the Duke and Duchess?'

'Nothing!'

Other than that the Duke terrified her. She had met him just two days before, introduced by Olivia, and his silvery-grey gaze—so like his son's—had swept over her, leaving her feeling as though he knew all her deepest, darkest secrets. Including that she was in love with his son and heir and had seduced him in the hope he might see sense. She shivered at the thought the Duke might find that out.

'I simply…it will be too grand. I do not care for such huge occasions. Now, please, stop pestering me. You will be perfectly safe attending with both Gideon and Mrs Mount and once you are surrounded by all your fawning admirers you won't have a thought to spare for me.'

Liberty spent the next day at home, even eschewing a ride in the Park. She could not face the growing excitement. It was just a ball, for goodness sake. What did the reason behind it matter? The Duke would no doubt announce the betrothal between Dominic and Lady Sybilla, and then the *ton*, in all its glittering, gossiping glory, would move on to the next shiny piece of news.

Much ado about nothing.

Except it wasn't nothing. Not to her. Romeo was beside her on the sofa and she buried her face in his soft fur. He licked her ear. Although it tickled, she could not summon even a giggle. Everywhere felt so numb.

'Miss Lovejoy?'

Her head jerked up at the maid's voice. 'Yes, Ethel?'

It was early evening and, having already dined, Liberty was alone in the drawing room, waiting to see the rest of the family, all dressed in their finery, before they left for the Cheritons' ball.

The maid looked flushed and flustered.

'It's Mrs Mount, miss. She's had the megrim come on.'

'Oh, dear!' Liberty stood. 'I shall go to her at once. Ask Mrs Taylor to prepare some willow-bark tea, if you will. That may help.'

'Yes, miss.'

When she reached Mrs Mount's bedchamber, Hope and Verity were both in attendance and Mrs Mount herself was in bed, the covers pulled up to her chin and a damp cloth draped across her forehead.

'My dear Mrs Mount.' Liberty went to her bedside, ushering her sisters out of the way. 'You must tell me if there is anything I can do to help.'

Mrs Mount moaned softly, her eyes shut. 'Nothing,' she whispered. 'I just need peace and quiet.'

'Of course.' Liberty scanned the room. The curtains were drawn, blocking out the light, and there was a glass of water on the bedside table. 'I have ordered willowbark tea and I shall send one of the maids up to sit with you, in case you require anything. Come, girls...' she waved Hope and Verity towards the door '...let us leave poor Mrs Mount in peace.'

Once on the landing, she said, 'Why aren't you dressed for the ball? I thought the carriage was ordered for half past?'

Verity pouted. 'How can we go now? We have no chaperon. Mrs Mount is indisposed and *you* have refused to go.'

'It's the ball of the Season,' Hope wailed, 'and we shall be the only ones not there!'

'Oh, good grief.' Liberty thought quickly, but could see no alternative. 'I... I must accompany you, I suppose. I can hardly expect Gideon to watch over you both.'

Verity flung her arms around Liberty and kissed her cheek. 'Oh, *thank* you. You are the *best* sister.'

Her heart expanded, knowing she had made her sisters happy. But what about her? She would have to face Dominic and, probably, endure his happy news. It was the last thing she wished to do. And yet...by staying away, would he not guess the reason why? She thought she had managed to hoodwink him so far, acting as though she could not care less, but he was no fool. Her absence would scream the truth more loudly than her stoical attendance.

Perhaps this was for the best. It would be but a few hours of her life. She had endured worse and coped. She would survive this.

'I suppose it will have to be the violet silk again,' she said. 'But no matter—no one will be looking my way, after all.'

'Oh! I forgot to tell you!' Hope's blue eyes sparkled. 'You won't need your violet silk. Do you recall that new gown I told you about? It was delivered this afternoon, but Lizzie stupidly put it in my bedchamber, thinking it was mine! She will bring it to you and she can help you with your hair, for mine is already done.'

The gown was perfect. If Liberty could have chosen a gown for herself, without consideration of cost, it was just what she would have chosen—a high-waisted gown of blush-pink crepe over a satin slip, the skirt decorated with two festoons of pink rosebuds at the hem. The bodice—with scattered seed pearls and tiny rosebuds stitched to the fabric—was cut low over the shoulders, in the current fashion, with short sleeves held up by narrow satin bands. Lizzie pinned her hair on top of her head, threading a string of pearls through her locks and leaving a few curls to frame her face. Her mother's single strand of pearls was clasped around her throat and matching pearl eardrops hung from her lobes.

Her sisters' gasps when she appeared at the head of the stairs were balm to Liberty's soul. She straightened her shoulders and raised her chin as she descended to where they waited in the hall. Gideon came in the front door.

'The carriage is waiting.' He let out a low whistle as he caught sight of Liberty and he walked to meet her and kissed her hand. 'You look like a princess.'

The line of carriages waiting to deliver their occupants to Beauchamp House stretched all the way around Grosvenor Square. As they waited, the evening dry, the sky spangled with stars, Liberty remembered the very first time she had called at Beauchamp House: the heavy rain, the thunder and lightning, the footman with the umbrella. And Dominic. The very first time they met. Little did she imagine then how she would come to feel about him. Little did she imagine he would break her heart. She swallowed, forcing down the aching mass that invaded her throat.

I will not disgrace myself. I am braver...stronger... than that.

By the time the Lovejoys entered the front door Liberty's nerves had wound so tight she could barely hear a word said to her as she climbed the magnificent marble staircase with Gideon, Hope and Verity, and then stood in line to be greeted by their host and hostess.

The Duke was resplendent in severe black evening clothes and the Duchess looked lovely in lemon gauze over a cream underdress. As they waited their turn, a quick sweep of the surrounding area revealed no trace of any of the rest of the Beauchamps and, for that, Liberty was grateful. One step at a time. Get the formalities out of the way and she could hopefully lose herself in the crush—and it truly was a crush. As they reached the Duke—Gideon bowing and she, Hope and Verity sinking into curtsies—Liberty caught a glimpse of the crowded ballroom, down a short flight of stairs. How on earth anyone would manage to dance was beyond her although, no doubt, the elders would soon disperse to the card rooms and salons, leaving the ballroom free for the dancers and their chaperons.

She rose from her curtsy to find herself being regarded by a pair of friendly golden-brown eyes.

'We have heard a great deal about you from Olivia, Miss Lovejoy,' said the Duchess. 'Thank you for being such a good friend to her…she puts so much pressure on herself to be the perfect mother to the twins, even though we keep telling her not to be so hard on herself, is that not so, Leo?'

Gideon and the girls had moved on, waiting now at the top of the flight of steps down into the ballroom, and the following guests had not yet moved forward, leaving Liberty in limbo with the Duke and the Duchess. She sucked in a sharp breath in an attempt to quell her nerves as the Duke's penetrating silver-grey gaze studied her unhurriedly.

'Indeed.' He smiled at Liberty, his eyes crinkling at the corners, and suddenly he did not look as intimidating. His gaze did not swerve from hers. 'It is a pleasure to meet you again, Miss Lovejoy. We are honoured that you accepted our invitation.'

Liberty managed a smile in return, even as she wondered at the strange phrasing used by the Duke. She joined Gideon and the girls at the head of the stairs.

Chapter Twenty-One

'The Earl of Wendover; Miss Lovejoy; Miss Hope Lovejoy; Miss Verity Lovejoy.'

Their arrival was announced by Grantham—very erect and clearly relishing his role as Master of Ceremonies—in resonant tones. They descended the stairs into the ball-room. Liberty rested her hand on Gideon's arm as Hope and Verity followed behind, and aimed her gaze resolutely above the heads of the crowd. As they reached the foot of the stairs, Gideon slipped his arm from beneath her hand.

'I see Emily over by the window. I shall see you later.'

He melted among the crowd, lost to sight within sec-onds. Liberty didn't even know which window he might be heading for—there were five sets of French windows along the far wall, but she had been so determined not to catch sight of Dominic or Sybilla that neither had she seen Lady Emily, or where she stood. She turned to Hope and Verity, but they were already surrounded by young men eager to reserve dances.

Liberty rubbed her upper chest, feeling the hollow swoop of her stomach as she did so. This had been her worst fear. Being alone, in the crowd, waiting for the axe to fall. She peered around anxiously, and froze.

Dominic. Two paces away, handsome and debonair in black evening clothes, a dark sapphire pin in his neckcloth. His gaze steady. On her. She swallowed and forced a smile. She would not evade this meeting. Her actions had been her own, the decisions her own. She had gambled of her own free will and it was not Dominic's fault that he still believed in duty over love.

'Good evening, Liberty.'

His rich voice sent shudders of helpless desire through her, as did the look of intent in his silvery gaze. He moved closer and she could smell the spicy, musky cologne he favoured. When she closed her eyes at night, it was that remembered scent that started the memories rolling through her head. She blinked, forcing her mind out of her feelings and into the practicalities of coping with this meeting without making a complete idiot of herself.

'Good evening, my lord.' Love—pure, despairing, eternal—squeezed her heart, catching at her breath. How could she bear this? But bear it she must. 'It is… it is a crush tonight, is it not? Your stepmother must be pleased with the success of her ball.'

He smiled. Tenderly. She blinked again, too accustomed to him blanking his emotions to believe her own eyes. But she was not mistaken. That tender smile was aimed directly at her. It reached his eyes, too—no opaque silver coins tonight, nor even mirrors reflecting the world back. For almost the first time since she had known him—other than *that night*—he appeared to be inviting her in. Inviting her to see the real man inside.

'I am sure she is.'

Her heart beat a little faster. That vice constricting

her heart eased a fraction and hope stirred as Dominic extended one hand. As though in a dream she placed her own hand in his. His fingers closed strongly around hers, warm, comforting, safe. Tears stung her eyes and she desperately swallowed her emotions down. She could not cope with comforting. Or with safe.

Her heart began to pound. Disjointed questions ricocheted around her head. *What...? Why...? How...?* Her knees trembled and her mouth dried, and all coherent thought scattered, as out of reach as the stars in the sky.

Dominic captured her other hand, bringing their joined hands together, between them, at chest height. Then, in a gesture that stole her breath, he opened his fingers leaving his hands side by side, palm up, almost in supplication. Her own hands lay on his, palm to palm, but she was not controlled in any way. She could remove her hands. She could move away, if she chose to. But she would not...could not...move. Her mind had ceased to control her body. She stood, helpless, waiting to hear what he might say. Dreading and yet hoping... yearning...*praying*.

He smiled into her eyes.

'If you do not want this, Liberty Louisa Lovejoy...if you do not want *me*...please tell me now and we shall say no more about it.'

She could not grasp his meaning, so she picked on the familiar.

'How do you know my middle name?'

One corner of his lips quirked up in a half-smile. 'Verity told me.'

Her gaze skimmed past him, to where she had last seen her sisters. Hope and Verity, beyond Dominic's right shoulder, were watching her, wide smiles on their faces. She wrenched her attention back to Dominic.

'V-Verity? Wh-why did she tell you that?'

'I asked her.'

'Oh.' Her throat ached unbearably. She still could not allow herself to hope…to believe…what his words meant. 'Wh-what is this? What are you doing?'

He ducked his head close to listen to her whispered question. His ear, his dark hair curling slightly over its rim, was tantalisingly close to her lips. He was so close she could see the texture of his skin, the faint shadow of his beard, even though he was freshly shaven. He raised his head again and she saw the glisten of his tongue as it moistened his visibly dry lips. She slid her palms over his and her fingertips found the pulse in his wrist. It pounded even faster than her own.

'I am about to propose to you.'

Her heart leapt. Her lungs seized. Her sisters were still watching avidly…with Gideon and…*Mrs Mount*? Liberty swallowed down a swell of tears as she processed his words. Propose? To her? But… 'What about Sybilla?' she whispered.

'Forget Sybilla,' he said roughly. 'It is you I love. You I need.' His chest expanded as he inhaled, then his words came out in a disjointed rush. 'Berty…if you can forgive me…if you can love me…if, when I ask you to marry me, your answer is yes…then stay here, by my side. But if you cannot, if your answer is still no, then we will say no more.'

He captured her gaze again. Heat swirled in his eyes and she could feel the dampness of his palms.

'My intention was to declare my love and to propose to you tonight—here, in front of everyone, so neither you nor anyone else will doubt my love for you is true. But I changed my mind.'

Liberty's heart had begun to soar. Now, she could not stifle her gasp of dismay.

'I changed my mind,' Dominic continued, 'because I will not back you into a corner in front of all these people. I will not put you in a position where you feel you *cannot* refuse me. You are in control, my darling Berty. Walk away now, if you wish, and no one will be any the wiser. But know that my heart will go with you.'

Her heart somersaulted. This private man—a man who concealed his heart and his emotions behind duty and obligation—was about to make a public declaration. To her!

The cacophony of surrounding voices was fading—a tide of sound receding. She sensed they now stood in a clearing and that the people around them were moving back, but she could not tear her gaze from his.

She slid her hands back until just their fingers overlapped and then she curled her fingers until they were linked with his. She smoothed her thumbs across his knuckles and put all of her love into her smile. 'I will not walk away, Dominic. I love you.'

His lips curved and his fingers tightened around hers. He raised his head, clearly seeking someone over the heads of the crowd. A gong reverberated throughout the room and now the hush of the crowd could not be mistaken.

'My lords, ladies and gentleman.' Liberty recognised Grantham's voice. 'Pray silence for His Lordship, the Marquess of Avon.'

The difficult part was over. So why did his knees still shake and why was his stomach still churning? She would not walk away. She had said so. But this was still the most important moment of his life and he was desperate to get it right. Dominic swallowed past the swell of emotion that clogged his throat and clasped Liberty's hands even tighter, revelling in the knowledge that he could hold her hands whenever he chose, from this night onwards, for the rest of their lives. He could feel her suppressed emotion in the tremble of her hands and he could see it by the quiver of her lower lip.

Then their eyes met. And she smiled and it was as though the sun broke through dark clouds and everything...*everything*...was all right. His tension fragmented and a surge of energy...of hope...of joy... radiated throughout his entire body. He hauled in a deep breath and, when he spoke, there was no hesitancy in his words or in his voice.

He had prepared what he would say—the proper words and sentiments for an occasion such as this—but he ignored all his careful plans. He gazed out at the sea of faces surrounding them and he spoke from the heart.

'There has been much speculation in the past weeks about my intentions. I arrived in town with the aim of finding the perfect wife for me and for my position as my father's heir. I have to tell you...' his gaze swept the crowd '...that I was possibly even more undecided than any one of you as to whom that lady might be.

'And then this lady—Liberty Louisa Lovejoy—burst into my life like a...like a...'

He paused, and stared down at Liberty. How could he sum up what she had come to mean to him in just a few words? What words could do her justice? She smiled, her gold-flecked blue eyes urging him on. And then the exact words didn't matter. He was talking with his heart, not his head—and if they came out less than perfect, he did not care.

'She burst into my life like a whirlwind of sunshine,

lighting my life with laughter, with love and with joy. And I had found my perfect partner in life. And, if she will have me, my perfect wife…my perfect Marchioness.'

It was his turn to smile, while Liberty looked serious.

'Liberty Lovejoy, I love you with every beat of my heart. I love you with every breath I take. You already have possession of my heart. Will you now do me the great honour of accepting my hand as well? Will you marry me?'

For what felt like an eternity her expression remained set and it felt as though his heart, too, stilled as he waited. The room around them was silent, not a sound to be heard. He concentrated on her mouth, those lush lips, willing her to answer. Slowly…excruciatingly slowly…her lips lifted at the corners…curved into a smile…and parted.

And he shouldn't have been surprised, but he was. Because she went up on tiptoes, threw her arms around his neck and kissed him, quite thoroughly, accompanied by a chorus of gasps and sighs from their audience.

And Dominic could breathe properly for the first time since Liberty had announced she was not with child and he could marry whomever he chose.

He chose Liberty Lovejoy.

And she said yes…in deed if not in so many words.

Chapter Twenty-Two

The ball was finally over. The guests, other than their families, had all gone home and the Beauchamps and the Lovejoys repaired to the family parlour for their first opportunity to discuss the betrothal. Publicly, of course, all his family had congratulated him. They had put on a good show…but was it just a show, or would they really be happy for him and welcome Liberty into the fold? The hard ball of anxiety that had lodged in Dominic's stomach over the past weeks had dissolved, leaving one tiny knot of unease, one unanswered question, behind.

Would following his heart mean a rift between him and his beloved family?

Dominic tucked Liberty close to him as they sat side by side on the sofa and the Beauchamps, Lovejoys—and Mrs Mount—assembled. Olivia, of course, piped up the minute the door closed.

'Well! I do think you might have told *me* what you planned, Dominic. Liberty *is* my friend, after all. I could have helped.'

He should have expected no less and he noticed Father and Rosalind exchange wry smiles.

'I neither needed nor wanted your help, Livvy,' he said. 'But thank you for the thought.'

Olivia pouted. 'Hope and Verity knew! And even Mrs Mount and she's not even family.'

'I had to confide in them, Liv. I wasn't confident Liberty would come tonight otherwise.'

'She was exceedingly stubborn.' Hope was sitting next to Alex, casting occasional coquettish glances at him through her lashes while Alex pretended not to notice. 'Poor Mrs Mount had to feign illness before she would give in.'

'Well, I still think—' Olivia fell silent as Hugo placed a hand on her shoulder.

'All has worked out for the best, my sweet, so you must concede that Dominic didn't need your help. He knew what he was doing.'

'Eventually,' said Alex.

Dominic frowned at his brother, receiving an innocent smile in return as Alex continued, 'You're slipping, Liv. It must be motherhood. Hugo and I knew which way the wind was blowing *weeks* ago.'

Olivia sucked in a deep breath, ready to retaliate, and Dominic saw his father getting ready to intervene, but it was Liberty who spoke.

'Are you disappointed you weren't told, or disappointed in Dominic's choice, Olivia?'

The slightest of tremors in her voice told him how much courage it had taken for her to ask such a direct question, especially when she had already confided in him how nervous she was at facing his family. Especially his father. He took her hand and squeezed.

Olivia paled at Liberty's words and she shot out of her seat and sat on the other side of Liberty, putting her arm around her shoulders.

'How could you even *think* I might be disappointed he chose you, Liberty? When I think of those haughty girls on that ridiculous list of his—no! There is no comparison. You are perfect, just as Dom said. It is just that I feel like I'm the only one who didn't know.'

'You always did want to know everything that is going on, Olivia, and you haven't changed.' Father stood and moved across to the mantelpiece, commanding the room as was his wont. 'If it's any consolation, your stepmother and I knew nothing either, not until the very first guests were already walking up the stairs this evening. That is the first time we knew Liberty's identity.'

Both Rosalind and Father had trusted Dominic when he had asked them to throw a ball for a special announcement without revealing any details. He prayed they did not now feel that trust had been betrayed. Liberty's fingers tightened on Dominic's and he heard her intake of breath.

'Is that why you said what you did to me when I arrived, Your Grace?'

Dominic stared at his father. Had he been unwelcoming?

'What did you say to her?' he demanded. He had to challenge him—he would not stand for any member of his family, even his father, upsetting Liberty. He had deliberately not revealed her identity earlier because he had wanted neither his father's help nor his hindrance. Nor had he wanted to know if Father disapproved because his approval or disapproval had been irrelevant, in the end.

Liberty was Dominic's choice and his alone.

He held his breath, awaiting his father's reply, but it was Liberty who spoke.

'He said it was a pleasure to meet me again and that

he and the Duchess were honoured that I accepted their invitation.' She smiled up at Dominic. 'Honoured! Your father made me feel welcome and that helped to give me the courage to face this evening.'

Dominic caught his father's eyes and sent him a silent apology. Father ghosted a wink in reply and that last knot of tension in Dominic's stomach unravelled.

But Liberty hadn't finished. Her cheeks turned pink as her gaze took in every person in the room, one by one.

'I was convinced Dominic was about to announce his betrothal to someone else and I wanted to be anywhere but here tonight.' She beamed then at her brother and sisters, and Mrs Mount, who had still come to the ball, but rather later than planned. 'Thank you all for not giving up on me.'

'That's all right, Sis,' said Gideon. 'We did it for ourselves more than you—how else could we get rid of Romeo?'

'Is that your dog, Liberty?' Rosalind asked, over the chuckles raised by Gideon's remarks. 'I hope he likes other dogs because there will be several around when you come to the Abbey in July.'

Liberty looked questioningly at Dominic. He hadn't even thought that far ahead. The Abbey was his childhood home and he couldn't wait to show Liberty around, although they would make their home at one of Father's minor estates.

'The entire family will all be together for the first time since Olivia and Hugo married, four years ago,' said Dominic. He lifted her hand and kissed it. 'I cannot wait for you—and Romeo—to meet the rest of them.'

She smiled at that. 'I am sure he will be on his best behaviour,' she said to Rosalind.

'Well, now.' Father crossed to where Rosalind was sitting and helped her to rise, then he led her across to Dominic and Liberty, who stood up also. 'I said it in the ballroom, Liberty, but I want you to be in no doubt... I am delighted to welcome you to our family. I can see you have made my son a happy man and that's good enough for me.'

He placed his hands on her shoulders and bent to kiss her cheek, then murmured something into her ear. Something Dominic could not hear.

'Goodnight, everyone.' He and Rosalind went to the door, then Father held it open, making it clear to the rest of the company it was time to leave. One by one they said goodnight to Dominic and Liberty and trooped out. Gideon was the last to go.

'We'll wait for you in the entrance hall, Sis,' he said.

And then they were alone. At last. Dominic wrapped Liberty in his arms, but still the question burned in him and he had to ask.

'What did Father whisper to you?'

Liberty beamed up at him. 'He said he knew it was me, from the night of Lady Stanton's ball.'

'And I was very pleased,' came a deep voice from the doorway, 'that you saw sense, my Son. After all, why spoil the Beauchamp tradition of following our hearts?'

'Why did you say nothing?'

His father never normally shied away from manipulating events to suit himself.

'Because it was your decision, Dom. It was for you to make your own choice—head or heart. I'm happy it was the right one. Eventually, as your brother would say. Goodnight.'

They were alone again. And now there were no more unanswered questions. Except... Dominic frowned.

'What is it?'

'You never did answer my question, Berty.'

'Which question?'

'Will you marry me?'

She smiled and traced his lower lip with her forefinger. '*I thought I answered you most explicitly, Lord Avon. But, if you want unequivocal, then you shall have it.*'

She slipped her arms around his neck, went up on tiptoes and, for the second time that night, she kissed him. Very thoroughly. Until his senses swam and his blood was on fire.

'Oh, yes,' she whispered against his lips. 'Yes. Yes. Yes.'

* * * * *

MILLS & BOON

THE HEART OF ROMANCE

A ROMANCE FOR EVERY READER

MODERN

Prepare to be swept off your feet by sophisticated, sexy and seductive heroes, in some of the world's most glamourous and romantic locations, where power and passion collide.

HISTORICAL

Escape with historical heroes from time gone by. Whether your passion is for wicked Regency Rakes, muscled Vikings or rugged Highlanders, awake the romance of the past.

MEDICAL

Set your pulse racing with dedicated, delectable doctors in the high-pressure world of medicine, where emotions run high and passion, comfort and love are the best medicine.

True Love

Celebrate true love with tender stories of heartfelt romance, from the rush of falling in love to the joy a new baby can bring, and a focus on the emotional heart of a relationship.

Desire

Indulge in secrets and scandal, intense drama and plenty of sizzling hot action with powerful and passionate heroes who have it all: wealth, status, good looks…everything but the right woman.

HEROES

Experience all the excitement of a gripping thriller, with an intense romance at its heart. Resourceful, true-to-life women and strong, fearless men face danger and desire - a killer combination!

To see which titles are coming soon, please visit

millsandboon.co.uk/nextmonth

JOIN US ON SOCIAL MEDIA!

Stay up to date with our latest releases, author news and gossip, special offers and discounts, and all the behind-the-scenes action from Mills & Boon...

 @millsandboon

 @millsandboonuk

 facebook.com/millsandboon

 @millsandboonuk

It might just be true love...

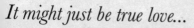

GET YOUR ROMANCE FIX!

Get the latest romance news,
exclusive author interviews, story
extracts and much more!

MILLS & BOON

HISTORICAL

Awaken the romance of the past

Escape with historical heroes from time gone by.
Whether your passion is for wicked
Regency Rakes, muscled Viking warriors or
rugged Highlanders, indulge your fantasies and
awaken the romance of the past.

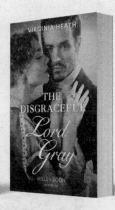

MILLS & BOON

True Love

Romance from the Heart

Celebrate true love with tender stories of heartfelt romance, from the rush of falling in love to the joy a new baby can bring, and a focus on the emotional heart of a relationship.